HOME ON THE RANCH:
FAMILY FOUND

———— ✗ ————

New York Times Bestselling Author
KATHLEEN EAGLE

REBECCA WINTERS

(H) HARLEQUIN® HOME ON THE RANCH

ISBN-13: 978-1-335-02045-1

First published as One Brave Cowboy by Harlequin Books in 2011 and Home to Wyoming by Harlequin Books in 2013.

Home on the Ranch: Family Found

Copyright © 2018 by Harlequin Books S.A.

The publisher acknowledges the copyright holders of the individual works as follows:

One Brave Cowboy
Copyright © 2011 by Kathleen Eagle

Home to Wyoming
Copyright © 2013 by Rebecca Winters

Recycling programs for this product may not exist in your area.

Printed in U.S.A.

CONTENTS

ONE BRAVE COWBOY

KATHLEEN EAGLE

Remembering Daddy

Honoring the American soldier

Chapter One

The driver of the black pickup was himself driven, fixed on the hulking two-story white house at the end of the road. It was an old house in need of a coat of paint with a brand new, freshly painted sign affixed to the porch railing.

Office
Double D Wild Horse Sanctuary

It was the kind of incongruence that automatically drew his eye and raised the hackles he'd been working hard to tame. He was back in the States, for God's sake. *South Dakota*. Land of the granite chiefs and home of the original braves. Just because something was a little off in a place that seemed too quiet didn't mean Cougar needed to crouch and prepare to pounce. He was there on a tip from a fellow soldier. About the only people he trusted these days were guys he'd served with, and Sergeant Mary Tutan was one of the most standup "guys" he knew.

She couldn't pull rank on him anymore, but she'd tracked him down, got him on the phone and talked like she could. *Get your ass in gear, soldier! Go check out the wild horse training competition my friend Sally Drexler is running. It's just what the VA docs ordered.* She'd corrected herself—Sally *Night Horse*—and explained that Sally had married an Indian guy. Did he know Hank Night Horse? How about Logan Wolf Track?

As if Indian country was that damn small.

Cougar wasn't interested in the sergeant's social life, but the mention of horses got his attention. *Training competition* and *cash prize* sounded pretty attractive, too. He'd been away from horses too long. The one he could see loping across the pasture a good half mile away made him smile. Nice bay with a big spotted colt in tow. He could almost smell their earthy sweat on the hot South Dakota wind blowing through the pickup cab.

His nose welcomed horse sweat, buffalo grass and the clay dust kicked up by the oversize tires on his "tricked out" ride, compliments of his brother, Eddie. He could have done without the tires. Could have done without any of the surprises he'd come home to, but he didn't want to do without his brother, and Eddie would have pouted indefinitely if Cougar had said anything about how many miles his brother had racked up on the vehicle in Cougar's absence.

The house looked pretty quiet for the "headquarters" of what was billed as the biggest privately maintained wild animal reserve in the Dakotas. Cougar didn't care how big it was as long as it was legitimate. He'd been down too many dead-end roads lately. The end of this one seemed pretty dead as far as human activity was concerned, but one by one the horses were silently materializing, rising from the ebb and flow of tall grass. They kept their distance, but they were watchful, aware of everything that moved.

As was Cougar. His instinct for self-preservation wasn't quite as sharp as the horses', but it surpassed that of any man, woman or...

...child.

Cougar hit the brake. He saw nothing, heard nothing, but eyes and ears were limited. Cougar knew things. Men and women were on their own, but kids were like foals. Always vulnerable. They gave off signals, and Cougar was a gut-level receptor. Which was a damn good thing. If it hadn't been for his gut, he would have done nothing.

And if it hadn't been for the red baseball cap, he would have thought he was going crazy again, and he might have slid his boot back over the accelerator. But the red cap saved both kid and driver.

And the goat.

Cougar's pulse pounded behind his staring eyeballs. The goat took off, and a small hand stretched out, barely visible beyond a desert camo armored fender.

Don't stop for anything, sergeant. That kid's coming for us. You slow down, he takes us out. Do. Not. Stop.

Cougar closed his eyes, took a breath, shifted into reverse as he took a look back, gunned the engine, and nearly jackknifed his trailer. When he turned, there was no goat. He saw a light-haired kid in blue jeans, stretched out on his belly. He saw the front end of his black pickup. He saw a red and white barn, sparsely graveled road and South Dakota sod. He secured the pickup and threw the door open simultaneously. His boots hit the ground just as the kid pushed himself up on hands and knees. He looked up at Cougar, eyes filled with terror, but no tears.

And he was up. *Thank you, Jesus.*

Cougar's shadow fell across the boy like a blanket dropped from a top bunk. His own knees wouldn't bend. "You okay?"

The boy stared at him.

"I didn't see you," Cougar said, willing the boy to stand on his own, to *be able to* get up all the way. "Are you hurt?"

The boy stretched out his arm, pointed across the road and smiled. Cougar swung his head around and saw a gray cat.

"Was that it?" He looked down at the boy. "A damn cat? For a second I thought I'd…" His legs went jittery on him, and his knee cracked as he squatted, butt to boot heels. "Jesus," he whispered as he braced his elbow on his knees and dropped his head into his hand. His heart was battering his ribs. He couldn't bring himself to look the kid in the eye quite yet. Might scare him worse. Might scare them both worse.

A small hand lit like a little bird on his shoulder. He twitched beneath it, but he held himself together. He saw the red cap out of the corner of his eye, felt the wind lift his hair, smelled the grass, heard the pickup purring at his back. His own vehicle, not the Army's. He held on to the here and now, lifted his head and gave the boy a quick once-over, every part of him but his eyes. He couldn't trust himself to look the boy in the eye. He wasn't strong enough yet.

"That was close, wasn't it? Scared the...livin'..."

Not a word from the boy.

Cougar took the risk of patting the hand on his shoulder. It was okay. His hand was steady. "But you're all right, huh? No harm done?"

No response. Kid was either scared speechless, or he was deaf.

Or blind. One eye, anyway. The other eye didn't move. Cougar looked him up and down again, but the only sign of blood was a skinned knee peeking through a stained hole in his jeans.

Wordlessly the boy turned tail and sped away like a fish running up against a glass wall. Cougar stood slowly, pushing off on his thighs with less than steady hands, lifting his gaze from the soles of the boy's pumping tennis shoes, down the road to the finish line.

The barn's side door flew open, and there was Mama. She was all sound and flurry. "Mark!"

Get set, go! Cougar heard within his head, where his pounding pulse kept pace with retreating feet. He got back into his pickup and let the tires crawl the rest of the way, passing up the house for the barn, where the woman— small, slight, certainly pretty and pretty certainly upset— would be somebody to talk to. The options—all but one—weren't exactly jumping out at him.

He parked, drew a long, deep breath on the reminder that he hadn't killed anybody today and then blew it out slowly, again thanking any higher power that might be listening. The doc's slow, deep breathing trick seemed to be working.

"Is the boy all right?" Cougar called out as he flung the pickup door shut.

The woman held the boy's face in her hands, checking for damage. Cougar watched her long, lush ponytail bob and weave as she fussed over her charge. It swung shoulder to shoulder as she turned big, bright, beautiful brown eyes on Cougar. "What happened?"

For the sake of those wondrous eyes he wished he had an answer. "Whatever he told you." He took a step, testing his welcome. "I'm still not sure."

"He hasn't told me anything. He doesn't speak."

Cougar looked down at the boy, who appeared to be taking his measure. "So you weren't holding out on me. But you took off before I got around to saying I'm..." He offered his hand. "I'm sorry. I didn't see you."

"What *happened?*" the woman insisted.

"I'd say he came out of nowhere, but that would sound like an excuse. All I know is that I slammed on the brakes, and..." He shook his head. "Then I saw his cap, then a hand and I thought I'd, uh...*hit*—" he glanced at the boy, and his stomach knotted "—somebody."

"You stopped *before* you saw anything?"

"Yeah. Well, I..." He owed it to her straight, just the way he remembered it. "I had a feeling. It's hard to explain. I guess I was admiring the scenery." He adjusted his new brown Stetson, stirred some gravel beneath his shifting boots. "I didn't see him. Didn't hit the horn, nothing."

"I was just getting some..." She gestured toward the door she'd left open. "Oh, God, I wasn't paying attention. I let him slip..." She gave her head a quick shake. "*I* slipped. For a minute. *More than a minute.*" She pulled the boy's head to her body. The top of it fit nicely between her breasts. He gave her a quick hug and then ducked under her arms and backed away, leaving her empty arms still reaching for him. "Oh, Markie-B, I thought you were playing with the kittens."

"I guess the mama got away. He was chasing her." Cougar's gaze connected with the boy's. "Right, Mark? You were just trying to bring Mama Cat back to her babies."

"Was it close?" the woman asked, almost inaudibly.

"He must've tripped. He was face-in-the-dirt. Blew the knee out of his jeans." He turned to the woman. "He can't hear, either?"

She shook her head. "As far as we know."

"Don't they have tests for that?" *You just crossed the line, Cougar.*

"Yes, of course. Tests. All kinds of tests." She offered him her hand. "I'm Celia Banyon. My son, Mark, is a mystery. We really don't know what's going on."

"Yeah, it was close." Either the truth or her touch made him weaken inside. He glanced away. "Really close."

"I'm… He looks…" She cleared her throat, stepped back, and her hand slid away. "Are you here to see Sally?"

That's right. He was on a mission that had nothing to do with a stray kid.

"I'm here about the training contest. The name's Cougar."

"First? Last?"

"Always." She gave him a puzzled look, and he took a shot at smiling. "Just Cougar. One name is enough." He glanced at the house. "Is she here?"

"Nope, it's just me and Mark holding down the fort today. Everyone else is either out in the field or taking care of business. You're a trainer?"

"I've trained my own horses, yeah. I heard about this wild horse contest from a friend, so I thought I'd have a look for myself, see if I can qualify."

"Mustang Sally's Wild Horse Makeover Competition. I'm not actually involved. We're volunteers with the sanctuary. Aren't we, Mark?" She touched the boy's shoulder, and he looked up at her. "We help Sally with the horses, don't we?" Then turning her attention back to Cougar, she shaded her eyes with her hand. "Sally and her husband had an appointment. Everyone else is working. I could get you an information packet from the office." She glanced at the boy. "We need to go in and take care of your knee anyway, don't we?"

Mark was staring at Cougar, who felt obliged to honor the eye contact since the boy seemed to be a few senses short of a full house.

"Where was he?" Celia asked. "He couldn't've been far away. Right? He was right here with me, and then…"

"He's pretty quick on his feet."

"I know." She sighed. "Boy, do I know."

"I'll come back later." Cougar stepped back, giving the woman plenty of space for worries that were no longer his business. The boy was unharmed.

"If you'd like to leave Sally your number…"

"I'll call her later. Think I'll head back over to Sinte and hang out for a while."

"I'll let Sally know." When he stepped back, she quickly added, "Where are you from?"

"Wyoming. Wind River country."

"Did you make a special trip?"

"Up until I met up with Mark it was pretty ordinary."

"I meant…" She reconsidered, and then she nodded, reached for the boy and drew him under her wing. "Next time…"

"Yeah." He gave a wink when he caught Mark's eye. "We'll be careful. We'll watch out for each other."

Down the road, Cougar ran across the gray cat. She was sitting exactly where he'd last seen her, as though she was waiting to be picked up. He stopped and did exactly that. The cat didn't object, not even when he slid his hand around her belly. He could feel her swollen teats. The gooseneck trailer he was towing complicated his U-turn, but he wasn't about to back down the road. He knew a thing or two about blind spots.

Celia appeared in the doorway, shaded her eyes and watched him warily. Probably thought he'd been casing the place and come back to cause mayhem. Couldn't blame her.

"I found the cat," he called out as he alighted, holding the animal to his chest. "Thought it might be a comfort."

"Thank you." She didn't reach for the cat, and he didn't offer it. She looked a little ashen. Delayed shock, maybe. They just looked at each other while he stood there like an overgrown kid, rubbing the cat behind her ears.

"She would have come back," Celia said as she led the way into the barn.

The cat started purring. He liked the feel of it. "I'm like the boy. Don't want her getting too far away from her litter."

"Mark's playing with them. I don't think he realizes. I haven't done a good job of impressing it on him that he has to…he can't just…"

Cougar squatted beside the boy and released the

cat into the newspaper-lined box, to the delight of her squirming, mewling kittens.

"Oh, look how welcome Mama is," Celia said.

Cougar watched the kittens latch on to Mama for lunch. Mark was busy making sure all seven were hooked up. He didn't seem to realize that disaster had zoomed in so close that its sickening taste still filled Cougar's mouth. Maybe the boy had already filed the lesson away, and it would serve him down the road. Cougar wished he could do the same—a wish he probably shared with the kid's mom. He turned, looking for confirmation, a little eye contact with her big, magnetic brown eyes, but she wasn't there anymore. Not the hovering kind, apparently.

But how did she know Cougar wasn't some kind of a whack job? She'd already told him he had the two of them pretty much all to himself. He'd drop a word of caution if he were the interfering kind of a...

He heard soft mewling—the human variety—coming though an open door to a dark room. He assured himself that the boy was thoroughly occupied before he stepped close to the door.

"Celia?" Her name rolled off his tongue as though he'd been saying it for years.

She drew a hiccough-y breath. "I'm...okay."

She's okay. Walk away.

"Doesn't sound like it."

"I just don't want him to see me," she whispered desperately.

Cougar stepped through the door. It was a tack room, and the woman stood tucked among the bridles. Small and slim as she was, she might have been one of them.

"How close was it, really?" she asked, her voice reedy.

"Close."

"You couldn't see him, but you stopped?"

"That's right." He didn't quite know what to do with himself now that he'd crossed his own line. He'd just met the woman, and he felt like he was looking at her naked. He took a leather headstall in hand and hung on, steadying himself for a bumpy ride. "Some people have eyes in the back of their head. I have something inside my head. It picks up where the eyes and ears leave off. *Sometimes.* Not…not always."

"Whatever it is, I need some."

He gave a dry chuckle. "It doesn't always turn out this good."

"It did this time. Mark's in his own world, and I'm on the outside, trying to look in. I blink, and he gets away from me." She drew a quavering breath. "But he's not hurt. What am I blubbering about?"

"I've still got the shakes, too. We know what could have happened. Mark doesn't, so he doesn't need to worry too much right now. We can do that for him."

"He *does* know what could have happened. Somewhere in the back of his mind he knows better than we do." She swallowed so loudly Cougar could taste her tears. "He had a terrible accident. Lost an eye."

"Car accident?"

"No. It happened…" She shut herself down. He had all the details he was getting right now. "This isn't the first time I blinked."

"Won't be the last. You got another pair of eyes in your family?"

"Mark's father and I are divorced." She paused, shifting gears. "I want what you have. A mother's instincts aren't enough with a child like Mark."

"Ordinarily I'd say *take mine,* but I'm glad I had it goin' on today."

"Me, too." She took a swipe at each eye with the back of her wrist as she emerged from her little harbor. "Just Cougar?"

"It's all I need. Pretty big name."

"It's a great name." He took half a step back as she edged past him. A singular moment had passed. "You know, the winner of the training contest gets twenty thousand dollars."

"Yeah, that's what Sergeant Tutan said." He followed her through the tack room door. "Mary Tutan. She's the one who told me about the competition."

"Oh, yes, Mary," she said, her voice brightening. "She just got married."

"I stopped in and met her husband before I came here. She's…"

"…back in Texas."

"Says she's put in for discharge. Kinda surprised me." Seeing the boy with the kittens made him smile. "Sergeant Tutan had *lifer* written all over her. She's a damn good soldier. Uncle Sam will miss her, but she's served well."

She took his measure with a look. "You, too?"

"I've been out for two months now. Officially." Which was like saying her son had had an accident. There was a lot more to it, but nobody wanted to go there. "Tell Sally I'll be at Logan's place. I'll check back in with her." He reached down and touched Mark's shoulder. "You've got a nice family there." The boy offered up a little calico. Cougar rubbed the top of its head with his forefinger and nodded. "They're too young to leave their mama."

"Maybe we'll see you when you come back for your horse," Celia said. "You'll get to choose."

"If Mark's around, maybe he could help me with that." He still had the boy's attention, maybe even some awareness of what he was saying. Cougar felt some connection. Close calls could have that effect. He'd experienced enough of them to know that. "I'll bet you know the mustangs around here pretty well. I could use your advice."

"He'd like that," Celia said. "Thank you. I…" She laid her hand on his arm. Against his will he turned, took her eyes up on their offer of a clear view into her heart. "Thank you."

He couldn't wait to get out the door. He couldn't handle that kind of gratitude. It wasn't about anything he'd done. It was about not doing the unthinkable. At best it was about an accident that hadn't happened, and he needed to put some distance between his image of what might have been and the faces in the image.

At the same time he wanted to hang around, which was pretty damned surprising. And it was about as uncomfortable as a new pair of boots.

Logan Wolf Track lived in a log house just outside the town of Sinte, where he served as a tribal councilman for his Lakota people. Cougar's mother had been Lakota, but he was enrolled with the Shoshone, his father's people. Cougar hadn't met Logan until he'd knocked on the Wolf Track door the previous night. Sergeant Mary Tutan Wolf Track was the person they had in common. A white woman, strangely enough.

Or maybe it wasn't that strange. Indian country was more open these days than ever before, what with the casinos and educational programs that opened up opportunities for people on both sides of what had long been an unchallenged fence. But before these changes and beyond Indian country, there had been the military. Cougar's people had been serving in ever-increasing numbers for generations.

Cougar had been an army police officer—an MP—and Mary had been a dog handler. She'd served as a trainer—most recently in Afghanistan—and as far as Cougar was concerned she was the best trainer in uniform. She'd paid him a visit in the hospital in Kandahar, and she'd written to him after he was transferred stateside. More recently, they'd spoken by phone. Their mutual interest in training animals had given her something cheerful to talk about, and when Mary had talked up the wild horse training competition, she had his full attention. She'd planted an idea that had pulled him out of the seclusion he'd sought after his release from a VA hospital.

Cougar was glad to see Logan's pickup parked in his driveway. It wasn't home—Cougar towed his house around with him these days—but Logan Wolf Track was the kind of guy who made you feel at home. Fellow Indian, fellow cowboy, husband of a fellow soldier. Logan opened the door before Cougar's knuckles hit the wood.

"Did you get signed up?" Logan asked as he handed Cougar a welcoming cup of coffee.

"Not yet." Cougar settled in the kitchen chair Logan offered with a gesture. "The boss was out."

"Nobody around?" He said it like such a thing never happened.

"There was a woman. A volunteer, she said. And her kid." Cougar took a sip of kick-ass and cut-to-the-chase coffee. He closed his eyes and drew a deep breath. "I almost ran over the kid."

Logan let the quiet take over, leaving Cougar to take his time, sort though the images. They were jumpy, like an old silent movie, until he came to the woman. Her face was clear in his mind, and her voice poured over the images like slow dance music.

"He's okay," Cougar said. "Came out of nowhere, but I hit the brakes in time. Scared the hell out of me, and I think *I* scared the hell out of his mom. The kid…" He shook his head. "Hell, he didn't seem to notice. Can't talk, can't hear and he's half blind. I didn't see him." Another sip of coffee fortified him. "Damn, that was close."

Logan put a plate of frybread on the table and took a seat across from his guest. "Your pickup sits up pretty high."

Cougar nodded. "I gotta get rid of those monster tires. My little brother had the truck while I was gone, and he thought he was doing me a favor tricking it out like that. Coming home present, you know?"

"How do they ride?"

"Like saddling up a plow horse. Somehow I gotta tell Eddie the monster truck days are behind me."

"That's hard. A gift is a gift."

"And the monster truck was a kid's dream." Cougar lifted his cup. "Good coffee. Tastes like Green Beans. Honor first, coffee second," he recited, paying tribute to one of the few things he missed about being deployed in the Middle East.

Logan smiled. "You and Mary were in the same outfit?"

"No, but she worked pretty closely with us. She's a real specialist. I'm the guy nobody invites to the party."

"But when the party turns ugly, it's the guy with MP on his sleeve who kicks ass in a good way."

"That's what we're all about. I've kicked a lot of ass." He helped himself to a piece of frybread. "You've been over there?"

"Gulf War." Logan claimed a piece of frybread and tore it in half. "I was a kid when I went over there. Came back desperate to find some kind of normal. I found myself a hot woman and married up. She cooled off real fast. Took off and left me with her two boys. Who became my two boys." He took a bite out of the chewy deep-fried bread. "Did Mary tell you we're gonna have a baby?"

"Already?"

"Hell, yeah. You know what else? Normal's the name of a town somewhere. Who needs Normal when you've got Sinte, South Dakota? Or… Wyoming, right? Where in Wyoming? You probably—"

"I probably didn't say. Right now it's wherever I park my outfit." He nodded toward the front door. "Room to haul two horses and sleep two people."

"What else does a guy need?" Logan asked with a grin.

"Not much." Cougar gazed out the patio door and past the deck toward Logan's corrals and pole barn. It wasn't a fancy setup, but it was trim and orderly. "My brother and I have some land west of Fort Washakie.

We own a quarter section, and we leased some grazing land, but he gave up the lease while I was gone." He lifted a shoulder. "Can't blame him. I was gone."

"Were you running cattle?"

"I had horses. Eddie had to sell them." But that wasn't what he wanted to think about right now. He turned back to his new friend. "You know the people over at the Double D pretty well?"

"I know Sally. She and Mary have been friends a long time. Hell of a woman, that Sally Night Horse. She has multiple sclerosis, but she doesn't let it slow her down much." Logan offered a knowing look. "She has a lot of volunteers coming in to help. What's the name of the woman you met?"

"Celia Banyon. The boy's name is Mark."

"Oh, sure. Celia's a teacher." Logan smiled. "Pretty little thing."

"Pretty enough." Logan's smile was slightly irritating, but Cougar caught himself half smiling, too.

"Careful," Logan said. "You crack your face, you're gonna feel it."

Cougar laughed. "Ouch. Damn, that smarts."

"It looks good on you. Like you said, no harm done. Shake it off, cowboy." Logan warmed up Cougar's coffee with a refill. "What kind of horse are you looking for?"

"A war pony. One that can go all day without complaining."

"You do know it's a contest."

"Mary said you can train the horse for anything you want."

"You have to turn out a useful horse. Not much call for war ponies these days."

"That's what *I'm* calling for. A war pony prospect." Cougar leaned back in his chair and stretched his legs under the table. "I did some endurance racing before I enlisted. Mustangs and Arabs are the best mounts for endurance, far as I'm concerned."

"That's how you'd prove your horse?"

"If they're pretty open on what you can train the horse for, I don't see why not. Endurance is a good sport. Good for the horse, great for the rider. From what I've read, it's even more popular than it was back when I tried it out. You think I can get approved to train a war pony?"

"I think you'd round out Sally's contestant collection pretty nicely." Logan grinned. "Especially now that I'm out of it."

"She needs an Indian replacement?"

"Indian *cowboy.*" Logan chuckled. "Talk about your dying breeds, huh? Cowboys are scarce enough, but us *Indian* cowboys…"

"Why'd you take yourself out?"

"The horses will be auctioned off after the thing is over, and my wife and I…" He smiled, clearly pleased with the words. "We decided Adobe was worth more to us than winning the competition, so we adopted him and took him out of the running."

"Sweet. The horse is out of the running. The owner's off the market."

"*Both* owners."

"Sergeant Tutan deserves the best." Cougar glanced out the patio door again, taking in Logan's setup. "You've got a round pen out there. How do you like it?"

"When you get your horse, you come try it out. I wouldn't be without one."

"They weren't expecting me at the Double D," Cougar admitted. "I told them I was coming, but I didn't exactly say when. Sunrise this morning, I didn't think about it too much. Felt like a good time to take a drive."

"And now you're here," Logan said. "So take your time. Stay here tonight, and I'll head over there with you tomorrow. I never miss a chance to go looking at horses."

"I just need a place to park."

"Plenty of parking space, but there's also a spare room." Logan indicated the hallway with a jerk of his chin. "It's yours if you want it."

Cougar wanted peace and privacy. He needed to build a new life, and he would start with what he loved most.

Horses.

Chapter Two

Cougar spent the night in his trailer. The bed was comfortable—great memory foam mattress one of his fellow patients at the VA had raved about until Cougar had promised to get himself one if the guy would shut up about it—and all the basic necessities were covered. The best part was the solitude. Privacy had been hard enough to come by in the army, but hospitals were worse yet. Not only did you have people around every minute of every endless day and night, but you had them poking at your body and digging into your mind.

The trailer had been another of Eddie's homecoming surprises. *Got a great deal on it for you.* Eddie had used the money he'd gotten for their horses to buy his brother a horse trailer. It sounded like a story Cougar had read in English class back in the good ol' days, only in the story it wasn't the same person selling the two things that went together. Cougar would have taken his kid brother's head off if he hadn't actually been a little touched by the whole thing. They'd been partners, but the trailer was in Cougar's name. And in the end it was a relief to know that he could still be touched in the heart, what with it being general knowledge that he was touched in the head. So who was he to accuse "Eddie Machete" of being a madman?

Logan had offered Cougar the use of his man-size shower, and he planned to take him up on it, but not without knocking on the door with a few groceries in hand for breakfast. After honoring sunrise with a song, he unhitched the trailer, drove into the little town of Sinte, parked in front of the Jack and Jill and waited for the doors to open.

The cashier gave him the once-over when he unloaded bacon, eggs and orange juice next to her register. He read the whole two-second small-town ritual in her eyes. Nope, she didn't know him.

"Anything else?" she asked tonelessly. Half a dozen smartass answers came to mind, but he opted for a simple negative.

With one arm he swept the grocery bag off the counter, thrusting his free hand into his key-carrying pocket as he turned to the door. Two big brown eyes stared up at him—one friendly, the other fake.

Cougar smiled. "Hey, Mark, how's it going this morning? Better than yesterday?"

"Yesterday?" A man about Cougar's size stepped in close behind the boy. His dark red goatee and mustache somehow humanized his pale, nearly colorless eyes. He laid a hand on Mark's shoulder, but his question was for Cougar. "What happened yesterday?"

So this is the ex-husband.

"We had a little run-in." Cougar winked at the boy as he scratched his own smooth jaw. "*Near* run-in. Mark was lookin' out for his cat, and I was looking at horses."

"Yeah?" With one hand the man adjusted his white baseball cap by the brim—the *Bread and Butter Bakery* emblem identified him apart from the woman and her boy—while he tightened the other around Mark's small shoulder and moved him two more steps into the store. "Where did all this happen?"

"The wild horse sanctuary. Are you…?"

"Mark's father."

Cougar drew a deep breath and offered a handshake. "The name's Cougar."

"What do you mean by *run-in?*" Handshake accepted, nothing offered in return. "Were you walking? Riding?"

"I was driving. I didn't see him. I drive a—"

"Where was his mother?"

"She was close by." Cougar eyed the hand on the boy's shoulder. He could feel the fingertips digging in. *Ease up, Mark's father.* "It was one of those things that happens so fast, nobody can really be—"

"In Mark's case, everyone has to be."

Man, those eyes are cold.

"I know. She told me. Guess that's why it scared me more than it scared him." He smiled at Mark, sending out *you and me, we're good* vibes. "But nobody got hurt, and we found the cat, and it was all good training."

"Training? She calls that *training?*"

"I call it good training." Cougar's keys chinked in his restive right hand. "Ever been in the army? If nobody gets killed, it's called good training."

"No, I haven't served in the military." Again he touched the brim of his cap. "But, you know...thanks for your service. Cougar, you said?"

"That's right."

"Could I get some contact information from you? I might want to get a few more details."

"About what?"

Not that it mattered. Cougar was all done with the pleasantries. He would have walked right through the guy and out the door if the boy hadn't been looking up at him the whole time, asking him for something. He didn't want to know what it was. He didn't have it to give.

"Mark is what they call *special needs,*" Red Beard said slowly, as though he was using a technical term. "I'm his father, and I have rights. Not to mention a responsibility to make sure he's getting all the services and care he's got coming. You never know what you'll be able to use to back up your case."

"Case against who?"

"Not *against* anybody. *For* Mark. Proof that his needs are special."

"His mother knows how to reach me," Cougar said. He only had eyes for the boy as he stepped around the two. "Look both ways, Mark. I'll see you around."

Cougar smelled bacon. Damn, he loved that smell. He didn't miss much about being deployed in the Middle East, but food in camp was surprisingly good, and breakfast in "the sandbox" had been the best meal of the day. Unless you were manning an outpost, in which case every meal came with a side of sand.

Logan had gotten the jump on Cougar's plan to prepare breakfast. He stowed most of his purchases in the fridge, set the bread on the table—gave the plastic Bread and Butter Bakery bag a second look and decided he wasn't in the mood for toast—and helped himself to coffee.

"I ran into that kid I told you about over at the Jack and Jill. He was with his dad."

Logan turned from the stove and the bacon he was lifting from the pan and raised an eyebrow. "When you say *ran into*…"

"I was on foot." Cougar watched the grease drip from bacon to pan. "His mother said he lost his eye in an accident. You know anything about that?"

"Not much. Happened on some kind of construction site, the way I heard it. Before she came here to teach. Her ex-husband started showing up a few months ago." Logan turned the stove off. "About all I know for sure is she's a good teacher."

"He wanted to know how to get in touch with me in case he needed some kind of witness or something. I don't know what he was talking about. It was a close call, but the boy wasn't hurt." Cougar drew a deep breath and glanced out the patio door toward the buttes that buttressed the blue horizon. "I'm sure he wasn't hurt."

"His mom checked him over?"

"Skinned his knee, but that's…" The image of the boy pushing himself up to his hands and knees brought back the wrecking ball swing—*boom!* panic, *boom!* relief. Even now his heart was racing again. "He doesn't talk. He can't really say what's…"

"At that age, they get hurt, most kids let you know with everything they've got except the kind of words that make sense. You get blood, bellowing, slobber, maybe the silent treatment, but you don't get the story until you've already assessed the damage."

"They break easy," Cougar said quietly.

"After they're grown, you look back at all the close calls and you figure somebody besides you had to be lookin' out for them." Logan handed Cougar a plate. "Go to the head of the line."

Cougar followed orders. Logan added finishing touches to Cougar's meal—the toast he didn't want and the coffee he couldn't get enough of—playing host or dad, Cougar wasn't sure which.

"My older son, Trace, he's a rodeo cowboy." Logan's plate joined Cougar's on the table. "He's broken a lot of bones riding rough stock. You gotta learn to bend, I tell him. Look at the trees that survive in the wind around here. We're survivors."

"Learn to bend," Cougar echoed.

He hadn't known Logan long, but he knew him pretty well. They'd worn some of the same boots— cowboy boots with riding heels, round-toed G.I. boots, worn-out high tops stashed under an Indian boarding school bed at night, beaded baby shoes. He knew the lessons, figured they'd both felt the same kind of pinching, done their share of resisting.

Considering all that, Cougar sipped his coffee and gave Logan a look over the rim of the cup.

"Pretty deep, huh?" Logan chuckled. "Spend a few years in tribal politics, you learn how to command respect with a few well-placed words of wisdom. Everybody around the table says *Ohan,* so you know when it comes time to vote, you've gotten the ones who were on the fence to jump down on your side."

"So that's the way it works." Cougar set the cup down with exaggerated care. "Whatever passes for wisdom."

"It helps if it's true."

"I'm having a hard time with that lately. I thought it would all come clear to me as soon as I got back to the States, back home. It hasn't happened yet. Truth, justice and the American Way." Cougar's turn to chuckle. "What the hell is that?"

"Superman," Logan said with a smile. "I heard he died. Never learned to bend, they said."

"Superheroes ain't what they used to be."

"No, but that cottonwood tree keeps right on spittin' seed into the wind." Logan nodded toward the glass door that opened onto a deck dappled by the scant shade of a young tree. "I don't know about you Shoshone, but the Lakota hold the cottonwood in high esteem. Adaptable as hell, that tree."

"Where I come from, we don't have many trees." Cougar finished off his eggs and stacked his utensils. "I could listen to you throw the bull all day long, Logan, but that won't get me into the wild horse training competition. Are we heading over to meet this Mustang Sally I've heard so much about, or not?"

Logan slid his chair back from the table. "My friend, let's go get you a horse."

Through the big barn doors Celia recognized the white panel truck when it was still the size of a Matchbox toy. It carried her heart's greatest delight and her mind's worst trouble. Part of her wanted it to slow down and take the Double D approach, and part of her wanted it to sail on past.

It turned.

It was too soon. She'd just seen her former husband last night when he'd come to get Mark for the weekend. He'd been civil enough, but that didn't make it any easier for her to be around him. Round two was bound to be uncivil. Either he'd invented some new bone of contention or devised another way to throw her off balance.

Or maybe something had come up and he was about to forego the rest of his time with Mark. No problem. No need to explain. *Just give my son back to me and say no more.*

Oh, if he would only say no more.

She finished dumping the contents of the wheelbarrow onto the manure pile, grabbed the handles and pointed the front wheel toward the barn. She didn't want to deal with Greg out in the open. Whenever there was a chance of an audience, he was *on.* His normal tone of voice was several notches higher than anyone else in the scene. And Greg loved a scene.

She wished she had time for a shower. Sure it was silly, but scent confidence always felt like a huge advantage. Stinker that he was, Greg rarely got his hands dirty.

Mark ran to his mother the moment he entered the barn. Celia got the message from his quick, strong hug—*I'd rather be with you*—and then he bolted for the cats' nest.

"We're on our way to Reptile Gardens," Greg announced. "We figured you'd be here, so we thought we'd stop in."

"This stop isn't on the way to Reptile Gardens." She pulled her rawhide work gloves off as she watched Mark claim a gray tiger in each hand and tuck them against his neck. She wanted to thank the mewling kittens and

their patient mama for the bright laughter in her boy's
eyes. "But Mark obviously needed to check on the kittens."

"The bakery changed my route. I've got the Jack and
Jill in Sinte now, and I made a special delivery there
this morning. Ran into your new friend." Greg greeted
her glance with a cold smile. "Calls himself Cougar?"

Celia tucked her work gloves into the back pockets
of her jeans. She'd learned to ignore the inevitable preamble and go on about her business until Greg got to his
point. He took fewer time-consuming detours that way.

"He said he almost ran into Mark yesterday. Could
have killed him."

Not a direct quote, Celia decided. She hardly knew
Cougar, but she was pretty sure he hadn't said that. Greg
was baiting her. If she kept her mouth firmly closed, he
would eventually go away. Maybe even without Mark if
he could come up with a glitch in his plan. News that the
rattlesnakes had escaped from Reptile Gardens, maybe,
or a tortoise quarantine.

"Why weren't you watching him?"

She hadn't braced herself for that one. It was a fair
question, and it had been haunting her since the incident happened. Sarcasm evaporated. Who was she to
criticize—even silently—when she'd failed so miserably?

"We were doing chores," she said quietly. "I thought
he was—"

"*You thought.* See, that's your problem, Cecilia.
You're always thinking. Meanwhile, he's on the move,
many steps ahead of you. And who the hell knows what
he's thinking?"

"He was playing with the cats."

"And what were you playing with? Huh? What were

you playing with, Cecilia?" He grabbed her shoulder. "Or should I ask, *who?*"

Celia jerked away, but she took only one step back, fighting him off with a defiant stare. "You can ask about Mark. Obviously I wasn't playing with Mark. I was busy doing chores, and, yes, that's my—"

"It's not your job. Your job is that boy right—"

"Hey, Mark." Cougar strolled into the barn, flashing Celia a reassuring glance on his way to the cat's nursery. He squatted, touched Mark's shoulder and then a couple of kittens. "Are they all there? Did you take a head count?"

Mark pressed a kitten under Cougar's chin.

"Have you figured out how many boys and how many girls? I think the calico's a girl." He stood easily, confident in the silence his appearance had created. Without moving from the position he'd taken, he looked directly at Celia and offered a soft, intimate, "Hi."

"Hello." Silken calm slid over her. "I understand you two have met."

"Yeah, Mark introduced us." Cougar reached down to ruffle Mark's hair. The boy looked up and smiled. "I'm glad you're here. You can help me pick out a horse."

"My son and I have plans," Greg said. "I just stopped in to see what she had to say about what happened yesterday. So far—"

"I came over with Logan," Cougar told Celia. "Called first this time."

"That must be why the boys brought some of the horses in," she said.

He glanced at Greg as though he were an image on a TV show that nobody was watching. "Mark and I can go take a look if you two need to talk."

"Mark's with me." Greg moved to block Celia's view of everyone but him. "It's my weekend. Long as you're both here, maybe you can explain exactly how my son came to be out in the road and why nobody saw him until he was nose to nose with—"

"Because he's quick, and he's small," Cougar said. "Fate cut us a break. Be grateful."

"Don't tell me to be grateful." Greg pivoted and postured, hands on hips. "You don't know what we're dealing with here. But you will if I see any more evidence of emotional or psychological trauma."

Cougar chuckled. "You wanna sue me for something that didn't happen? What are you, a lawyer?"

"No, but I have one."

"Have at it, then. If I harmed this kid, I'll make sure—"

"He wasn't hurt," Celia insisted quietly. "He's fine, and he doesn't need to hear this."

"He can't hear, remember?" Greg's challenge swung from Celia to Cougar. "Doctors don't know why, but I do. It's because his mother left him to—"

"Greg, please. Let's not do this now. You know what's going to happen." She continued to speak in hushed tones while Mark went right on attending to the kittens. He was protecting himself in ways that she could not, but still she would do what she could. Maybe he *didn't* hear, but she believed he *could,* and when he was ready, he would. Meanwhile, he had keen senses, and she would not have him treated otherwise.

She moved past Greg and caught Mark's attention. "Let's go have a look at the mustangs."

"Hell with the mustangs," Greg bellowed. "Next

thing I know, you'll have him wandering into the path of a pack of wild horses."

"They run in herds," Cougar said.

"Put the cats down, Mark." Greg grabbed Mark by the elbow and urged him to his feet. "We're going to Rapid City. We'll catch the snake show." His big hand swallowed the child's small one. "Like I said, I've got a lawyer. We're not done yet, Cecilia. Not by a long shot."

Cougar stood in the doorway and watched the boy tag along with his father, stretching his leash arm to its limit, dragging his toes in the dirt. He tamped down the urge to go after them, spring the ham-fisted trap and release the kid. Why wasn't there some kind of law against adults using kids to even a score? Maybe Cougar should make one. He'd gladly enforce it.

Come on, Mark's father, sue me.

"I'm sorry about that." Celia's soft voice drew him back into her company, where his anger began to cool. "I guess you could tell, we aren't exactly on friendly terms. I try not to say very much when he gets going like that. It's pointless to try to talk with him." She touched his arm. "Thank you for understanding."

"The guy already pissed me off once today, so the understanding part was easy. The hard part is watching Mark. He doesn't want to go."

"I know. But Greg has his new court order." She didn't sound too happy about it. "And his lawyer."

"It's none of my business," he reminded himself aloud. "Unless he wants it to be. In that case, bring it on."

"I hope not," she said with a sigh. "I'm tired of fighting. It's a distraction from figuring out what's best for Mark."

She sure sounded tired, and he felt bad about that, even though he was pretty sure whatever distraction he'd just caused hadn't been a bad thing. The truth was, he'd headed straight for the barn when he saw the bread delivery truck parked beside her little blue Chevy. He was in the habit of filing away the details of every vehicle he saw, where he saw it and whether it might blow up in his face down the road. After the conversation he'd had with Mark's father at the store, he'd done the math in his head—ex plus ex—and he'd chosen to butt in. It had taken him all of two minutes to develop a strong dislike for the man and become Celia's natural ally.

Which might have just added to her difficulties, dumbass. You don't know what's going on between these two people. When did you become lifeguard on this beach?

I saved a life yesterday, didn't I?

You came within an inch of ending one. Two, if you count yours.

"I don't have to pick out a horse today," Cougar said. "I can wait for Mark." Which was just a thought, in case anyone inside his head was listening.

"He loves them all. Whichever you choose, tell him you'll share. Come look." Celia gestured toward the far side of the barn. She led, and he followed.

They rounded the corner of the building, clambered up the tall rail fence and peered past a set of corrals. At least a dozen young horses milled about in a small pasture.

"They'll let you handle it any way you want. Run them all into the pens for a close look, turn out the ones that don't interest you, let you run your own test on those that do." She grabbed a piece of her sorrel-colored hair away from the wind and anchored it behind her ear. "It's fun to watch people make their selection. Sometimes they want the wildest one in the bunch. Other times you just know they're looking for one that looks like he's half asleep."

"I want one that's almost as smart as I am." He smiled at her. "But not quite."

"You said Logan was here? He's the one you should confer with. Have you read his book?"

"His book?"

"The one about how he trains horses," Celia said. "I can never remember titles, but it's the author's name that's important, and Logan Wolf Track is the real deal."

"The real deal, huh?" Cougar smiled. *So that's what a real deal looks like.* "I figured he was a good trainer. Didn't know he'd written a book, though."

"It's wonderful." Celia scrambled back down the fence, and Cougar jumped down after her. "I knew nothing about horses when I started volunteering here, and my friend, Ann, gave me Logan's book. Ann's Sally's sister. She's a teacher, too. We both teach at…" She waved at something that caught her eye behind his back. "He's over here!"

Cougar turned to find "the real deal" striding in his direction. Logan had parked in front of the house, and Cougar had promised to be along in a minute. No questions had been asked, no comments exchanged.

"Sally's waiting for you to fill out some papers, cowboy," Logan announced. "That's one woman you don't wanna keep waiting."

"Why not? She kept me waiting."

"That was yesterday. You keep her waiting today, you'll just be giving her time to think up something the sanctuary needs that nobody but you can provide." Logan clapped his hand on Cougar's shoulder. "Because you're just that special."

"What's your specialty?" Cougar asked Celia.

"Well, with a B.S. in education—Sally calls it a B.S. in BS-ing—we've found that I'm really good at distinguishing horse manure from boot polish."

The men looked at each other.

"Shinola?" Celia insisted. *"Boot polish?"*

Both men grinned. "Long story short, there was a time when she kept Sally waiting," Logan told Cougar.

Chapter Three

"I'm going with one of the Paints."

Cougar laid the form on Sally Night Horse's desk, most of the blanks, including the horse's ID number, finally filled in. He'd been leaning toward a bay that showed strong Spanish Mustang traits when Celia mentioned her son's attraction to the spotted horses, and the Medicine Hat gelding was the flashiest horse in the bunch.

"Good choice," Logan said. The two men exchanged looks—Logan's knowing, Cougar's *what the hell*. "Medicine Hats are sacred, and that one has classic war bonnet markings. Brown ears, little brown cap on his head. He'll show nicely."

"He'll cost you," Sally said.

Sally Drexler Night Horse had a way of filling a room with energy. She was the positive charge in the

Double D's power grid, and her latest project had her chugging ahead full steam, even when she had to power up her wheelchair. Her office furniture gave her wide berth, and even though she wasn't tied to the chair, she wasn't apt to explain or deny it, either. Sally was in charge.

Clearly when she said *pay up,* a guy was expected to ask, "How much?"

"Your cowboy ass planted firmly on the line. Or the fence." Sally leaned to one side as though she were trying to get a look at the new applicant's backside. "In the saddle is good, too. We need eye candy for a documentary we're shooting."

"That Paint is pretty sweet." Cougar slid Logan a what's-up-with-this look. Logan chuckled.

"True, but you're the real bonbon. Put the two of you together…" She gave Cougar a sassy wink. "YouTube, here we come. And we'll be goin' viral."

"What do I have to do?" Cougar asked. He barely knew what YouTube was, which was already considerably more than he cared to know.

"The woman who's doing the video—Skyler Quinn—Logan's son, Trace, knows her pretty well. Right, Logan? The Double D is giving Match.com a run for their money lately. They hook you up on paper—or what passes for paper these days—but we make matches on the ground right here in horse heaven."

Logan laughed. "Skyler has Trace carrying her camera bags and loving every minute of it, all right."

"Sally's got talent," Sally quipped as she started scanning his application. "My husband, Hank, may be the singer in the family, but I know a thing or two about harmony. I know future soul mates when I see them."

She glanced over the edge of the paper and gave Cougar a loaded look with an enigmatic smile, which almost scared him. He was a private man, and right now she was holding some of the keys to his privacy on what had always passed for paper.

She went on reading, all innocence.

"Anyway, Skyler's out in Wyoming, and you're located in that beautiful, rugged, picturesque Wind River country. She'll love that." Sally flipped the application in Cougar's direction and pointed to a blank space. "You forgot to fill out this part. Location, location, location."

"I'm…kinda between locations."

"What does that mean?"

"Between a VA hospital and a home site in Shoshone country," he said impatiently.

The sergeant was supposed to have laid the groundwork here. If anybody had a problem with his recent history, he wasn't going to waste his time with any damned application. He'd been banged up a little and spent some time getting his head straight. He wasn't about to open up his medical records to get into a horse contest.

"But you ranch," Sally affirmed, adjusting her glasses as she took another look at what he was beginning to regard as his test paper.

"Did I say I'm ranching now?" The muscles in the back of his neck were threatening to knot up beneath the short hairs she was tugging on. "It doesn't say I'm still ranching. It says that's one of my qualifications. Right?"

In the time it took him to draw one of those cleansing breaths he'd been taught to practice, he was able to put everyone in the room out of his mind. It was just a piece of paper. "The answer to this question is ranching," he said calmly as he tapped the word with an instructive finger. "And this one… Wind River is where I'm from." He pushed the paper across the desk. "I put Sergeant Tutan down as a reference. Call her."

Sally turned the paper over. "Mary's your only reference?"

"Why didn't you put me down?" Logan asked him. "You're bringing the mustang over to my place."

"For a few days." Had he accidently walked into a damn bank? He had half a mind to turn on his heel and walk out.

But his other half a mind remembered how far he'd have to walk to get to Sinte, where he'd left his roof and his ride—the two things he owned the keys to.

And the whole of his mind was set on taking on that Paint gelding with the sweet brown "cap" pulled down over his ears. He had no idea what kind of endurance horse he'd make, but he didn't care about winning an endurance event. Running it from start to finish would do fine.

"I have a few acres. My brother and I turned our lease back and sold…" Be damned if he was going to stand here and recite his whole life story. He was glad Celia had gone back to the straightforward BS in the barn. "Look, I'm a civilian now, pretty much starting over."

Sally looked up with a genuine, no BS smile. "All we need is a location and a description of your facilities."

"Put down my place," Logan told her. "Are you coming to the celebration? You and Hank?"

"Wouldn't miss it. I hear Mary's coming home."

He turned to Cougar, grinning like a proud papa. "Don't say anything, but the celebration's for her. She just got a Commendation medal. Meritorious achievement. Did she tell you?"

"She didn't. That's some eagle feather to cap off a career."

"No kidding." Logan tapped Cougar's chest with the back of his hand. "You're coming, right? I need a color guard. You got your uniform packed away in that trailer of yours?"

"Your Lakota VFW will want to do the honors." Cougar had put his army green away for good. "But I'll be there. I'll step up to the microphone and pay tribute to her the Indian way."

"Put down my place," Logan urged Sally with the distinctively Indian version of a chin jerk.

"Cougar?" She wanted his word.

"Is that okay with you?" Cougar asked her.

"For now," she said. "But if anything changes…"

"I'm not gonna run off with your horse."

"I'm not worried about that, Cougar, and he's not my horse. I answer to the Bureau of Land Management, and you know how that goes. Red tape from here to Texas."

"Stand down, soldier," Logan said. "You're set for now. But you'll have to let Sally get some of that Shoshone country video footage she's lookin' for."

"*Footage* is boring," Sally said as she signed the form. She swung her chair and fed Cougar's commitment into her copier. She punched a button and followed up with a punch to the air. "Woo-hoo! Chalk up another Indian cowboy for the cause. Women are our target market, and they're not looking at your boots, boys."

Cougar had to laugh. He took damn good care of his boots. Spit and Shinola.

"You have a clean barn, Sally."

Cougar turned toward the voice. Celia stood in the office doorway, her shiny pink face framed by zigzagging tendrils of damp hair. The smudge on her jaw—some kind of boot polish, no doubt—called out for a friendly thumb to wipe it off. He rubbed his itchy palm on the outside seam of his jeans.

"Hey, Celia, thanks," Sally said. "You want some lunch?"

"I wondered if you wanted me to grain the horses they just brought in."

"Actually, I'm short-handed today, and there's something else I had in mind for you." Sally's dramatic pause drew Cougar's attention. "We really depend on our volunteers. They're mostly women, and I just hate piling so much on such slim shoulders."

Celia laughed. "Since when?"

"I know I don't thank you often enough, Celia, but I'm trying to do that right now," Sally deadpanned. "And in a meaningful way."

"I could help out while I'm here," Cougar said. "What do you want done?"

Sally hiked up the corners of her mouth, nodded and winked at him in a way that just didn't seem right for a married woman. "Put the man to work, Celia," she said.

Logan cleared his throat. "He rode over with me, and I have a—"

"Few hours to contribute? We're hauling bales and riding fence. Take your pick."

"I'll have to take door number three," Logan said. "The one marked Exit."

"But you're already committed," Sally said, cocking a finger at Cougar. "You'll be helping Celia, and she'll give you a ride back to Sinte." She glanced at Celia. "Is that okay with you?"

"What's the assignment?"

"Find out how six of our horses got into Tutan's pasture." Sally took off her glasses and waved them at Logan. "Your father-in-law—my damned neighbor—called the sheriff again. He doesn't believe in handling these things between neighbors."

"My father-in-law." Logan shook his head. "That's a real kicker."

"I sent a couple of the kids out, but they came up empty, said they couldn't find any fence down. I just want to make sure. If there's a hole in that fence, we'll get it fixed before Mary gets back." She made a smooth-sailing gesture. "Peace in the valley for Mary's sake. You think he'll show up at the celebration?"

"I doubt it. But she'll want to see her mother. She's only got three days this time." Logan lifted one shoulder. "Kinda sorry I planned this party now. Only three days."

"She's a short-timer," Sally said. "Pretty soon she'll be home for good. But I wouldn't put it past your *father-in-law* to run our stock into his pasture just to stir things up again. Which is fine by me—he cranks on his egg beater, I'll come back at him with my Mixmaster—but it's not fair to Mary."

"You can pick your wife, but not your in-laws. Listen, I'm all for mending fences, and I'd stay and help with it, but I've got a meeting," Logan told Cougar. He nodded at Sally. "Watch out for that one. She'll have you thanking her for letting you paint her fence."

Sally laughed. "If he's lucky he'll get to stretch some wire, but there's nothing out there to paint. I'll tell you what, though, I can't wait to paint this house. I don't care how many people try to horn in, I'm saving it all for myself." She wagged a finger at Cougar. "I might let you watch, but nobody's taking over on me."

"She'll get takers. You watch." Logan clapped a hand on Cougar's shoulder. "I gotta get goin'. I'll move the pickup so we can load up your mustang. I'll buy these two lunch, Sally. The Fence Rider's Special, on me."

"One volunteer sponsorship. That's going on your tab, Wolf Track."

"This woman knows how to rake in the donations," Logan told Cougar. "Better than a cable TV preacher." He gave Sally a two-fingered wave. "You oughta get yourself a show, Sally."

"People in love are so generous. Gotta strike while they're hot," Sally called out after Logan. Then she gave Celia the calculating eye. "A weekly TV show. How could we work that?"

Celia glanced at Cougar. She was smiling. The horses weren't the Double D's only attraction for a woman packing some heavy cares. Cougar nodded, and her smile brightened even more.

"Oh! Speaking of hot irons," Sally said. She was checking her watch. "Hank should be pulling in any time now. He's been out shoeing horses for a team-roping club, and I'm not gonna let him cool off just yet." She rolled back from her desk, put her wheels in park and levered herself to her feet. "Just the thought makes me weak in the knees.

"So you guys get that horse loaded up and then help yourselves in the kitchen, will you? Pack up the Fence Rider's Special. Sandwiches, chips, water and a wire stretcher. Enjoy the ride." She winked at Cougar as she reached past him for her cane. "I know I will."

"Can't wait to meet her husband," Cougar whispered to Celia as they headed for the front door.

"Hank's a lovely man, and Sally's the rising tide that lifts all boats," Celia said. "She's unsinkable."

Ordinarily Cougar might have doubted the notion on the grounds that the person simply hadn't waded in deep enough, but Sally was far from ordinary. And Celia? If he drowned in the woman's eyes, it wouldn't be a bad way to go. As long as he didn't come bobbing back up to the surface and find himself in a mud puddle. He'd been there, and he wasn't going back.

He wasn't looking forward to loading a wild horse into a trailer, either, but Logan had him covered. No pushing, no pulling, no slapping. The closest thing Cougar had ever witnessed to Logan's display of patience was a dog training session with Staff Sergeant Mary Tutan, which led him to conclude that theirs was a match made in the kind of heaven where dogs and horses— the Lakota *sunka* and *sunka wakan*—dwelled side by side with human spirits. The notion made a pretty picture for Cougar to file among the good places he regularly sought for refuge when ugly thoughts crowded his damaged head.

"The Paint doesn't have a schedule," Logan said. "And we won't try to give him one. If our time runs out, we'll walk away and come back later."

Logan instructed Cougar to approach the trailer *beside* the horse, not ahead or behind, and to remember that horses were naturally claustrophobic. Cougar had no trouble sympathizing with that particular fear. It was one of several he'd brought home with him.

It turned out he'd chosen a horse that was compliant by nature, and Logan was able to drive away with him in time to make his meeting.

And then it was time to take a ride. Celia insisted on packing food for a picnic, which was a foreign concept to Cougar. But he liked the way she hustled around the kitchen, checking in with him to find out whether he liked this or that. He tried to tell her he wasn't picky, but she kept asking, and he kept saying "Sounds good" until she had that canvas lunch bag so full she could hardly close it.

Celia was able to walk right up to the big gray gelding she would be riding, but Cougar had to throw a loop over the buckskin he was assigned. Celia wasn't going to let him saddle her horse for her until he claimed it to be a man's duty according to his tradition. He didn't know whether he was feeding her a line—he figured saddling a woman's horse had to be covered in some soldier, cowboy or Indian code of conduct—but the way she bought into it made him feel good.

The horses were two of Sally's favorites. Tank—the big gray—was the only horse Celia would ride. He'd been Sally's first adoption, and he was a good example of the mustang-draft horse cross that had developed when farmers had opened the gates and turned their plow horses free to fend for themselves. Hostile times, hard times, changing times, the horse had survived it all.

So far.

Cougar rode Little Henry, a horse that liked to play. He was exactly the ride Cougar needed. Coming home to find that he no longer owned a horse had been a staggering blow, the bullet that broke the soldier's heart.

Hoka hey! he'd cried. *It's a good day to die!* He'd flipped out, gone on a killer drunk, ended up behind bars and then behind locked doors on the psych ward.

And all he'd really needed was a playful horse and a good day to ride.

Celia's ponytail bobbing around up ahead of him was a nice bonus. The way it swished back and forth from shoulder to beautiful bare shoulder was an unexpected turn-on. His little buckskin danced beneath him, eager to pass the big gray, but there was no way Cougar was giving up this view. It took them nearly an hour to reach their destination.

Time well spent.

"There it is," Celia said of the grassland beyond the three-strand barbwire fence. "That's Mary's father's land. Dan Tutan territory. Here at the Double D he's known as Damn Tootin'. He's one of those ranchers who think any grassland that's not being used by cattle is wasted."

"In Wyoming it's any land without an oil or gas well." Cougar rested his forearm across the saddle horn and drank in the view. He was not a desert man. He'd take rugged mountains, high plains, river bottom breaks or prairie sod over never-ending sand any day. Even in late summer shades of green and brown, an endless expanse of living, breathing, gently swaying grass was a beautiful thing. "You know how people say nothing's sacred anymore?" he mused. "If that's true, guys like that are probably way ahead of the game."

Her voice slid up behind him coupled with the warm breeze. "What game?"

"Whoever dies with the most kills wins."

"Is this a video game or a war game?"

"Doesn't matter. It's always open season, and every hit counts. You choose your—what do they call it? Avatar? Driller and grass grabber must do okay, and it sounds like Mary's father is still rackin' up points." He turned to her, adjusting the brim of his hat against the sun. "Once you're into it, you can find all kinds of ways to play."

"What about you? Are you in the running?"

"I thought I was. Tried to be." He smiled a little, remembering the gung-ho would-be warrior who'd once greeted him in the mirror. "But I was only going after the bad guys, you know? Only the ones who wore the bad-guy outfits and carried the bad-guy flags."

"What happened?"

"I ran into a little trouble." He sighted down the fence line. "Is that a wire down?"

"Good eye," she said as she tapped the gray with her heel, wheeling him toward the loose wire, no further questions asked. "It's only one wire," she called back to him.

"Can't be the spot we're looking for, but we'll fix it."

Celia dismounted and started untying the tool bag from Cougar's saddle. He reached back and pulled the slipknot on the other side of the saddle skirt.

"You sure tie a tight knot," Celia grumbled. He turned, took the slip string from her hand and gave it a quick jerk. She looked up, squinting against the sun or frowning at him, he wasn't sure which.

He gave her a proper wink. "I sure do."

"I hope that means you can stretch a tight wire."

"I'll stretch it as tight as you want, but—" They both grabbed for the slipping tool bag, and their fingers overlapped. For an instant neither of them moved. "Just don't ask me to walk it," he finished quietly.

"No," she said, quieter still. "I wouldn't."

He gave a little on the bag. "Got it?"

She nodded, and he pulled the saddle strings out of the way. He dismounted, took a pair of leather gloves from the canvas bag, and they set to work on the barbed wire. Few words were exchanged other than "Hold this," and "Hand me that." He gave no thought to what she might be thinking. Watching her hands move, catching the expression on her face when she watched him, simply being with her filled his head completely. How long had it been since his head had been filled so agreeably?

When the work was done they stood back and admired it, as though they'd created something truly outstanding. They looked at each other and nodded.

"We'll report this to Sally and chalk up some points," Celia said. "Makes it worth the ride even if we don't find a real opening in the fence."

"Riding is worth the ride." Cougar adjusted his hat. "Riding in good company is even better."

"Agreed." She glanced away quickly. "Ready for lunch?"

Figuring they might be getting on each other's nerves in a good way, Cougar reconsidered the sea of grass. A single cottonwood tree beckoned from Tutan territory. "Where's a good hole in the fence when you need one?"

"You'd trespass for one skinny tree?"

"Damn tootin'."

Celia laughed. "What counts as a 'kill'? If it's the same as a coup, you could score two in one day."

"It's part of my nature to be satisfied with counting coups as kills, but in the army, a coup doesn't earn you any feathers." Cougar gave a tight smile. "Uncle Sam issues you an M16, a near miss gets you nothing but dead."

"You've turned in your combat gear," she reminded him.

"Yeah, but I was trained to trespass." He stepped into the stirrup and swung into his saddle. "I'm still getting used to civilian rules. Transitioning, they call it."

Her saddle creaked as she pulled leather and hauled herself onto the big gray's back. Cougar mentally whipped himself for not offering a leg-up. *Civilian rules.*

"Is everything knotted up nice and tight?" She shaded her eyes with one hand and pointed to the next rolling hill with the other. "First one gets to the top without losing tools or lunch wins."

He grinned. "Say when."

The big gray beat the little buckskin with an easy, long-legged lope. Cougar called Celia the winner and counted himself a civilian gentleman, at least for one day. The draw below the hill not only offered better shade than the lone tree on the other side of the fence, but an end to their search. They could see a break in the fence at the top of the next hill.

Celia's canvas saddlebags yielded sandwiches, fruit, water and cookies, which she laid out on a faded blue bandanna-print tablecloth on the shady side of a thorny buffalo berry thicket. Cougar loosened the saddles and staked the horses in a shady spot. He plucked a few berries.

"They're not ripe yet," Celia said.

"I know. I used to have to pick these for one of my

grammas. It wasn't my favorite chore, but it was worth it for her jelly. She made pemmican, too."

"Must be a lot of work. They're so small." She took off her boots and socks and settled cross-legged, showing off toenails painted the same color as the tablecloth. "They grow in Wyoming?"

"Uh-huh. Ever been to the western part of the state?"

"I haven't traveled much since I moved here from Iowa." Grass crackled beneath the cloth as she patted an empty corner. "Come sit with me."

"More sitting?" He chuckled as he squatted on his heels. He didn't much like eating on the ground anymore, but he liked the way she phrased the invitation. "Why not? Indian style for you, and cowboy style for me."

"What makes that cowboy style?"

"Saddle sores." He raised a cautionary finger as she handed him a sandwich. "Never sit cowboy style with your spurs on."

"Really? Saddle sores?"

He shook his head, laughing. "Not yet. Can't find my spurs, and I haven't ridden a lot lately, so who knows?" He nodded toward her feet. "Were you standing in your stirrups?"

"My toes need a breather. They hate shoes."

"Shoes, yeah, but those are boots. They're not even related." He grinned. "Cute toes."

"You like?" She wiggled all ten. "Mark painted them for me. Blue is his favorite color."

"Kid's got a future in, uh…"

"Cosmetology?" She offered Cougar a bottle of water. "He wants to fly airplanes. It's been a while since he's talked about it, of course, but he still cruises around the backyard with his arms outstretched." She demonstrated with arms stiff, eyes closed, face lifted toward the sky. The tip of her nose and the high points of her cheeks were pink. "It could happen. Modern medicine, you know, new miracles every day." She opened her eyes suddenly. "How's your sandwich?"

He took a bite, but he couldn't taste anything with the boy gliding silently through his head and the woman tugging on his heartstrings. He nodded and gave her a thumbs-up.

"How did you get involved with the sanctuary?" he asked after some quiet time had passed. He'd finished his sandwich and stretched out in the grass. "Through the Drexlers or the horses?"

"Through my son."

She was ready to tell him. Where he came from, people listened without staring the speaker in the eye, but he could feel her need to exchange signals the way her people did, through the eyes. Hers were frank and fragile. All he knew about his was that, like his ears, they were open.

"The accident happened three years ago. He went through surgery three times and therapy…all kinds of therapy. We were running out of options. Sally's sister, Ann— Did I mention we both teach at the school in Sinte? Anyway, Ann suggested I bring him out there to see the horses. He took to them immediately."

"Maybe the horses took to him."

Celia smiled. "You sound like Logan. He says things like that in his book. You know, that horses relate to people the way they relate to each other and that they're very sensitive to people who are open to…

equine vibes." She shrugged, laughed self-consciously. "Something like that."

"But you're not a believer."

"I want to be. I *desperately* want to be. So far, no one can tell me why Mark doesn't hear or speak or what can be done about it. They tell me it's probably psychosomatic, which usually puts him in some kind of a program, some new and different kind of treatment, some complicated insurance category. I don't care what they say, Mark doesn't hear, and he is unable to speak. I haven't found anyone who relates to him any better than the horses here do." She glanced at the two that grazed nearby. "But they don't speak to me, either, so I can't tell what's going on."

"Give him time."

"I have. I bring him here as often as I can. It's good for both of us. But I have to find a better doctor, a better... something."

"You...wanna tell me what happened?"

"We were with a friend who was having a house built. She was showing me around—this goes here, that goes there—and I was really into it, sort of building my dream house vicariously. Mark was almost six. Curious about everything, you know? He was, um...he put his eye over a hole...in a floor...and someone who was working down below..." She held an imaginary dagger in her fisted hand and thrust upward.

Cougar braced for the blow he'd lived and relived, the white heat of stabbing steel, the breathtaking terror, the staggering pain. As long as he was awake and in control of his faculties he could hold himself together and let it pass through him. The physical pain in his own body always turned out to be bearable, but it was everything that went with it—all the jacks in the boxes, ghosts in the closet—the doubts were what kept him up at night.

"It was a metal rod." She spoke softly, for which he was grateful. "It took the eye, every bit of it, but nothing more. It could have been so much worse."

Questions sprang to mind, but he ignored them. She would have been asked more times than she could count, and she would have answered and answered and answered. But she would never be sure of anything except that she could have done something differently. And every time she replayed the incident, she would try something else, and it would always change the outcome for the better.

He reached for the hand she held fisted on her knee, uncurled her fingers with a gently probing thumb as he drew it to him and pressed his lips to her palm.

"I know," she said, barely audibly. "It's over. Just breathe."

"It sounds easy." He closed his hand around hers and smiled sadly. *"I know."*

Chapter Four

Celia sat on the front step watching each little vehicle as it appeared on the hill half a mile away and slid down the highway. Watching traffic was relaxing when Mark was home. Passing cars were few and far between on their remote highway—a welcome change from their apartment overlooking a busy street in Des Moines—and Celia had made up several guessing games for them to play on summer evenings. Mark loved anything with paws, hooves, wheels or wings, and Celia loved anything that made Mark happy.

Mark's father was not one of those things, and watching for his delivery truck was not relaxing.

A house full of silence had her back. She would take Mark from Greg's clutches, thank him very much, go inside and close the door. Still quiet but not utterly silent, the house would surround them and keep him out for two blessed weeks. She loved her new house. It was only new to Celia—certainly nothing fancy—but the walls were solid and the doors had locks. And it was *hers*. The mortgage was in her name. She'd bought the house and forty-two acres of grass land in an estate auction, and she'd spent the past six months struggling to fix the place up.

Celia took off her gardening gloves, laid them beside the clay pot she'd just filled with mums and rubbed her hands together. One palm felt warmer than the other. She turned it up, imagined a lip imprint and smiled to herself. It was one of many places she'd never been kissed, and she'd been deeply touched by the gesture. Prickles-in-the-throat touched. Butterflies-deep-in-the-belly touched. Cougar was anything but a cool cat. He was warm and sensitive, a little mysterious, *a lot* attractive, a surprise at every turn.

She would see him tonight at the powwow grounds. Just thinking about it made her feel like a teenager.

But waiting for Greg made her feel anxious and worn out at the same time. Their marriage had been over before Mark's accident. He'd never taken much interest in Mark even though he liked to say he was looking forward to riding bikes with his son or playing ball or having some real conversation. As soon as Mark got over being a baby, they were going to be great buddies. Mark's milestones passed without Greg's notice, while Celia's every move was closely monitored. Who was that on the phone? Why was she showing off her boobs in that dress? What was she really doing when she said she was taking the baby to the park? Celia signed them up for counseling, but the handwriting was on the wall.

The accident made it official. Celia had done the unthinkable. She'd dropped the ball. God only knew what she was doing when she was supposed to be watching, but Mark was broken beyond repair. Now it was one surgery after another, more doctors, more treatment plans, more sleepless nights. Greg had no stomach for "medical stuff," and he had all but taken his leave. He cut his visitations or skipped out on them altogether. But that was before the "know your rights" guy had stepped in.

The sight of the bread truck sent dour memories packing. As soon as the truck stopped, Mark was out the door and in her arms.

Greg strolled up behind him. "We didn't get to the Reptile Gardens, but we did some other stuff. We hit Mickey D's a couple of times." He ruffled Mark's hair. "Didn't we, son? Golden arches?" He whistled as his hand dove over an air arch. "They had a playground. Good times, huh?"

"I missed you, Markie-B. You had fun?" Celia touched his chin, and he turned to her with a smile. "You and your dad had fun?"

"Are you hoping he'll say *no?*"

"I'm hoping he'll say something. I don't care what it is." She kissed the top of his head. "You will. I know you will."

"What have you heard from the insurance company?"

And there it was. Greg's new baby's name was Lawsuit.

Greg's renewed interest in Mark had been clear from the moment he'd followed Celia to South Dakota and petitioned for the visitation rights he'd shrugged off when they'd divorced. With the help of his new ambulance-chasing lawyer—he relished saying the words *my lawyer*—Greg had claimed Celia wasn't looking after Mark's best interests in court, any more than—according to Greg—she had looked after his safety the day he'd been injured. The medical bills had been covered, and Celia agreed that there was no way of knowing what other needs might arise for Mark in the future. But there was a sure way of knowing what Greg was up to. All it took was watching him operate.

Celia could think of nothing she'd rather do less.

"I'm sure the insurance company has your lawyer on speed dial," she said. "Or *vice versa*."

"I have a feeling you'll hear first. You still have everyone thinking you're Saint Cecilia."

"As far as I know they're still dickering."

"Cheap bastards," he spat. "We should get… You know, *Mark* should get millions. You hear about multimillion dollar damage awards every day."

"I don't want to talk about this, Greg. Not now."

"Don't you want our son to get what's coming to him?"

"That's what the lawyers are for." She put her arm around Mark's shoulders and turned to mount the steps. "We'll see you in—"

"What's with the Indian guy?" he said quietly. "How long has that been going on?"

She stopped between steps.

"Not that it's any of my business, you and him, but he nearly ran over my kid. That's my business."

Fortunately, Celia, you're the only one who can hear him. Go inside.

"If he's in such a killing hurry to get to you that he'll mow down anything that gets in his way—" his shoe—

one shoe—scraped the gravel "—and it's my kid that's in his way, you damn well bet that's my business."

"Don't threaten me, Greg." She opened the front door and nudged Mark inside before turning to face him. "I *will* get a restraining order."

"How did I threaten you? What did I say? I'm not touching you. All I'm saying is that I will protect my son."

Celia stepped inside.

"Somebody has to." Greg wedged the words in edge-wise through the shrinking crack as she closed the door.

Mark put his arms around her and hugged her.

"We're fine, Markie-B." She rubbed his back. "You and me, babe. We're going to..." She lifted his chin. "Look at me. We're going to a party tonight. We're going to have supper, and there'll be lots of kids. I think there will. *Of course,* there will. It's a celebration. *And*..." She smiled. "You remember Cougar? He'll be there. We like him, don't we?"

She went on chattering the way she had done when he was a baby, without talking down to or babbling at him. He was a person, and he was present, and he would soon participate in the conversation. It was more than a wish on her part. It was an expectation. She talked about horseback riding and fixing fences and Bridget the cat going hunting again and catching a mouse in the tack room.

Mark was eager to throw his clothes in the laundry room, shower and wash his hair. While he was in the bathroom she checked his clothes. They reeked of cigarette smoke. Greg wasn't a smoker. She had the feeling the weekend entertainment—likely involving gambling—had not been kid-friendly.

She wasn't going to grill Mark about it. He was glad to be home, and he didn't need to be asked questions he couldn't or wouldn't answer. But she wished they could go back to the days when an occasional supervised visit with his son was all Greg had time for.

Mark emerged from the bathroom looking handsome in his khaki shorts and polo shirt, light brown hair all slicked down. Little gentleman that he was, he opened the front door for his mom. But rather than follow her, he ran back into his room.

He'd changed his mind. He'd had enough socializing. He didn't understand what was going on. He *did* understand, and he wanted no part of it. Celia was trying to learn new signs and signals, but she would have given anything for a word from her son. One word, one…

…foot in front of the other, scurrying down the hallway, bringing her a boy who'd almost forgotten his favorite red baseball cap, which he never took with him when he went with his father. He was giving her all the signs and signals a mother could want in one beautiful gap-toothed smile.

It was a quiet, stonewash denim sky evening. The sun had lost its command, and the swallows were gaining on the mosquitoes. Somebody was testing out a microphone, somebody else toying with a drumbeater as Celia parked her car in the grassy parking area at the powwow grounds. She didn't see Cougar's pickup, and she gave herself a mental scolding. She knew she would have parked near him, as close as she could get, and she felt silly about it. Eager and silly. *Totally regressive, Celia.*

Kinda fun, though.

But his mean-looking black pickup wasn't there. Maybe he wasn't coming.

"Hey, you made it."

Celia whirled toward the sound of the voice and found Cougar striding toward her. He looked wonderful in a crisp white Western shirt, sleeves rolled just above his wrists, and a pair of Wranglers he was clearly wearing for the first time.

Mark accepted Cougar's handshake without hesitation, man to man. He greeted Celia with a hand press. She didn't want him to let go. His eyes said he got it, and his smile said he was glad of it.

"Lots of people here," Cougar said as he touched the small of her back. She took Mark's hand, and they started walking toward the bowery, the big circular structure—open in the center, thatched with leafy cottonwood branches around the perimeter—that had stood for ceremony and celebration for the Lakota since before recorded memory. "You probably know most of them."

"I know more kids than adults. I teach sixth graders. I know some parents. I've met Mary once at the Double D." Celia nodded toward the far side of the arena, where familiar faces were sharing animated conversation. "There she is, over there with the Drexler crew. Except Sally and Ann are no longer Drexlers. I wonder where Ann is." She was rattling on awkwardly. She never missed a school function, but her social calendar was pretty empty. "Have you met Ann Beaudry, Sally's sister? We both…"

"Teach," Cougar remembered, smiling. "You've mentioned that a few times. You must really enjoy it."

"Most days I do. I struggled the first year, but now

that I have a few years' experience under my belt, I think I'm getting pretty good at it."

"Is that what that bulge is?" He dropped the smile and gave a chin jerk toward her small waist. "I was wondering."

Celia laid her hand over her belt buckle and gave him the squint-eye.

"Mrs. Banyon!" Celia turned to greet a bright-eyed girl with a sagging ponytail. "We're playing dodge ball. Can your son play?"

"Dodge ball?" She glanced at Mark, who was playing on the bench with a Matchbox airplane. "I don't know, hon, that's so dangerous."

"We'll be careful," the girl promised. "We're using a soft ball."

"A softball?"

"A *soft* ball. It's practically a cotton ball, it's so soft." She looked up at Cougar. "It's the only one we could find."

"It's so nice of you to include Mark, but you know, his eye…"

"I'll make sure he doesn't get hurt." She leaned sideways to peek at Mark's face. "I'm gonna be in your class next year, Mrs. Banyon."

Logan joined them, laughing as he laid a hand on the girl's shoulder. "So there's no way Maxine's gonna let anything happen to your son. I'll vouch for her. She's my niece's kid. The Indian way, that makes her my granddaughter. Right, Maxine?" He winked at Celia. "Last week she told me to stop calling her Maxie."

"Geez, Lala Logan. That's so embarrassing."

"I didn't know. I'm just a man." Logan gently tugged Maxine's ponytail. He nodded toward the long serving table the younger women and teens were loading up with kettles and pans. "Why don't you take Mark over to get some chow? The kids are lining up. Go ask Grandma Margaret whether she wants you to help with the little ones or take plates to the elders."

Maxine folded her arms and glared at the row of chairs holding elders-in-waiting near the serving table. "I'm helping the kids."

"What happened?"

She gave a nod toward the group. "That one said I walk like a duck."

Celia couldn't tell from the gesture whether the wizened woman with the black scarf tied over her head or the leathery man with the walker was the deadpan tease.

"Do you?" Logan asked.

"No!"

"Then don't worry about it. He used to tell me I walked like a bear."

"Are Ann and Zach here?" Celia asked on the tail end of the laughter.

"I saw them somewhere." Logan glanced over his shoulder and forgot who he was looking for. "Hey, here's my decorated warrior."

Dressed in Army green, Sergeant Mary Wolf Track took her husband's hand and stood by his side. "And I see Cougar's already made a friend," Mary said, offering her free hand. "Celia, right? You volunteer at the Double D."

"She's a teacher," Cougar put in. "When I signed up for the wild horse training competition, that quick, Sally had her teaching me how to fix fence."

"Cougar's the one who deserves the medal," Mary told Celia, as though he needed a reference. "He might not be a soldier anymore, but this man is one brave cowboy."

"More like a cowboy brave," Cougar said diffidently.

"A cowboy brave. Now there's a... What's that called?" Mary snapped her fingers and pointed at Celia. "Teacher?"

"An oxymoron." Celia smiled. "Just remember *stupid laundry soap*."

"Ignore them." Logan clapped a hand on Cougar's shoulder. "Either way, you're the man. When we turn on the mike, would you step up first?"

"You said you'd keep it simple," Mary pleaded.

"That's just me," Logan told his wife. "Can't speak for everybody here." He turned to Cougar. "She just married into an Indian family. She's got a lot to learn."

"He's a tribal councilman," Cougar told Mary. "Sure sign he never met a microphone he didn't like."

Logan laughed. "The Shoshone are well known for their pretty faces and their coarse tongues."

"The Lakota are just the opposite," Cougar said. "Scary faces and silver tongues."

"The way I heard it, you're part Lakota," Logan said.

Cougar smiled. "I got the best of both worlds."

"Get yourselves something to eat," Logan said. "I can't wait to hear this guy put his money where his mouth is."

Celia was thinking the same thing. Cougar didn't strike her as the speech-making type, but he spoke of his fellow soldier—he called her an outstanding warrior—from the heart. She was a dog handler and trainer, and when the time came, Cougar spoke reverently of the lives Mary's dogs had saved. The handlers in his MP unit "talked up their Tutan-trained dogs like they were smarter than the average GI. And the average GI wholeheartedly agrees."

There were several testimonials, including one from Mary's shy but very proud mother, but there were even more expressions of appreciation and camaraderie in arms from veterans. Celia had heard about the generations of American Indians who had served in the military, but she was seeing the evidence, hearing the voices for the first time. She paid close attention and mentally recorded each comment having to do with a way of life that hadn't really touched her until now. For all her close listening and mental note-taking, her thoughts were with Cougar. What was he remembering? How did he feel about it?

She felt chosen when he came to get Mark and her for the Honor Song. They cued up behind the VFW color guard, followed by Mary and her husband and family. The slow iambic cadence of the drum echoed the earth's heartbeat, and the procession grew. The singers pitched their voices ever higher, calling the stars, one by one, to the purpling sky.

And then came the dancing. The young Fancy Dancers' colorful feather bustles covered their back from head to toe, and when they twirled it was like watching a spinning carnival ride. Shawl Dancers used their flashy fringed shawls to create wings worthy of hovering on the wind, and the Traditional Dancers' porcupine roach headdresses bobbed in perfect imitation of a tall grass prairie chicken all puffed up and "booming" to attract female attention.

"Look at Mark." Cougar laid his hand on Celia's knee and nodded toward the drum circle, where children gathered like groupies.

Mark was dancing! He was imitating the other boys—whirling, stomping, nodding like a playful grouse—but he was moving in perfect rhythm with the drum.

"Pretty damn good," Cougar said. "How long has he been at it?"

Celia couldn't take her eyes off her son. She shook her head slightly, spoke softly, as though he might hear her and feel self-conscious. Her heart fluttered wildly. "He's never done it before."

"He's sure feelin' it."

"That's it, isn't it? He feels the drum." Not quite the same as hearing it, but it was an acknowledgment, wasn't it? He was being reached. "I dance with him at home, but he just stumbles around. It must be the live music. The bass drum. I should've tried this before."

"Haven't you been to a powwow?"

"We've been to a couple, but only to watch. We sat on the bleachers. This is the first time he's…"

"First time you've let him get in there with the kids?"

She glanced at him warily. "I try to keep a close watch on him. I really do."

"Anybody can see that, Celia. Anybody with honest eyes." He smiled and nodded toward the clutch of kids. "Either Maxine's trying to make some points with you, or she's a little mother hen. Probably both, huh?"

"A little prairie chicken hen, right?" Her shoulders settled down. She hadn't even realized she'd hiked them up. He had a way of smoothing her ruffled feathers with a single stroke.

She laid her hand over his. "Do you have children?"

"Nope."

"You connect with them. Most men don't unless they have their own."

"Really?"

"Some don't, even if they have their own." She tipped her head back and gave a small, sardonic laugh. "I'm sorry. I'm making generalizations. I don't know what I'm talking about."

He turned his palm to hers and closed his hand around hers slowly. "You see the people hangin' outside the bowery?"

She glanced over her shoulder, between a couple of droopy branches and into the dusky perimeter. Shadows strolling, shadows giggling and chasing shadows. Shadows loitering and lingering in tête-à-tête pose.

Celia smiled. "Ah, yes."

"There's some old-fashioned courting going on out there."

"I thought this represented courting." She nodded toward the dancers.

"It does if you're a bird." He laughed. "I tried Fancy Dancing, but with two left feet, I was the one who laid an egg. Picked myself up off the ground, climbed on a horse and suddenly the chicks noticed me."

"And you were how old?"

"About fifteen." He squeezed her hand. "What else do you wanna know? I don't have a wife, or an ex-wife or a girlfriend. I do have an ex-girlfriend." He lifted one shoulder. "She got tired of waiting. Can't blame her."

Holding hands. She was holding hands with a man, and her insides were jitterbugging. *Ask an intelligent question, Celia.*

"How long were you over in the Middle East?"

"Altogether, thirty-two months."

"That would be hard on a relationship."

"Some people have done three, even four tours between Iraq and Afghanistan. People who have families at home…" He glanced across the circle. Arm in arm, Mary and Logan were receiving well wishers. "…should be with their families. I could do another tour, easy. So somebody with a family could come home."

"Do you want to go back?"

"I don't know where I want to be. Except maybe…" He turned to her, looked into her through her eyes in a way that thrilled and terrified her. She was the connection he had on his mind, and she wasn't sure he wanted it there. But there it was.

He cocked his head toward the perimeter. "Care to go for a stroll?"

She wanted to look away from the eyes that held hers, check with Mark, find something to hold her back, but she couldn't. The look in his eyes shifted from challenging to amused.

"He's still there."

She smiled. "Still dancing?"

"Still dancing. Havin' a hell of a time."

She stood up from the end of the bench, and he followed suit. She gave his hand a squeeze. "You're making a statement here."

"*You're* making a statement, teacher." He gave a return squeeze as they emerged from the bowery onto the beaten path. "Nobody knows me here. I am—what's the expression? *Off the reservation.*"

"But this *is* the reservation," she accommodated him, laughing.

"Not mine. But, hey." He leaned down close to her ear. "Let 'em talk. I ain't afraid of Indian country."

"Off the reservation," she echoed as they strolled. "Indian country. Does any of that bother you?"

"You know what bothers me? Chief. I don't wanna be called *chief.* First sergeant was good enough. Any rank with *chief* attached…" He shook his head.

"How about commander-in-chief?"

"They couldn't call me *chief,* then, could they?"

"Have they always just called you Cougar?"

"Nope." He looked at her, and for a moment she thought he might tell her his secret. Or one of them. He grinned. "But they do now."

She glanced into the bowery as they passed the drum circle. There was Mark trying out a new step, and there was Maxine, tending to her assignment.

"Hey." Cougar tugged on her hand. "It's our turn to swing."

"What?" She stumbled over the angle her sudden pivot required. "We're walkin' here," she quipped.

"Did you see this?" He led her down a small grassy slope, jumped a dry washout and scrambled up the other side.

She couldn't see anything. The stars were out, the horizon held on to a rosy sliver of leftover sunset, and the moon had yet to show its face.

"Do you have night vision?"

"Of course."

Now she saw a huge, dark, hulking tree. It wasn't until he grabbed something hanging from it, tugged and didn't detect any give that she realized what kind of swinging he had in mind. He assessed the distance from the ground to the thick, wide plank seat, muttered, "Too low," and tossed the seat over the branch that held it until the length of the ropes met his requirements.

"I can't wait to see you climb up there and fix it when you're finished playing," she said.

"Don't hold your breath." He gave the ropes a firm tug.

"But what about the kids?"

"They'll fight over who gets to make the climb."

"Somebody might fall."

"I never did." He took a seat. "How much do you weigh?"

"Two-twenty. What's it to ya?" She grabbed the rope, stacking her hand on top of his, and circled toward his back. "I'll start you off with one push, but then—"

He caught her at the waist with a long shepherd's crook of an arm. "Come sit on my lap and let's ride double." He drew her to stand between his knees. "This is a two-passenger swing. They don't make 'em like this anymore."

"Because seats made out of leftover lumber…" She took a rope in each hand, kicked off her shoes, stepped up and planted a foot on either side of his hips. "…somebody could get hurt." She lowered herself onto his lap.

"Keep most of that two-twenty off somebody, he'll be fine."

She stared at him for a moment. She shouldn't reward such talk. But, then, she shouldn't be sitting on him like this. Her next bold move—tipping his hat back— exposed bright expectation in his eyes. He was waiting. She dropped her head back and laughed.

He took his hat off and tossed it in the grass, pushed off the ground with his booted feet just as she stretched her legs out behind his back. "You're a hundred or so off in your estimate, I'd say."

They were flying low, chasing evening shadows with bright smiles.

She leaned back on the upswing. "This is crazy!"

"You never did this?"

"Okay for two little people, maybe, but this limb could break."

"Pretend we're one big person, and we'll blend." Forward on the backswing, she lent him an ear. "A good tree feels sorry for a kid this heavy—" he nipped her earlobe between whisperings "—coming out here all alone in the dark—" nuzzled her cheek "—looking to take a few minutes' flight."

His first kiss came mid-flight. Lips to lips only. No hands, no arms. It felt like a warm greeting, a discovery so welcome as to warrant a replay. And another, and another, each tasting sweeter than the last with her sitting on him like this and him growing on her like that. Barely perceptible, a tickle between her legs that begged to be pressed. But the shared awareness and the delicious resistance was worth preserving. A good lover would know that. And Cougar, she now knew, would be such a lover. The lover she'd known in dreams.

They let the motion wind down by slow degrees. Just before standstill he took her face in his hands and kissed her lusciously, thoroughly, to the point of knowing nothing but the joy of kissing.

He touched his forehead to hers, rolled it back and forth, surely leaving an imprint. She hoped it contained that kiss.

"I'll say it for you," he whispered. "This was fun, but you have to get back."

"It was." Her lips brushed his. "I do."

He smiled against her lips. "The next move is all yours."

She laughed. "And there's no graceful way."

But she was barefoot and agile, and she untangled herself from man and swing without losing dignity.

Which, surprisingly, she suddenly felt in abundance. Dignity and class and beauty and all kinds of confidence magnified by a simple kiss.

He recovered his hat, and she her shoes, and they walked hand in hand, the bright bowery up ahead. He pointed toward the rear view of a man carrying a child on his back.

"That's Mark!" Celia exclaimed.

"Riding the master trainer," Cougar said with a chuckle as they approached the narrow washout. "Kid's got style."

"How long have we been gone? Ouch!" She grabbed for his arm. "I lost my shoe."

"I see it." He bent to retrieve her comfy, clunky slip-on. "You do know this is boot country."

"They're hard to take off."

"Let's see if I can lift two-twenty."

He gave her the shoe, and she laughed as he swept her up in his arms, jumped the narrow crevasse and scaled the grassy slope in three steps.

"Wow, you really *are* strong." And they were getting closer to the bowery. "Now, if your manly ears have heard enough music, please put me down before someone sees us."

He stopped short. "Too much style?"

"A little overstated." She kissed him sweetly. "But thank you."

He lowered her to the ground and into her shoe, and they lingered a moment longer, a pair of outsiders clinging to each other in the dark like children reluctant to go in for the night. They watched Maxine lay claim to Mark while Logan grabbed his wife's hand for the *kahamni,* the traditional Lakota circle dance.

"I know where I don't wanna be tonight," Cougar said, picking up on the question she'd asked earlier. He jerked his chin toward the Wolf Tracks as they side-stepped out of view. "And that's camping out in their backyard. She's home on a three-day pass."

"I have a huge yard," she offered, sounding more eager than she'd intended. "Is that all you need? I have electricity and running water, too. And an old barn." Eagerness shamelessly amplified, she thought. "And most of a corral. It's only missing a few pieces."

He grinned. "Are you offering me a place to park?"

"A place to camp." She lifted one shoulder. "At least as long as Mary's home. I'm sure you'll want to go back to their place to work on your program."

"For sure. Gotta work my program."

"But it looks as though the honeymoon is still on." The couple had danced back into view on the far side of the circle. "It's really no trouble."

"I'll pay you," he said.

"I'll take that offer as acceptance of mine. No strings attached." She glanced over her shoulder toward the silhouette of their tree. "I don't know about where you come from, but we don't charge for parking in these parts. One thing we have in South Dakota is plenty of parking space."

"Just because I let you kiss me doesn't mean I'm looking for favors."

She turned back with a mock scowl. "*Let* me—"

"I don't mind paying in services. So what can I do you for?"

"How good are you with tools?"

"I'm a man. I know tools. What do you need?"

"What *don't* I need? I bought a fixer-upper and a few

acres of pasture in an estate sale. The farm land was sold separately, and nobody wanted the home place. Nobody but me. But there's more to this fixing up business than I thought."

"Now we're on the same side. No confusion. We both know what's on the table." He offered his hand. "You got yourself a deal."

Chapter Five

Dust billowing around the truck made it hard to see where he was going, but he couldn't slow down now. If he did, something bad would happen. There were people out there, faces looming in the dust clouds, but they didn't matter as long as they stayed clear of the truck. He had to get to a place where he wasn't eating dirt every time he tried to take a breath or say a word.

Sand.

The place was made of sand. Grittier than Wyoming dust, sharper sting in the eye, bigger clog in the nose, worse threat to the throat. He was fine with faces. He could fire back at bullets. Sand was the enemy. Hot wind and godawful sand.

Suddenly one fiend sucked the other up, and the faces were unveiled. Unreadable eyes, most of them, all but the children. He slowed down for the children.

They were dancing, whirling like the wind, arms outstretched like little airplanes, eyes bright.

Eyes right. Right side of the road, right here right now, pedestrians have the right of way. Right foot, Cougar, brake right.

Don't stop for anything, Sergeant. That kid's coming for us. You slow down, he takes us out. Do. Not. Stop.

Cougar sat up screaming. Shaking, shooting out of the sandbox like a bottle rocket and screaming to beat hell. He knocked the blind off the window and hit his head on the ceiling above the trailer's loft bed. He was in for a killing headache.

Headaches don't kill people. People kill people.

Head noise killed sleep. Cougar couldn't remember his last full night of quiet sleep. The first part of the night almost wasn't worth the last part, but a guy had to take what he could get. Otherwise the hole got deeper and the walls felt tighter.

He went to his medicine chest and sorted through his options. He kept them all handy these days. Pills, packaged injections, a pint of whiskey, a pack of cigarettes. He'd used them all. He wanted to be free of them all. "It's a process," the doctors kept telling him. And banging his head against the wall—ceiling, whatever— was part of it.

He grabbed two bottles—pills and booze—pulled his boots on, burst out the side door and into the vast and velvety night. He set the bottles side by side on top of a fencepost and backed away. Maybe the fresh air would do it. Maybe all he needed was wide open spaces and a chill chaser. He went back for the pint, uncapped it, drew a long, deep breath full of whiskey fumes and capped it back up again.

"Are you okay?"

Cougar spun on his heel, crouching like a Hollywood gunfighter.

Celia squared up, looking surprised, like he'd been the one who'd just sneaked up on her. He straightened slowly. His reaction was nothing to be embarrassed about. Hell, he was glad to know that getting himself locked away by the white coats hadn't dulled his reflexes too much. As long as he wasn't looking for anything sharp or loaded, he was doing fine.

"I'm sorry," she said quickly. She was clutching a small, fringed blanket around her shoulders, and her legs were bare.

He gave a dry chuckle. "What for? Catching me in the act?"

"Of…"

He gestured with the bottle. "I have orders to stay away from this stuff."

"Orders from whom?" She tipped her head to one side, as though she'd just asked whether he'd rather have a glass of warm milk.

"*Whom?* I like that. Whom. It sounds proper." He studied the bottle. "Dr. Choi, that's *whom*."

"Which isn't proper, but we won't get into that. You sounded…" She swished through the dry grass toward the fencepost, but she paid no attention to the pills. Instead she peered into the deepest part of the cricket-filled night. "I ran into a badger out here one night. Scared me half to death."

"Did he come after you?"

"He ran one way, and I ran the other." She turned to him, one hand spread over her chest holding the blanket in place. Moonlight washed over her worried face. "Do you mind if I ask why Dr. Choi gave you those orders?"

He nodded toward the pill bottle, poised on the post like a shooting target. "He wants me to take those. He says they'll mix it up with the spirits."

"You mean you're not supposed to mix the medication with spirits?"

"Is that the proper word for booze? Spirits?" He laughed and shook his head. "I don't mind if you ask. You should ask. I'm sleeping in your backyard, and you've got a kid to protect. Not to mention..." He scanned her makeshift cloak, neck to knees, and his imagination shifted into high gear. "Sorry I woke you up."

"You didn't. I was sitting outside." She shrugged. "I heard you, um..."

"Friggin' embarrassing as hell." *Sitting outside?* Right. He glanced at the sky. It must have been three in the morning. "I scared you."

"A little. Only because..." She was staring at the bottle in his hand. "It sounded like you were in terrible pain."

"Just a dream." He set the pint back on the fence and stood back. "I don't like taking the pills. They feed the spirits they're supposed to fight off."

"The things that go bump in the night?"

He chuckled as he plowed his fingers though his thick hair. "Yeah, my damn head. I can't get used to that low ceiling."

"Mark has nightmares, too. He crawls in bed with me sometimes, and the only way I know he's crying is that his face is wet."

Cougar froze. Instantly the scene played out in his

mind. Screaming, crying, cussing, head-banging—a kid doubled over in terror and none of these outlets were available to him.

He shoved his hands into his pockets. No shirt, but he'd had the presence of mind to keep his jeans on. "You think he hears anything in his dreams?"

"That's a good question." She let the blanket slip as she linked her arm with his. T-shirt and shorts. No bra. His arm was tucked against the side of her breast. "Come sit with me. I can't sleep now, either."

"I could sure sleep if I picked a poison." But he let her lead the way, which was not in poison's direction.

"What woke you up, Cougar? Was there some kind of noise? In your dream, I mean."

"Not exactly. It's hard to tell. Hell, it was a dream."

"If I knew what was going on in Mark's head, maybe I could…" With her free hand she flipped the blanket over her shoulder. "Logan's book is all about understanding what goes on in a horse's head. They can't tell you in words, so you have to pay attention to other signs, other language." Her tone dropped from instructional to personal. "I know what happened, but I didn't actually see it happen."

"Neither did the guy who did it."

"No, he didn't. The poor man, he was devastated. He came to the hospital and just sat there, waiting. He ended up losing his job. There was no warning, no signs, no barriers, but that was the contractor's fault. No one actually saw what happened. Everyone heard him scream."

"You hear it in your dreams?"

She nodded.

"Hey. I'm sorry. Last thing I wanna do is go diggin'

around in somebody else's dreams. I know the sound
of…" They'd reached the house. He planted a boot on
the first rickety step of two leading to the ground-level
deck. It squeaked and sagged but didn't crack. He surveyed the deck and noticed crude patches in the plank-
ing. "…worn-out wood. Ready to retire."

"I've made some temporary repairs." She pointed to
a glider at the far edge of the deck. "That part's pretty
sturdy. I covered some holes, and then started replac-
ing planks."

"It won't take much to fix up one of those pens so I
can get started with the mustang. You want me to start
on the deck after that? Or do you have something more
important that needs doing?" He glanced left and right.
"I don't see a swing."

"A swing would be…" She laughed. "Swings can
be dangerous. Come try this glider out." She sat down
beside him, mentioned the night chill as she tossed the
blanket across their laps and pulled her side up to her
shoulders. "I don't have many tools, but there's lots of
good lumber in the barn. It came with the property. I
think I need some sort of an electric saw."

"You did this much with just a handsaw?"

"I found pieces that fit. I looked at saws once, but I
couldn't find one that wouldn't cut fingers."

"Did you try the toy department?" With no thought
of making a move he reached under the blanket and
drew her legs onto his lap. Her feet stuck out, rubber
flip-flops dangling off her polish-tipped toes, and her
skin felt smooth and cool. "You might as well be walking barefoot on a bed of nails."

"What do you mean? These shoes have great soles."

He groaned. "That's cute, but this is hay needle and

prickly pear country. You don't know what you'll run into in the dark."

"When I came outside I wasn't planning to leave the deck." She leaned back for a double take. "You do realize that, don't you?"

"Yeah, but you did. It would've been smarter not to."

"I suppose. But I don't feel stupid." She laughed. "Okay, maybe about the footwear."

He ran his hand over the top of her leg until he reached cloth. "What's this?"

"Pajama shorts," she said in a clipped tone, as though any idiot would know. And then she groaned. "Yes, they're pajamas, but they're also shorts. I'm not running around naked, and I'm not trying to…"

"Seduce me?" He laughed. "It wouldn't take much." His hand retreated to her knee. "I'm just saying you could get hurt. You heard somebody in trouble, and you came running. You don't know what kind of trouble you'll find."

"I know you wouldn't hurt me," she said quietly.

"I wouldn't want to." He lifted his arm over her head and pushed against the deck with his booted foot. The glider creaked as he set it in motion. "I'd rather rock you gently."

"A swinger and a rocker." She laid her head on his bare shoulder. "Aren't you cold?"

"I woke up in a sweat. The night air is just what the doctor ordered."

"Dr. Choi?"

The question was loaded, and his instinct was to duck. But he let it rest with him for a moment, testing it out. It was heavy, but coming from Celia, it didn't feel like a threat. She'd stuck her neck out saying she believed she was safe with him, and she deserved answers since he was parked in her backyard.

"I got hit in an explosion," he said quietly. "I was lucky. I didn't lose any limbs. Had a little head damage, but it could've been a lot worse." He tipped his head back and drank in more night air. "I won't lie to you, Celia, I was a mess when I came home. When I came *back*. I don't know about home."

"Things had changed?"

"No. Not much. I mean, I thought so at first, but then I realized that life had gone on exactly the way people had been living it before I left. What was I expecting?"

"You felt like a stranger?"

"I was. But it was me. My problem. I felt betrayed, but the truth is, I didn't wanna be with people who'd known me before. I didn't know who I'd become, but I knew I couldn't be that person again. So they were right to move on." He glanced at her and smiled. "And that's a whole lot more than I ever told Dr. Choi."

"It's the glider. It's like a watch on a chain." She mimicked the motion with her hand. "Watch the watch."

"That's the one thing they didn't try on me." He tipped his head back again and kept rocking. "What a night," he said. The moon had disappeared, and there was nothing overhead but an infinite black canvas stippled with stars. There was no yard light, no city, no town, nothing throwing man-made competition up against natural gems. "You know, there are a lot of people who have never seen the Milky Way? Never."

"They see it in Afghanistan, don't they?"

"Oh, yeah. It's almost as pretty as this. Unless you're wearing night vision goggles that turn everything glow-in-the-dark green. Which is fun if you're into video games. You line up a target, you score a hit, you rack up the points. Points, people, whatever. The bad guys." He glanced at her. "The people over there are tribal."

She smiled. "So are yours."

"Shh. Don't tell anybody." He looked up again, still rocking, his hand stirring over her smooth skin. Two strangers in a strange land, he thought. Somehow they were able to cut through the chaos and see each other clearly. "What a night," he said again.

"Shooting star!" She pointed to a ribbon of fire streaking across the sky. "Did you make a wish?"

He shook his head. "It's a gift. Halfway around the world you see something like that, it clears your head." He smiled against the night. "*Look at me,* it says. *I'm going down in a blaze of glory.* And everybody gets the same gift. You don't have to fight over it."

"Even so, a girl can wish."

"If it has anything to do with this deck, I can tear it out and replace it in a day or two, depending on what's under there for footings." He ran his hand along her shin and closed it around her slender ankle and gave a playful shake. "If it's as flimsy as these shoes…"

"Stop knocking my shoes." Laughing, she started to pull away, but he held on until she looked up. "You don't scare me, Cougar."

"That makes one of us," he said as he lowered his head and went in for a kiss.

He knew he was hungry for the taste of her, but he thought he could sate himself with just that—a taste. Even if he couldn't, he would make do, maybe take a little more, a touch of the tongue, a nip of the lip. He drew breath from her breath as he slid his hand up slowly, stretching his fingers to accommodate the widening of her thigh, feeling every fine hair, sensing her excitement. He paused when he encountered clothing, deepened his kiss and let his fingers slide farther until he felt the catch in her breath, and then he stayed his hand as he kissed her through the moment.

"Two of us now," she whispered when she could.

"I'll stop."

"That's what I'm afraid of."

He kissed her again while his fingers explored the swell of her hip, the peak of her pelvis, and the dip into her belly. His thumb found coarse hair marking another peak, a hard place, a protective boundary. The feel of her all-over, deep-down trembling thrilled him, pushing for quick, decisive action. It pleased him to test his own resistance even as he challenged hers.

He rubbed her belly. "I don't make wishes," he whispered, and he tried to offer up a smile with his little joke, but it wouldn't come.

"I do." She touched his cheek. "But… I can't…"

"I know."

He knew what?

Celia lay on her bed staring at the ceiling, enjoying the instant replay. All but the talk. And wasn't that a fine how-do-you-do? Yes, indeed, she made wishes, and one of them involved heartfelt words. He'd talked. He'd told her things he hadn't told anyone else. All she'd said was that he didn't scare her, and he knew that.

What else did he know?

That she couldn't believe how potent his kiss was? That she couldn't believe the urgency it made her feel, the need to reach out and hold on and kiss back? That she couldn't believe the power of a little pleasure, couldn't ask him to make love to her, couldn't stop thinking he should stop and hoping he wouldn't?

Of course he knew all that.

But did he know she wasn't really a flirt? If he thought about it, it was probably pretty obvious, considering how inept she was at it. Could he tell how happy she was to have him there and how upset she was with herself for showing it? She'd been feeling alone and vulnerable lately, and she wanted someone on her side.

She'd also wanted him to kiss her, told herself she was wishing for it in an ephemeral, shooting star sort of way. A wonderful, first date kiss. Okay, second date. Third. A have-your-cake-and-eat-it-too kiss. What made her think she could just order it up? *I'll have one of those with a little petting on the side.*

She felt like an idiot. Being tongue-tied was probably a good thing. Whatever was on the tip of it hadn't escaped. *I can't go to bed with you, can't have sex with you, can't run away with you.*

Nobody's asking you to, Celia.

And I certainly can't fall in love with you.

He'd get a good laugh out of that one. A welcome laugh, no doubt. Nightmares left people shaken, unbalanced and slightly chagrined. A good laugh would have helped him throw all that off. She could have made him laugh by jumping from conclusion to conclusion like a kid playing in a trampoline park. Not that it was something she normally did anywhere but inside her head, but brightening a dark corner for a good man plagued with bad dreams seemed like a worthy cause. And Cougar wasn't the kind of man who would judge or take advantage or...

Damn. Was that a warning cramp? Celia slipped her

hand under the elastic waistband of her pajama bottoms and rubbed her concave tummy. She wanted to slide her little finger lower very gradually, a fraction of an inch at a time, pick up where he'd left off, but she was feeling dangerously lightheaded, and her lips tingled. If she wasn't careful, she'd soon be giving birth to premature trust.

She awoke—surprised to be waking from what had surely been a night without sleep—to the sound of hammering somewhere outside. She looked at the clock, sprang from her bed and checked Mark's room. *No Mark.* She dashed to the kitchen and peeked through the yellow curtain on the back door toward the broken down corral.

Sigh of relief. Mark wielded the hammer while Cougar held a plank in place. Relief drew another breath and became full-blown delight. Mark was hammering! And Cougar was patiently supervising, helping him adjust his grip and strike the target.

Celia took a quick shower, put on a T-shirt and a pair of jeans so that she could wear her boots, and dashed outside, her damp hair clipped high on the back of her head.

"Good morning," she chirped. Her glance ricocheted from Cougar's eyes, shaded by the brim of his hat, to her son, who didn't notice her. He was bent over a cinder block trying to tap the curve out of a bent nail. "You two are up early."

"Some of us are grateful to see the sun rise." His short-sleeved shirt was unbuttoned, and the sun was doing a glorious number on his bronze chest. "Coffee?"

"I haven't started it yet. I was surprised to see Mark

out here. He's not supposed to leave the house without telling me. Did you…?"

"Nope. He came out to help. If I didn't know better, I'd've thought he heard the racket." He gave her an enigmatic look as he reached around her for the blue plastic mug he'd left sitting on the wheel housing of his trailer. "Thought maybe you were ignoring us. I made coffee. Want some?"

"I'm sorry. I'll get breakfast—"

"Sorry about what?" He gestured with his coffee toward the camper door. "We had Lucky Charms. There's some left if you're interested."

"Sorry about the cold breakfast."

"It wasn't cold. It was just a little dry. But who needs milk when you've got Lucky Charms? Right, Mark?" It didn't seem to matter to him that Mark didn't look up. "This guy sure can swing a hammer."

"So can I." She glanced at the front end of the trailer. It would be interesting to find out how he liked his coffee. Even more interesting to see what was behind that door.

But she pivoted on her heel and turned her attention to her business. "What can I help with?"

"We're gonna need more nails." He nodded toward a collection of building supplies he'd gathered on a makeshift workbench fashioned from a pair of sawhorses and part of an old Dutch door. "That was the only box I found in the barn. I looked around pretty good."

She brightened. She had just what he needed. "There's a whole keg of them in the barn. An old wooden keg. It's probably been out there for fifty years or more."

"A nail is a nail." He nodded a come-on toward the

trailer door. "What made you decide to buy a place like this?" he asked as he opened the door and gestured *after you*.

"Like what?" Stepping up on the running board, she glanced over her shoulder. "Rustic? Don't I strike you as the rustic type?"

"You don't strike me as a *type*." He smiled. "But you do strike me."

"And you do have coffee." And a tidy little kitchen with a tiny stove, sink, refrigerator, microwave, miniature cabinets that might have been part of a downmarket trailer or an upscale playhouse. There were three books stacked on the bench seat—the top one written by Logan Wolf Track—and an iPod dock hanging on the wall. Music and books, she thought. Good signs.

"It's a good place." He was standing in the doorway. "There's another cup above the sink. But you're pretty isolated."

"Not that far from Sinte, which is where I work, where Mark goes to school." She poured her coffee. "Is it okay if I nuke this?"

"Blast away. Sinte is pretty far from the beaten path," he noted. "People come to a reservation for a job, it's usually temporary. You buy a place like this, you're putting down roots."

"The price was right, and no one else wanted it." She pressed a button and smiled when the light came on in the little box above the stove. *So cute.* "My roots were tired of pots. They wanted solid ground. They like it here."

There was more to it, of course. She'd needed a place that was off the beaten path, but not so far off that she couldn't get Mark the help he needed. She thought she'd put the worst of her difficulties behind her. They could both sign the alphabet, even though Mark didn't seem interested in using it. Give him time, the specialists advised. Mark was still a mystery. She'd been able to keep him insured, and the Mayo Clinic, where he'd been treated originally, had recommended a good therapist for him in Rapid City. She hadn't expected Greg to follow her and insist on resuming his visitations with Mark after admitting he didn't know what to do with a kid who wasn't "normal."

But there was his lawsuit to consider.

"It's a good place," Cougar repeated as he backed away to let Celia out the door. "You can build on a place like this."

"The one thing I worry about is that Mark might be a little too isolated, especially when school's out. That's why I got started with the horse…" She squinted into the sunlight, shaded her eyes with her free hand and scanned the site. "Where did he go?"

"He went in the barn. He took me in and showed me around a while ago. He's the one who found the nails. Hey, what's the story on that old car back in the—"

"You asked him for nails?"

"I picked up the hammer, and he saw." He gave her a silly grin.

Cute again, but Cougar didn't get it. Working together was one thing, but Mark wasn't supposed to play in the barn alone. She set her coffee on the workbench and headed for the barn. "Celia," he called after her. But she kept going. First things first.

It took a moment for her eyes to adjust to the barn's murky shadows, but she heard a scraping sound, and when she saw what was making it, she stopped in her tracks. Mark was struggling with the nail keg.

"Cut him some slack," Cougar said quietly.

She turned, her heart pounding with excitement. "He *heard*."

Cougar glanced past her toward Mark and then back again. He nodded, but when she started to speak, he signaled her to hold it. "Take a breath, Celia, you're scaring us." He smiled. "We've got nails."

She turned back to Mark. "Let me help you with that, Markie-B." She hoped to see his eyes before she touched him to get his attention, and she was disappointed when it didn't happen. In fact, he gave her a less-than-welcoming look when she laid hands on the keg. "No?"

"Mark's got it," Cougar said quietly. "We'll have ourselves a corral before dinnertime. I was just telling Mark before you came out, I can hardly wait to show him the Medicine Hat mustang. Told him the horse loaded pretty easy, which is a good sign."

She looked at him curiously.

"That's what *he* wanted to know. Sign of what? Sign that the horse is ready. Some signs speak louder than words."

"You think so?"

He thumbed his hat back. "'Course, I haven't written a *damn book* on the subject, but I know a thing or two about coming back from a wild place. It takes some adjustment."

"And you can't be sure who your friends are?" She watched as her son mastered rolling the heavy keg on the bottom rim. She felt rejected. Maybe she was the one who didn't get it.

"I think you know who your mother is. She's the one who's been there since day one. Mine's gone, but if she was still alive, I'd probably want to lean on her if she'd let me."

"Would she?"

"I don't know. It's been a long time. I like to think she would." He laid his hand on her shoulder. "For a little while. Maybe you don't want her to step back right away. But then something new comes along and you forget yourself for a few minutes. And then a few more and a few more."

"You're saying I'm too protective." Mark rolled the keg through the open door, set it down, looked up at her and grinned. She gave him a thumbs up. "So you don't think he *heard* you ask for nails."

"I'm saying he might just be listening more than you realize. I don't know if he's using his ears, but I think he's trying to hear and be heard." He slid his hand over her back and nudged her toward the door. "And I'm saying it'll be good to get this corral fixed so we can sneak over to Logan and Mary's place and try to load up the mustang without disturbing the honeymooners."

She nodded. "I see what you're saying."

"And seeing is one way to catch on. So you're good." He draped his forearm over her far shoulder. "Not fast, but good."

Chapter Six

There was no sneaking in and out at Logan and Mary Wolf Track's home. The couple was outside playing ground games with their claybank mustang with the flashy black mane and tail. Logan had the horse batting a big rubber ball around the paddock with his muzzle, much to the delight of his wife, who had devoted her professional life to training dogs. The honeymooners were "in the zone," and Mark fairly glowed as he watched. Any minute he's going to cheer, Celia told herself. She could almost hear his voice.

"Time out for substitutions," Mary called out. "Mama needs rest."

"Come on, Shoshoni, show us what you got." Logan patted the super-size beach ball and beckoned Cougar. "The name of the game is Horse's Pass."

"I just started the book," Cougar shouted. "Haven't

gotten to that chapter yet? Are you in the pictures? 'Cause if this gets out, you won't make the Indian Cowboy Hall of Fame." But one look at the excitement in Mark's face had Cougar vaulting over the fence. He reached back over for Mark. "You and me, partner. What we've got is game."

"What would you like to drink?" Mary asked Celia as they hiked themselves up on the open tailgate of Logan's pickup. Mary reached into a small cooler. "The choices are juice and water. And I have crackers and fruit. Try some strawberries." She offered up a pint box. "Please help me with these. It's like eating flavored packing peanuts, but don't tell Logan. He thinks he's getting me fresh fruit. He's forgotten what local fruit tastes like." She nodded toward the paddock, calling attention to the boys, the horse and their big red ball. "It looks like Cougar has a new tail."

"Simpatico," Celia mused as she bit into a nearly flavorless red and white strawberry. "I've never seen Mark take to anybody like this, especially after the accident."

"Logan said it started with a *near*-accident."

"No, I meant…"

Celia watched her son push the ball toward the horse, who whacked it right back and knocked the boy over like a bowling pin. She took a step toward the fence, but Mark came up grinning, and the words *it started* hit her between the eyes. *The accident* did not refer to the same seminal event for everybody.

"Well, yes," she amended, "Mark ran out in front of Cougar's pickup. He was chasing a cat. Cougar's pickup sits up so high, he didn't see him, but somehow he stopped the truck in time. It was pretty miraculous, actually."

"It was Cougar. That sixth sense of his has saved a few lives, including his own." Mary tossed half a strawberry into the grass and reached into the cooler without taking her eyes away from the game. "That is one brave cowboy."

"He said he spent some time in a VA hospital." Celia reached into the cooler for a cold bottle of cranberry juice. "I know he's struggling with his own demons. He doesn't need Mark's."

"Oh, but he'll gladly take them on. He's been decorated, too. One medal he has that I don't want is a Purple Heart."

"What… I mean, can you tell what me happened?"

"There was an explosion," Mary said on the tail-end of a swallow of orange juice. She sounded matter-of-fact, as though she were reporting a fireworks display.

"One of those roadside IEDs?"

"Improvised explosive device," Mary mused. "It sounds almost clinical, doesn't it? It's the improvised part, the creativity that makes things interesting. Each one is unique."

Celia studied the label on the juice bottle—an upended crate with a scattering of red fruit. "I haven't asked him for details."

"Neither have I, but I've read the report." Mary leaned forward, elbows braced on her thighs, juice bottle cradled in both hands in the chasm between her knees. "Some of my dog handlers were in Cougar's unit. An incident report can read pretty dry, too, kinda what it might be like to read a movie script, you know? This character moves here, this vehicle comes in over there."

Cougar called for "heads up," and he play-tackled Mark, swept him off the ground and swung him around, slinging him over his shoulder like a sack of meal. The game had apparently been called with the ball in the mustang's corner. Grinning, Mark swiped Cougar's cowboy hat and put it on his own head.

Mary sipped her orange juice. "What looked like a couple with two kids crossed their truck's path. Cougar was driving. He saw that something didn't look right, but he slowed down anyway because one of the kids lost this goat he was dragging along behind him.

"Long story short, Cougar suddenly thought he was riding a cutting horse. He used the truck to cut the kid out of the little pack, and then he jumped out and called to the woman to send him the other kid. Somehow he knew the woman was wired and the kids were being used to keep her in line. She exploded, and the child close to her was killed. Cougar caught some shrapnel. The goat and its little herder were okay. It was an up-armored truck, and it was far enough from the explosion—thanks to Cougar—that nobody else was injured."

Logan served the ball over the fence volleyball-style. It bounced to within a few feet of the women's dangling boots. "What are you drinking?" he shouted to his wife.

"Sunshine." She held the bottle aloft, and he gave a thumbs-up.

Sunshine. Sergeant Mary Tutan Wolf Track was filling up on sunshine in the wake of living with long, dark stories made short for eyes and ears on the home front. Celia imagined witnessing an explosion of human beings. Unimaginable, yes, but her mind's eye came up with a picture that was clearer than her memory of her son lying face down in a pool of blood. In her head she could see through Cougar's eyes, but not her own. Her mind protected her from her memory.

"What about the man?" Celia asked Mary quietly. "You said it was a couple."

"I said it *looked like* a couple. The man got away. Apparently lived to fight another day."

"Oh, God, how is that fair?"

"Only God knows, I guess." The men were on the move from paddock to pen, where Cougar's Paint gelding eyed them warily. "Cougar's a good man who's had a rough time. But I can't think of anyone I'd rather have in my foxhole except one of my dogs."

"What about Logan?"

"Logan?" Mary grinned. "He'd be too much of a distraction. Stay alert, stay alive."

"No kidding." Celia drew a deep breath. "How serious were Cougar's injuries?"

"That's for him to say." Mary shut down for a moment, and they both watched as Logan approached the mustang while Cougar and Mark stood back and let the "master" work his magic.

Wrong question. Celia's face felt flush. She'd overstepped, and she'd gotten some push-back. She wanted to bite her tongue.

Mary smiled wistfully. "He looks a lot better than he did the last time I saw him, I'll say that much."

"We haven't known him long, but that doesn't seem to matter. I mean, we've both really…" She was watching Logan and Cougar prepare to load the mustang in Cougar's trailer. He'd made sure Mark was safely out of the way but well within view of the activity.

"Taken to him?"

"I guess you could say that. The thing is…" She tried

to remember the last time her son had seemed at once connected to what was going on around him and care-free. "Mark doesn't need any more demons, either."

"From what I understand, neither do you."

Celia glanced warily at her new friend wondering what she'd heard, and from whom, and what she thought about it. With a challenging new job, new friends, dra-matically different surroundings, she had hoped to make a new life for herself. She'd spent way too much en-ergy trying to keep up appearances over the years. She wanted to be done with that, to revive the simple what-you-see-is-what-you-get kind of a girl she'd once been. But something inside her jumped up and down shout-ing, *Oh, no, we're fine.*

Her demons had always ridden pogo sticks.

And that image made her laugh, which allowed her to nod in agreement. "But what're ya gonna do?" she quipped. "No demons, no angels."

"I like that one. Do you mind if I add it to my book of mottos?"

"Be my guest. I'm appropriating, *Stay alert, stay alive.*"

"Be careful with that one. If you're drinking Red Bull and popping pills to stay awake so you don't get killed, you've gotten yourself into some seriously un-friendly territory."

"Shouldn't have to live that way," Celia said soberly.

"Shouldn't," Mary agreed.

"Did you see that?" Cougar called out, turning both women's heads. The three guys were standing beside open trailer doors. Cougar gave a sweeping gesture. "He loaded right up." He laid his hand on Mark's shoulder and gave an affectionate squeeze. "We're on our way, partner."

Mark looked up, grinning to beat the band.

"Right?"

Mark nodded. Celia's breath got hung up in her chest. Understanding a one-word question without hearing it was not such a big deal, but Mark's ready response was remarkable.

Don't jump all over it, Celia. Let the turtle feel the sun on his face.

"So you're partners now." She greeted Mark with a mother's unconscious reach for the mat of damp hair on the sweaty forehead, which Mark ducked for the first time ever. *Give me a break, Mom. I'm not a baby.*

"Oh, yeah," Cougar said. "We're a team. We're rescuing horses and houses, giving each cause equal time— half the day training, the other half fixing up. We're gonna be busy."

"Mark's going to be in summer school camp next week."

"Summer school *camp?* That sounds cool." Cougar was sorting through the bottles in the cooler, assessing the choices. "What kind of school does he go to?"

"He goes to school in Sinte. I hope I never have to send him away to school. I hope..." She watched Cougar exchange signals with Mark. *How about some water? Catch.* So clear. So easy. So natural. "They're trying something new with his group this summer. The kids sign up for a week at a time, so they can take time off or hang in there the whole summer. And it's fun. It's like camp, but with the three R's deftly woven in."

"His group?" Cougar swallowed half a bottle of

water in one gulp and then gave her a look that said, *I'm listening.*

"Special needs."

"Well, we'll weave in two more R's—ridin' and ropin'." He grinned at the sight of Mark gulping down his water. "Oh, man, I went to summer school *wishing* I could go to camp. Then I went to boot camp and wished I was back in school. This guy already knows how to put his horse in front of the cart. Right, partner?" They shared an enthusiastic high-five.

"You boys are gonna do fine with that horse," Logan put in as he took his turn at the drinks box. "You got a name for him?"

"Mark's gonna name him. Soon as he comes up with just the right one, he'll tell me." Cougar tapped Logan's arm with the back of his drinking hand. "Hey, we'll have a naming ceremony."

"You know, Mark can write," Celia said. "He won't always do it for me, but he does it in school all the time."

"He won't pass notes to you?" Cougar laughed. "I'll teach him how to pass notes. I was always pretty good at stuff like that."

"I'll bet you were," Celia said with a smile. *We're a team,* he'd said. Her son was on a team.

"I don't know much about special needs, but Mark has special gifts."

"I know he does." Celia lifted one shoulder. "But I'm a bit biased."

"I'm not, so you can take my word." He waited for her eyes to connect with his, and when they did, he nodded. "And do whatever you want with it."

Somewhere in the periphery, Logan said to his wife,

"I don't think he's coming back to our place anytime soon, do you?"

Cougar laughed. "Like I said, I appreciate the offer, but Celia's got some work for me to do."

"My place needs a lot of work," Celia explained to Mary. "I bought the old Krueger place a few months ago. West of here about ten miles. Do you know it?"

Mary nodded. "How long was that place empty?"

"Long enough to bring the price down to within a teacher's reach. The house has good bones with deteriorating flesh and peeling skin."

Cougar tapped Mary's arm with the back of his hand. "I've got a few skills you don't know about, First Sergeant Tutan."

"I'll bet you do, Staff Sergeant Cougar. I'm glad you're putting them to use." She smiled wistfully. "I'm leaving tomorrow. Next time I see you, I'll be wearing civvies twenty-four seven." She rolled her eyes heavenward. "If all goes well."

"Hey, you tell them they'll still be able to get Tutan-trained dogs," Cougar said. "They show you the money, you'll show them the contract. Hell, everyone else is doing it."

Mary laid her hand on her belly. "Before long I'm going to be showing more than a contract."

"Congratulations," Cougar said, and Celia chimed in with, "That's wonderful."

"Which might have been reason enough to stay in the army a while longer, but..." She glanced at her husband. "Did I tell you I qualified for post-separation delivery?"

Logan jacked up one eyebrow. "Meaning?"

"I can have the baby on Uncle Sam's dime." She smiled. "Because I'm worth it."

At the sound of his horse getting restless in the trailer, Cougar offered Mary a handshake. "Stay safe."

"Stay *here,* Cougar. You have friends here."

He laughed. "You don't think I have friends in other places?"

"Not like these two. It's hard to come back to the same old stuff. It looks like what you've always called home, but it feels different. And it's not because it *is* different. It's because *you're* different, and they haven't changed."

Cougar gave a dry chuckle. "Ain't that the truth."

The rubber had barely met the blacktop before Mark was fast asleep in the backseat of Cougar's pickup. He'd had a good day. Celia was smiling as she turned back around in her seat, catching a glimpse of the man at the wheel. She loved that cowboy hat, which was amazing. *A cowboy hat?* It wasn't a costume. It was Cougar. She tried to imagine him wearing a uniform, and the image wouldn't take form. The hat, the shirt, the jeans, the boots, they were Cougar.

He glanced at her. "Sounds like Sergeant Tutan's all wound up. Did she give you an earful?"

"Not quite. There's room left if you want to add more."

He nodded, intent on the road ahead. "This is where I'm supposed to say something like, I've done some bad stuff, war's hell and I can't talk about it. But trust me. I'm one of the good guys."

"If that's what you're saying, I believe you."

He glanced at her again. "Which part?"

"It all sounds true." She smiled. "My son has good instincts, and he trusts you."

"What about you?"

"I like you very much, Cougar. I think you know that. As for my instincts, they're still on probation."

Mark was dying to get down off the fence and get up close and personal with the horse with no name. Cougar was doing his damnedest to concentrate on keeping the horse moving about the pen—he'd lose the horse the minute he lost his focus—while he kept the boy in the periphery of his field of vision. His training served him well. Mark's enthusiasm was palpable, and he felt good about that.

No Name was aware of it, too. He knew Mark was his kind. Speechless and sensitive, the two would connect when the time came, and Cougar looked forward to seeing it happen. What animal didn't have special needs? Especially the young ones. Make a safe place for them, let them stretch their legs and test their senses while you chase the vultures away and pick off the poachers.

He would have welcomed the sound of an approaching vehicle had it been a small car instead of a noisy panel truck. *Bread and Butter Bakery.* Celia hadn't said anything about Greg Banyon possibly stopping in while she was doing her errands, so this must have been somebody's unexpected pleasure. Cougar couldn't imagine whose.

Banyon parked close to the corral, but he didn't get out of the truck. Instead he hung his head out the window and shouted at Mark. "How's my boy?"

Cougar could see him through the fence. The odd salute he affected didn't merit a response. "You gonna teach him to ride?" Banyon shouted as he emerged from the truck.

"This is a mustang," Cougar said. "We're gentling him."

"That's a wild horse? Mark, get down off that fence!" Banyon lunged for the fence, shouting the boy's name. He got a piece of Mark's T-shirt, but it slipped though his fingers as Mark fell or jumped—Cougar wasn't sure which—into the pen. The horse's ears flattened, and he started dancing back and forth on the opposite side. Cougar stood between the boy and the nervous animal.

"Jesus," Cougar muttered. He backed into Mark's corner quickly, picked him up and set him on his feet, keeping his eyes on the mustang. "It's okay, Mark. You're okay."

"What the hell is wrong with you?" Banyon yelled. "That's a wild animal."

"Meaning what?" Cougar shepherded Mark over the fence. "He's liable to do something crazy?"

"You've got a wild horse and a deaf mute child here," Banyon ranted. "I was trying to grab him down, get him out of harm's way." He eyed the boy, who wasn't going near him, and then the horse, who was taking the same precaution. "What's going on here, anyway? She's bringing those wild mustangs over *here* now?"

Cougar pulled on his fireproof suit, covered himself with calm. "Celia isn't here right now. Was she expecting you?"

Banyon looked befuddled, thrown off course. "I… I tried calling. Got no answer, so…so I thought I'd stop on my way by. Where is she?"

"She had some business to do."

Banyon's eyes narrowed. "And she left my son with you?"

He was back on course.

"Mark wanted to stay. I don't know if it's me or the horse, but at least one of us must be pretty interesting."

Banyon humphed, turning his attention to a car passing on the highway. "When do you expect Cecilia back?"

Cougar's calm was waning. He needed to keep quiet, keep the last of it from draining away.

"Did you hear me? I said, *when...*" Banyon stepped back as reality suddenly hit him between the eyes. He lowered his voice, but he couldn't quite bring himself to drop the bluster. "I had some news for her. Now I *really* have news for her. She can't go off and leave him with just anyone." He shrugged. "No offense, but we don't know you."

When they say no offense, you know the offense is incoming. Just stay cool. Let it drop on the ground and roll away.

Cougar laughed. Dr. Choi knew the triggers.

"Look, we're not putting on a show here." Cougar gave Mark's shoulder a soft squeeze to let him know he hadn't forgotten where the boy stood. "If you want to watch, why don't you sit in your truck?"

"I gotta get back to work, and I should be taking Mark with me." But he moved in the direction Cougar suggested. "I'm gonna trust you this time." He pointed at Cougar and then toward the corral. "But don't let him near that horse. That's one of the things his mother's been doing without my approval. Being around those wild horses." He jerked the door open on his truck with one hand, leaving the other free for more pointing. "You tell her I stopped by. Tell her she'd better pick up when I call."

Cougar could feel the tension melt from Mark's

shoulders as they watched the truck speed away, leaving a dust wake in the air and a bitter taste in the mouth. He steered Mark back to the fence and helped him climb up and straddle the top rail. They watched the mustang regain his balance. His ears rotated, testing out the vibes.

"I'd like for you to name him for me," Cougar said as they watched. He didn't think of it as talking to himself. Just planting seeds. "You don't have to come up with anything right now, but just be thinking about it. Let me know when it comes to you."

Mark unsnapped the flap on the big pocket of his cargo pants, reached in and pulled out a toy airplane. Cougar looked him in the eye, letting him know he was all ears and then some. The boy showed him the name on the side of the fuselage.

Flyboy.

Cougar swallowed hard and nodded slowly. There was no doubt.

"That's a good name. We'll try it out on him and see if he likes it." He smiled. *Not too big. Not too scary. Let him pace himself.* "Your mom says you get to go to summer camp pretty soon. Do they ride horses at this camp?"

Mark rubbed the word *Flyboy* with his forefinger.

"I'm guessing that means no, so we'll have our own camp here. You get your own personal trainer. You and Flyboy."

Cougar drew a deep breath. *Keep talking. You're giving no offense, and something's getting through.*

"I didn't have horses at my camp, either. Plenty of guns, but no horses. I was a soldier. I wanted to be a warrior, you know? Defend the people. Whoever's getting pushed around." He patted Mark's knobby knee.

"Anybody tries to push you around, you've got Cougar to back you. That's my last name, Cougar.

"In the Army you get a nametag with just your last name, so the day I put on that uniform, I stopped using any other name. Why would anyone name her kid Calvin Cougar, huh?" He touched his finger to his lips. "That's just between you and me, okay? Don't tell anybody. I guess Cal ain't such a bad handle, but when you have a name like Cougar, why use anything else?

"You know what a cougar is? They live around here, out in the hills. They're wild." He gave an expansive gesture. The boy was with him. He was sure of it. "Ever been to a zoo? You don't wanna see a cougar in a zoo. It makes you wanna puke."

And you don't want to be a Cougar in a cage. It makes you wanna kill the guy who put you there.

"Flyboy's checking us out. See his eyes?" Cougar pointed, and Mark followed his finger. "Watch his ears. He's got his own radar, like they have at airfields. He'll learn to trust us. No other horses around, so we're all he's…" The sound of a little four-banger engine drew Cougar's head around. "Hey, your mom's back."

He'd been engrossed in his therapy session. He wasn't sure who was getting more out of it, but Cougar must've been heavily invested if Celia's car could reach the yard without raising either defenses or anticipation.

He jumped down from the fence and reached for Mark. "Should we tell her? You know, about your dad." Mark gave him a funny look. "Yeah, you're right. Mind your own business, Cougar."

They sauntered over to the little blue car like a pair of watchmen checking out a visitor. But when Celia emerged, both faces brightened.

"Hey," Cougar said.

"Hey." She looked at him curiously, as though she thought he might be up to something. And she expected to be pleasantly surprised.

"We have something to show you." It wasn't much, but it would do. He took her by the hand and signaled Mark to lead the way to the corral, where they showed her the plywood hay feeder they'd built. He nodded toward the far side of the pen. "It's going in that corner. Got the water hooked up so we don't have to haul it by the bucket."

"So you got the pump... Mark?"

He'd crawled through the newly repaired fence.

Cougar scaled the fence and started to intervene, but Mark took two steps and stood quietly. The horse stood just as quietly.

"Cou—"

Cougar signaled Celia to be still.

The horse lowered his head and took one step. Mark made a quarter turn and started walking away from the Paint the way he'd seen Cougar do earlier with little success. Muzzle near the ground, the horse followed.

"I'll be damned," Cougar whispered.

Mark glanced at Cougar first, and then his mom. He was all smiles.

"Mark named him Flyboy," Cougar said as he unloaded a couple of cloth grocery bags and a cooler on Celia's kitchen counter. Mark grabbed a small box out of the way and took it to the kitchen table.

Celia looked up from ditching her shoes just inside the back door. "Mark did?"

"The name's written on the side of one of his planes.

He showed it to me." Mark was pulling more planes out of the box, seemingly oblivious to what was being said about him. The excitement of his moment with the horse had apparently passed. Cougar felt a little deflated.

"And you decided to use it. He'd like that."

Cougar nodded. He was damn sure the kid tipped his hand over the name. Whether Mark knew what he was doing was another question. Whether he was even *doing* what he was doing. He glanced at Mark, lining several plastic planes up for takeoff. If he heard what was being said, he wasn't responding.

If he heard what was being said, he had amazing control.

Cougar would tell her and let her judge for herself. But not yet. He wasn't sure whether Mark had in his own way confided in Cougar, and if he had, he wasn't sure what the boy really wanted him to do with the information. Or maybe Mark didn't know, either, and they were both feeling their way along.

"How about I take you guys out to supper?" Cougar suggested impulsively.

"How about I make us some supper?" Celia laid her hand on his arm. "I want to."

"After I earn it," he insisted. "I haven't started on the deck yet."

"You fixed the corral."

"I needed to use it. That's not something you… Hey, you never told me about that old car in the back of the barn."

"Like the rest of that stuff, it came with the barn," she said. "Do you fix cars, too? If you do, you're welcome to it. I have no use—"

"Not so fast, woman. You don't just give away a sixty-six Ford Fairlane."

"I don't even know if it has an engine. It's probably home to colonies of—"

"It's clean." He shrugged, a little embarrassed about nosing around. "I checked. It's a car covered with tarp, what can I say?"

She laughed. "Say you'll stay out of my closet."

"Hell, I'm a man. I don't care what's in your closet." He grinned. "But you've got potential muscle in your barn."

"So you're a car man."

"I'm a horse man," he averred. "But my brother, Eddie, he's crazy about cars."

"So there's a brother," she said as though she'd just bought herself a clue.

"Now who's diggin' around in the closet?"

"We'll talk about the car and the deck over supper. It's been ages since I made my special lasagna." She gave him a teasing glance. "Unless you're worried we might be buttering you up."

"I like butter. How much butter do you serve with your lasagna?"

"As much as you want. I didn't get any bread at the store because I'm not a fan of their bakery, but…" She waggled her delicate eyebrows. "I prefer to bake my own. And I don't have to ask how homemade bread sounds. You're a man."

"You got that right. I'm definitely a man." He smiled wistfully. "And I'd be lying if I said I don't know what I'm doing here. I like it here, and I don't want to wear out my welcome. I keep wanting to see you again, and this way…by helping out…"

"I know what you mean."

"No, you don't," he said quietly. It felt as though they'd known each other a while because they'd hit it off right away, but he had stuff in his closet he didn't want dragged out. He'd barely managed to get the door closed on it. He'd figured on traveling around with it for a while, letting it settle after all the wrestling around he'd done with it.

He looked into her eyes. "You don't know anything about the man who wants to see you again."

"Yes, I do. I trust you, Cougar."

"I don't. I have too many raw places, Celia." He glanced at Mark, whose planes were lined up by size, and the smallest one was taxiing toward the end of the table. "I came here looking for a simple connection. I know horses. I *love* horses. These horses, there's still that wildness in them, but it's natural. The wildness in me is…" His eyes connected with hers again. Not the connection he'd been looking for, but the one he'd be hard-pressed to walk away from now. "I don't know what to do about it. I thought the horse could teach me."

"Mary told me a little bit about the incident that put you in the hospital. Only the official report. She said the rest was up to you." She laid her hand over the back of his. "I know you saved lives. How can you not trust a man who would risk his life for someone he didn't—"

"It wasn't like that." He wasn't claiming any heroics, and he didn't want anyone else doing it in his behalf. "I didn't think about it. I acted. After something like that happens, *then* you get to thinkin' about it. There were other people in my truck. I don't know what would have happened if I'd just floored the damn thing like I was trained to do. Maybe what I really did was I set the guy off. I acted, and he reacted."

"What do you think would have happened?"

"All the thinking I do now ain't worth…" He shook his head as he slid his hand out from under hers. "But I do it anyway. I think about it, and I dream about it, and here I am talking about it." It was his turn to claim her hand. No sympathy. No seduction. "I just want to see you again. I want to be a normal guy who meets a woman, likes her right away, she likes him and they can go on seeing each other and find out where it takes them."

"If I make lasagna, will you have supper with us? Because I'm not going to make that recipe if I'm going to be eating leftovers for a week."

"I'm gonna start on the deck tomorrow." Mark looked up from his toys. *"We,"* Cougar amended. "My partner and I will get started tomorrow."

Chapter Seven

After the supper dishes were done, Cougar took a few measurements on the deck while Celia put Mark to bed. Through an open window he could hear her reading a story about an owl, which creeped him out some since having an owl stay near the house all night was a bad sign for an Indian, and telling owl stories might draw them in. An owl could hear a mouse step on a blade of grass. But he didn't give away his position. He just sat there and took it all in, much the way Mark did, waiting for the right time. Time for the owl to attack, time for Mark to…

He wasn't sure what Mark was waiting for. Perimeter security, maybe. He was staying inside until somebody secured the perimeter.

Security was Cougar's specialty. Hell, he'd been an MP for ten years. Protect and defend. *We take care of our own.* He could do that, no problem. He'd thought about looking for a job as a cop. They'd want to train him a little differently, and they'd find him to be a quick study.

But his medical records would be a quick study, too. Combat-related disability. Most people didn't know what to make of post-traumatic stress disorder. Was it safe to be around him? He didn't know for sure. He'd scared himself a few times. Heavy-duty meds had become part of the problem, so he was weaning himself off, trying to clear the cobwebs, and he was almost there. But the dreams were back. And the dreams were deadly.

"That didn't take long," Celia announced as she emerged from the house. "He was tired. You must've kept him busy while I was gone. Or was it the other way around?"

"We're a team." Down on one knee, Cougar dropped the tape measure into his toolbox and closed the lid. "We have a connection. It's hard to explain, but…" He stared out into the night, toward the corral. "The horse is in on it, too. The connection. The therapy program I was in…" Damn. Nobody was asking for an explanation. He needed to take a cue from Mark and keep his damn mouth shut. He flipped the latch on the toolbox. "You know, they used horses."

She was quiet. He stood up, tucked his hands in his back pockets, felt a little awkward. Fits and starts, he thought. He wasn't a big talker, but when he was with Celia, it was easy to *start* saying whatever was on his mind, which didn't really *fit* with who he was, where he was or what he was doing there. But it felt okay until his mind caught up with his mouth.

Don't go there. Not now.

"I couldn't find anything like that for Mark," she said finally. "But I've read a lot about therapy with animals, especially horses, and I know that volunteering at the sanctuary has helped us both." She held her hand out to him. "Walk with me?"

Her hand felt small and cool in his. She set the pace for slow and the course for meandering. A warm breeze discouraged mosquitoes, and the enormous sky provided enough starlight and moonlight to cast across their path the shadowy shape of a couple joined at the hip and sliding along the grass.

"You think he'll wake up and be scared?" Cougar asked.

"He'll sleep soundly. If he gets up, it's usually not until two or three o'clock in the morning."

"Yeah, that's about the right time for a nightmare." They were wandering in the direction of the corral. "You said there's no physical reason for him not to be able to hear."

"That's what the doctors say. They've done all kinds of testing."

"I'm gonna go out on a limb and tell you he heard me when I asked him to come up with a name for the horse."

She stopped and turned to him. "Are you sure?"

"He had to. He wasn't watching me, couldn't have read my lips. And that's not the only time." He cradled her hand in both of his. "He's protecting himself, Celia."

"From me?"

"I don't know what's in his mind. I know I've got some scary stuff in mine."

"That could be part of the connection between you." She sighed. "But I have some of that, too. Not the real pain, but the…" She covered her stomach with her free hand. "Phantom pain, I guess."

Cougar nodded. "He doesn't have much connection with his father."

"His father thinks Mark is a potential cash cow." She groaned. "That sounds awful."

"He stopped by here today. He doesn't like me much, and the feeling is mutual. I get the feeling he's looking for ammunition he can fire off at you, and I look like a possibility."

"What did he want?"

"Said he had some news for you."

She sighed. "It's always about that damn lawsuit. You know how long those things can drag on? If it wasn't for that, he'd leave us alone."

"You're not on board with it?"

"I'm not going to sit around counting chickens. Mark's medical needs are covered, along with any therapy or training or special needs relating to his injuries. If anything comes of these other claims, the lawyer will get a big chunk of it."

"The man doesn't think you should leave Mark with me." He drew her hand around the back of his waist, put his arm around her shoulders, and started them moving again. "You don't know me well enough."

"Where have I heard that before?" She gave his waist a quick squeeze. "My only worry is that I might be taking advantage of you. Not that I would ask you to…"

"You didn't. I offered. Mark…"

"…wanted to stay with you today. I know a lot about you, Cougar." She looked up at him, offering a moonlit smile. "Except your name. I'm pretty sure there's more to it."

He returned her smile by half. "Cougar isn't enough for you?"

They'd reached the corral, where Flyboy stood hipshot, probably wondering why he wasn't walking around in the grass with his new herd.

Celia turned to Cougar. "Not when there's more to it. I want the whole story."

"Why?" He traced the curve of her chin with his thumb. "Take my word, it ain't gonna get any better than Cougar."

"Be careful. I don't take words lightly." But she took his hips lightly in her hands, tucking her thumbs in his belt. "That was a pretty big deal, wasn't it? For the horse to follow Mark the way he did?"

"It was beautiful, but don't weigh it or measure it. Just take it to heart."

"Mark spoke to him, didn't he? Somehow they spoke to each other."

He reached for her hands as though he were drawing six-shooters from his holsters. But rather than aim and shoot, he lifted each one in turn to his lips. "I don't want my being here to bring any trouble down on you."

"You're not… You mean from Greg? No." She squeezed his hands. "No, he can't…" She shook her head. "No. We're past that."

"Sounds like there's more to the story."

She released his hands, and he turned toward the corral, leaned back against the pickup, separating himself but standing right beside her. Her sentry.

She drew breath, as though she were about to go under for a while, but she let it out quickly, and she spoke quietly.

"I used to think jealousy was a sign of… I don't know, love, I guess. I took it lightly. It was high school stuff, kind of sweet. But then we had Mark, and we weren't kids anymore. We were both supposed to be parents." She gave a dry chuckle. "Greg was jealous."

"Of Mark?"

"Of anybody that wasn't Greg. He was always suspicious, always checking up on me. We tried to fix things. I mean…well, we got some counseling." She shook her head. "After Mark's accident, there was nothing left. Mark needed attention, and Greg couldn't deal with any of it. But he couldn't leave us alone, either. Especially after he got started on *his son's lawsuit*." She looked up at him. "I'm sorry for…if he said anything insulting. I want you to stay, Cougar, but I'll certainly understand…"

"He's not gonna run me off."

"Good."

"I don't wanna get into it with him, so I'll try to steer clear. But if you need me, you say the word."

"What word would that be?"

"Cougar." He toyed with a wisp of her hair escaped from the clip that had the rest trapped. "Just don't use it lightly."

"Are you a lethal weapon?"

"I can be." His finger lifted the strand of hair, traced the curve of her ear and, joined by three more fingers, made a path toward the back of her head. "But I'm learning how to turn it down a notch."

"A notch below lethal?"

"I just need more practice." He smiled as he released the clip and sprang her hair loose.

"The word is *Cougar*."

He turned to her again, sank his fingers into her hair and held her head in his hands, took his time parting his lips as she prepared for him by moistening hers.

His mouth hovered until he felt her breath on his face, and he drew it in quickly, touching his tongue to her lower lip as she lifted herself to him. He claimed his kiss fully, held her head, rubbed her hair between his fingers, pressed his hips close, but not tight. Not yet. He was well below lethal. Plenty of room to maneuver.

He backed off, kissed her softly, flirted with her tongue, let his hands drift over her shoulders, his thumb brush her nape and discover the down that must have covered her head when she was a baby.

"Cougar," she whispered, and this time the sound of his name borne on her breath sent a shock wave deep into his belly.

"Careful." He shifted his legs apart, gathered her close, kissed her just beneath her ear and whispered in a way meant to warm her and make her shiver in the same instant. "Careful, careful."

"I don't say it lightly."

"Yes, you do." He slipped his hands under her T-shirt and slid them up her back. From the small of her back to her shoulder blades, nothing but soft skin over firm muscle. She put her arms around his neck, and his thumbs brushed the outer fullness of her breasts. "You make it float," he whispered into her hair.

She turned her face to him, nuzzled his ear, nipped his lobe and made a soft, sweet sound deep in her throat when his thumbs edged close to her nipples. He rocked his hips against hers. Damn, his jeans were getting tight. She took the lead on the next kiss, slipped him some tongue and took his hungrily when her turn came. Her nipples had beaded up even before he touched them.

He rested his forehead on hers and fought to contain himself long enough to ask, "Do you want to go inside?"

"No." She buried her fingers in his hair. "Because I can't take you with me."

"My camper is closer."

"I can't." But she kissed him as though she could, and then she said, "Step by step, Cougar. You're making *me* float."

"I've barely started."

"I know." She hugged his neck and whispered in his ear. "Not so fast, cowboy."

Celia and Mark stood at the end of their dirt road under the puffy blue and red umbrella of a morning sky. During the school year Mark rode to school with Celia, and she'd been leery of letting him ride the bus to summer school, but the program director had urged her to give it a try. The first few times had been a little iffy—not for Mark as much as for Celia—but now she felt good about putting him on the bus. He was stretching out those baby steps, and she was keeping hands off, feet still, eyes on her precious prize.

The bus door folded open, and the driver greeted them with his usual report. "We're finally gonna get some rain today, looks like."

"We'll see," said aide Vicky Long Soldier, appearing at the top of the steps. "Merle makes the same prediction every day. He's bound to get it right eventually." She descended the steps slightly sideways, owing to sore knees and extra pounds. She'd assisted in special education through a parade of teachers with younger knees and impressive degrees, and she was still going strong. "Right, Mark? Are you ready to go on a field trip today?"

Mark looked up at his mother. *Do I have to go?*

"There'll be plenty of time for you to work with Cougar when you get back. He'll have Flyboy ready and waiting." *Show me you understand. Give me a sign.*

"You have a cougar and a flyboy?" Vicky extended her hand to Mark. "I can't wait to see what that's all about." She glanced at Celia. "He might write something about it. I know he'll draw me something."

Flashing a smile over his shoulder, Mark took Vicky's hand. He was suddenly fine with something that was happening. Maybe something he'd heard. Celia glanced at the always magnificent, ever intimidating sky. Change was in the air.

"Call me if he needs me to come get him." Celia gave a wan smile. "For any reason."

"He's doing good. We're going to see alpacas and llamas today."

"We visited that farm once. Mark loved it. They also raise rabbits." She remembered Mark's reluctance to surrender the baby bunny he'd been allowed to hold, and she reached out impulsively. "Don't let him—"

"Don't worry," Vicky called out as she slid into the seat behind the driver. "Nobody rides a llama without a helmet."

Celia smiled as she watched the bus head back down the road. She had a feeling Mark was on the verge of a breakthrough. Granted, it wasn't a new feeling, but it was gaining strength. Mark was going to be okay.

And Celia was finding her way. For a woman whose carefully planned household had unraveled quickly once the first thread was pulled, she'd been feeling pretty good lately about boldly choosing the road less traveled and sticking to the path. Even when Greg had shown up, she reminded herself that she was there first. And when Cougar had shown up, she'd had no expectations, and she'd discovered that surprises could be pleasant. Waking up in the morning to the sound of demolition didn't seem so great at first, but when she looked at the clock, she'd been grateful for the wake-up call, along with the sound of a man keeping his promise.

He hadn't seemed to notice her moving around in the kitchen, and she felt oddly shy about bouncing outside to greet him first thing, so she'd made coffee and hustled Mark down to the bus stop. Back in the house she saw no sign that he'd helped himself, so she filled a cup with coffee and opened the back door in time to watch him heave a tattered plank off the deck. He turned, ready to grab another one. His expression softened, business to pleasure, and he greeted her with a cowboy salute—the touch of a finger to the brim of a hat—a little different from the crisp salute he'd given Mary on the heels of paying her public tribute, but offered with equal ease by the same man.

One look and she was ready to leap.

"Whoa!" The salute became a warning flag. He pointed toward the hole she was about to put her foot in.

"That's your second save this morning." She doubled the stretch in her step-off leg and flip-flopped over to his side of what was left of the deck. "I forgot to set the alarm, so your racket was timely." She handed him the coffee. "Mark made it to the bus."

"You might want to use the front door for a couple of days, especially after it rains." He cast a glance overhead as he sipped.

"That's two rain forecasts. You and the bus driver." She scanned the sky. "Those don't look like rain clouds."

"They aren't. They're warnings. Put them together

with the barometer in my head, and you've got a sure thing."

"You have an imaginary barometer?" Under his hat, buried in his beautiful black hair. She smiled at the image.

"Oh, it's real. Got one in my head and one in my back."

"Cougar, you don't have to do this now. You don't have to do it at all."

He handed her the coffee and bent to pick up another splintered plank.

"Cougar!"

He tossed the plank onto the grass and turned with a tight smile. "Okay, now's the time to use words lightly. The headache is down to a dull roar, and I'd like to keep it that way."

"But you don't have to—"

"I want to. Actually, I *need* to. I've learned the hard way. I give myself an injection, and I keep moving. I don't think about it until I realize, hey, it's almost gone."

"Can I help?"

"Sure, if you put some shoes on." He took the coffee back and ushered her to the edge of the deck, where he motioned for her to take a seat with his red toolbox between them. He pulled out two pieces of paper. "I have two plans, A and B.

"I started out with Plan B, and then I started dreaming up options. See?" He pushed the toolbox aside and sidled closer, presenting his drawings as though he actually had a stake in all this—a grade, a medal, a check, something more than parking space. "Plan A has some extra cool stuff. Two satellite decks. This one's a play area for Mark, and this one's for stargazing." He pointed out each part of the pencil drawing, neatly executed with a straight edge. "And then up here, you can have this workbench for whatever project you've got going. I see you do some gardening, and you build little things and decorate stuff."

He pointed to a cross-hatched area. "I wanna put up some shade here and here. Build a frame and maybe throw some cottonwood cuttings on to start with."

"Like a bowery," she enthused.

"To start," he stressed, as though she might take exception to the lovely traditional touch. "You and Mark are both pretty pale until you turn pink for a day or two, and then it's back to pale."

"Peel first. Then back to pale."

"I wasn't gonna mention that, but, yeah. I read that you people get a lot of skin cancer out here on the prairie." He gave her a lopsided smile. "Don't worry—I'm not feeling sorry for you or nothin'. It's me. That peeling part is pretty disturbing."

But she was studying his sketch. "This is too much work."

"It'll take a little time."

"That's true." She looked up at him. The playful smile was gone, and the message was clear. *Do you want me around, or not?* "You said I could help."

"*Real* shoes." The smile was back. "If there's enough lumber, I can do this for little or nothing. You take an inventory of what's in the barn while I finish ripping this up. From what I can tell, the stuff out there is all treated lumber, which this isn't. So I'm thinking..." He slapped the paper with the back of his hand. "This was meant to be."

"Meant to be." She nodded. "I never met the people

who lived here, but they left so much of themselves behind, I feel like I know them. They were going to build something out of that pile of lumber. An outdoor something, right?" She laid her hand on the lid of his toolbox. "Can I use your tape measure?"

He lifted one shoulder. "You can just eyeball it."

"I tend to estimate on the wishful side."

"Oh, yeah." He laughed. "They say that's a woman thing."

"They also say it works to a man's advantage sometimes."

"But not in this case." He handed her the tape measure. "Width, length and thickness. All of it matters."

"Gotcha. I'll write everything down and prepare a report. I have both Excel and PowerPoint."

He winked at her. "So do I." He leaned across the toolbox and gave her a kiss. "Look, Ma. No headache."

The storm rolled in suddenly. Barn swallows went silent, and the air stopped moving in prelude, but Celia kept counting, pulling the tape out, letting it snap back into place and making notes. She was almost finished.

Then daylight dimmed, and the wind took charge of the world. Celia began clutching her notes and searching for the cell phone that only worked half the time, but she froze mid-rush. The skies had opened, and the deluge hammered the barn's ramshackle roof. Celia truly hated being alone in a storm. She considered making a dash for the house, but a flash of lightning turned her away from the door. She wasn't even going to try to roll the mammoth thing shut.

Water had already started to fall through the holes in the roof. There were three steady streams. Fortunately they ended on the floor's two empty stalls and a concrete slab. She'd have to fix those. She was going to use this barn for something. Someday.

She decided to get back to work on her building materials inventory. Better than sitting there listening to heaven clashing with hell.

"Celia!"

Her heartbeat leaped into overdrive as she turned to find Cougar standing—barely—one arm braced on the doorjamb, chest heaving, hat gone, hair dripping.

"You can quit now," he called to her.

And she came running. "My goodness, you're soaked."

He looked at her as though she'd grown a beak. "Do you see what's out there?"

"A storm." She gestured toward the track door. "I couldn't close it." Not that she'd tried. "This will blow over."

"This place could go with it," he shouted as he grabbed the door and gave it a mighty shove. The noise level dropped by half. "What the hell are you doing? I thought you'd be in the house."

She rammed one hand against her hip. "Do *you* see what's out there?"

"I closed up the camper, turned Flyboy out and then went back to the house thinking that's where you'd be. In the basement, for God's sake."

"I didn't realize…"

He was looking around. "The car." He grabbed her by the arm and pulled her toward the far side of the barn. "Just in case the roof caves in," he said as he set about rolling the canvas from bumper to trunk and over the roof. He jerked the back door open and gave a sweeping gesture. "Party of two?"

She scooted across the cracked leather seat, and he followed her. "Wow, this is some backseat," she said. "Actual leg room. And it really is pretty clean." She braced her forearm on his shoulder and felt around for the hard lump under her bottom. It was a giant buckle. "Hey, they had seat belts in those days. You're soaked, Cougar. Are you cold?"

"If I say yes, will you tell me to take off my wet clothes?"

He smiled at her when she touched his wet hair. "You lost your hat."

"I tossed it in the back door of the house." He laughed. "Hell, that's the first thing I thought of."

"And the horse was the next, and then the camper."

He shrugged out of his shirt and hung it over the front seat. "How long have you lived here?"

"Almost a year and a half."

"Okay, I should've gone looking for you right after I took care of the hat." He lifted his arm around her shoulders. His chest was brawny, bronze and smooth, and his arms exuded power. "You look up and see those wall clouds forming, you get yourself underground, woman."

"I really don't like the way you say *woman*." She shrugged. "Okay, I didn't look outside."

"Geez."

"I was almost finished with my inventory." She thrust the paper under his nose. "Look."

"I'm wet."

"Well, it's a lot of lumber." She tossed the paper over the front seat. "Did you happen to hear anything on the radio? Anything about where the storm is headed?"

"Mark should be okay," he assured her quietly as he unclipped her hair. "This thing came out of the Hills, tracking east."

Her voice rose when she said, "They went north," then dropped. "But you can't be sure."

"You can never be sure."

"I shouldn't have let him go."

"Yeah, you should've kept him here. He could've been sittin' here in the car with us, wondering whether we're gonna get to see Oz." He ran splayed fingers through her hair. "But he isn't."

She glanced askance. "I wonder if that radio works."

"I wonder if this baby's been sittin' here since 1966. It's in great shape. Somebody sure loved her." He leaned over the seat and turned a couple of knobs, which brought nothing forth. He came back to her laughing. "Can't believe I did that."

"Neither can I, but thanks for trying." She cuddled up to him again. His skin had gone from wet-hot to cool-clammy. "You're cold, aren't you."

"I'm gonna say *yes* and see where it gets me."

She smiled and stroked his shoulder. "I wonder if anybody ever went to a drive-in movie in this car. Or went parking by the river."

"Or got his girl pregnant."

"Or just lost her virginity."

He tucked one hand beneath the hem of her T-shirt, his eyes plying the depths of hers. "Did you?"

"Not in this car. Did you?"

"Not in any car." He ran his fingertips across her abdomen slowly, following her waistband around back. "I've never owned a car. Or gotten a girl pregnant."

"Would you like to?"

His hand stilled, and he gave her an incredulous look.

"Own a car," she said with a smile. "I can tell you like this one."

"Right now, between owning an old car and doing what it takes to get a girl pregnant in the backseat of an old car..." He closed his eyes. "Let me think."

She felt her bra go slack. The wind whistled through the barn walls.

"Better make up your mind. We could end up in Oz, where there's no car and no sex."

"I ain't no tin man, honey."

He shifted her in his arms and planted a warm, wet, breath-stealing kiss on and around and within her mouth as proof. She unbuckled his belt, unzipped his pants and found more evidence. His flesh expanded. There was no rust in his joints and no uncertainty in his brain. He was all human, all man, all there for her and easily made ready. He whisked her T-shirt over her head, taking her bra with it, and coddled her breasts with gentle hands and plucking fingers until she was all about getting him inside her, and he pushed her to the point of telling him so.

He loosened her shorts and slipped his hand between her legs. She pressed his flesh hard and heavy until he took her hand away with a reluctant, "Uh-uh. Just let me."

"Cougar..."

"I have no protection for you." He nibbled her earlobe as he explored her with kind, caring fingers. "If I go in, I'll explode before I can get out."

"Cougar..."

"It doesn't get any better than Cougar."

He slid his finger inside her, and she gasped and gave

welcome—moisture drawn out by his wondrous finger to the so, so sensitive flesh between her outer folds. Her whole being followed his woman-centered stroking until it was she who exploded. He held her, pet her, protected her with his sheltering body, giving her the most while she made the best of his gift.

And then she returned his gift in kind. She pressed him back against the car door, lowered his jeans, took him in her mouth and made him let go and let Celia.

They held each other, hands stirring over each other. The car smelled of nothing but their sex, and the storm swirled around them like music, rocking, rolling, finally winding down.

"It's letting up," he said, and she looked up at him, smiling. He smiled back. He rolled his eyes heavenward. "Outside."

Reluctantly they covered themselves, straightened and zipped and buttoned.

"It's gonna be mud city," he said. "What kind of shoes are you wearing?"

"The good kind." She lifted her foot for his inspection. "The washable kind."

"South Dakota gumbo will eat those things up."

"My feet are washable, too. You have some footwear snobbery going on, Cougar."

"I'd pity you if I didn't know you had boots." He sat up. "It's a long way to the house, but, hell, I've done ten times that with at least two-twenty on my back."

"Oh, goodie, a piggyback ride."

"But that was before I took a load of shrapnel." He glanced down at his knees. "And I've got my boots to consider."

"But you saved your hat."

"Let's just stay here a while." He put his arm around her. "This is my first time."

"Right."

"First time in the backseat of a car. I've always wanted to steam up the windows like this." He drew a heart in the vapor and wrote *CB* +. He glanced at her, the corner of his mouth twitching. And then he drew a *C*. "It fits."

She pulled his head down and kissed him soundly. A second kiss, and a third, and then they looked at each other. *To be continued.*

"My place or yours?" he asked as he opened the car door.

"How big is your shower?"

"About half the size of this backseat, but with a little more head room."

"I'll race you to the house," she proposed as she emerged from the car. "Bare feet versus boots."

They reached the barn door, he pulled it open, and they surveyed the scene. Cottonwood branches, roof shingles and tumbleweeds littered the yard, but it was the gigantic puddles in what had been dry ground that impressed them the most.

"Yard of a thousand lakes," he said.

"That's what I love about this country," she said. "No half measures."

He sat down on a three-legged stool and pulled one boot off. She laughed. "You can start now if you want," he said without looking up. "I'll still beat the pants off you."

"Not if I get to yours first."

Chapter Eight

Celia took off running, pumping her arms and paddling the air with a flip-flop in each hand. Suddenly reborn, the kid in Cougar sprang from the stool and dashed past her. He carried his boots like a running back, deftly dodging puddles until she started gaining on him by running straight up the middle. He cut in front of her, and she let out a girlish shriek. Music to a bad boy's ears.

He did a one-eighty and sloshed backward. "Take me down, woman. I dare you."

She kicked water in his direction, but he was out of range.

"Aw, c'mon." He fired back, and she was fully splattered. "Try again. The ol' college try. You went to college for this, didn't you?"

A girlish screech added some power to her second try, and he took some spray.

"Better, but not by mu—" One foot went out from under him and down he went, flat on his ass in six inches of water.

Squealing with delight, Celia hurled herself on top of him. Her rubber sandals floated away as she pushed against his shoulders, going for the pin. He couldn't let her get it, but he admired her cowboy try.

"Takedown!" She scooped water on him furiously with both hands. "Say it! I've got you down!"

"Takedown? Ha! It's first and goal." Tucked under his elevated wing, the ball was still in his possession.

"Typical man." She sat back and scowled. "Not only do you change the rules to suit you, you switch games." Her eyes narrowed. She wagged her finger at his boots and smiled impishly. "But your boots are wet."

He glanced askance. Sure enough. "I don't care about a little water."

"Oh. Now you change your whole bottom line."

"Which is underwater." He grinned, and then he gave her a quick kiss. "As long as my boots aren't caked with mud, I'm happy."

"What about winning the race?"

"What about you beatin' my pants off?"

She hit him with a parting handful of water as she sprang off his lap. Then she reached for his hand. He gave her a wary look, and she laughed. "I'd pity you if you hadn't shown your true colors." She risked a closer reach. "Can we call it a draw?"

"*You* can." He took her hand. "I call it a time-out."

They sloshed through the water, unflinching now that caution and dignity had been released to the wind. He couldn't remember the last time he'd indulged himself in the feel of being ankle-deep in mud, but it felt vaguely familiar. Celia was dragging him toward the grass around the house, but he pulled back at the edge to partake of a thorough mud squeeze between his toes. He looked up and found the teacher smiling, like he'd just mastered some skill. They both laughed. They wiped their feet on wet grass and hosed each other off before they went inside.

He hung back and watched her make the switch from playful girl to real mother. She went directly to the phone, called the school and was, from what he gathered, reassured that the storm hadn't disrupted the field trip.

"Where's your dryer?" he asked as she bustled around in the kitchen—out of sight, back in, out again. He was just standing there, trying to figure out what to do with his hands. "I'll just throw my pants in since you didn't beat them off me." She leaned back around the corner and leered at him. "What?" He yanked at his belt, grinning. Her eyes narrowed. "You've already seen the best parts."

"Oh." The word was injected with a full measure of disappointment. She extended her palm with a supple twist of the wrist. "Hand them over, then."

"Yours are wet, too."

"Yeah, but I've just decided to save mine."

"Fair enough. This way to the shower?" He jerked his thumb over his shoulder. She waved a gimme gesture. "You're not beating anything off me, woman. Turn around."

He took his jeans off, draped them over her arm, and headed for the shower. No rush. He could tell when she turned to take a peek at his bare ass. He had the ears of an owl.

"I'll leave the door unlocked," he said.

He helped himself to soap and shampoo, which was cascading over his face when she slid in behind him, slipped her arms around his waist and pressed her belly against his backside. She slid up a little, down and up again, buffing him with her soft skin and springy hair, her fingertips lightly circling his belly. She stilled momentarily when the tip of his penis touched the back of her hand, but she started in again, pressing a little more, testing him. She'd find him solid if that was what she was testing for. Physically, at least.

He turned in her arms and pivoted with her to give her a turn under the running water. She sputtered, tipped her head and let the water wash her hair as she caressed his backside. "You're a hardass, you know."

"You like that?"

She laughed. "Who knew such a thing existed in real life?"

"You're a soft touch." He slid his hands up her sleek back, pressed his lip to her forehead. "You know that?"

"I meant literally."

"I meant inside and out." Which both pleased and troubled him, but rubbing up against her in the shower, he wasn't in any mood for trouble. "Let me touch both."

"I want this." She slipped her hand between their bodies and claimed his penis. "This was made to touch me inside."

"You sure? I had the feeling you weren't impressed."

"I didn't say it was made to look at." She hooked her leg around his back and lifted herself as though she would shimmy up his body. "I said… I meant…"

He put one arm around her and used the other to ease himself down in the tub with her in his lap, right where she'd been when they'd played in the mud puddle like kids. "I'm made to go deep," he warned.

She rose on her knees and positioned herself to take him where he was made to fit her, to swallow him by degrees, feel him make his way in a place built to house him and home in on him and welcome him with her undying "Yesss…" until the whole of him made her catch her breath.

He went still. "Hurt?"

"No. Yes."

But she was in charge. She looked into his eyes as though he were a mirror and she was learning a new dance, taking it slow, trying one rhythm, then another, all the while watching his eyes. He had no idea what she saw, but he saw pleasure. Behind those beautiful brown eyes there was pleasure and nothing else. There was Cougar and no one else. He would be good to her, and she would make him even better.

He took charge. He found ways to reach her that made her body quake and her mouth pour molten words in his ears. Ah, she was flying, and he wanted to stay where he was and fly with her, first class.

But he did not.

"No!" she gasped, but she could do nothing to keep him from pulling himself away. In his arms she was boneless and mindless and beautifully spent, oblivious to the water pelting her back.

"Oh, I could have gone on all day," she whispered against his shoulder.

"That's where we're different. Where we have to part ways if I'm unprepared." He kissed her wet hair. "I'll do better next time."

Her throaty chuckle felt like a bee buzzing against his chest. "It doesn't get any better than Cougar."

"Oh, yeah. Cougar gets better than Cougar." He lifted her shoulders away from his. "What? You're laughing at my name?" She braced her hands on his arms and glanced down between them. "No, don't look down. If you look down and you're still laughing, I'll be—"

She kissed him hard and quick. "I'm laughing for joy, silly."

"That's something I've never been called. Silly." He raised a palm against the spray. "Get up, woman. It was nice while it lasted, but the water's going cold on us."

They laughed at themselves in their awkward recovery. He reached past her and shut the water off. "Joy, huh?" He grinned. "That good?"

"You're that good, Cougar." She slid the shower curtain aside, grabbed a bath sheet from the rack and flung it around his shoulders. "Not it, Cougar. You."

"Joy seems way out there. Just tell me the sex was good. I get that." He took a couple of swipes at his legs with the towel, and then he wrapped it around her. "It's been a while, Celia. I kept it together tour after tour, and then I got hit, and I lost it. I can't even tell you what I lost and how much I got back. You're taking a risk with me."

"It's always a risk."

She climbed out of the tub, and he stood there, watching her dry off. She stepped into a pair of silky-looking white panties and slipped lacy bra straps over her shoulders. He stepped out of the tub, took the two sides of the bra band from her hands and fit the tiny wire hooks together. Pleased with the steadiness, he kissed her shoulder.

"Are you trying to scare me?"

"That's the last thing I wanna do. Scare you, hurt you. If it happens, tell me. Okay? And I'll go."

She turned to him. "I want you here, and so does Mark."

"For now." He glanced at the door. "When does Mark get back?"

"Soon. I'll go get your jeans out of the dryer." She pulled a fresh, pale green T-shirt on over wet hair and climbed into a pair of clean shorts. "We could use some wind now to dry everything out." She twisted her hair up the back of her head and clipped it in place.

He listened to the sound of bare feet go down the hall, then up again. The door opened, and his pants came in on the end of her arm.

"Here you go. I need to be at the highway to meet the bus pretty soon. I just hope my road's passable."

"We'll take the pickup," Cougar called out after her, chuckling at the way she bounced between shy and seductive.

And then Celia gasped. He knew distress when he heard it. Before she'd finished demanding, "What are you doing here?" Cougar was at her side.

"He's quick," Greg said. He was seated comfortably in an easy chair in the least conspicuous corner of the living room. "Quick as a cat. What do you do for a living, Cougar?"

A pale red haze closed in from the periphery like rising smoke. Cougar stared through it, focusing impassively at the intruder. Inches away, Celia's body exuded tension.

But she spoke quietly. "What are you doing in my house?"

"I heard about the storm. It kinda blew through ahead of me." Banyon cut his eyes at Cougar. "Looks like that's not all."

Cougar's blood was heating up.

"Get out of here," Celia demanded, her tone on the rise. "This is *my house*. You can't just walk in here."

"Anybody could. The front door was unlocked. And the road *is* passable." Banyon pushed himself out of the chair and closed in. "Where's my son?"

"Mark is in school."

"How do you know? For all you know, the school could've blown away." He turned to Cougar. "I guess you noticed, Cecilia's a great lay during a—"

Cougar had the intruder in a headlock with his arm behind his back before the sentence could be finished with anything more than a choking sound. "Yeah, I'm quick. And you're trespassing."

"Cougar..."

"What do you want me to do with him, Celia?"

"I just want him to go away." He couldn't look at her, but her hand felt cool on his arm. "Don't, Cougar. Please."

"You can't just walk into somebody's house," Cougar calmly told his prisoner. "It's against the law."

"Cougar, let him go. He'll leave." The hand on his arm tightened. "Please, Cougar."

He released the head of the prisoner first and then the arm.

"I think you broke my arm," Banyon whined, cradling one arm in the other.

"I know something about breaking bones. I thought about it, but I decided against it." Cougar stepped back. "The smart thing for you to do now is leave."

"This man's dangerous." Banyon stepped to one side, effectively using Celia as a shield. "Why is he here?"

"Because I invited him, Greg. And he—"

"And he was here first? But he isn't the first, is he?" Another sidestep, menacing eyes, loading up the idiot finger and aiming at Cougar...

Buster, you're about to blunder.

"You aren't the first. I was the first, but between me and you there was a whole damn parade. A whole—"

Cougar backhanded the fool's mouth shut, spun him around and neutralized his "broken" arm.

"Aaa! I'm...calling...the police."

"You." Pressure applied. "Are." More pressure applied. "Trespassing." And Banyon was out the door.

Cougar closed the door and stood for a moment, cooling himself, calming himself, collecting himself. He turned to face Celia, whose eyes were big with surprise but not—so far—horror.

"He'll call the police," she said in a small voice.

Meaning what? "Did I do something wrong?"

"I would have called the police." She took a tentative step. "If he'd tried to hurt anyone, I *would* have."

"What do you think he was he trying to do?"

"I don't care what he says, and it doesn't matter anymore what he suspects. He's a bully and a coward."

"One thing I'm not is a coward."

"You're not a bully, either." She wrapped her arms around her slender middle. "When Greg comes here, I don't ask him to come in. He had no business..." Her face went funny with a touch of sadness, a hint of fury. "He doesn't come in my house, but he comes to take my son." She shook her head. "*Our* son according to the court."

He wanted to hold her, but he wasn't sure what category he fell into. Maybe she wasn't looking at a bully, but what business did he have?

"He won't get past me, Celia."

"He'll make trouble for you." She closed the distance between them. "He has a way of twisting things. Finding you here…"

"Are we doing something wrong?"

"No, of course not." She put her arms around him. "Mark and I are both glad you're here. But I don't want you to get mixed up with Greg."

"Too late." He rubbed her back. "He's the one who got mixed up with me."

"And I'm so sorry for that. If I hadn't brought you your jeans…"

"I *really* would've scared the crap out of him." He leaned back and smiled at her. "Let's go down to the bus stop and wait for Mark."

The bus was late, but the word from the school was reassuring. The group had been treated to ice cream and playtime while they waited out the storm. Like hood ornaments on his pickup, Celia and Cougar sat high above the river in the right of way on the muddy island that her turnoff had become. They didn't speak of the day's roller coaster ride. For her part, Celia put doubts aside and took pleasure in the lingering afterglow of love made with exquisite care. Blowing fresh off rain-washed prairie grass, the cool breeze toyed with her hair and soothed her head. The growing connection between her heart and that of the man at her side could only be a good thing.

At first glimpse of bright yellow, Cougar jumped

down and turned to offer her a hand. "Mark won't be hungry right away, will he? We should check on Flyboy. How's your fence out there?"

"I haven't checked."

"Well, you've had no reason to. If the horse is gone, we'll put out an APB."

"Really? Can you do that?"

He smiled. "We'll find him. There's no driving out there now, but I think I can borrow a horse from Logan."

She loved that warm, reassuring smile of his. He had one for Mark when he got off the bus, and Mark gave him one right back. Celia didn't mind seeing Mark reach for Cougar's hand without a thought for where hers might be.

Vicky Long Soldier leaned around the safety pole and reported, "We had a good day."

"Heard the Thunder Bird flew south of you," Cougar said. "You missed a hell of a show."

"You guys get any damage?"

"Nothing a good hired man can't fix."

Celia gave him a look as the bus pulled away. "Hired man?"

"Yes, ma'am." Cougar adjusted his hat as he glanced at the bulbous layers of white clouds pressing against the horizon. "I thought *remodeling contractor* might be pushin' it."

Celia loved the way he made her laugh. She grabbed his face and pulled his head within reach of her quick, firm kiss. The surprised look on his face delighted her even more. She looked down at her son and saw the innocent marriage of Cougar's surprise and her own delight. Life was good again.

Cougar's four-wheel drive attacked mud like an army

half track. As they approached the fence, he signaled Mark in the backseat, pointed to the windshield, and then turned his hand into an airplane. The spotted mustang stood half a mile away.

Cougar got out of the pickup and loaded Mark onto his back, but once they reached the fence, the boy had other plans. He got down and started trying to pull up grass. Cougar waved off Celia's pending objection, took out a pocket knife and squatted beside Mark to lend a hand. Wheatgrass and big bluestem with edible leaves and nodding heads—the boy knew what he wanted. He took the handful Cougar cut for him, walked to the fence and waved it like a semaphore. Ears forward, the horse trotted in their direction.

"Wow," Celia whispered. "Oh, wow."

Mark kept waving, and the horse kept coming. He stopped a few yards short of the fence. Mark got down on hands and knees and started ripping the grass again. Flyboy lowered his nose to the ground and took several steps closer.

"I'll be damned. If it wasn't for the fence…"

Mark looked up at Cougar. Celia held her breath. The light in her son's living eye spoke volumes. *If it wasn't for the fence.*

Cougar stepped the bottom strand down and pulled the middle one up enough to allow Mark to slip through. He stood quietly, clutching his handful of grass. Flyboy hung his head and slowly closed the distance. He snuffled the boy's shoulder, nickered and sniffed the grass.

And Mark nickered back.

Mark made a sound.

Celia's mouth dropped open. She wanted to whinny or howl or crow. She wanted to squeal and squeeze and jiggety jig. She'd wanted and waited and wished, and she was about to explode.

Cougar took hold of her hand. She looked up at him, and he shook his head almost imperceptibly, as though the slightest motion might destroy the magic. They watched the two sensitive creatures bring all their senses to bear for an E.T. moment. Mark stood quietly while Flyboy ate the grass from his hand.

A car drove up behind them and killed the moment. Cougar ignored it, but Celia looked over her shoulder. It was brown and white with a lightbar on the roof. Her heart sank. She heard the horse retreat and felt the loss of Cougar's hand. He was stretching wire again, making a hole for Mark to climb through. Celia reached for him as soon as he crossed over. Whatever was going on, her child would not be touched by it.

The county sheriff was an older man, slightly paunchy, but he carried himself smartly, sported a tan Stetson and wore a star affixed to his neatly pressed khaki shirt. Celia had heard him speak at a teacher's meeting, where he and the chief of tribal police had explained the nature of their separate but cooperative jurisdictions in Indian country.

"Is your name Cougar?" he asked without preamble.

"That's right."

"First, last?"

"Both."

The sheriff put hands to hips. "We got a call about an assault. Are you a tribal member?"

"Not here. I'm from Wind River."

"Mrs. Banyon?" Celia nodded, and the sheriff touched his hat brim. "Sheriff Pete Harding. Can you tell me what happened here today?"

"Why don't we let Mrs. Banyon take the boy inside, and you have your talk with me, Sheriff?"

Sheriff Harding looked down at Mark and appeared to consider the suggestion. "Was the boy here when the incident happened?"

"Mark just got home from summer school," Celia said. "Would you like to come inside?"

Celia was unsure of the protocol for an official visit from the sheriff. Should she ask to see a warrant or refuse to say anything without benefit of counsel? So far, Cougar hadn't batted an eye. But, then he'd been icily calm earlier, too, and the only thing he'd batted was Greg. Who'd deserved it.

She set Mark in front of the TV with a video game and joined Cougar and the sheriff at the kitchen table. The sheriff had opened up a metal clipboard and was filling out a form.

"My ex-husband came into my house uninvited," Celia blurted out. Cougar looked at her, his expression unreadable. Had she spoken too soon?

"Broke in?"

"Walked in." Celia folded her hands on the table. "The door wasn't locked. He scared me, insulted me. The very fact that he walked in was a threat."

The sheriff flipped a page in his clipboard. "He said he was looking for his son."

"Today wasn't his day."

"I guess not," the sheriff said without looking up from his previous notes. "He thought his arm was broken."

"It wasn't," Cougar said. "Did he file a complaint on me?"

"He complained, yeah." Harding turned to Celia. "Do you have a restraining order against Mr. Banyon?"

"Not yet."

"If he's threatening you, you should get one." Back to Cougar. "He says you tried to strangle him."

Cougar gave a humorless chortle.

"Said you knew karate or something." Harding scanned his report and appeared to read from it. "He's pretty sure your hands could be considered dangerous weapons."

"Are you gonna arrest me?"

"I don't know." The sheriff gave himself away with a hint of a smile. "Are your hands dangerous weapons?" No answer. "Army or Marines?"

"Army."

"Were you in the Middle East?" Cougar nodded. The sheriff turned to Celia. "Is Mr. Cougar living here with you?"

"Talk to me, Sheriff. I'm Cougar. I'll answer your questions."

"Are you living with—"

"He's working for me," Celia said.

"Okay, so who's answering my questions?"

"I live in that camper out back." Cougar leaned in. "You need probable cause to arrest me, so let's get to the story, Sheriff. Yes, I know how to handle an intruder without breaking any bones or scarring him for life."

"I was in the Marines," Harding said.

"That's not my problem."

The sheriff stared for a moment. Finally he chuckled. Nothing uproarious, but a bit of an icebreaker.

Celia sighed. *Let's get this over with.*

"I came into the living room, found Greg sitting

there—scared me half to death—and I asked him to leave. He said some things, and Cougar took exception."

"Mr. Banyon took exception to Mr. Cougar's exception," the sheriff concluded. "Turned out Banyon had no injuries. I took his statement at the clinic."

"So you're not going to arrest anyone," Cougar said.

"Do you want to make a complaint, Mrs. Banyon?" Sheriff Harding pulled another form from his clipboard. "I can take yours now and file them both."

"About Greg just walking in here?"

"It's up to you. If you decide to ask for a restraining order, a record of this incident would be…" He gave her a pointed look. "It's up to you."

She took his point. Clearly Greg had acted like a jackass when he'd reported his outrage to the sheriff. Celia knew Greg's routine better than anyone. She'd hoped to put it behind her. She'd pulled up stakes and *moved,* for pity's sake.

"Yes, I want to make a complaint," she said with a sigh. "I want the whole incident on record."

The sheriff slid the form across the table and laid his pen down on top of it. Celia picked it up and set about telling her side of the story. She kept it brief and purely factual, squeezing her emotions between the lines, where no one would see them. But she knew they were there. She owned them. And she was unapologetic about filing the report, the kind she'd never wanted to make because things just weren't that bad.

But neither was filing the complaint.

"There's no room at the County Inn right now," Harding said as he slipped the new reports into his handy metal case. "You're right. If you did what Banyon accused you of, you did it well. Not a mark on him.

Since he's the one trespassing, I have no cause to arrest anyone here." He turned to Celia as he snapped his clipboard shut. "The number is 911."

"I didn't handle that very well," Celia said quietly. They sat together on the sofa. Several feet away, Mark was busy communicating with jumpy Lego figures through a joystick. "I should have called right away, the minute I walked out and found him here. I was afraid of…"

"Of what? Him? Me?" He turned on her as the truth hit him. "*For* me? Don't worry about me, Celia. You do what's right for you and Mark."

"I was taken off guard. Blindsided, really."

"Celia…"

"It's been quite a day." She laid her hand on his thigh.

He covered it quickly with his as though he took exception. She almost said, *I'm not going to do anything,* but she started to pull her hand away instead.

He held fast. "If he showed up that way again, I can't promise I'd do anything different."

"We'll call the sheriff."

"*You'll* call the sheriff. You'll do what you need to do. As for me…" He gave a wistful smile. "Greg was lucky."

"He's all talk. Don't let him get to you. He's one of those people who would sue you because he broke into your house and got bitten by your dog." She squeezed his hand. "No more fighting."

"That wasn't a fight. All I did was shut him up and move him out."

"I'm glad Mark wasn't here." She leaned closer. "You heard him, right? His voice?" Cougar smiled. "That was his voice. It's been so long since I've heard it, Cougar, but I knew it would come back. *He* would come back."

"Let him do it in his own way, his own time."

"You said horses were part of your therapy. Did you…?" *His own way.* "I mean, were you…?" *His own time.*

"I've been around horses most of my life. Thought I knew all about them. I could use them. I could get them to do what I wanted them to do. And I knew they were smart, too. People think the smartest animals are the ones you can train to be most like humans."

"The ones who let you put diapers on them and teach them to smoke?"

He laughed. "Can you see a horse putting up with that? No." He shook his head. "When I was in the hospital— and I was there for months—they said I needed to do something besides read and go to the gym. I needed to connect. So I looked at what they had to offer, and there was this horse therapy. I laughed. Horse *therapy?* Okay, I could connect. I knew horses." He smiled. "But I never realized how much they knew about me."

She glanced at Mark. "Can you explain it to me?"

"You read the book, honey." He grinned. "You're right about Logan. He's the master. He's the one to ex-plain it all." He jammed his thumb to his chest. "I know it in here. I know where Mark's been, and I think I know where he is now. You're right, Celia. He's coming back."

She closed her eyes and drew a deep breath. "I'm so glad he wasn't here today."

"Yeah. I am, too."

Celia would never know how glad he was. Cougar's heart ached with it. He knew it wouldn't have made a difference who'd been there to witness his battle with himself. Banyon was no match for him. He wasn't dealing with a trained watchdog. Celia had a wildcat patrolling the premises. A good hardass could run interference for her, but she needed more than that. She needed a man, and she deserved a whole one. Cougar was on his way back, too, just like Mark was.

But would he ever get there?

"And it *has* been a hell of a day." He slapped his knees. "We're going out for supper."

Chapter Nine

"Truce, Cecilia."

The bread truck door sounded like a lid slamming shut on a tin box. Celia had seen it coming, but she'd kept right on currying the big gray saddle horse, so much more deserving of her attention than the driver of that damn truck. Grooming a horse on the shady side of the barn was her favorite chore at the Double D. It was therapeutic.

Dealing with Greg would require all the tranquility she'd attained.

"See?" He took off his cap and waved it above his head. "White flag. We have business to discuss."

"I don't want you coming here, Greg." She turned to the tool bucket and traded the currycomb for a body brush. "I work here."

"You volunteer here. It isn't like you're punching a time clock." He pulled up short as soon as he hit the shade. "If you're reasonable about this, it'll only take a minute, and look—" He made a sweeping gesture, taking in the view of three teenagers stacking square bales with Hoolie Hoolihan, who'd been ranch foreman since Sally and Ann were children. "Witnesses."

Hoolie noticed Greg's gesture and started moving in their direction. Any other time Celia would have welcomed the older man's conversation, but she didn't want anything to prolong Greg's stay. "No, we're okay, Hoolie," she called out as she waved him back.

"Just here to say hi," Greg added.

"And what else?" Celia asked quietly.

He jammed his hat back on. "Hey, I went by your place, didn't go inside, didn't even get out of the van. Your car wasn't there, but his pickup was. Sounds like you've got him doing a little carpentry out there." He glanced over his shoulder. "Anyway, I saw your car here."

She was going to start parking behind the barn. She stared at the big sliding door. Maybe she could fit her little car in one of the stalls. Her question was still hanging in Greg's aggravating limbo.

"Where's Mark? Did you leave him with that Indian?"

"Mark has school this week. You have his schedule. What business do we have to discuss?"

"We got a settlement offer."

Celia turned to apply the big brush to Tank's gray coat, running her free hand over the warm hair.

"Tichner says it's good, but they'll do a lot better. Insurance companies don't want to go to court on a case like this. Loss of an eye is bad enough, but there's obviously serious brain damage. Speech, hearing—no matter what the doctors say, none of that's functioning. I mean, it's been how long now?"

She turned and stared at him, knowing her eyes looked as cold as he made her feel.

"Almost three years, right? So Tichner says we turn the offer down. Look at this. He says we can do way better. We have to, right? I mean, the lawyers take a third after they pay every cost they can come up with. So we both need to sign off on this."

"I'm not signing anything."

"Why not?"

"I'll get in touch with the lawyer myself." She kept on talking while she put the brush back in the rubber bucket and gave Hoolie a high sign, pointing to the horse. Hoolie signaled back. "We're going to go back to communicating through third parties. I feel like you're stalking me."

"So you got yourself a bodyguard?"

"I'm going inside," she told him. "I'm not signing anything except a restraining order if you don't stop this. And I don't care how many lawyers you hire."

"You're lucky I didn't press charges on your boy-friend."

She kept walking.

"My lawyer has a private investigator—"

Damn. He was following her. She didn't want a scene. Not here. This was *the sanctuary*.

"Leave me alone, Greg."

Sally's husband, Hank, appeared on the porch. "What's up, Celia? Is this guy lost?"

"I wish he'd *get* lost," she grumbled as she mounted the steps to the big covered porch. Greg cursed under his breath and began to head back toward his truck.

"I'll be glad to give him the message."

"No, Hank, it's okay. The sheriff's already taken dueling complaints over Greg's little tussle with Cougar."

"That must've been fun to watch. You didn't get a video, did you?"

"It's not something I want to see again. Once was…" She smiled at the tall, rangy Indian cowboy with the stony face and kind eyes. "Actually, once was pretty thrilling, but don't tell anyone. Is Sally…"

"She's taking a little siesta." He glanced past her. "The bread man is leaving."

The truck door slammed, the engine roared and the tires squealed.

Celia closed her eyes and sighed. "I'm sorry, Hank."

"For what? He's your ex for a reason. If he chooses to go around with the reason as good as tattooed across his forehead, that's not your fault." She opened her eyes and was greeted with a smile. "Just makes us love you all the more."

"It's Mark I'm worried about. That man's his father."

"We love Mark, too. Sally has a special affinity for him."

"That's why I wanted to talk to her. Mark has made real progress since we've been coming here, and now with Cougar's horse…" She was almost afraid to tell anyone. She might jinx it. "Something really amazing is happening."

"You want to have a seat and tell me about it?" Hank gave a nod in the direction of a pair of high-backed porch rockers. "I know a little something about therapy. And rodeo cowboys get their share of head injuries."

Celia dropped into the chair and rocked back, taking comfort in the soothing motion. Hank was a physician's assistant who worked the rodeo circuit with a sports medicine team. He was also a farrier. He understood the nature of healing and what it took to promote the process.

"The mustang—they named him Flyboy—twice now Flyboy has walked right up to Mark and put his head down so they could check each other out."

The other rocker squeaked as Hank took a seat. He gave her his full attention, eyes lowered respectfully in the Indian way. "They haven't done that much with him," Celia explained. "No hackamore or halter, no saddle blanket, nothing like that. Cougar just finished repairing the corral."

"At your place?"

"That's another thing I wanted to tell Sally. She can add that to Cougar's paperwork. The horse is at my place now."

She didn't know why she felt compelled to explain the horse's whereabouts in the middle of her miracle story. Maybe her news didn't surprise him that much. Or maybe he was respectfully multi-tasking.

Keep it light, Celia. The neighbors don't need any more complications.

"I'd love to have her come out and inspect it."

"Oh, I'm sure she'll wanna look into this situation. You and Cougar?" Hank chuckled. "She'll be on the phone with Mary Wolf Track as soon as she gets an update. Those women had you pegged for a couple the night of Mary's medal celebration."

"Sally must not have enough to do."

"Right." Hank rocked back. "I'd like to see Mark with his Flyboy myself. Seems like it might be a little risky, putting them together this soon."

"Mark marches to the beat of his own drum. He got in there with the horse when we were standing close by.

Cougar was right behind him, but then it just happened. It was like they made a connection. Mark and Flyboy."

"I believe it. Horses are wondrous creatures. I never realized how amazing they are until I fell in with these mustangs." He flashed her a bright-eyed smile. "And Mustang Sally."

"I was thinking… I know you've got a lot going on here, but what about a horse therapy program?"

"For who?"

"Cougar…" She was going too far too fast. She lifted one shoulder. "Well, Cougar's had some experience with a…special program."

"For kids?"

Celia shook her head tightly.

"For veterans." He needed no confirmation. "So what are you thinking?"

"Right now I'm thinking, *hoping* my son's about to give me ideas. Give *us* ideas. He's on the verge of a breakthrough, Hank. He's been to so many doctors, and not one of them has been able to reach him the way these horses have."

"We've got our hands full here. 'Course you start talking to Sally, she'll grow another hand." He patted hers. "Or match up a new pair."

"It's just the germ of an idea."

"Don't tell her that. Sally loves germs." He gave a chin jerk in the direction of the window on the far side of the front door. "She's got files full of them in there. It's a wonder her computer hasn't been quarantined."

"Hey, Night Horse, are you out there rockin' and rollin' with another woman?"

Celia and Hank exchanged mock-guilty glances. He

turned his head toward the window again. "She came to see you, but when she found out I was available…"

"Hey, Celia." The front door opened, and Sally stepped onto the porch. She was limping, but she wasn't using her cane. "I didn't know you were on the schedule today."

"I had—" Celia and Hank took to their feet simultaneously "—some extra time."

"Not by my calculations. I had you keeping time with one of our most promising contenders." Sally tucked herself under her new husband's arm. "And not this guy. He doesn't compete." She looked up at Hank. "Or is that compute?" Back to Celia with a sassy smile. "Put it this way, he has no idea what's in my files." She poked her husband three times just above his belt buckle, once for each word. "Must love germs."

Hank laughed. "I thought you were asleep."

"I was, but I put the squeak in these chairs so I don't miss anything." She turned to Celia. "I like your idea. What's Cougar planning to do with that flashy horse he picked? Endurance?"

"I haven't mentioned this therapy thing to him. It's something that just started…incubating. As I was telling Hank, Cougar hasn't gotten that far yet, but I think he has his heart set on endurance. He's done it before."

"That man's made to endure, no question. As far as the heart's concerned, though, these horses have a way of changing hearts. Human hearts. Horse hearts are pretty steady, but human hearts…" She patted Hank's chest. "People think they're headed in one direction, they meet up with wild horses and they get turned around. Find themselves coming full circle."

"Maybe they just find themselves," Hank said. He

was clearly the no-nonsense side of the Night Horse equation.

"I like your idea." A slow-rising Sally smile boded well for *some*body's idea. "Could we make a little video? Mark and Flyboy?"

But maybe not Celia's.

"I don't know about…" Celia glanced at Hank. He rolled his eyes. "What kind of a video?"

"Just a little home movie. Of course, it couldn't be used for anything without your permission, and maybe it wouldn't even turn out to be useful for anything except my extensive files. But it sounds like you've got something going that could help people."

"And horses," Hank said. "The more we discover about them, the better people like having the wild ones around."

"And we need to see the work in progress with Mark," Sally said.

"He's not a guinea pig."

"He's a kid who's building confidence his own way. You try to minimize the risk the best you can, but let him take the next step. These are the good times." Sally spoke from experience. "I like your idea. It's exciting, Celia." She looked up at her husband. "Isn't that right, cowboy? It would be a challenge, but how exciting!"

"What, were you experiencing a dull moment?" Hank raised an eyebrow. "Thanks for spreading your germs around, Celia. Seems my wife had an empty petri dish hidden somewhere."

"I keep them in files, not dishes." Sally laughed. "Ah, cowboys. They love their poetry, but they're forever mixing their metaphors."

"I'll do some research," Celia said.

"Even more excitement," Sally enthused. "Life gives you a little mold, you make penicillin. Without the germs and the people who spread them around, life would be nothing but a bowl of boring cherries."

Now who was mixing metaphors?

Cougar heard the car coming. Celia had gone off to do her thing at the Double D, and she was bringing Mark back with her from the bus stop.

Damn, he needed one more hour to finish up his first satellite deck. But it was usable for tonight. Mark could roast marshmallows in the new fire pit while the Western sky put on its nightly show. Cougar stashed his toolbox out of sight and hurried to meet them as they got out of the car in front of the house.

"Come this way. Eyes closed. Here." He tucked a hand from each of them into the back pockets of his jeans. "Close your eyes and come along like good little tail feathers." He smiled when he reached back to lay his hand over Mark's eyes and found them already closed. The ears were working now.

"Ta-*tum* ta-*tum*," Cougar chanted, bending knees on the downbeat as he led the dance. Celia had pinned the word *silly* on him, and it seemed to be sticking. "Ho!" The big tail feather crashed into him. The small one did not.

He reached back, pulled precious hands from his pockets and squeezed them as though they were On buttons.

"Ta-da."

Cougar, you are one lovesick puppy.

"Oh, yes." Wide-eyed and thoroughly charmed, Celia stepped up on the wooden hexagon.

He'd cut a square hole for the fire pit in the center—

the most time-consuming part of the project—and lined it with fire bricks, which he'd bought without telling her. He'd showed her his plans, but he had the feeling she hadn't expected him to come through. Once he got going on a project, he tended to improvise. He'd added the fire pit during the improvising stage. *Pure genius.*

"Oh, Cougar, this is wonderful."

Music to his ears.

"There'll be a full bench around the edge." He drew a picture in the air. "For tonight we'll use chairs. I picked some sage and got some marshmallows." He caught her looking at him as though he'd really done something, and a wave of diffidence washed over him. "Marshmallows first, then sage. You don't want to mix the two."

Fortunately, he wasn't capable of blushing.

"This is beautiful, Cougar." She took a quarter turn around the structure, touched one of the posts that would become part of his benches, and sought his gaze across the corner of his creation. "I hope this isn't taking you away from Flyboy too much. I mean, this is amazing, but I thought the time in the competition was getting short."

"Well, it is. I worked him some this morning." He signaled the boy, who had checked out the fire pit, probably noticed the sand at the bottom and wondered how he was supposed to play in that little thing. "Mark and I are gonna get back to it right now if you wouldn't mind throwing some chow together."

Celia smiled. "No ifs, ands or buts about letting me cook for you?"

"None."

"I love it, Cougar. I love…"

He hung on the word. *Tell me, Celia. I know it's too soon, but say it anyway.*

"...everything you've done here," she said, disappointing him a little, but she walked back to him and hung her arms around his neck.

And his heart soared. "Everything?"

"Every blessed thing."

"Show me." His lips twitched. "Plant one on me, woman."

Her kiss was slow, soft and sweet. There was sure as hell more to it than a simple *Good job, Cougar.*

She leaned back and smiled, all dreamy-eyed. "I'd cook you a royal feast if I knew what went into one."

"Home-cooked meat and potatoes." He kissed her back, but he wasn't matching her on the slow, soft and sweet. Quick and hard said it better. He stepped back and tucked a wisp of hair behind her ear. "It doesn't get any better than meat and potatoes."

"Home-cooked." She laid her hand on his cheek. "Thank you. I don't know what else to say."

"You'll think of something. You're good with words." He signaled Mark. "C'mon, partner. Let's go fly our pony, boy."

It was a quiet supper. Cougar had given his big gesture some more thought, and he was feeling a little silly. There it was again. He didn't much like the word, but he liked the feeling even less. He'd gone overboard. He probably looked like one of those cartoon characters with the googlie eyes and throbbing lump in his chest. He could only wish he was a tin man right about now.

Especially since something was bothering Celia, and her skill with words wasn't serving her. Which would have been strictly her business if Cougar hadn't been pretty damn sure her business had a lot to do with him.

Not that he was so damned important—she had a kid, for God's sake—but he was a lost soul trying to find himself in her backyard. Pretty bad for a man to give the woman he loved that kind of business.

She asked him about his horse therapy with the VA, and he probably wasn't any more forthcoming than she was, but he wasn't eager to talk about his time in the hospital. He was trying to move on. Plus, he was pretty sure Mark was really listening, and he didn't want the boy to start thinking of Flyboy as some kind of tool or Cougar as another so-called specialist with a theory. They were just three slightly dislocated males who spoke the same language.

"So all we'll need is a few sticks," he ended up telling her when neither of them could come up with anything the other was looking to hear. "Soak 'em good so they don't burn. There's one puddle left out there we can use."

"I'll do the dishes while you—"

"I'll help you first," he said. "We've got plenty of time."

They cleared the table and did the dishes—she washed and he dried—while Mark played outside. The sun had set, and magic light held its fleeting sway—bright enough to see by, soft enough to smudge all the sharp edges.

Celia leaned closer to the window. "What's he doing?"

"Cutting sticks."

"With what?" She turned to him, horrified. "You gave him a knife?"

"I let him use my pocket knife to cut some twine off a square bale. Forgot to get it back."

"Cougar!"

"You see him, Celia. I showed him how to use the knife. You see this?" He showed her the tiny cut on the pad of his thumb. "I gave some skin to show him what happens." He turned his hand to take a look for himself, just to make sure the evidence was still there. A traditional Indian sacrifice—a bit of skin, a drop of blood. It made sense. Give a little, maybe you won't be shedding a lot.

He nodded toward the window. "There's still plenty of light out. He can see what he's doing. He *knows* what he's doing. Certain things a kid has to learn living out in the country like this."

"Did you show him where to find sticks and what to…"

He shook his head as he dried the last of the plates. "No more than what you heard me say at the table."

"What we both heard." Tears welled in her eyes. "It's true, isn't it?"

"Oh, yeah." He draped the towel over her hands and gently blotted them dry. "It's true."

One of her little wells ranneth over. He caught the runoff with his wounded thumb, and then touched his tongue to it, thirsty for her joy.

"He has to spend this weekend with Greg," she whispered.

He went still. "You haven't seen any sign of any kind of physical…"

She shook her head. "Except that he wants to stay with me. With *us*. He trusts you, Cougar. Maybe more than he does me right now. I'm the one who hands him over to his father."

"You want me to do that for you?"

"No. That's my responsibility. I signed the damned agreement." She drew his hand to her cheek and kissed his callused palm. "And you couldn't do it anyway. I know you better than you think I do."

"I'd rather eat nails, but I could do that, too, if I had to." He glanced out the window. The first evening star pierced twilight. Mark was arranging his sticks on the new deck. "Maybe I should take a cue from your ex-husband and do some stalking. Nobody stalks better than a Cougar."

"You're a man of many talents," she told him as she pulled a package of marshmallows from the cupboard.

"Master of none." He folded the dishtowel and laid it next to the sink. "Which doesn't matter. Let somebody else write the books. I ain't gonna run for office."

The embers still glowed in the firepit. Curls of blue-gray smoke filled the air with the scent of wild sage. Mark slept in Cougar's arms. He hardly stirred when Cougar plucked a puff of sticky white stuff from the boy's upper lip, thinking someday he'll grow hair here. He'll kiss a girl. He'll say silly things. He'll laugh when she says silly things back to him. He'll kid her about having his eye on her, and she'll let him kiss her again.

Cougar licked the marshmallow off his finger. His satellite deck had been christened with fire. He'd pointed out ancient star-to-star sketches in the inky sky and told Indian legends about the way they'd formed. He knew different ones—Shoshoni, Lakota, Navaho—even a few Pashtun tales. He especially liked the one about shooting stars chasing devils.

One of his fellow warriors in Afghanistan—Ahmer, who was a translator and whose name meant *red*—had explained his traditional code of honor, which had a lot in common with some of the values Cougar's own grandfathers had taught him—hospitality, loyalty, community support, the role of shame, ways to settle scores. "Oh, so you would do it this way," one would say, and the other would listen, take exception where there was misunderstanding, and then maybe tell his side.

Ahmer had liked it all over when Cougar told him that red represented goodness and warmth and pleasure in his mother's Lakota tradition. It was the color of the sky at sunrise, and the red road was a good path. Ahmer said, yes, he was a red road kind of a guy. After all, the sun rose in the east. Ahmer's squad would be headed west tomorrow, he'd said. He would consider turning his face to the sun and marching backward, but since guys like Cougar came from the west, such a move would not be prudent.

The next day had been Ahmer's final tomorrow. The direction of the setting sun, where the symbolic color was black, had taken him to his death. Every time Cougar thought of the previous night's conversation, he saw red. He saw the red sky of the rising sun, and he felt its warmth. And then he saw a red explosion.

Go get 'em, shooting stars, he'd cheered as he'd folded his hand around Mark's and combined their power in a skyward fist pump. *Chase those devils to the far corners of the universe.* For Ahmer, he'd added silently. For Ahmer's sons. For mine.

And Mark had made a joyful noise. It was small, and it came from deep in his throat, but it was joyful.

Chapter Ten

Before Greg arrived, Cougar and Celia had a quiet discussion safely out of Mark's range. Was it time to take a stand? And if it was, would she give him the place of honor—the badass post between good and ugly? The little smile she gave him was appreciative, but it said *stand down.*

And that had to be the hardest nail he'd ever been given to chew on.

He promised not to use force, but he refused to stay out of sight. Greg would take Cougar along for the weekend, if only in his twisted mind.

Mark knew exactly what was going down. He stood at the front window until the bread truck showed up, and then he disappeared. Celia found him under his bed, but she could not reach him. On the verge of tears, she asked for Cougar's help. Bad assignment, but that was the kind he'd asked for.

"I'll go out and meet him," she said. "I don't want him coming to the door."

"C'mon, partner. We don't let our women go first. They follow us so they don't get..." *Shot.* "Well, they follow us. We're their shield. C'mon." The little hand slipped into his. It felt cold. As soon as he had the boy out from under the bed, he rubbed the small hand between his two big ones and then slung the kid on his back.

He tried to lighten up the moment a little. The darker the moment, the better the time for Indian humor. "Get behind us, woman. Five paces."

The fact that she complied told him she wasn't herself.

Banyon sat there in his bread truck, having himself a smoke. Right there Celia had good cause not to put her kid in the vehicle. He was doing it just to show her he could. Cougar had to work hard to keep the flashes of things *he* could do from taking control of his hands. He put them under the soles of Mark's tennis shoes like two stirrups to remind himself of his priority. *Support.*

And then, suddenly, he heard a third voice.

"Cougar, don't."

Words? So quiet, so small. *But words.*

Cougar paused and turned his head slightly until he could feel the boy's breath in his ear.

"Don't let him take me."

Oh, God. Oh, God, oh, God. Cougar reached across his own belly and patted the knobby little knee resting in the crook of his elbow.

"Does he have school next week?" Greg asked Celia

as they approached the vehicle. He pretended not to notice Cougar walking in front of her. No surprise, he wasn't getting out of the van. He flicked his cigarette into Celia's driveway. "I'm supposed to have vacation time with him sometime this summer."

"You didn't schedule it," she said.

"I know. I wanna schedule it now."

The velvet noose tightened around Cougar's neck.

Banyon finally looked up and gave him the stink eye. "I haven't bothered you about that incident we had, but you have an anger management problem, buddy, and I have a complaint on file with the authorities."

"I'm not your buddy."

"Yeah, well, I've checked you out. You've got a little shell-shock thing goin', right? A little brain damage?" Stink eye turned smirky. "That's right, Sergeant. The rumors are flyin'." He leaned out the window just far enough to get a look at Celia.

Cougar imagined slamming his hand down on the back of Banyon's head and smashing his Adam's apple on the window ledge. The only thing stopping him was Mark.

"Did you know that about your war hero, Cecilia? They cracked his melon."

"Jesus," Cougar growled.

"I know him," Celia said. "And I know you, Greg. And this is not the time to discuss—"

"When?" Greg barked. "When would be a good time? Because I've got a few more things I intend to discuss. Like the terms of the custody agreement. You've got this guy living here, and he's got a hair-trigger temper. I've seen it for myself. It's a matter of police record."

"I won't let you do this, Greg."

"Put my son down. He's coming with me." He leaned sideways to take another shot at Celia. "And you'd better give a little more thought to signing those papers I brought you. You're about to hand me primary custody, and then maybe I won't need your signature."

Cougar gently loosened the human collar around his neck. "I gotta put you down, partner."

Mark buried his nose behind Cougar's ear. "Don't."

"You gotta say it out loud, Mark. You gotta tell him yourself."

"Cut the crap," Banyon spat. "He can't hear you, thank God, and he can't talk. And I'm gonna see that we get paid for that. We'll be set for life. He'll have nursing care, twenty-four seven. No worries. Right, son?"

"No," Mark said.

"What?" Banyon's eyes widened. He could've been some kind of a bug under a microscope. He turned his damn bug eyes on Cougar. "What are you, a ventriloquist?"

Mark slipped his legs free and slid down Cougar's back. He stood steadily on his own two feet and repeated the word.

Bug eyes shifted to Celia. "How long has this been going on? They've got him talking, and you didn't say anything to me?"

"*They?* You mean the doctors?" Celia stepped forward and put her hands on the boy's shoulders. "Mark has himself talking for the first time. Not the first time *ever*—you don't even remember, do you, Greg—but the same first word. Clear as a bell." She glanced over her shoulder. She had a smile for her man. "Clear as a bell," she whispered.

"Can he hear, too?" Banyon looked down at the boy. "Can you hear me, Mark?"

"Staying here," Mark said.

"No, you're not." The Adam's apple Cougar had wanted to smash was bobbing up and down now like a happy frog. "I'm your father, and this is my weekend."

"I'm taking him to see his doctor, Greg." She took a step back. Mark moved with her. "You call your lawyer."

"You know what? I carry all my paperwork with me. I'll go to the cops. I'll show them the court order, and I'll be back with the law on my side." With a flat hand he banged the buns painted on the side of the bread truck. "I'll take him to the doctor myself. I wanna know what's goin' on here."

"Staying with Flyboy," Mark said.

"Now, that doesn't even make any sense. Baby talk. He's mentally impaired, just like…" Banyon risked a finger by pointing it at Cougar. "Your friend here."

Cougar laughed. "You don't dare step out of that van, Banyon, and Mark says he's not getting in. Go find yourself a cop."

"Do you think he will?"

Celia lay beside Cougar on the bed they hadn't turned down in the clothes she hadn't taken off. His shoulder pillowed her head, and his shirt smelled of wood smoke and sage. She wanted to peel it off and make love to him even though it seemed like an unseemly wish after all that had happened. But he had made it happen, and it was all good, and she longed to draw him into her body and make it even better.

At least part of her did. But she had to put that part on the back burner. Mark was asleep in the next room.

"Bring a cop? Not tonight." He pressed his lips to her forehead. "What I'm thinking about is you. You're a strong woman who's raising a warrior."

"A warrior?"

"Somebody who can stand his ground. You're doing it just right, Celia. He's coming. He's been a shooting star, chasing his own demons away. You know what that's like? He's coming back to you."

She smiled against the dark. "He's coming back to Flyboy."

"Yeah." He went quiet for a moment. Too quiet for her comfort. "And Flyboy should stay here. But I need to find myself another parking space."

She went numb. "You said you wouldn't let him run you off."

"It's not him. It's the law." He sighed. The night air was too heavy. It was clearly weighing him down. "Look, I don't know much about child custody, but I do know it's no good to take chances with kids' lives."

"I would never do that. Not…not intentionally."

"I didn't mean it that way, Celia. Stop beating yourself up. I don't understand why any court would ever side with that ass—" He drew a deep breath and blew it out like some kind of cleansing agent. "He's right about one thing. I have a history. I have a record of… I went off the deep end when I got out of the hospital and came back stateside. I got wasted for days at a time, got into fights, got hold of a pistol and I—" deep, dark, painful silence "—decided against using it."

"On yourself?"

"I wanted to check out. I was no good to anybody. I

was on another planet, and the people around me looked at me like I was wired. I could explode anytime, and I knew what that looked like. I've seen it. It kills.

"So, my brother, Eddie—used to call him Eddie Machete because he can be tough when he has to be—anyway, my little brother checked me back in. And I'm doing pretty good. Even better since I met you. But you don't need me and my crazy past parked out in your yard."

"I need you right here, Cougar. In my home. In my bed." Her hand stirred over his powerful chest. "I need you in my life."

"You're on a roll with your life. Your son is on the mend. You're making a home here. You've got a good career going, good friends." He covered her hand with his. "I feel like I've just climbed out of a dark hole. I've got the sun in my face, thanks to you and Mark. I can feel the wind at my back. But I'm not sure what I'm gonna do now."

"Aren't you a warrior?"

She had some nerve asking a question like that, and she knew it. But it wouldn't do to coddle a warrior. He'd been telling her that all along. She waited for an answer.

It came in a soft chuckle, a quaking chest. "I'm a wounded warrior. Early retirement with a service-connected disability. Ever hear of a thirty-four-year-old retiree?"

"No. But I don't know too many decorated wounded warriors, either. None, actually. But I'd like to meet a few more."

"Why?"

"Maybe do a little comparison shopping. I'd like to take you off the market, but if you're going to sell yourself short now that you've shown me your plethora of talents…"

"Plethora?"

"That's like the mother lode, Cougar, and I happen to be a single mother."

"Hmm. Plethora of talents." He was on the verge of a good comeback—she could feel it. "Name me five."

She laughed. "*You* name your five. And then I'll name you five more."

"First one that comes to mind is one I didn't know I had. I have a talent for loving."

"Don't start with a lie. You've never doubted that one."

"I didn't say making love. I said *loving*." He turned to her. "I'm loving you every minute of every day, Celia. I didn't know I had it in me."

She could hardly draw breath.

"You don't have to say it if you don't want to, but I wish you would."

She slammed her fist against his chest. "Then what's the deal with finding a different place to park your damn—"

"Why can't you say it? I know you're afraid of me, and you should, be, but I also know—"

"I love you." She pounded on him again. "Of course I love you. *Me* scared of *you*? You're the one who's ready to drive off into the sunset."

"Sunrise. I'm a red road kind of a guy." He held her fist close to his chest. "Please don't hit me again. You need as much muscle as you can get out of me, and believe me, I've got my weak spots." He lifted her hand to his lips. It was one of her favorite gestures of his. "Like

I said, Celia, we can't take our chances with each other until we're sure I can't hurt Mark."

"There's no way."

"Greg thinks he has ways. He's got this lawsuit."

"It's *his* lawsuit. A thing like that—especially the way Greg's trying to work it—it could drag on for years. Mark's medical needs are already covered, and he has a nice little trust fund. And, Cougar, he can talk. He can *hear.*"

"I could maybe get a job as a tribal cop. If I can pass the background check, I've got the training."

"Is that something you want to do?"

"I haven't thought that far ahead. Not seriously. All I've been thinking about is how to be with you without adding to your problems."

"What problems?" She propped herself up on her elbow. "I have challenges. You have challenges. Mark has—"

"—challenges. I can handle all of it, Celia. All except one. Now that Mark's had a breakthrough, he's gonna tell us why he didn't wanna get into that bread truck. And if I have to choose between chewing nails and putting Mark in that truck... I'll be spitting nails in Banyon's face." He gave her a moment to digest that image. And then he offered quietly, "You think you could marry me?"

"Why wouldn't I be able to marry you?" He caught her upraised fist before she could do him any more harm. "Do you think you could come up with a better proposal? You're a decorated warrior, for heaven's sake. And you're obviously not retiring. You're moving on. So don't give me this—"

"Hey!" He uncurled her fingers and kissed her palm.

"Will you take a Purple Heart as a down payment on a diamond ring?"

Her heart pounded inside its little cage. It wanted so much to take off and fly.

"I don't need a diamond," she whispered.

"I want to be the man you need. Not just part of him. All of him."

"Oh, Cougar, what I need is a true heart. I'll never know what you've been through—"

"I don't want you to."

"—but I know who you are. Mark knows you. Flyboy knows you. If you were to come up with a clear-cut, unambiguous proposal, then, yes, I think I'd be able to marry you." She laughed. "It would be worth it to watch you sign the license."

"You want my name?"

"I'm old-fashioned. I want your name."

"You'll get it, then. My wedding gift to you, my secret name." He put his hand on the back of her head and drew her to him for a kiss. "But trust me. It don't get any better than Cougar."

One week later, Cougar's outfit was still parked in Celia's yard. He still had his bed, and she still had hers. But that would all change soon. Maybe they were both a little old-fashioned, and that had its advantages. Anticipation was delicious. The big day would mark the beginning of beautiful nights spent in *their* bed and glorious sunrises viewed from their yard. Cougar was busy making his mark in both places—clear-cut, unambiguous and straight from a true heart. Maybe his head got a little screwed up sometimes, but he was working on some retraining. He and Mark were both on the red road.

He'd mounted Flyboy bareback and was working him on a hackamore when he saw Celia's little car top the rise on the highway. He dismounted quickly. He wanted to surprise Mark.

"What's the good word today, partner?" he asked as the two he awaited approached him.

"Flyboy."

The horse peered over the top fence rail, ears standing at attention.

Cougar chuckled. "If that horse could say a word, it would be Mark. How was your visit to the doctor?"

"Good." Mark's hand slid away from his mother's as he headed for the corral. "Flyboy!"

Cougar slipped his arm around Celia. "Any more good words?"

"Cougar." She offered her lips up to him for a kiss that ended in a smile. "And *brainpower*. Mark's brain has the power to turn itself around. The therapist says he wasn't refusing to talk or pretending not to hear. His brain cut him off for some reason. Limited his interaction with a world that kept poking and prodding at him."

"He wants to take it slow. A step at a time, a few words at a time. I know how that goes." He walked her over to his pickup and opened the passenger side door. "I have something for you."

"A Purple Heart?"

"I couldn't even tell you where that is right now. Let's see if I guess right." He took a straw cowboy hat from a bag, put it on her, adjusted the brim and grinned. "Perfect."

She took a look at herself in the pickup's big side mirror. "You really think it's me?"

"I think it's a hat." He admired her reflection. "It looks great on you, and it'll protect you a little bit. Wear it for me."

"Thank you." She kissed him again.

"I got one for Mark, too."

"He'll love it." She turned to lean back against the pickup door and folded her arms around herself. "I called Greg's lawyer and told him that I'm going to consult with another attorney. I told him that Mark's suddenly showing improvement, and all of a sudden there's a rush to accept the insurance company's offer. I'm pretty sure Mark's interests are not at the top of the list of concerns."

"You're a wise woman."

"Any money that comes out of this has to be put aside for Mark. Once Greg gets that through his head..."

"Yeah." He leaned back beside her and folded his arms. Two of a kind. "I know I won't miss him."

"I haven't heard anything from him this week. He said he was going to push for primary custody, and I'll be prepared for that battle."

"That's the one you can't take chances with."

"Well, I've been there, so I know the drill. Another court, another lawyer. As I said, I'm getting prepared."

"Look at that." Cougar nodded toward the corral, where Mark was nose to mustang nose between fence rails. "You'd think they were talking something over. According to *the book*..."

Celia flashed him a warning glance. "If you're sitting on a jealous streak, I might have to reconsider your proposal."

"Jealous of Logan Wolf Track? Not me." He tipped his head back and smiled. "Okay, maybe a little envious of the book. Somebody writes a book, you gotta respect him for that."

"Respect is one of those good words."

"I'll give you plenty to respect me for. I've got a good head on my shoulders. You know, basically." He tugged at his hat brim. "I know, I know. I've got heart. You know, back in the day—I learned this from Dr. Choi, and I think it was the Civil War—PTSD was called *soldier's heart*. So that means I've got a soft heart. Not a good thing. See, we call it a warrior's heart. *Strong*." He gestured with a fist. "I guess that's why I'd rather believe it's all in my head."

"There's nothing soft about your heart. Nothing soft about caring for people, putting others first."

"When I don't think too much, I get right in there and do what's necessary. Other times…" He looked into the eyes he was learning to trust beyond any he'd known. "Sometimes I'm scared, Celia. So scared I can hardly move. Trouble is, when the fear comes after the fact and the deed's already done…" He shook his head.

"That tells me a heart like yours is stronger than most. It holds on to who you really are, no matter what's going on around you." She slid his unbuttoned shirt aside and touched his chest. "You amaze me, Cougar. You've helped me understand my son."

"I wanted to hurt his father. Really, really bad."

"But you didn't." She glanced down at her hand. "You know what? Greg has never struck me physically. But emotionally… Well, he's never cared about me, either. Or Mark. It's all about Greg. It took me a while to realize how awful that is. It wasn't my fault. It wasn't me. It was *him*."

"You asked me about the program I was in, the one where we used horses…" He gave a self-deprecating chuckle. "The one where the horses were the ones giving the humans a leg-up. What are you thinking?" She questioned him with a look, and he touched her chin. "See, I'm getting to know you. I can tell you're thinking up some kind of a plan."

"Says the man who made plans to turn my deck into an entertainment center. You've been talking to Hank Night Horse, haven't you."

"Oh, now it's Night Horse." He winked at her. "Who has my greatest respect. Actually, it was Sally. She wants me to take her to the VA hospital and show her around."

"Are you going to? Can Mark and I…" She turned toward the corral, and he followed her lead. Mark was inside the pen. With nothing but charisma he'd lured the mustang close to the fence, which he was about to use as a ladder. "Uh-oh."

"Can't keep a good man down," Cougar said as he pushed away from the pickup. "I'll take care of it."

Cougar eased his way into the corral through the gate and sidled up to Mark, who was determined to mount the horse. "Wait for me, partner. The three of us, we'll do this together." He rubbed Flyboy's shoulder with his left hand while he lifted Mark in his right arm. "If he says no, we back off. Okay?"

"Okay," Mark said. "Flyboy says okay."

"Put your arms over his back. Let him feel your belly against him." Mark followed instructions. The horse was relaxed. Cougar noticed Celia standing behind the gate. "Come join us," he told her quietly.

"I can ride now," Mark said.

Cougar lifted him onto the horse's back. He looked up and saw the face of a shooting star. He felt a warm hand slip into his, and he turned to find his woman, his wise and warm-hearted woman.

And the look in her eyes said, *It doesn't get any better than Cougar.*

* * * * *

Rebecca Winters, whose family of four children has now swelled to include five beautiful grandchildren, lives in Salt Lake City, Utah, in the land of the Rocky Mountains. With canyons and high alpine meadows full of wildflowers, she never runs out of places to explore. They, plus her favorite vacation spots in Europe, often end up as backgrounds for her romance novels, because writing is her passion, along with her family and church.

Rebecca loves to hear from readers. If you wish to email her, please visit her website, cleanromances.com.

Books by Rebecca Winters

Harlequin Western Romance

Sapphire Mountain Cowboys

A Valentine for the Cowboy

Lone Star Lawmen

The Texas Ranger's Bride
The Texas Ranger's Nanny
The Texas Ranger's Family
Her Texas Ranger Hero

Hitting Rocks Cowboys

In a Cowboy's Arms
A Cowboy's Heart
The New Cowboy
A Montana Cowboy

Visit the Author Profile page at Harlequin.com for more titles.

HOME TO WYOMING

REBECCA WINTERS

Dedicated to all the selfless, wonderful, heroic grandmothers raising grandchildren after raising their own children. What greater love can there be?

Chapter One

The station wagon pulled up to the curb in front of the airport in Colorado Springs. "Son, won't you please consider coming back home? I mean...for good."

He knew what she meant. Buck Summerhayes stared into his mother's pleading eyes before releasing the seat belt. They'd been through this half a dozen times since last March when he'd been given a medical discharge from Walter Reed National Military Medical Center in Bethesda, Maryland. The military had flown him home, where his family had been waiting to welcome him.

"You know I can't do that, Mom," he said, breaking into a cough. "I've made a commitment to Carson and Ross. I only flew here for a three-day break. Now I have to get back to Wyoming. Another family of a fallen soldier from California will be arriving in Jackson this evening. The guys and I take turns. This family will be my main responsibility for the next week, so I have to be there to pick them up."

"I realize that, but you have no idea how much we all miss you. Your father and brothers could use you in the business. At his last physical, the doctor told Dad he needed to slow down."

"Is it anything serious?" Buck asked in alarm.

"No, darling. He's just getting older, and all I'm saying is that Summerhayes Construction could use your help." Her face took on a sad expression. "Is it possible you're still staying away because of Melanie?"

A mother wasn't a mother for nothing. There was no point in avoiding the subject of Melanie Marsden, his high school girlfriend and the woman he'd hoped to marry after college.

But after his oldest brother, Pete, told him she and his brother Sam had fallen in love while Buck had been away at school and that they were afraid to tell him, he wished them all the best. After their wedding, he'd joined the marines and it would have become his life-long career if he hadn't been diagnosed with acute dyspnea.

He frowned. "That might have been the case twelve years ago, but the war changed my life. When you see your buddies blown up in front of your face, it changes the way you think about things. I got over it a long time ago. Don't you remember? When I was first sent overseas, I wrote them a letter telling them how happy I was for them?"

"Yes, of course. They told me what you did after you were deployed and it meant the world to them, but I was just afraid that because you haven't met a woman to settle down with—"

"You thought I was still pining for her?" He cut her off. Incredulous, he said, "Mom—put your fears away. That's in the long-forgotten past. There've been many women since then and there will be many more to come. Jackson Hole is a mecca for Western goddesses decked out in cowboy hats and spurs."

His comment caused her to laugh. "If you want to know the truth, I love what I'm doing *now*. I need it."

She patted his cheek. "I believe you."

"I'm glad you do, because you don't know what survivor's guilt is like. When I was in the hospital, it tore me apart to think that some of our buddies didn't make it home to their wives and children. My friends and I decided the only way to get over it was to find a way to help people. Carson came up with the idea of turning his ranch into a dude ranch to give some of the victims' families a vacation. It struck a chord with Ross and me."

"It's a very noble idea, but what about your health?"

"We all see the doctor regularly. It could've been a lot worse. We like to think of it as our mark of bravery for breathing all that nasty stuff over in Afghanistan."

She leaned across and gave him a big hug and a kiss. "I love you, honey." Her voice was filled with tears.

Emotion swamped him as he reciprocated. "I love you, too. Stop worrying so much. I'll see you in six weeks."

He was saying that now, but he couldn't guarantee it. Their dude-ranch business for regular tourists was growing faster than they'd anticipated. As for their first experiment entertaining a war widow and her son, it had gone so well that Carson had just married Tracy Baretta, and her six-year-old son Johnny was the cutest little kid Buck had ever seen.

It seemed unbelievable that she'd flown out from Ohio at the beginning of June and now they were man and wife and raising a child together. It was only the third week of July. Johnny would be celebrating his seventh birthday next Thursday night. Carson and Tracy were in the middle of planning a big party for him.

In truth, Buck was envious of Carson. Bachelorhood was all right until the right woman came along, but Buck could see how fulfilling it would be to be a father and he felt that yearning growing stronger. Johnny had gotten to Buck in a big way.

Buck smiled when he thought about Carson. The second he'd laid eyes on Tracy, the ultimate bachelor cowboy was a goner. He couldn't be happier for his friend, but his nuptials had cut their numbers to an overall bachelor status of two.

After getting out of the car, he reached for his duffel bag on the backseat. "Drive safely, Mom. You're the only mother I've got. And please, don't worry. One day the right woman will come along and I'll get married and give you grandchildren."

"Oh, you." She chuckled. "Take care, my brave boy."

He was still her boy instead of a thirty-five-year-old vet with an annoying disease. As for *brave,* there were degrees of bravery. Like the heroism of one of their buddies who volunteered to be a target to save half a dozen of their platoon. He'd saved Buck's life. Now, *that* was brave.

Buck shook his head after watching his mother pull away, and then he hurried inside to make his afternoon flight to Jackson via Denver.

His forty-minute trip went smoothly, but after changing planes for the second leg, the pilot made an announcement. Bad weather and high winds over Wyoming meant their flight had to be diverted to Salt Lake.

Terrific.

Once he arrived at Salt Lake International to check his bag, he phoned Carson and Ross, but got voice mail for both and had to leave messages. Frustrated, he called the front desk at the ranch and was able to reach Willy and tell him about the delay. The part-time apprentice mechanic who alternated shifts with Susan and Patty told him not to worry. Alexis and Jenny Forrester—the mother and daughter he was supposed to meet—would probably be late, too. But no matter when they arrived, someone on staff would pick them up. Buck was to give them a call whenever he touched down.

Rather than sit it out in the passenger waiting area, he found a Starbucks on the lower level and grabbed a sandwich and coffee and a copy of *The Salt Lake Tribune*. The place was packed with tourists. A lot of flights had been delayed. After he'd eaten, he went back upstairs and walked behind the last row of lounge seats until he came to the end where he found a free one. In the next chair was a blonde girl, maybe six or seven years old, curled up asleep next to her mother.

After sitting, he opened his newspaper to the business section. Unlike many other states, Utah was experiencing some growth of new housing in an otherwise depressed economy. He hoped things would pick up in Colorado, but it probably wouldn't happen for some time.

Beside him, Buck could hear the mother talking to someone on her cell phone. "I know a week seems like a long time, but it's something I feel I had to do for a lot of reasons....You know why....Please try to understand, Frank....Love you, too."

The call ended just as Buck had finished the editorial page. When he felt a spasm coming on, he coughed into the newspaper to muffle the sound, hoping he hadn't startled the little girl, who straightened in her seat and rubbed her eyes.

"Now that you're awake, let's go to the restroom, sweetheart," the mother said in a well-modulated voice. Buck would bet it wasn't a coincidence that she'd made the suggestion at that particular moment. Chagrined to think he was probably the reason they got up, he kept his face hidden behind the paper and flipped to the financial section.

The guys had joked about wearing signs that said their coughs weren't contagious; maybe it wasn't such a bad idea.

When he'd finished reading the paper, he tucked it between him and the side of the chair. As he sat leaning forward with his hands clasped between his knees, waiting for the announcement that his flight was now boarding, the little girl walked in front of him to take her seat.

Behind her came the most gorgeous pair of long legs he'd ever seen on a woman. Her linen-colored skirt fit snugly around shapely hips and legs to flare at the knee, and she was wearing beige wedge sandals.

Compelled to look up, he took in the top half of her shapely body clothed in a summery crocheted top. Her wavy chestnut-colored hair hid her profile as she sat down next to her daughter. Surprised by his strong reaction to the stranger, it took all the willpower he possessed not to stand so he could get a better look at her. No one appreciated a beautiful woman more than he did.

When he'd told his mom there'd been many women in his life, he hadn't exaggerated, which was why he was so surprised that this particular female had so captured his attention. It appeared that she and her daughter were taking his flight, but that didn't mean Jackson was their final destination. The mother and daughter he was supposed to meet were flying in from Sacramento, California—could they have been rerouted to Salt Lake City, as well?

In the middle of his reverie, he heard the announcement that his flight was ready for boarding. The woman and her daughter had already gone ahead to join the lineup. He was the last one to board the midsize passenger plane. Since his flight had been diverted, he was the last to be given a seat assignment and had to sit at the rear of the plane.

Before he reached his seat, he spotted the mother who'd caught his eye sitting on the left a couple of rows ahead. She was helping her daughter with the seat belt. He noted there was no wedding ring on her left hand. She could still be married, he surmised, or then again, Frank—the man she'd been talking to on the phone earlier—could be a boyfriend. Buck was forced to keep moving down the aisle and he still didn't get a look at her face, because her hair had fallen forward.

The flight was a short one, but bumpy toward the end. After the plane landed, three-fourths of the passengers got off, but he saw no sign of the woman and her daughter. Oddly disappointed, he made his way over to the baggage claim to retrieve his duffel bag and call the ranch.

"Buck!"

He wheeled around to see Willy carrying a sign for the Teton Valley Dude Ranch. "Hey, Willy."

The twenty-six-year-old pushed his cowboy hat back on his head. "I didn't know you'd be on this flight. You didn't by any chance see a woman and little girl on board, did you? The Forresters didn't come in on the last flight. I was supposed to pick them up in front, but they weren't outside, so I figured they'd be in here getting their luggage. Some of the bags still haven't been claimed."

So the woman and her daughter were the Forresters!

After overhearing part of her phone conversation with "Frank," he'd pretty much ruled her out as possibly being the widow of Daniel Forrester.

The marine's heroism had been lauded after he'd taken a grenade to save members of his platoon from certain death. He'd been buried only nine months ago. Not that his wife couldn't have found herself in another relationship this fast. The woman was a raving beauty.

Come to think of it, Melanie and Buck's brother had gotten close much faster than that while he'd been away at school. But Melanie hadn't lost a husband in the war. Somehow, Buck would have expected a grieving widow to take a little longer to recover. The woman had already removed her wedding ring. Still, it was none of his business.

"I sat next to a mother and daughter in the airport lounge in Salt Lake, but I had no idea they were the family we're hosting. Unfortunately, I was the last one off the plane." He frowned, wondering if the turbulence had made one of them ill. They were his responsibility, after all. "Maybe they're in the restroom. Stay here."

He started across the terminal lounge to look around when he saw them come out of an alcove and head for the luggage carousel. The little girl clung to her mother's hand. Buck closed in on them.

"Mrs. Forrester?"

She swung halfway around, giving him the frontal view he'd been trying to glimpse earlier. Midnight-blue eyes connected with his. He thought she looked surprised to see him. She probably hadn't expected the man with the cough at the Salt Lake airport to be the one greeting her.

She was maybe thirty. A generously curved mouth and high cheekbones were set in an oval face. Her classic features appealed to him as much as the rest of her. She was a very attractive woman. He thought of Carson and the way he'd felt when he'd first laid eyes on Tracy.

Damn.

He looked down at her daughter, who showed all the promise of growing up to be a beauty herself. "I'm Buck Summerhayes, one of the partners at the dude ranch. Welcome to Teton Valley." He shook her hand.

"Thank you, Mr. Summerhayes. We're very happy to be here." Although her tone sounded cordial enough, she seemed a bit subdued. Maybe the flight had made her ill.

"Let me introduce Willy Felder. He's one of our staff and will be taking us back to the ranch."

"My name's Alex. How do you do?" She shook hands with him.

"If you'll tell Willy which of those bags are yours, he'll take them out to the van."

"They're the red ones."

"Red's my favorite color," the little girl piped up.

Buck smiled. "So I can see." He squatted in front of her. She was wearing jeans and a red top with a princess on the front. "It's nice to meet you, Jennifer. I'm glad you're coming to the ranch. I forget—are you six or seven?"

"Seven."

"Jenny had a birthday last week," her mother explained.

"Well, congratulations, Jenny!" he said. "The owner of the dude ranch, Carson Lundgren, has a son named Johnny who's going to turn seven next Thursday. You'll meet him at breakfast in the morning. He'll want to show you his pony, Goldie."

"I've never seen a real pony."

"We've got four of them."

"Can I have a ride on one?"

He smiled. "You can pick your favorite and start riding first thing in the morning. Do you know you have the prettiest green eyes?"

"So do you." Her comment took him by surprise. She seemed so grown up for a seven-year-old. "My daddy's were green, too."

"That explains their color." A lump lodged in his throat. This was Daniel Forrester's little girl, who would have to live without him for the rest of her life. "Your daddy was a very brave man. We invited you to the ranch as our way of honoring him."

Her features sobered, but she didn't tear up. "Were you in the war?"

"Yes."

"How come you're not there now?"

"That's a good question. It's because I got sick while I was in Afghanistan and had to come home. So did my friends Carson and Ross who run the ranch. They have coughs, too."

"I heard you coughing at the airport."

"I saw you sleeping, and I'm sorry if I woke you up. I cough a lot, but just remember you can't catch it from me."

"Why not?" She was curious like Johnny, a trait he found endearing.

"Because it's not a cough from a cold. It's from breathing the bad air in the war."

She looked up at her mother with an anxious expression. "Do you think Daddy got that cough, too?"

"I don't think so, or he would have said something in his emails."

Jenny looked a trifle pale. The mention of her father must have upset her. "Let's get going to the ranch. It's only a short drive away. I'm sure you're tired and hungry."

"I got sick on the plane."

That explained her pallor. "I'm sorry about that. Our plane did get bounced around, but we're on the ground now. Are you thirsty?"

"Not yet."

Buck got to his feet and turned to the girl's mother. "Are you ready to go?"

"Yes, thank you."

He guessed that she couldn't wait to get to the ranch and put her daughter to bed. "Then let's go. The van's right outside."

When they exited the terminal into the darkness, the wind was blowing so fiercely it was a good thing he wasn't wearing his cowboy hat. He saw lightning flashes followed by thunder. It was going to rain before they reached the ranch. Willy opened the van door to help Jenny and her mother get in. A strong gust caused her skirt to ride up those fabulous legs just as Buck climbed in behind her. Once behind the wheel, Willy pulled away. Two minutes later, the downpour started.

"Where's that big mountain?" Jenny wanted to know. She rested her head against her mother, who had a protective arm around her. He noticed she squeezed her daughter harder every time there was another clap of thunder.

"The Grand Teton is to the right of us, but with the storm, you won't be able to see it until tomorrow."

"I'm scared."

Willy had turned on the windshield wipers, but it was still hard to see.

"You don't need to be, Jenny. We're perfectly safe in the van, and in a few minutes we'll have you tucked in bed in our cabin. You'll be as cozy as the red squirrel who lives in a hole in the fir tree near the main ranch house."

"It's really red?"

When Buck smiled, Jenny's mother reciprocated. "Not exactly like your top. More of a burnt-orange-red color. Moppy likes pine nuts."

"Moppy?" Jenny squealed in delight, her fear forgotten for the moment.

"That's Carson's name for her."

"I want to see her."

"Tomorrow she'll be running up and down the tree, chattering her head off. You won't be able to miss her. She has a huge bushy tail."

"What if it's still raining tomorrow and she doesn't come out?"

"By morning, this storm will be long gone."

"Promise?"

Buck had checked his smartphone for the weather report before he'd exited the plane. He caught her mother's eye before he said, "I promise the sun will be out."

She kissed her daughter's forehead. "If Mr. Summerhayes made a promise, then you can believe it, sweetheart."

"Please, call me Buck."

"That sounds like a horse's name."

Jenny's comment made him laugh and brought on a cough. When it subsided, he said, "A lot of people say that and you're absolutely right, but I was named Bradford after my great grandfather. My dad nicknamed me Buck because his grandfather liked the Buck Rogers comic books and thought I looked like him."

"Who was Buck Rogers?"

"A spaceman."

The girl glanced at her mom. "Have you heard of Buck Rogers?"

"Yes. I loved science fiction growing up."

Buck had been enjoying their conversation so much, he didn't realize they'd driven up in front of the guest cabin until Willy turned off the engine.

He leaned toward the two of them. "The worst of the storm has passed. I'll unlock the cabin door and then you make a run for it so you don't get too wet. Willy will bring in your luggage. But before we go in, I have to put on an oxygen mask."

Jenny looked startled. "How come?"

"Because housekeeping has made a fire for you and smoke hurts my lungs. The guys and I have started carrying an oxygen apparatus in all our vehicles because we never know when we'll need it." He opened the small locker on the floor and pulled out a mask and canister. "Don't be scared."

"I won't."

"If my great grandfather saw me now, he'd think I really was Buck Rogers from outer space." He put on the mask and turned on the oxygen before leaving the van. In a minute, he had the cabin door unlocked.

Jenny and her mother hurried over the threshold into the living room where the glow from the hearth illuminated their faces. Judging by their expressions, they found the cabin welcoming and moved closer to the heat source.

When he and the guys had built the cabins, they'd decided on wood-burning fireplaces for their authenticity.

"Ooh, this feels good, doesn't it, sweetheart?"

"I wish our house had a fireplace."

Pleased with their response to their temporary home away from home, Buck helped Willy take the bags into one of the two bedrooms adjoined by a bathroom. "Ladies," he said as he came back to the living room, "you have all the comforts of home here. There's a coffeemaker and microwave. The fridge is stocked with drinks and there's a basket of fruit, along with packets of hot chocolate and snacks on the table. If you'll look in the closets, there are extra pillows and blankets."

"This is wonderful," she exclaimed, looking around at the rest of the room, her eyes landing on the state-of-the-art entertainment center.

"If you need anything, just dial zero on the house phone by your bed and the front desk will let me know, no matter the hour." He studied his guests. "Is there anything I can get you before I say good-night?"

Jenny stared up at him with a worried expression. "Do you feel okay?"

"I feel fine. Do I look too frightening?"

"No, but I feel bad for you. Where do you live?"

"In the main ranch house. It's close by, but you couldn't see it in the storm. I hope your stomach will feel better by morning. We serve breakfast in the big dining room from six to nine. Lunch is from twelve to two and dinner from five to eight."

"Will you be there?"

"I wouldn't be anywhere else."

"That's good." Jenny's quiet response touched him. "Do you have to wear the mask at the ranch house?"

"Only if they make a fire in the big fireplace, which doesn't happen very often."

"You're brave."

"No. Your dad was the one who was brave. If you've noticed, the thunder and lightning have already moved on. It isn't scary anymore. I bet Moppy is already peeking out of her hole and planning her breakfast for tomorrow. The rain will have made a lot of pine nuts fall to the ground."

The little girl's face broke into a sweet smile. Daniel Forrester's daughter was a treasure. It tore him up to think she'd lost her father. "I want to watch."

He cleared his throat. "She'll be up early."

"I don't know if we can say the same thing for us," her mother remarked.

Buck was trying hard not to think too much about Daniel's wife and his unwanted attraction to her. He threw her a glance. "Tomorrow will be your first day here. After coming from Sacramento, you need to get used to the altitude."

"You can certainly tell the air is thinner here."

"It's a bit of a change and that flight had to be unsettling to a lot of the passengers. Jenny? You're a courageous girl to have handled it. Something tells me you're just like your daddy."

When she didn't say anything, he glanced at her mother and saw tears pooling in her dark blue eyes. "You don't know how true that is." Her comment piqued his curiosity, but now wasn't the time to probe.

"Good night."

"Good night, Mr. Summerhayes."

"Buck."

"Yes, Buck. Sorry."

"No problem. What would you like me to call you?"

"Alex. It's short for Alexis," Jenny volunteered. "Frank calls her that, but she doesn't like it."

"Jenny—"

Amused, Buck's gaze swerved back to the seven-year-old. "Who's Frank?" Might as well learn the truth right now. Hopefully it would help kill his interest in her.

"He's going to be my new grandpa."

"You mean, your grandmother is getting married to Frank?"

"Yes. After we get back from our trip."

"That's an exciting thing to look forward to."

The little girl's face crumpled. "No, it isn't." Before he could blink, she ran out of the living room into the bedroom where he'd put their bags and shut the door.

Alex looked shattered. "I'm sorry. She's been upset lately, but never around anyone other than me."

"It's probably just because she's not feeling well and

the storm scared her. I'll leave so you can take care of her. I can show you around the ranch tomorrow."

"Please don't go yet. There's something you need to know. I was going to tell you at the airport, but it didn't feel like the right time. Jenny needs to cry this out and she'll be fine by herself for a few minutes. I'm afraid this can't wait."

He felt her urgency. "What is it?"

"Do you mind if we sit down?"

Wondering what this was all about, Buck sat in one of the chairs, while she took the end of the couch. "I'll make this as short as possible. My name is Alex Wilson. I'm Jenny's grandmother, *not* her mother."

Buck shot up from the chair. *Grandmother?* It wasn't possible. She looked so young! His mind had to do a complete thought reversal.

"Two months after Daniel was killed, my daughter, Christy, died. She'd suffered from leukemia for a short time before her passing. I became Jenny's legal guardian."

A slug to the gut couldn't have come as more of a shock.

"When the letter arrived from the Teton Valley Dude Ranch inviting Christy and Jenny to come, I was so touched you couldn't imagine. But the invitation was meant for my daughter." He heard tears in her voice.

"I called Daniel's commanding officer so he could explain my situation to Mr. Lundgren—Carson—and tell him the reason why we couldn't accept such a great honor. He told me that since I was Jenny's legal guardian and had virtually raised her since Christy fell ill, no one had more of a right to come and bring Jenny than I did.

"I struggled with it. In fact, up to a week ago, I was ready to call the ranch and tell you about my daughter's death. I wanted you to give this honor to a well-deserving widow and her child. But the commanding officer wouldn't hear of it. By that time Jenny was so excited to come, I couldn't disappoint her. With both her parents' deaths, she's been through so much grief. But I wanted you to know the truth."

Buck couldn't begin to fathom it. "I'm glad he insisted you come. After hearing what you've told me, I speak for Carson and Ross when I say we couldn't be happier that Daniel Forrester's daughter and mother-in-law have accepted our invitation. He was a real hero. We're hoping this trip will let Jenny know how special we thought her father was."

Her eyes glazed over. "You're very kind, Buck. Daniel was a terrific son-in-law. My daughter couldn't have chosen better. Which brings me to what happened tonight. I'm planning to be married to a man I met over two years ago. He's been careful because of Jenny's feelings and has only proposed recently.

"Jenny knows we're planning marriage and I'd hoped she was getting used to the idea, but tonight's outburst has shown me she's not ready to share me with Frank yet. To be truthful, he was worried about my bringing her on this trip and is still unhappy about it. She adored her daddy and Frank thought meeting more ex-marines might be too painful a reminder of her loss.

"But she acted so excited about coming here that I couldn't disappoint her. I'm embarrassed for the way she acted out just now. If I see any more of this behavior while we're here, we'll have to leave, and I'll reimburse you for the airline tickets and any expense you've gone to for us."

"I'm sure that won't be necessary. Once she meets Johnny, she'll be so preoccupied that she'll forget to be upset. There's something about this ranch that gives people a new perspective."

She stood and walked over to the door. "I hope you're right. I can tell you one thing. You knew exactly how to calm Jenny's fears tonight. For that, I'm indebted to you. Thank you for inviting us here. You'll never know what that letter from the ranch did for me and Jenny. At a very dark hour for her, it gave us the hope that a brighter future was in store."

Buck could hardly swallow for the sorrow he was feeling for their family. "I'm so glad it did that for you. Good night, Alex. See you in the morning."

Without lingering, he hurried outside and whipped off his mask. After the rain, the scent of sage hung heavy in the air. Willy was waiting for him in the van. "Everything all right, Buck? You look…disturbed."

He put his apparatus back in the locker. "To be honest, disturbed doesn't come close to what I'm feeling." His thoughts were in chaos.

Willy started driving them along the puddled dirt road toward the parking area at the side of the main ranch house. "Mrs. Forrester is a knockout."

That she was. "Just so you know, her name is actually Alex Wilson. She's Jenny Forrester's grandmother."

"Grandmother—" At that revelation, Willy pressed on the brakes and looked at him. "Come on… You're joshing me, right? How could she be a grandmother?"

Buck's eyebrows lifted. "I don't know. I've been

trying to do the math. Her granddaughter just turned seven." He could hear Willy's brain working.

"She would have to be forty or damn near close."

"Yep." But she could pass for ten years younger and was planning to get married. "Her daughter died soon after Daniel Forrester was killed by a grenade."

Quiet reigned until they reached the ranch house. "That's awful. The poor little kid."

"You can say that again." They'd both suffered too many losses. Buck opened the door. "Thanks for the lift, Willy. See you tomorrow."

Buck entered the ranch through the front door, coughing his way back to the office to find the guys. What he had to tell them would blow their minds. During those weeks in the hospital when they'd come up with the idea to run a dude ranch to honor soldiers' families, Buck could never have dreamed up a scenario like this one.

Chapter Two

Relieved that Buck Summerhayes knew the truth about everything, Alex locked up and walked back to the bedroom. Jenny was lying on top of one of the twin beds with her head buried in the pillow. Alex sat at her side and started rubbing her back.

"Did Buck leave?"

"Yes."

"I wish he didn't have to go. He's nice."

"I agree, but it's late. He needs his sleep and so do you. Before he left, I told him about your mom."

"I'm so glad we came. Do you think he's in pain?"

"No. As long as he doesn't breathe smoke, I'm sure he's fine."

"I like him."

"I know."

"He has pretty green eyes. They're lighter than Daddy's."

"You're right."

With his full head of thick light brown hair and his well-defined physique, Buck Summerhayes was undeniably an attractive man—and he had a way about him that had charmed her granddaughter. She suspected he charmed most females. Alex hadn't seen a wedding band. Since he hadn't mentioned a wife or children, Alex presumed he was still a bachelor.

"I have something to tell you that will make you happier, but you have to turn over so we can look at each other."

Jenny flipped over on her back. "What is it?"

"When we go home, I'm going to tell Frank I'm not ready to marry him yet."

She sat up straight. "You're not?"

"No. You and I need more time." Tonight's outburst in front of a stranger had given her ample proof that it was too soon for any more changes in Jenny's life.

The girl's slim arms caught Alex around the neck in a powerful hug. "I love you, Nana!"

"I love you too, sweetheart. How does your tummy feel now? Would you like a soda?"

"Yes, please."

"Good. I'll see what I can find."

Alex went in the other room and opened the minifridge. There were a variety of drinks. She drew out a ginger ale and a cola. Before she went back to the bedroom, she checked on the fire. It was burning down. With the screen in place, she didn't need to worry about sparks catching something on fire.

"Here you go." Alex sat on the other twin bed and pulled out the brochure that had been included with the letter she'd received from the dude ranch. Together they made plans for the next day while they drank their sodas.

She knew Frank was waiting for her to call him, but for the first time, she didn't feel like talking to him. He hadn't wanted her to come to the ranch, and Jenny was thrilled to be there. Alex felt as if she was in a tug-of-war. It took too much emotional energy. Instead of calling, she reached for her cell phone and texted him that they'd arrived safely but were exhausted. She'd phone him tomorrow. Alex meant it about being worn out.

With that decision made, she and Jenny opened their suitcases to get out the things they'd need for bed, including the framed photograph of Jenny's parents that Alex placed on the telephone table for her.

"We'll put everything else away in the morning," she said. After brushing their teeth, they said their prayers, and then she turned out the lights and they climbed under their comfy quilts. Alex liked their yellow-and-white-checkered design. The whole log cabin had a cheery ambience. There was no doubt that she and Jenny needed a little cheer in their lives.

In her heart of hearts, she was relieved about the decision she'd made where Frank was concerned. Alex had refused to wear his engagement ring yet because deep down she'd known Jenny wasn't ready. She'd seen the signs, but tonight's incident had crystallized things for her.

Marriage was a big step for anyone, but an even bigger one for a woman who'd be forty-one in a few months and had never been married. Frank was fifty-five but looked fifty because he played a lot of tennis and kept fit. They'd met when she'd started working at the bank where he was the vice president. After he lost his wife to cancer, they became friends. That friendship deepened following Christy's death and they fell in love.

She liked his two married children and grandchildren. He had a maturity and stability that were especially appealing to her. Jenny liked him fairly well, but the mention of marriage was something else. Obviously it was too soon after her daddy's death for her to imagine a man living with them under the same roof.

Alex knew it would come as a blow when she got home and told Frank she couldn't marry him yet. For her, intimacy was out of the question until their wedding, because she refused to anticipate their vows as she'd done with Kyle when she was seventeen.

Although she hated the thought of disappointing Frank further, Jenny had to come first. Alex had raised one daughter, and now she was raising another. The responsibility was enormous. Frank would help her, but not until Jenny was ready. And as much as Alex was looking forward to marriage, they had to get past this problem first. She guessed she was going to find out how patient Frank could be.

With a troubled sigh, she turned on her other side. When Jenny had been in the first grade, Alex had arranged various playdates for her. One girl named Mandy was turning into a friend Jenny really liked. They got along great, but she needed more friends. She hoped that she would make some friends at the ranch for the time that they were there. Maybe there would be some other families with a girl. And Buck had mentioned a boy....

She and Jenny had been through so much in the past year, but if there was any consolation, it was that her daughter and Daniel were together in heaven. Alex loved her granddaughter and was determined they were going to have a wonderful life and enjoy this special week, which had come as an unexpected gift.

To her surprise, her thoughts drifted to the handsome ex-marine who'd flown on the plane with them to Jackson. Who would have guessed he was one of the owners of the dude ranch.

Buck's words rang in her ears: *There's something about this ranch that gives you a new perspective.* She had the feeling he'd been speaking from personal experience and prayed it would be equally true for her and Jenny.

"Nana? Somebody's knocking at the door. Do you think it's Buck?" Jenny asked with an eagerness that surprised Alex.

"I have no idea." Alex had awakened thinking about him and how good he'd been with Jenny last night. She knew married men who didn't handle their own children's fears as well as the way he'd handled Jenny's. She shot up in bed and brushed the hair out of her eyes to check her watch. It was five after eight.

There was another knock. "Can I get it?"

"Go ahead." Alex had slept in her sweats and felt decent enough as she followed Jenny into the other room. Her granddaughter had inherited the best features from both Christy and Daniel. She looked so cute in her Sleeping Beauty pajamas. Alex thought she was the most adorable girl on the planet.

When Jenny opened the door, they were met by a brown-eyed, brown-haired boy in a black Stetson and cowboy boots. He wore a holster around his hips and was holding a cap gun in one hand. Alex decided she was looking at the most adorable *boy* on the planet.

"Hi! I'm Johnny Lundgren. Are you Jenny?" Her granddaughter's green eyes widened in astonishment before she nodded. "Do you want to have breakfast with me?"

She turned to Alex. "Would that be okay with you, Nana?"

"Of course." She moved to the door. "Hi, Johnny. I'm Alex."

"I know. You're her grandmother."

Alex couldn't help smiling. He had amazing confidence for his age. "That's right. Last night Buck told us you're Mr. Lundgren's son."

"Yep."

"We're very pleased to meet you." She shook his hand. "We understand you have a pony named Goldie."

"Yep. I'll show you to her after breakfast. Do you want to see me ride her?"

"Yes. I want to ride, too."

"Okay. We'll go after we eat. I like Fruit Loops. What about you?"

Jenny thought for a minute. "Do they have Boo Berry?"

"I think so, but it makes your mouth blue."

"I know." Both children laughed at the same time. A small miracle had occurred with her granddaughter. Buck Summerhayes wasn't the only male around the ranch who had charm. "Come on in, Johnny. We'll be ready in a few minutes."

"Thanks."

"Where did you get your cap gun?"

"In Jackson. Maybe your nana will buy one for you." Jenny turned to her. "Would you?"

"We'll see. First we need to get dressed."

"Okay."

Alex hustled Jenny into the bedroom. They took turns quickly showering, and then both dived into their suitcases for jeans and tops. She guessed that Buck was behind this and knew what he was doing. Here Alex had been hoping there'd be a girl for Jenny to play with, but Johnny Lundgren was so cute and interesting that he had her granddaughter mesmerized. Better strike while the iron was hot.

In fewer than twenty minutes, they'd freshened up and brushed their hair. "I think we're ready." They joined Johnny and the three of them stepped out of the cabin. The Teton mountain range rose majestically in the distance. The sight of it in the sunshine took Alex's breath away. You would never have known there'd been a storm last night.

"There's the big mountain!" Jenny cried, pointing to it. You couldn't miss it.

"Yep. That's the Grand Teton."

"What does *Teton* mean?" The question didn't surprise her. Her granddaughter was the most observant, curious person Alex had ever known.

Johnny looked puzzled. "I'll have to ask Dad."

"Have you ever seen anything more beautiful, sweetheart?"

"I didn't know it was so tall!"

Alex looked all around. There were a few other cabins besides their own, and they were all surrounded by sagebrush. A distance away, she could see the main ranch house—a big rustic two-story affair with a copse of trees to the side. It was the type of home the man on the horse in the Great American Cowboy ad might live in. Alex was being fanciful, but this ranch was the kind of place dreams were made of.

The children moved ahead of her as they walked along the road.

Johnny turned to Jenny. "Do you want to camp out on the mountain?"

"Have you done it?"

"A couple of times."

"Is it scary?"

"Only once, when we got caught in a storm."

"I don't like storms."

"It was okay. Dad was with me. We stayed in our tent and drank hot chocolate until it was over."

Alex caught up to them. "That sounds fun."

Jenny's expression sobered. "I don't have a dad anymore."

"I know."

Her blond head lifted. "You do?"

"Yep. I know all about you. Your daddy was a marine like mine, and they both got killed in the war."

"But I thought you said you went hiking with your dad."

"I meant my *new* dad."

After a pause, Jenny said, "Your mom got married again?"

"Yep. To Carson."

"Do you like him?"

"He's my favorite person in the whole world besides my dad."

Alex knew what her granddaughter was thinking. Frank wasn't her favorite person in the world, but she didn't say it out loud, for which Alex was grateful.

Suddenly a lovely blonde woman in a blouse and

jeans came walking around the side of the building where Alex could see half a dozen vehicles of different kinds were parked. "There you are, Johnny. I was just coming to look for you."

"I'm afraid it's our fault." Alex smiled at her. "Jenny and I needed to get showered and dressed while he waited for us. You must be Johnny's mother."

"Yes. I'm Tracy Lundgren and you have to be Alex Wilson. Welcome to the ranch." They shook hands.

"Thank you. Your son makes a wonderful guide. We're thrilled to be here."

"No more than we are to have you." She walked over to Jenny. "Buck told us you just had your seventh birthday. Johnny's turning seven next week. It's an amazing coincidence. You'll have to come to his party. We're going to go into Jackson to the Funorama. They have all kinds of slides and games, and you can eat all the pizza you want."

Johnny eyed Jenny. "Do you like pizza?"

She nodded. "It's my favorite food."

"Mine, too."

"I like pepperoni."

"Me, too."

Alex and Tracy exchanged amused glances. Johnny's mother was probably in her late twenties and seemed so friendly. Christy would have liked her. Alex's heart ached for what her daughter was missing, but today wasn't the time to be sad. Johnny's arrival at their front door had brought its own brand of sunshine, something they badly needed.

"Which tree does Moppy live in?"

Johnny looked surprised. "How do you know about her?"

"Buck told me last night."

He ran over to a big fir. "See that hole?"

Jenny moved closer. "Do you think she's inside?"

"I don't know. When she hears voices, she hides. We'll come back after breakfast and sneak up on her."

"Okay."

They rounded the corner to enter the main doors of the lobby. Suddenly Jenny cried, "Look, Nana—"

Alex turned in time to see what had to be the biggest moose head ever. It was mounted above the door frame. "My heavens—he's enormous."

Johnny tilted his hat back. "Dad calls him Mathoozela."

"Mathoozela?" At this point Jenny's eyes had rounded. "I never heard that name before."

"It's because he was so old when he died."

By now Tracy's shoulders were shaking along with Alex's. She put an arm around her granddaughter's shoulders. "The Bible says Methusela was the oldest man who ever lived."

"Yep. Dad says he lived to be 969 years. He thinks maybe that's how old this moose got to be."

"Maybe he's even older," sounded a male voice behind them.

"Dad!"

Alex watched as the attractive dark blond Stetson-wearing cowboy gave his stepson a bear hug before picking him up. "So, introduce me."

"This is Jenny Forrester and that's her nana, Alex. My dad's name is Carson."

Carson Lundgren smiled, his eyes a bright blue. "Welcome to the ranch." He coughed. "We've been waiting for you, especially when we found out your granddaughter was the same age as Johnny. The more kids around here, the better."

Alex agreed. "We're very excited to be here." What wasn't there about these people to like?

"Our other partner Ross would be here, but he's on an overnight pack trip with some of our guests. You'll meet him tomorrow."

After the greetings were over, Carson put Johnny back down and curled an arm around his wife's waist. They appeared to be crazy about each other. Alex remembered being in love like that with Christy's father once, but once she told him she was pregnant, she never saw him again.

Jenny looked up at him. "Is Buck here?"

"Did I hear someone say my name?"

At the sound of the deep, familiar male voice, Alex spun around to see the former marine walk toward them from a doorway beyond the front-desk area. Last night he'd been wearing a jacket and chinos. This morning he was dressed in cowboy boots, a Western shirt and jeans that molded his powerful thighs. His rugged good looks caused her pulse to race for no good reason.

"*I* did." Jenny smiled up at him. "But we didn't see Moppy this morning."

"Don't worry. We'll catch her after dinner when she doesn't think anyone is watching. Have you had breakfast yet?" Jenny shook her head. "Are you hungry?" She nodded. "Good. Then let's go in the dining room. We could eat the three big trout I caught early this morning."

"You did?" Jenny looked amazed.

"Do you know what a trout is?" Johnny asked her.

"Yes, it's fish."

Alex was glad her granddaughter could hold her own on something. Mirth filled Buck's green eyes as he lifted them to Alex, bringing on an unexpected rush of adrenaline. What on earth was wrong with her? "How about you?"

"One medium trout sounds delicious."

His low chuckle traveled to her insides. "I caught a couple of those, too." He turned to Carson. "Are you going to join us?"

"I'm afraid I've got a meeting with the stockmen, but I'll try to catch up with you at the barn later in the day." Alex remembered reading that the dude ranch was also a cattle ranch. These men led busy lives. He hugged Johnny again. "Have you got a pony picked out for Jenny yet?"

He whispered to his father. Carson nodded. "Good choice."

"Hey, Dad? Jenny wants to know what *Teton* means."

Suddenly both men broke out in wide grins. "I'll leave that to your mom to explain. Got to run."

"Coward," Tracy said to her husband with a grin as he kissed her. "Come on, everyone. We need to eat breakfast while we still can."

The five of them walked through the great room with its floor-to-ceiling fireplace and entered the main dining room. Wagon-wheel chandeliers hung from the ceiling. Alex saw several families seated with older teenagers. Only one table was empty. All of them were covered in red-and-white-checked cloths with white daisies forming the centerpieces. Alex loved the decor.

Once they were seated and had been served their orders, Buck looked at Alex and Jenny. "Last night you were too tired for me to tell you much about the ranch.

Carson Lundgren's great-great-grandfather purchased this land in 1908 and turned it into the Teton Valley Ranch where they ran cattle and we still do, today.

"His grandparents raised him and he became a rodeo champion known as 'King of the Cowboys.' Since I went into business with him and Ross Livingston, we've also begun operating the ranch as a dude ranch for tourists who make reservations with us and are paying guests. But once a month we use part of the money to invite one war widow and her children to stay with us. You two are our honored guests for this week and have access to all the facilities free of charge."

"We're thrilled to be here," Alex exclaimed. "Jenny and I read the brochure. You offer so many activities we can't believe it. I think it would be impossible to do them all."

He chuckled. "Most everyone wants to try horseback riding, so you'll probably want to invest in some Western gear. We also offer fishing. If you want to go down the Snake River in a raft or a kayak, we'll take you. Some people want to do mountain climbing or go hiking.

"We also have a swimming pool off the games room on the other side of the dining room. Ping-Pong, cards, television—it's all at your disposal. We plan pack trips to the lake for overnight campouts and there are hot-air-balloon rides you can enjoy over Jackson Hole. You can also attend the Jackson Rodeo if that appeals to you. If you need a car, we'll provide you with one so you can go into town to shop, see a movie or try out one of the restaurants.

"Housekeeping makes up your cabins and supplies you with laundry service. Just put what needs washing or cleaning in the laundry bag under the sink and leave it on the peg of the door. It'll be returned to you later in the day.

"As the brochure explained, this is also a cattle ranch with a foreman and stockmen. They work up on the mountain with the cattle. If Jenny wants to see the herd, that can be arranged, too."

Alex smiled at him. "I'm still trying to take it all in."

"What do you think you want to do first?"

Jenny glanced at Alex. "Can we go buy me a cap gun like Johnny's?"

Buck chuckled. "Sure we can. I'll drive us into Jackson and we'll get you some other stuff, too."

"Can I go?" Johnny eyed his mother for permission.

"If it's all right with Buck."

"We couldn't get along without him."

"Be sure to mind Buck and be helpful." Tracy gave her son a kiss and excused herself. "I'm overseeing some heavy-duty cleaning. I'll see all of you later."

She left and Buck finished off a second trout and hash browns with another cup of coffee. Alex was already full from her fish and biscuits. "That was delicious."

"That's good," Buck said, smiling at her. "Johnny? Are you about ready to go?"

"Yep."

"Why don't you come and help me unload some supplies from the truck? Then we'll pick you ladies up at your cabin in, say, half an hour."

Alex nodded. "That sounds perfect." She needed to phone Frank before they went into town.

Johnny slid off his chair. "See you guys soon."

"Okay." Jenny ate her last spoonful of cereal. "We'll be ready."

"Hey—you've got blue teeth."

They both giggled.

Alex hadn't heard such a happy sound come out of her granddaughter in a long time. She herself felt lighter as the four of them parted company outside and they made their way back to the cabin.

"Why didn't Johnny's dad tell us what *Teton* means?"

She remembered the way Buck's eyes lit up *and* the way it made her feel—as if little sunbursts had exploded inside her. "Well, it's only a guess, but I imagine the range got its name from the Indians and early trappers who thought those peaks reminded them of a woman. You know what I mean?"

Alex had learned early that the unvarnished truth was the only way to get her granddaughter off a subject. Euphemisms didn't work with her.

"Oh." Jenny's eyes twinkled as she looked at Alex. Sometimes, she seemed older than seven. "Do you think Johnny knows?" They'd reached the cabin and went inside.

"No, or he wouldn't have asked his father in front of everyone. One day his dad will tell him."

In the midst of their illuminating conversation, her phone rang, interrupting a special moment. *Frank.* He had to be wondering why she hadn't phoned him yet. It was because Johnny had wakened them out of a sound sleep and they'd rushed to make breakfast on time.

"Jenny? Be sure to brush your teeth."

"I will. Nana? Will you tell Frank what we talked about last night?"

Oh, Jenny. Nothing got past her granddaughter.

* * *

Johnny helped Buck unload some supplies at the new house Carson was having built on the property for his family down near the Snake River. So far everyone was living in the ranch house with Buck and Ross upstairs, and Carson and his family on the main floor.

Buck had been overseeing the construction. After the foundation had been poured, he'd spent the next three days on a brief vacation in Colorado Springs with his family while he waited for it to settle. He hadn't seen his parents since March. Now it was back to work.

He talked with the construction workers who'd already started the framing. When everything appeared under control, he shoved his cowboy hat back on his head and turned to Johnny. "Come on. Let's go get the girls." They walked back to the truck and climbed in.

"Jenny's nana isn't a girl."

"You're right, but she doesn't look like any grandma I ever met."

"I know. My Grandma Baretta looks a lot, lot older."

Buck was having a devil of a time coming to grips with that fact. He started the engine and they took off.

"Hey—can we go to town in the Jeep? It's more fun."

"Sure."

"Will you take the top off?"

"Why not." According to the weather forecast, they wouldn't have to worry about rain for at least three or four days. Buck drove them to the parking area at the side of the ranch house and they got in the Jeep. But before they went anywhere, he had to remove the soft top at the garage south of the house.

Once that was accomplished, they set out for the Forrester cabin. The second they pulled up in front, Johnny threw open the door. "I'll get them."

"You do that." The less involvement he had with Alex Forrester, the better. After they got back from town, he'd turn them over to Carson for the horseback-riding lesson while he helped with the framing. Ross could take them fishing in the morning. A good rotational plan was called for if he wanted to survive this week with his emotions intact.

He didn't have to wait long for their guests. The ladies came right out. Correction, Jenny practically flew down the steps, her blond ponytail swaying back and forth. "I've never ridden in a Jeep before!"

"It's cool!" Johnny raced after her. "Can we sit in back, Uncle Buck?"

"Uncle—"

"He's not really my uncle. Neither is Ross. But Daddy told me I could call them that if I wanted."

"You must love them a lot."

"I love them as much as my uncles in Cleveland, but don't tell my mom I told you that."

The things Johnny said got to Buck's heart. More and more, he found himself wanting to be a father. "Ross and I love you, too. Now, make sure your seat belts are fastened."

"We will," they said in unison.

Buck stepped down and walked around to help Alex in the front passenger seat. She was wearing a crew-neck sweater in a sage-green color with khaki pleated trousers. Although her legs were covered today, the length of them combined with her womanly hips and generous curves made nonsense of his intentions to remain indifferent.

Her fragrance put him in mind of a vale of spring wildflowers, adding to the assault on his senses. Damn. Frank had more than one reason to wish the two of them hadn't come on this trip. Buck knew he wouldn't have been able to handle it.

"Thank you," she said as he shut the door.

He nodded and took his place behind the wheel. "Before we leave, did anyone forget anything? Now is the time to speak up."

Alex glanced at him with a mysterious smile. "Or forever hold our peace?"

Buck could feel himself falling into those eyes that looked like impossibly dark blue pools. "Something like that," he murmured.

"Thanks, Buck, for taking us into town," she said. "You've been so wonderful to us and this is such a beautiful day. I can't believe there was ever a storm last night. It's getting hot already."

"It's always that way here in the mountains."

"Yep," Johnny piped up from the back as they drove off. He had big ears. As usual, he was multitasking and could take in every word the grown-ups had to say, while maintaining a conversation with his new friend. "Hey, Jenny? Do you want to go swimming later?"

"Yes. I love swimming."

Buck smiled to himself. "You mean, after you've shown her your pony?"

"Yeah. I think she should ride Mitzi. Have you ever been riding?"

"Yes."

"Do you like it?"

"It's okay, but the horses are so big. Frank's friend owns horses and he's taken us a lot of times."

"Oh. Who's Frank?"

"Nana's boyfriend."

"I didn't know grandmas had boyfriends."

Buck burst into laughter. He couldn't help it. Thankfully, Alex joined him.

Buck heard whispering coming from the backseat. Alex turned her head. "Jenny? It's not polite to whisper in front of other people."

"I'm sorry."

Johnny had always amused Buck, but he couldn't remember ever being this entertained before. He turned onto the highway leading into the town of Jackson. The place was crowded with every kind of four-wheel-drive vehicle loaded up with kayaks, bikes and rafts. After he made a left down one of the streets, they passed a movie theater.

"Hey—" Johnny cried out. "Can we go see that after we get her a cap gun?"

"Could we, Nana? See *The Big Blue Macaw?* It's that show about those birds from Brazil! My teacher said we should go."

"Sweetheart, we came to a dude ranch. Buck has more exciting things for us to do than watch a movie."

"Actually I haven't been to see a movie in a theater in years. It sounds fun."

"Yippee!" Johnny exclaimed.

"Mandy says it's really good."

"Who's Mandy?"

"One of my friends from school. But we've been off track for a week and I haven't seen her. I have to go back to school after our trip."

"My school doesn't start for another month."

"You're lucky."

Alex shot Buck a glance. "Do you think the theater would even be open this time of day?"

He nodded. "They have matinees. You'd be surprised how many guests at the dude ranch take in a show while they're in town. When you're on vacation, you should be able to do whatever you want." For the moment, this was exactly what Buck wanted to do.

One more corner and they came to the Boot Corral. He shut off the engine and they all climbed out. Johnny led the way inside the store. The college-aged girl at the counter broke into a smile when she saw Buck. "Hello again, you guys."

"Hi," Johnny greeted her. Buck followed suit.

The brunette was cute and flirted with him every time he came in, but there was no chemistry and she was too young for him. "Today we need a cap gun, a holster and enough ammo to last a week."

"It's for Jenny," Johnny explained.

"I see. Well, let's get her outfitted. Is there anything else you need while I'm at it?"

"Do you have any cowboy boots?" Johnny asked Jenny.

"No."

"Then she needs boots and a hat!" Johnny was starting to sound more like Carson every day.

"Could I have a white one?"

"I think there's one your size."

"Maybe I'll get some cowboy boots, too," Alex spoke up.

Buck had been on the verge of suggesting it.

"Great. Come on and follow me to the other end of the store."

Before long, they'd bought everything they needed.

Buck enjoyed sitting back while he watched Alex try on several different kinds of boots. With those legs…

When all the decisions had been made, he threw in a white hat for her. "Now you and Jenny will be the good guy twins."

After flashing him a smile that lit her eyes, she walked to the front desk and pulled out her credit card.

"Sorry." Buck picked it up and handed it back to her. He felt her warmth when their hands brushed in the process. "These purchases are compliments of the ranch. They go with the territory."

She shook her head. "I don't feel right about it."

"Too bad, because that's the way it is." He turned to the clerk. "Put it on my bill."

"You bet."

"Would it be all right if we leave the bags here? We'll come back for them a little later."

"No problem. I'll leave them behind the counter."

"Thank you." Excited for what was to follow, Buck left his cowboy hat with their purchases and walked the four of them out to the Jeep. When he'd flown into Jackson last evening anticipating the Forresters' arrival, he couldn't have imagined this happy scene or a woman like Alex. Although Frank was waiting in the background, Buck refused to think about that right now.

Chapter Three

Alex had noticed the way the clerk who'd waited on them only had eyes for Buck. That didn't surprise her. There were a lot of guys walking around the store and out on the streets, but none of them had captured Alex's attention, either.

And although he was nice to the attractive girl who'd looked to be in her early twenties, he didn't give off any signals that he was interested. If Alex had been that clerk, it would have been disappointing not to make any headway with him. A man with his appeal and charisma didn't come along often.

Alex couldn't remember the last time she'd found a younger man so attractive. In fact, it frustrated her that he'd been on her mind this much since their arrival in Jackson.

After Christy was born, Alex had lived with her parents and had gotten a job so she could afford day care for her baby. Later on, when Christy started kindergarten, Alex went to college on student loans at night and worked during the day while still living at home.

Once she'd graduated with a degree in finance, she started a new job at a bank near her parents' house and eventually earned enough money to move into an apartment with Christy. Over those years, she'd dedicated herself to her child and her work. She'd gone out on the occasional date, but getting married hadn't been her focus.

Her teenage love affair resulting in a child had changed her life and priorities. She'd worked so hard at everything and was so grateful for her parents' help that her mind hadn't been on guys. To her chagrin, her teenage daughter fell in love at seventeen, too. Since she and Daniel wanted to get married, Alex gave her permission. It was a good thing because they had a baby right away and Alex helped them all she could so they'd have a stable home. Soon after Jenny came along, Daniel joined the marines.

It was about the same time that Frank lost his wife. While Alex commiserated with him at work, their friendship grew. Then came double tragedy. Alex lived to console her granddaughter and give her the life she deserved. Frank was there to talk to and filled a huge void in her life.

In time, she fell in love with him and was thrilled when he proposed. To have a wonderful, constant man in her life and Jenny's meant everything. But when she'd broached the idea of marriage with Jenny, it hadn't gone as she'd hoped.

Her granddaughter's feelings seemed all mixed up

inside. Some days she was angry and threw her Lego bricks all over her room. Other times, Alex found her by the window in her bedroom after school, so lonely and quiet it pierced her heart. Last week, she'd talked constantly about her daddy and cried because he and her mommy were gone.

The invitation to spend an expense-free week at the dude ranch had brought the only light to Jenny's eyes in the past year. When Frank drove them to the airport to come on this trip, Jenny had acted as if he wasn't there. Alex was mortified over her behavior and suspected her granddaughter was glad they were getting away from him for a week. He *had* to have noticed, but there was nothing to be done about it.

But since their arrival in Jackson last night, Jenny had been acting like a normal girl again. Alex had a hunch Buck's entry into their lives had something to do with Jenny's lighter spirits. The man sure knew how to make everything exciting.

Frank wasn't exciting in the same way to Jenny, because he was older. Of course, it wasn't only that. Frank had a completely different personality. But the aspects Alex loved about him didn't do it for Jenny. He was too set in his ways for her and not spontaneous enough.

Buck, on the other hand, appeared ready to do anything and delighted the kids by getting them hot dogs and popcorn to eat during the movie. Alex felt like a kid herself as they entered the crowded theater with their food. Johnny spotted four seats together three-fourths of the way back and urged Jenny to follow him. Alex and Buck joined them. The film had a clever story and some catchy music. But as much as Alex enjoyed it, she was far too aware of the man seated on her left to be able to concentrate fully.

He smelled good and looked fantastic. Buck Summerhayes was a man in his prime who was plagued by a cough he'd inherited from the war. Like her son-in-law, Daniel, he'd done something exceptional with his life by fighting for his country. He and his friends were still doing something exceptional in their own way by making this trip possible for her and Jenny.

Her eyes smarted at the dedication of these men who had to keep oxygen on hand, yet didn't let it bother them. Johnny obviously admired Buck who could be fun and kind, yet firm when necessary. Jenny had liked him right off. That never happened with strangers.

Alex couldn't remember the last time she'd felt this carefree. When she got home, she would have to write to Daniel's commanding officer and thank him for urging her to bring Jenny on this trip.

"Are you all right?" Buck whispered.

Besides everything else, he was sensitive, too. "Yes," she whispered back. "I was just thinking how glad I am we came. Already you've made my granddaughter so happy."

"That's Johnny's doing."

"I think she feels an affinity with him because they've both lost their fathers, but he's had help from you and your friends. You're all true heroes."

After a long silence, he asked, "What about you? How are you holding up? I've never been a parent, but I know it had to be devastating for you to lose your daughter."

Her throat swelled. "I wouldn't have made it if I

didn't have Jenny to raise. She gives me a reason to get up every morning."

"For what it's worth, your devotion to her is heroic. Carson's grandfather raised him after his parents died. I see how he turned out and can only marvel over the older man's ability to be there for Carson in every way. He left this ranch to him. It's now Carson's goal to make the ranch successful and pay back the man who was a hero, just like you."

Tears escaped her closed lids. She wiped them away. "Don't praise me. My work has barely begun."

"That's what I'm talking about." His deep tone flowed through her. "You'll be there for her all your life. After what you've had to endure, I admire you more than you know."

"Thank you."

Deeply touched, she remained silent for the rest of the film. When it was over, they left and drove to the Boot Corral for their packages. On the way back to the ranch, Jenny got out her new gun. Johnny showed her how to fill the cartridge with a roll of caps. Pretty soon they were both firing their weapons at imaginary bad guys.

The noise didn't seem to bother Buck. Frank would have asked them to stop until they got home. He was so different from Buck, who seemed to say and do all the right things around Jenny. But it wasn't fair to compare them. Frank was probably twenty years Buck's senior.

He drove them to her cabin, and then looked over his shoulder at the kids. "What do you want to do now?"

"Play cowboys!" Jenny spoke up. She and Johnny scrambled out of the back and ran around the side of the cabin, whooping it up.

Buck's lips twitched, mesmerizing Alex. "I thought he wanted to go riding, but those cap guns are a strong draw."

"Jenny's never had one. The novelty will wear off, but I'm just glad she's having a great time with Johnny. Since I know your work is never done here on the ranch, why don't you go and do what needs doing. I'll watch both of them and walk Johnny back to the ranch house later."

From beneath the rim of his Stetson, he gazed at her through shuttered eyes. Jenny had been correct about their color. In the sunlight they were the shade of new spring grass. "You're right about the never-ending work, but my main responsibility is to take care of you this week. Behind the scenes, we've nicknamed this place the Daddy Dude Ranch for obvious reasons."

And they did the daddy part better than she could have imagined. "Then I'll relieve you of that awesome responsibility for a little while, because you deserve some rest."

"Well, thank you, ma'am," he drawled. His eyes seemed to focus on her mouth. "In that case, why don't I come inside with you? While you put the things you bought away, I'll make us some instant coffee. I could do with a cup."

Alex's heart thumped. This was something she knew she should avoid, but after all he'd done for them, she didn't dare offend him. "Well... I won't say no to that."

As they went inside with her packages, the feeling grew stronger that she'd just been on a date with him, and now they were coming home to spend the rest of the evening together. She had to remember this was the middle of the afternoon and it wasn't a date!

For one thing, he was probably ten years younger than she was, despite his maturity. For another, in the absence of Jenny's father, it was Buck's job to make certain this turned into a real vacation for her grand-daughter, nothing more. She wished to heaven she could see it that way, but he'd managed to get under her skin. The only way to get him out was to leave Wyoming, but she and Jenny had only just arrived.

On her way into the bedroom with their packages, her cell phone rang. She glanced at the caller ID. It was Frank calling her back. She'd tried to reach him earlier that morning, but he'd been in a meeting. Guilt pricked her when she thought about Buck being in the next room. The fact that she felt any guilt told her she was in trouble.

"If you'll excuse me, I need to answer my phone."

"Take all the time you need. I'm not going any-where."

She shivered, knowing it was true. After shutting the door, she sank down on the side of her twin bed to talk. "Frank?"

"Finally! I waited for your call this morning, but when it didn't come, I had a business conference to at-tend. How are you?"

"Good." Better than good, but he wouldn't like hear-ing her say that, since he hadn't wanted her to leave Sac-ramento. He was afraid it would open up old wounds for her and Jenny by being around the marines who'd invited them. To her surprise, it was doing the exact opposite. But after meeting Buck, she felt…vulnera-ble. She could never remember feeling that way before.

"I miss you more than I can say, Alexis." He'd always called her that at the bank and it had stuck.

When she thought about it, she hadn't had time to miss him and that made her feel guiltier. "I miss you too. Will you be seeing Cindy and the kids soon?"

"I'm going over there for dinner tonight."

"I'm glad."

"Where are you right now?"

"At the cabin. We've just come home from town with cowboy boots and a cap gun."

"Cap gun?"

"Yes. There's a boy here, Jenny's age, who has one. They're outside, running around with them. In a few minutes we're going to the barn to see his pony. Frank—I-I'm afraid I can't talk any longer," she stammered, aware Buck was waiting for her. She couldn't think with him inside her cabin. "Call me tonight when you're back from Cindy's and we'll talk."

"I should be home by ten at the latest."

"Talk to you then."

"Alexis?"

"Yes?"

"I love you. Let's hope this trip does Jenny a world of good, because we have plans to make when you get back."

"We'll talk about that tonight. Love you, too." She hung up and hurried back into the living room.

Buck was standing on the front porch with a coffee mug, obviously keeping an eye on the kids. He'd made coffee for her. She pulled it out of the microwave and joined him. "Sorry. That was a phone call I had to take. Thanks for the coffee." She took a sip.

He eyed her over his mug. "You're welcome. Everything okay?"

She took a steadying breath. She wasn't okay, not

really. Frank would be horribly hurt and upset by what she had to tell him. She was upset, too. "Yes."

He turned toward the main ranch house. "They've gone to see if they can spot Moppy. If they're not back in a few minutes, I'll go get them."

"I suspect they ran out of caps."

"You're right." He chuckled. "But they decided to take a detour before they loaded up again so they wouldn't scare the squirrel."

"Johnny seems to be a busy bee. I think Jenny has met her match."

"Soul mates at seven," he mused aloud. "Wouldn't that be something?"

"Did you ever meet yours?" The question flew out of her mouth before she could prevent it. She shouldn't have asked him anything that personal, but couldn't seem to help herself.

"I thought I had in high school. But when I went away to college, she didn't wait for me."

"Is that when you joined the marines?"

"Am I that transparent?"

"Not at all. But getting away from the pain is probably something I would have done in your position."

He gave her a penetrating glance. "What about your soul mate?"

"I met Christy's father when we were in high school. We were both seventeen. Like you and the girl you loved, I thought we'd be together forever. But when he found out I was pregnant, all that ended. I wanted the baby more than anything, and he didn't, so we parted ways. His family moved and I never saw him again."

"Your daughter never knew her father, then?"

"No."

His features sobered. "How did you manage?"

"My parents were terrific and still are. They helped me. I got a job. After Christy was born, I put her in day care and paid for my share at home. When she started school full-time, I went to college at night and kept working. After I got my degree in finance, I started working for a bank and moved us to an apartment. Christy was seventeen when she fell in love with Daniel."

He smiled in understanding, but she was embarrassed because she knew she'd been babbling. He was easy to talk to, but it was still no excuse.

"They wanted to get married. I talked with his aunt and uncle who'd raised him. Knowing how Daniel and Christy felt about each other, we all agreed to give them our permission. It was a good thing. Before long, Jenny was born. For a few years, life was wonderful for all of us."

Buck studied her with a compassion she could feel. "Take it from me, it will be again."

"It already is with Frank in my life. As for this trip, it's doing wonders for Jenny, thanks to you and your friends. I know I keep repeating myself, but your invitation came at just the right time."

She finished her coffee and relieved him of his empty mug, which she took inside. He followed her. "Since they haven't come back, let's get in the Jeep and find them. It's hot. Johnny probably took her into the house for a drink."

"I don't want her to be a nuisance."

"That would be impossible, but now would be a good time to pick them up and drive over to the barn to see the ponies. It's only a short distance from the house.

Later on, there'll be a barbecue out on the patio by the swimming pool."

"That sounds terrific."

Alex was much more excited than she should have been over their plans. Although she could come up with several reasons why, she knew Buck was at the center of the unexpected charge of energy she felt. Considering their age difference and the situation, it was ridiculous. He'd done nothing to make her think he was attracted to her. This was all on her side and it needed to be squelched.

Buck stayed inside the corral while Jenny got used to her saddled pony. Johnny rode around, and soon both of them were doing figure eights, playing follow the leader.

Alex stood outside the fence to watch. She'd put one leg on the lower bar and rested against the top, beaming at her granddaughter and taking pictures with her cell phone. Her femininity stood out a mile. The blond streaks in her hair caught the light.

"Hey—you're a pretty good rider!" Johnny called to Jenny, drawing Buck's attention away from her grandmother.

"Thanks. So are you. I wish I could take Mitzi home with me."

"That's what Rachel said."

"Who's she?"

"A girl from Florida who came to the ranch last month. She was nine."

"Was she a good rider?"

"Yep."

"Better than me?"

Buck already felt an attachment to Jenny and was all set to pipe in with something positive when Johnny said, "Nope." Sometimes he sounded exactly like Carson. The one syllable answer brought a smile to Jenny's face.

"Why don't you guys walk the ponies around the outside of the fencing for a little while."

At his suggestion, Johnny led them out of the corral and they started making broader circles. Buck walked over to Alex.

"Your granddaughter has been taught well. I'm almost as impressed as Johnny, who's so surprised he can hardly talk right now."

She chuckled softly. "Frank's friend Hugh has had horses for years. He taught his own children and grandchildren and has been happy to give her pointers."

"It appears she was an apt pupil. So was Johnny. When he came out here with Tracy last month, he'd never been on a horse. Carson was a rodeo champion and is teaching him one step at a time."

"It shows. See the way he holds himself in the saddle? Wearing that cowboy hat, he already has the look of a junior champion."

"That's Johnny's dream. Would you like to ride with them? I'll ask Bert to saddle one of the mares for you. He's been running the stable for years."

"Thank you, but I'll wait till tomorrow. Right now I'm just enjoying watching the kids having a great time."

Johnny rode up to them. "We're going to ride over to the ranch house to see Moppy. She ran away from us before. We'll be right back."

"I think it's a little too soon for that," Buck stated.

"But I can do it!" Jenny insisted.

"That's not the point, sweetheart," Alex intervened.

"Buck's right about your staying close to the corral until your pony is used to you and trusts you. When you ride her again tomorrow, she'll be more comfortable with you. Remember what Hugh told you about trust?"

"Hey—" Johnny cried. "That's what Dad says."

Alex smiled. "Since your father was a rodeo champion, he knows what he's talking about."

"Your dad's a champion?" Jenny's voice was full of wonder.

"Yep. I'll show you his belt buckles and pictures."

"Belt buckles?"

"Those are the prizes he won."

"How funny."

Buck's chuckle over their conversation turned into a cough. "Tomorrow we'll go on a ride. For now, why don't you head into the barn. Bert will help you down. Then we'll start back to the ranch house for dinner. How does that sound?"

"What are we going to have?"

"It's Saturday-night barbecue out by the pool."

"Oh, yeah. I forgot. Come on, Jenny. If we hurry, we can go swimming before we eat."

"I'll have to get my suit."

"Me, too."

Maybe after dinner Buck could talk Alex into a game of water volleyball. The Lundgren family against... He realized he'd gotten awfully possessive over two females who'd been strangers on his flight fewer than twenty-four hours ago. He had to stop his thoughts right there.

By tacit agreement, they walked over to the Jeep. The children came running and he started the engine. Within a few minutes they'd made the trip to the ranch house. "Be sure to let your mom know you're back, Johnny."

"I will."

After the boy disappeared, Buck left for the Forresters' cabin. When Alex got out, she darted him a glance. "Jenny and I want to thank you for a fabulous day and all the gifts."

Her granddaughter nodded. "The movie was really fun. I love my cap gun."

"I'm glad, but just remember this day isn't over yet." He was determined about that.

"See ya later, Buck."

"You can count on it," he murmured. With reluctance, he looked away from Alex before driving straight to the building site by the river. He'd expected to see Carson at the barn, but maybe he'd gone to see the progress on his new home.

The work crews had left for the evening, but sure enough, he spied Carson's truck and discovered him walking around inspecting everything. Relieved to find him alone, Buck jumped down from the Jeep and joined him.

"What do you think?"

Carson smiled. "It's exciting to see how fast the framing is coming along."

"I've been pushing them."

"Everything looks good."

"You'll be moved in here before long."

"Frankly, I can't wait to have some real privacy, if you know what I mean." Buck could only imagine. "How did it go with Johnny?"

"He and Jenny have hit it off. She's a pretty good little rider for her age." For the next few minutes, Buck gave him a rundown of their day, including the moment when Johnny had said he didn't know grandmas had boyfriends. That brought a roar of laughter from Carson.

"My new son still has a lot to learn. Tracy and I love his innocence, but we know he's growing up a little more every day and will lose it eventually."

"Jenny seems a little further along in that department, but then she's had to be." In the next breath, Buck found himself telling Carson about Alex's life and her struggles.

When he'd finished, his friend let out a low whistle. "That family has really been through it. No wonder Jenny's not ready to let Frank into her life. Sharing her grandmother will be another kind of loss she's not prepared for yet."

"I think having lost both parents in such a short period of time has made her extra afraid," Buck theorized.

Carson's blue eyes searched his. "According to my wife, it appears she doesn't have a problem sharing her nana with *you*."

He'd hit a nerve, causing Buck's head to rear. "What are you saying, Carson? Hell—leave me out of this! They just got here and Alex is on the verge of marrying Frank. But she can't until Jenny learns to accept him."

"Hey—take it easy. All I meant was, isn't it a good thing Jenny doesn't resent you being around her nana, since you'll be hosting this family until they leave?"

Buck eyed him warily. "That wasn't all you meant, but I'll let it go for now."

"Hey, buddy—it's me. Carson. For what it's worth, if I were in your shoes and hadn't met Tracy, I'd be walking around like a shell-shock victim, too. In a word,

Alex is breathtaking. Ross will have a heart attack when he meets her. How old is she?"

"I didn't ask. It's none of my business."

"Whatever you say," he said with a sly grin. "Come on. Let's head back. Tracy's expecting me to help with the barbecue."

Feeling out of sorts after his conversation with Carson, Buck got in the Jeep and started out for the ranch house. Carson followed in his truck. By the time they reached the parking area, he'd gotten himself under control. He was taking all of this way too seriously and Carson had just been teasing him.

Chill out, Summerhayes.

Taking a deep breath, he exited the Jeep. While Carson hurried inside to find his wife, Buck walked around the other side of the house to see what was going on. Sounds of shouts and laughter came from the pool area where tables of food had already been set up on the patio. Some of the guests were eating and others were in the pool, Tracy among them.

He would have been all right if he hadn't seen Ross cleaving the water to bear down on Alex, ready to dunk her. Buck didn't know Ross had returned from the overnight campout.

She screamed, laughing, trying to get away from the inevitable. Watching his friend horse around with her should have made him laugh. Instead he was knocked sideways. Ross usually swam laps in the pool before calling it a night, but he did it when the guests weren't around.

Buck hadn't known a feeling like this since he'd first learned about Melanie and his brother. How could he possibly be jealous? Ross was one of the greatest guys he knew.

As for Alex, she'd arrived only last night and would soon belong to another man. She and Ross were just fooling around and having fun. Last night, Alex had told him that fun was exactly what she and Jenny needed. But Buck had no other answer for what was bothering him. There had to be something seriously wrong with him.

"Buck—come and help us!" Jenny cried out the second she saw him. At least Buck had one fan: a precious little girl who was making inroads into his heart.

Johnny's brown head bobbed next to hers. "We're having a water fight with Ross. Come and be on our side!"

Whatever he was feeling, he needed to put it away for now. "I'll get on my suit and be right out."

"Yippee!" the kids cried.

He dashed through the side doors of the games room into the hall and hurried up the stairs to his bedroom to change. Once he'd put on his trunks, he grabbed a towel and rushed outside again. He'd be all right if he stayed with the children.

Ignore what's going on with Grandma and the thirty-year-old ex-marine who ought to know better.

Except that Ross probably didn't know the whole story about Alexis Wilson.

Taking a running leap, Buck did a cannonball in front of the kids that spread water in every direction like a tidal wave. Their screams of delight were followed by more screams as Carson plunged in, practically emptying the pool. When he surfaced, he was holding a ball. "Okay, everybody. It's the girls against the guys for a game of volleyball. Girls over there." He pointed to the shallow end.

Buck didn't put it past Carson to have seen Ross zero in on Alex and decide to do something about it. Whatever. Buck joined his friends and a couple of the older teenage boys. Johnny swam over to their side.

"Hey, sport." Carson immediately put Johnny on his shoulders while Ross spiked the ball to the other side.

One of the older teenage girls returned it and the game was on, but Buck had trouble concentrating. Alex's hair was in a braid she'd pinned to the top of her head. The style emphasized her angelic face. When she jumped to hit the ball, he caught a glimpse of her shapely body in her two-piece emerald suit. His lungs gave out in reaction, leaving him coughing up a storm.

The battle wore on for ten minutes. "Give up yet?" Carson called out with a gloating expression.

"Never!" Tracy retorted and spiked a ball that Buck never saw coming because he was looking somewhere else.

Carson turned to him. "Hey, buddy. We're supposed to be throttling them." But his eyes were crinkled with laughter, conveying a private message that he knew exactly what was going on with Buck.

Making a quick recovery, Buck served a fast ball that had the girls scrambling. Within minutes it was all over. Thirty-one to nine in favor of the guys.

"It's not fair," Jenny complained when Buck swam over to her. She looked so cute in her red suit, but she was so upset that he needed to turn things around for her.

"I know, but there's something we *can* do to make

things equal. If you get on my shoulders, we'll have a water fight with Carson and Johnny."

"Goody!" She'd adopted one of Johnny's words. In the next instant, she flew toward Buck so he could lift her onto his shoulders. Ignoring Alex, who was treading water while she watched them, he headed for the other end. Johnny saw them coming and yelped.

"I hope you guys are ready, because Jenny and I are going to whomp you."

"Oh, yeah?" Carson countered.

"Start chopping the water, Jenny."

"Okay."

The game was on while the kids fought like warriors. Buck and Carson were laughing so hard, they started coughing and Johnny got dumped in the water by accident.

"We won!" Jenny squealed, hugging Buck around the neck so hard he almost choked.

Johnny hung on to his daddy's arm. "We'll get you tomorrow night."

"No, you won't. Buck and I are the best!"

Yeah. Buck loved it.

By now everyone had gotten out of the pool, including Alex. She was covered in a beach robe that hid her exquisite figure and long legs from view. She stood at the edge of the pool to throw another large beach towel around Jenny who bragged to her grandmother about winning the contest against Carson and Johnny.

"You two deserve a prize."

"What kind?" she wanted to know immediately.

"I don't know yet." Those deep blue eyes found Buck's. Maybe it was the exertion from the water fight that caused adrenaline to pump through him, but he doubted it. "I'll have to think about it while we eat. Come on."

Buck ran back inside the house to change into jeans and a polo shirt. Once dressed, he came out to help himself to steak and corn on the cob. Jenny waved him over to one of the candlelit tables where she and Alex were sitting with Carson's family and Ross. He was telling them about the elk his group had seen while camping.

"You know something, Johnny? I believe it was the same elk as the one on the dude ranch brochure."

"You mean, the one with the giant antlers?" He nodded. "I bet that's another one of your fish stories, Uncle Ross."

"I swear, it isn't! I took a picture with my phone."

"Dad doesn't think it's around anymore."

"Then maybe it's his brother."

"His brother?" Jenny laughed over the comment, causing Buck to smile. Despite all the pain she'd lived through, Alex's granddaughter had a great sense of humor. His heart warmed to her more and more.

"Where's your phone?" Johnny asked.

"In my bedroom."

"Could I go get it?"

"Sure. It's on the top of the dresser."

"It can wait," Tracy reminded her son. "Ross can show it to us at breakfast. Right now let's all finish our dinner."

"Your mother's right," Carson backed her up.

Johnny turned to Buck with pleading brown eyes. "If it's the granddaddy elk, can we go on a campout tomorrow in the same place? I want to see it." He glanced at Jenny. "You want to see it, too, don't you? It's *huge.*"

"I know. I saw it on the brochure." She turned to Alex. "Can—I mean—may we go see it, Nana? Please?"

"Maybe in a few days, sweetheart. Remember what Buck said? You and the pony need to get used to each other. After a few days of short rides, you'll be ready for a longer ride. Doesn't that make sense?"

"I guess."

"But what if the elk isn't there by then?"

Carson put an arm around Johnny. "You have the rest of your life to find him."

"Yeah, but Jenny will be going home pretty soon and might not see it."

"I don't want to go home," she piped up out of the blue.

Alex looked chagrined. She put her fork down and got to her feet. "You know what, sweetheart? You sound tired. So am I. Let's thank everyone for this delicious meal and go back to the cabin."

Jenny mumbled her thanks before standing up. "Good night everybody. It's been really fun."

"Good night," Johnny muttered back, clearly unhappy. "See you in the morning. We'll go hunting for bad guys with our guns."

"Buck? Can we ride back to the cabin with you?"

It thrilled him that Jenny wanted his company. He got up from the deck chair. "I was just going to suggest it. The air is cooling down too fast for you to have to walk in your swimsuit. Even though the Jeep will be cold, we'll get there faster. But as soon as we arrive, I'll start a fire and make the cabin cozy for you."

Jenny hurried around the table toward Buck with a smile that reached down inside him.

"Can I come with you?" Johnny was already on his feet.

Tracy put the kibosh on that idea. "Not tonight. You've had a big day and need a good sleep, too."

Good. Buck wanted to be alone with Alex and Jenny. In Afghanistan he'd been around a lot of buddies who were family men and talked about their wives and children. During that period, Buck found himself wanting the same thing but he hadn't met the right woman yet.

When the guys had been hospitalized and they'd conceived of the idea of a daddy dude ranch, he'd had many fantasies about being married and having a family. Now that Alex and Jenny had arrived on the ranch, he found himself hungering for the experience.

But to fantasize about the three of them being a family was wrong. She'd pledged herself to another man. Buck needed to remember that or he'd go a little insane.

Chapter Four

Troubled by the direction of the conversation in the past few minutes, Alex said good-night and followed Jenny and Buck around the side of the ranch house. But Jenny didn't wait for Alex to catch up. To her dismay, she saw her granddaughter reach for Buck's hand the way she might have done with her father.

It all happened naturally. That was because he took such good care of them and made Jenny feel safe, just the way Daniel had done. Though that was his job while they were here, she knew instinctively that Buck would always be attentive and fun that way. Being there at the ranch, she could see the contrast between him and Frank, who'd already raised a family and had grandchildren. Frank was good to Jenny, but it was different because Frank was more attentive to Alex.

When they reached the Jeep, Alex climbed in front

and settled Jenny on her lap to help keep her warm. Buck drove them to the cabin in record time. After putting on another oxygen mask he kept in the Jeep, he got a fire going while they showered and washed their hair.

After dressing in their pajamas, they went back to the living room to dry their hair in front of the fire with the bathroom towels. Buck checked their stock of supplies while Alex put Jenny's hair in a ponytail.

Her granddaughter stared at Buck, seemingly fascinated by everything about him. "Do you have to leave now?"

"In about three more minutes. That's when my oxygen runs out."

"I wish you could stay longer." She looked up at Alex. "Tomorrow night let's not have a fire. Then Buck won't have to leave."

"He might have other plans, sweetheart."

Jenny's eyes switched to Buck with a worried expression. "*Do* you?"

"I was thinking that after dinner tomorrow we could watch a movie here with Johnny. There are a half dozen family DVDs in that armoire."

"Could we, Nana?"

It wouldn't be wise for Alex to spend any more time in Buck's company if she wanted to forget he existed, but it would mean the world to her granddaughter. "Sure. Maybe we can get Tracy and Carson to come, too. It sounds like fun. You and Johnny can pick the movie."

"Then it's a date."

Not that kind of a date. No, no, no.

Buck got to his feet and moved his hard-muscled frame to the door. Alex averted her gaze to avoid feasting her eyes on him. "I'll see you lovely ladies at breakfast tomorrow. Afterward we'll go fishing with anyone who wants to come."

"I want to catch a big one!"

"Then we'll do it." He grinned. "And you'll have to eat it."

"I'll get Johnny to help me."

"Good thinking." He started for the door. Jenny darted after him. "Good night, Buck."

"Good night, Red."

She laughed. "Red—"

"That's your favorite color, right?" She nodded. He sent Alex a brief glance before shutting the door.

Alex knew the unexpected nickname had slipped out in the same natural way Jenny had reached for his hand earlier. She could see Buck and Jenny bonding before her eyes and moaned inwardly.

The second he left, Alex hurried over to lock the door, but she found her fingers trembled.

"Do I have to go to bed yet?"

"You can stay up until I finish doing my hair." Alex dried it a little more before securing it at the nape with an elastic.

"You're going to talk to Frank tonight, huh?"

Her heart pounded harder. "Yes."

"Is he mad at me?"

"Of course not!" Alex picked her up and hugged her.

"I wish you didn't like him so much."

They'd been over this many times before. Alex could see how much Jenny needed reassurance of her love. "It's because of all the good things he does. But don't you know there's nobody in the whole world more important to me than you? I love you with all my heart."

Jenny clung to her. "I love you, too. I wish we could stay here forever."

That was the second time in an hour her granddaughter had expressed the same sentiment. "I love it here, too, and I know exactly how you feel, sweetheart. Everyone needs to go on vacation once in a while. You forget all your problems and just have fun."

"Do you think Buck goes on vacation sometimes?"

Alex groaned. Buck again. Where had that question come from? "I'm sure he does. Now, let's go in the bedroom. It's time to get some sleep."

Tears escaped Alex's lids when her granddaughter ended her prayer by asking God to cure Buck's disease. Jenny had a tender heart made much more sensitive by the loss of her parents. Alex supposed it was possible Jenny worried Buck might die because of his condition. The thought was too terrible to contemplate.

Once she'd gone to sleep, Alex went back to the living room and stretched out on the floor in front of the fire. She checked her watch. It was twenty after ten. There was an hour's time difference between Wyoming and California. Frank might be home from his daughter's by now, but there was time to spare before she needed to phone him.

Unfortunately the longer she put off making the call, the guiltier she would feel. Turning on her side, she pressed the speed dial for his number. He picked up before the second ring. "I've been waiting to hear your voice."

"Hi. I just got Jenny to bed. How was your dinner?"

"My daughter's a great cook. Phil got a promotion, which is good news, but I want to know about you. I keep thinking about you being there without me. I have to tell you I'm having a hard time. Work isn't the same."

"I know what you mean. It's too bad you can't be here. You'd love it."

"I've been to the Tetons several times in my life. It's a beautiful place, no doubt about it. Does Jenny like it?"

If he only knew. "Yes. She spent all day with Johnny, that boy I told you about. His father was a marine who lost his life, so they have that bond between them." But Jenny had formed another bond, too. That was the one that made Alex break out in a cold sweat.

"If you think it's helping, then I'm glad you went."

"To be honest, I haven't seen her this carefree since before Daniel's death. Tomorrow we're all going fishing."

"Who all?"

Her pulse picked up speed when she thought of Buck. "Different members of the staff and guests. Today Jenny rode one of the ponies."

"They have ponies?"

"Yes. Thanks to Hugh, she was able to ride around with a lot of confidence." After a pause she said, "Frank, tonight she opened up to me about some of her feelings. We have to talk about it."

"I can hear you hesitating. What's wrong?"

Alex closed her eyes tightly. "She isn't ready for me to get married yet."

"That's not news. Will she ever be? Honestly?"

"I realize that's the last thing you want to hear, but it's clear she's not over Christy's death."

"Alexis—"

She sat up. "I know what you're going to say. We've been over this before, so here's my idea. When we fly back to Sacramento, I'm going to get us into counseling. When Daniel died, I was advised to seek help and I would have, but then Christy got so ill, I put it off."

"Counseling could take months."

"Maybe, maybe not. The point is, I can't marry you until she's able to accept it, otherwise we'll have a nightmare on our hands. I'm so sorry it has to be this way. You *have* to know this isn't what I want."

"But let's be truthful about one thing. She has resented me from the beginning and is holding you hostage."

Alex bristled. "It's not personal, Frank. She's scared she's going to lose me. She'd feel that way about any man I wanted to marry."

"In that case, I have an idea. Why don't you stay there one more day and have fun, then fly home and start your counseling. I'll go with you."

In her head, his idea made a lot of sense. The sooner Jenny got professional help, the sooner their marriage could take place. But in Alex's heart of hearts, she knew her granddaughter too well. To leave the ranch before their time was up next Saturday was unthinkable. "Jenny's planning on us being here the full week. I can't disappoint her."

"You never disappoint her and she takes advantage of that fact because she knows she's the apple of your eye."

His resentment had been growing, and now he couldn't hold it back. "Frank—"

She heard a labored sigh. "All right. I'll leave it alone, but I don't like it. I miss you too much."

To her horror, she couldn't tell him the same thing. "I'll phone you tomorrow night about the same time."

"Alexis?"

"What is it?"

"You seem different."

"I do?"

"Yes, but I can't put my finger on it."

"I don't mean to be. Jenny's still going through a difficult time."

"It's this separation. I'm afraid I'm not used to you being gone. I love you."

"I love you, too," she said honestly. That would never change, but circumstances had. "We'll talk tomorrow. Good night." She ended the call, thankful not to have to discuss this any further tonight.

Alex *did* love him, but coming to the ranch had given her a perspective she wouldn't have imagined, just as Buck had said it would. Being away from everything familiar had already put a different slant on things for her and Jenny.

For so long, their lives had been wrapped up in Christy and Daniel, with Frank playing a growing part in the background. But for a little while, this trip had taken them out of that sad world and was bringing Jenny some real happiness. If Alex were honest with herself, she could admit she liked this feeling of freedom, too. It was as if she'd put her worries on hold and could be a free agent with no deadlines, no one to answer to.

When Frank had suggested she fly home in another day, she'd rebelled at the idea. Not just for Jenny's sake, but for her own. She recognized that she'd desperately needed this time away, but she would never have taken it if it hadn't have been for that letter from the ranch.

She still had it in her purse. It was lying on the table. Compelled to read it again, she got up and pulled it out. The fire was burning down, but she could still make out the words.

Dear Mrs. Forrester,

My name is Carson Lundgren. You don't know me, but I served as a marine in Afghanistan before I got out of the service.

Along with Buck Summerhayes and Ross Livingston, also former marines, I own the Teton Valley Dude Ranch. We put our heads together and decided to contact the families of the fallen soldiers from our various units.

Your courageous husband, Daniel Forrester, served our country with honor and distinction. Now we'd like to honor him by offering you and your daughter, Jennifer, an all-expenses-paid, one-week vacation at the dude ranch anytime in July or August. We'll pay for your airfare and any other travel expenses.

You're welcome to contact your husband's division commander. His office helped us obtain your address. If you're interested or have questions, please phone our office at the number below. We've also listed our web address. Click on it to see the brochure we've prepared. We'll be happy to email you any additional information.

Please know how anxious we are to give something back to you after his great sacrifice.

With warmest regards,

Carson Lundgren

Tears gushed down Alex's cheeks. She'd been touched when she'd first read it, but nothing compared to the feelings she had now. These men, suffering from an awful disease, were breaking their backs and their pocketbooks to bring joy to families who'd been torn apart by war. Their selflessness was beyond description.

The image of Buck wearing his oxygen mask refused to leave her. In order for them to enjoy a fire in their own fireplace, he'd put himself in jeopardy because he'd wanted to make Jenny feel welcome.

Christy would have been overwhelmed by their kindness. Alex hoped she and Daniel were looking down and knew what was going on.

Finally exhausted from crying, she put the letter back in her purse and went to bed. That letter would go in a scrapbook after they got home, along with a lot of pictures Alex was taking of everyone, including Buck, when Jenny wasn't looking.

Alex heard the house phone ringing and it brought her fully awake. Her watch said it was a quarter to eight. She turned on her other side to pick it up, aware of her pulse beating faster at the thought that it might be Buck on the other end. Maybe there'd been a change in plans for the morning. "Hello?"

"Hi, Alex. It's Johnny!"

He had more personality than any child she'd ever known. "Hi! How are you this morning?"

"I'm good. Can I speak to Jenny?"

Her mouth broke into a smile. "Sure. Just a minute." She handed the receiver to her granddaughter. "It's for you."

Jenny sprang out of bed. "Hello?"

Alex got up and loosened the hair from her elastic while she listened to Jenny's end of the conversation.

"Nana? Can I go over to the ranch house right now? Johnny has to clean his room before he can go anywhere. He wants me to help him so he can go fishing with us and Buck. His mom said it's all right. Can I? Please?"

"You mean, *may* I?" Alex tried to use any teaching moment to correct her granddaughter's grammar.

"I forgot. May I?"

She chuckled, never having seen Jenny this excited to help with chores. "If that's what you want to do."

"Thanks." A smile broke out on her precious face before she spoke into the phone again. "Nana says I can come. I'll hurry. Bye." She hung up and dashed into the bathroom to brush her teeth. When she hurried back in the room for a clean pair of jeans and a top, she said, "He wants me to wear my holster and cowboy stuff." In a flash, she was ready.

"Just a minute, young lady. Let me do your hair."

"I don't want a ponytail. Sometimes the elastic hurts."

"Then I'll just brush it out." Her silky blond hair had a lot of natural curl like her mother's and Alex's. It was a trait that spanned three generations. "There." She put the white cowboy hat on her head. "Do you know what? In that getup and with those fancy cowboy boots, you look like a real cowgirl." She kissed her cheeks. "As soon as I'm dressed, I'll walk over to the ranch house to eat. Come and find me in the dining room for breakfast."

"We will." She fastened her cap gun in her holster before racing out the door. The famous Road Runner from the cartoon couldn't have moved any faster. If Frank could see the change in Jenny, he wouldn't believe it. And Alex guessed that, while he'd be happy for her, he wouldn't like it because it meant Jenny wasn't getting any closer to accepting him.

More guilt consumed Alex, as she found herself looking forward to seeing Buck. On a whim, she put on her new cowboy boots and hat, more gifts from him. Why not? They were going fishing and horseback riding today. She might as well look the part.

When Alex walked into the dining room, looking like a rodeo queen, Buck's heart did a fierce kick. In fact, every male in the room appeared to freeze, including Ross, who'd stopped munching on his toast. "Last night she could have been a mermaid," he murmured. "This morning…"

Buck didn't want to hear the rest. "Damn—I just remembered I need to talk to the contractor at the building site about something urgent before the crews get started." He got up from the table. "Do me a favor and take Alex and her granddaughter fishing after breakfast? I'll be back soon to relieve you, but this can't wait."

Ross eyed him with a puzzled expression. "Sure. They can come with my group."

"I owe you."

Hoping Alex hadn't seen him yet, he escaped through the swinging doors into the kitchen and headed for the other exit. No sooner had he reached the back hallway than the children's cries forced him to spin around. "Hey, you two—what's going on?"

With her eyes shining, Jenny ran up to him. "I just finished helping Johnny clean up his room. It was a big mess. While we were changing the water in his baby garter snake's aquarium, it got out and we had to look for it."

Buck chuckled. "Did you find it?"

Johnny nodded. "It was curled up in my laundry bag. Fred likes to hide."

"It's a good thing you found him before your mom did."

"She would have freaked."

"He put him back and gave him water," Jenny explained. "His mom did her inspection and said we were free to go fishing."

"Have you had breakfast?"

She shook her head. "We're going to eat right now."

"Then it's good timing, because your nana just walked into the dining room. While you go find her, I have an errand to run at the building site."

"Buck is helping build our brand-new house," Johnny informed her.

Her eyes rounded. "You can build a house?"

"I learned how from my father. While I'm gone, Ross will get you guys outfitted with a rod and bait. I'll join you in a little while."

A frown appeared on the girl's face. "I'd rather come with you."

"I'll take you to the new house another time when it's not so dangerous."

"How come it's dangerous?"

Jenny Forrester looked so cute in her cowgirl outfit, Buck felt his heart melt. He hunched down in front of her. "A lot of men are carrying big long boards around. They have to wear hard hats in case they get hit by accident. Sometimes they still get hurt and I don't want anything to happen to you."

She stared into his eyes. "Do you wear a hard hat, too?"

"Yes."

"Do you promise to keep it on the whole time?"

"I promise."

Her sweetness and caring haunted him all the way to the site. He had eight nephews and nieces and loved them all, but they didn't tug at him emotionally the way Jenny did. She'd been deprived of her daddy. He suffered to think about the pain she'd gone through losing her mother, too.

Buck's mother and father had always been there for him. He hadn't been deprived of anything. He thought about Alex, who'd raised her daughter alone and was now raising her granddaughter by herself. That woman's strength awed him.

Needing an outlet for the nervous energy building inside him, he helped the guys haul lumber for the next two hours to give himself a workout. But when he left and caught up to everyone at the river, he didn't see Alex or the kids.

Surprised, he got out of the Jeep and wandered over to Ross, who was helping with some of the guests. "What happened to our family? Didn't they come with you?"

Ross gave him a speculative glance. "Jenny decided she'd rather play Ping-Pong with Johnny in the games room." His eyebrows lifted. "I think we know why, so I decided not to push it."

"What are you talking about?"

"Johnny whispered to me that Jenny had her heart set on you helping her catch a big one. I'd say she has a little crush on you. Kind of reminds me of the way Johnny ignored everyone but Carson after he got here. As you remember, that relationship happened fast. I'm beginning to feel like the invisible man." He said it with a smile, but Buck worried there might be some truth behind his words.

As much as it pleased him that Jenny had been enjoying herself when he was around, the last thing he wanted to do was make the situation harder for Alex where Frank was concerned. That was why he'd asked Ross to take over for a couple of hours.

"Thanks for being willing to help out."

"Any time. You know that."

He nodded. "See you later."

In a different frame of mind since learning what had happened, Buck drove back to the ranch house and went inside. Some of the teenagers were in the games room, but there was no sign of the kids or Alex in there or out by the pool.

"Susan?" The redheaded, part-time receptionist looked up from the computer. "You wouldn't by any chance know where Johnny and Jenny have gone, would you?"

"Tracy took them into town with her. She needed to mail a couple of packages to her in-laws. Johnny's grandpa has a birthday coming up. She said something about eating lunch there, but they ought to be back pretty soon."

"Did Jenny's grandmother go with them?"

"I'm not sure."

"What about Carson?"

"He's gone to the upper pasture."

"Okay. Thanks for the info. Call me on the cell if you need me."

"Will do."

Buck had planned to take everyone riding, but that would have to wait till later. He made a beeline for the kitchen, where he fixed himself a sandwich and grabbed a couple of doughnuts. After leaving the table earlier without finishing his breakfast, he was starving.

Still feeling at loose ends, he left the ranch house, figuring he'd drive back to the building site. But after he started up the Jeep, he found himself headed for the Forrester cabin. It was probably a wasted trip, but something nagged at him to find out if Alex was inside, so he could explain.

After a few knocks, Alex opened the door to him. Her fragrance assailed him along with her beauty. He heard a quiet gasp, revealing her surprise at seeing him. "Buck—"

"I'm sorry about this morning, but something came up at the building site that I needed to see to." Buck didn't consider it an outright lie. After all, he'd manufactured it as a preventative measure. If he hadn't shown up at her door just now, he might have actually believed his own explanation.

"Johnny told me you're supervising the construction of his family's new house. You don't need to apologize for that."

"Yes, I do. Jenny was counting on us going fishing."

"When I explained, she understood."

He was knee-deep in guilt about now. "When Ross told me what happened, I didn't know if you'd gone to town with Tracy or not. In case you were here, I decided to see if there was anything you needed."

When she shook her head, her dark hair flounced back and forth across her shoulders. "Jenny begged to go with them, so I decided to take advantage of the peace and quiet and write a letter to Daniel's commanding officer. If I hadn't listened to him, Jenny and

I wouldn't be having this vacation of a lifetime. That's what it is, you know."

Buck braced his body against the door frame. "Living in the shadow of the Grand Teton is a vacation for me, too. I have to tell you, it's indecent to enjoy your work as much as I do. Just so you know, I'm free for the rest of the day if you and Jenny want to go riding later."

"Jenny will be thrilled."

She's not going to invite you in, Summerhayes. What in the hell is wrong with you?

"Call the front desk when you're ready, and I'll swing by for you." He pivoted and reached the Jeep in a couple of strides.

Ross had implied Jenny had a crush on him. He could relate to that. He wished a crush was all he had on Alex, but he knew in his gut his feelings were involved and went deeper than that, but he couldn't begin to describe what made meeting her different from all the other women he'd met in his life.

Alex was committed to the man she'd been seeing for two years. They had a long history and worked at the same bank, where according to Johnny, Frank was the vice president. He'd been there to support her through both losses and had watched out for Jenny. They were planning to be married. So how could he stand on that porch, hoping she'd ask him to stay and talk for a while? What kind of a person was he?

For the first time in years he had a different take on what had happened when Melanie and his brother had found themselves attracted to each other during Buck's absence. Strong chemistry could draw you to another person against your will, no matter how hard you fought it or didn't want it. Before they realized they were playing with fire, they'd been burned by it. He understood that now. He got it.

Good grief. He'd seen Alex's legs walking in front of him at the airport lounge. By the time he'd come face-to-face with her in the terminal, something profound had happened to him. Nothing but chemistry could explain such a powerful physical reaction. But in two days it had gone beyond that, even though he knew that she and Frank were a couple.

Buck didn't know if she felt that same chemistry for him. He couldn't tell. If she did, he envied her ability to hide it.

But the more he reflected, the more he realized that this was completely different from what had gone on with Melanie and his brother years ago. Then, there'd been no child involved whose feelings had to be considered. Jenny came first with Alex. Her granddaughter's existence complicated an already complex situation for her and Frank.

As Buck had told Carson yesterday, Buck wanted to be left out of that equation, despite how much he was attracted to Alex or cared for Jenny. He'd meant it then, and meant it even more so now. Somehow he had to find a way to insulate himself until they left the ranch and she and Jenny went back to Frank and a future that didn't include Buck.

His first rule of thumb—don't ever be alone with her.

Second rule—don't involve yourself if you don't have to.

Third rule—keep Johnny close.

Chapter Five

Alex moved over to the window and watched him drive away. Would he have stayed if she'd invited him inside?

For what, Alex? So they could talk?

She didn't have an answer for that, because she didn't know what she wanted.

Oh, yes, you do.

Simply put, she had the hots for Buck Summerhayes.

The signs had been there from the night she'd seen him walking toward her in the Jackson airport. It made no sense. It hadn't made any sense when she'd met Kyle and had been struck by an energy she couldn't explain. But that was twenty-four years ago and she'd long since given up believing such a thing would ever happen again. She didn't want it to happen again, considering Kyle didn't turn out to have staying power.

It was as if a bolt of lightning during that summer storm over the Tetons had struck her, charging every atom of her body when she'd least expected it. She hadn't been the same since.

Earlier on the phone, Frank had told her she seemed different.

Yes, she was....

When Buck appeared at the cabin door just a few minutes ago, her body had sizzled at the very sight of him. She couldn't do anything about the feelings he aroused in her without even trying. They were a fact of life. If she ran away to the other side of the earth, they'd still be with her.

If Frank were here kissing her right this very minute, she wouldn't be able to feel it, not since her body had been ignited by this new energy radiating from Buck.

So deep was her fear of her feelings that she didn't realize Jenny had come back from town and was trying to get her attention. "Nana? Can't you hear me?"

Startled, Alex spun around. "Sweetheart—"

"What's wrong?"

"Nothing." Heat swept through her. "I was thinking about something else." Someone else. "I'm sorry. Did you have a good time?"

"Yes, and guess what? It's Buck's birthday on Friday. He'll be thirty-six. Johnny says he's older than Carson or Ross."

Adrenaline coursed through her body. "I didn't know that." Johnny knew just about everything that went on around the ranch. Buck was closer to her age than she'd assumed. He'd insisted that losing the girl he'd loved hadn't played a part in his decision to join the armed forces, but Alex marveled he hadn't fallen in love with someone else since then and wasn't married by now.

"Johnny's mom says we're going to celebrate it on Johnny's birthday the day before so it will be a surprise," she chattered away. "She let me and Johnny pick out a present for Buck and she'll wrap it for us. It's a T-shirt."

Alex took an extra breath. "What does it look like?"

"We went to a shop where they put on whatever you tell them. It's a dark green one with the Grand Teton on it, and we had them put Super Dad on it."

Of course. The Daddy Dude Ranch. How absolutely perfect for the man who was being a super dad to Johnny and Jenny and would definitely be a super dad if he had his own children one day.

"Do you think we could go into town to that same shop and make a T-shirt for Johnny? But it will have to be a secret."

"Of course. Since we have the use of a car while we're here if we want it, we can drive into Jackson tomorrow before breakfast. Do you have an idea what you'd like his shirt to say?" Interestingly enough, Alex had been thinking about buying matching T-shirts for Jenny and Buck for winning the water-fight contest last night.

"Not yet."

She squeezed her granddaughter. "Well, you've got plenty of time to decide."

"Can we go riding now? Buck's going to take us."

I know. "I was planning on it. Have you eaten lunch?"

"Yes. Johnny's mom bought us hamburgers and milk shakes."

"Lucky you!"

"She's really nice and fun. I wish we lived here all the time."

"I know you do. Hurry and freshen up, and then we'll walk to the barn. It's not that far."

"Okay. Be sure and wear your hat, just like in the cowboy movies. Johnny says his dad has a DVD we have to watch. Have you ever heard of Hopalong Cassidy?"

"I have. When I was little, I saw a few of his movies."

"Was Hopalong really his name?"

"I think so."

"That's funny. Wait till I tell Johnny—"

Alex chuckled and put the hat on her head. One thing she wouldn't do was phone the desk to reach Buck. No doubt he would find out Johnny was back and would meet them at the corral. The stable manager would help get their animals saddled.

When Jenny was ready, Alex grabbed a granola bar and an apple from the basket and they left the cabin. She munched her way along the road, so filled with a sense of well-being in spite of her guilt that she didn't notice her cowboy boots touching the ground.

They arrived at the barn to find Johnny already astride his pony. "What took you guys so long?"

She smiled at the boy who'd quickly become Jenny's friend. "It's such a beautiful day that we decided to stretch our legs."

Bert led Mitzi outside and saddled her. Jenny looked around while she was waiting, and then the older man helped her on. "Thanks, Bert. Where's Buck?" There was no sign of the Jeep.

They all heard a cough. "I'm right here."

"Goody!"

Alex felt as if she was falling into space when he emerged from the shadows of the barn, leading a saddled horse by the reins. In his hat and jeans and wearing a Western shirt that accentuated the size of his chest, he looked sensational.

He raised his head, causing their gazes to collide. Buck had to know she'd been staring at him, because he'd caught her before she could look away. One side of his compelling mouth turned up, giving her senses a jolt. "This is Blossom. She's a mare you can trust."

Don't touch me, Buck. Don't come near me.

But it was too late, because he steadied the horse while she climbed onto the saddle and his hard-muscled arm brushed hers, sending liquid fire through her body. "Thank you," she said in an unsteady voice.

"You're welcome."

While she attempted to recover, he went back to the barn and rode out on a dark brown horse.

Jenny made an excited sound. "What's his name?"

"Dopey."

She laughed hilariously. "No, it isn't."

"Buck's just teasing," Johnny explained. "His real name is Dynamite. Can we ride to the new house so Jenny can see it?"

"Sure. It's midafternoon. The workmen should be gone by the time we get there. Why don't you lead the way?"

"Okay. Let's go."

Alex hurriedly drew alongside him with Jenny on his other side and they were off. Buck brought up the rear. It had seemed like a good idea to go ahead with the children, but she couldn't forget that he was right behind them. Alternating thrills and chills bombarded her as they left the sagebrush and entered a forested area filled with the sound of insects and birds whirring about.

The children talked incessantly, but their voices couldn't drown out the sound of her own heart pounding mercilessly in her chest. Alex breathed in the fresh smell of pine and simply absorbed the wonder of her surroundings, made more intoxicating by the man trailing them.

When they came out of the trees into a clearing near the river, the skeleton of a house appeared before them. Beyond it, the Grand Teton stood like a sentinel. Alex had never seen anything so spectacular.

"What a beautiful house!"

"Yep. Uncle Buck built it."

Alex turned to look at Buck. "I thought you were a rancher."

"I grew up learning how to do construction. My father and brothers run Summerhayes Construction in Colorado Springs."

"Why didn't you go back to the business after you left the military?"

"I met the guys in the hospital. We had a lot of time to talk and think about our lives once we were no longer deployed. Compared to what we'd lived through, Carson's life as a rancher sounded like a piece of heaven. It got to me and Ross.

"We were filled with guilt that we'd survived the war and others hadn't. The idea of turning his ranch into a dude ranch for helping children who'd lost their dads in the war grew on us until we couldn't think about anything else. I figured I could put all the training I'd learned from my father to work building cabins and remodeling the ranch house. One thing led to another."

"And now he's built us our house! He made the loft just for me!" Johnny declared with a happy face.

Alex smiled. "Well, aren't you just the luckiest boy in the world to have a daddy like Carson and an uncle like Buck."

"Buck can do anything!" Jenny exclaimed.

"I know," Johnny said in that way of his. He rode over to a nearby stand of jack pines and dismounted by himself. Jenny needed help. While Buck jumped down to assist her, Alex swung her leg over and got down from Blossom. They tied the reins to tree trunks and started walking around. Johnny pointed out where every room would be.

"Mine's going to be in the loft. How long before I can go up there to look around, Uncle Buck?"

He was already inspecting the work. "In a few more days." The last word came out on a cough.

"That long? I want Jenny to be able to see it." Alex expected some kind of remark from her granddaughter about not wanting to go home, but oddly enough she remained quiet and kept following Johnny around. "We're going to go down by the river and watch the beavers."

"Don't get too close," Buck warned.

"We won't."

As they ran off, Buck came to stand by her. She turned to him. "It's going to be spectacular when it's finished. Paradise for a boy like Johnny."

"Carson hired an architect to design something contemporary. There'll be a lot of glass. He and Tracy want as much light as possible."

"I'd want the same thing so I could enjoy every season here. With a view like this, it will be beautiful in winter, sitting in front of a fire." The second the words came out, she cried, "Oh, no—I forgot."

He smiled. "We'll be putting in a fireplace, but it will be more for effect. Whether gas log or wood, the smoke is real."

"I'm so sorry you have to suffer," she whispered.

"It's a small price to pay to be alive." Shadows marred his features. "Daniel's death shouldn't have happened," he said in a hushed tone.

"Even so, he chose to go into the marines and knew it was possible he wouldn't come home. What no one expected was the sudden illness that attacked Christy and took her life. If I've learned anything so far, it's that life is precious and fragile. Coming to the ranch has taught me something else. You need to make every moment count in case it's your last."

He eyed her beneath the rim of his Stetson. "You sound as if you've made some kind of decision."

"I have. Last night Frank asked me to cut our vacation short and return home to get started on some counseling I'd planned for me and Jenny. You know, to help her adjust to our impending marriage. But watching her smile and laugh again, I know I don't want to leave until our vacation is over. Truth be told, Frank didn't want me to bring Jenny to the ranch in the first place."

Buck's eyebrows met in a frown. "Why not?"

"Since you're all marines, he worried she'd think too much about her father's death and it wouldn't help her to get on with her life." Alex swallowed hard. "But I haven't found that to be true. In fact, it's just the opposite because Johnny lost his father, too, and they talk about it. I think it's been healthy for her."

"For Johnny, as well," Buck concurred. "Kids have

their own system for relating. Carson's been worried about Johnny since he and Tracy got married. He knew it would be a big adjustment for him even though he does love Carson."

"Well, you can tell Carson for me, that boy is one of the happiest, cutest, most well-adjusted children I've ever met. I know Tracy has a lot to do with it, but Johnny told me himself that Carson was his favorite person in the whole wide world besides his birth father."

Buck inhaled sharply. "That'll make his day."

"I guess it doesn't come as any surprise that Jenny thinks the world of you." He had to have seen the way Jenny was smiling at him earlier.

"I'm flattered, but the truth is, every child enjoys attention." Apparently, Buck didn't do well with compliments. His modesty was one more thing to add to the list of his virtues.

"That's true, but she's given you a lot of thought, like, for example, do you ever go on a vacation?"

His eyes darted to hers in surprise. "Why do you think she would ask that?"

"Maybe she worries you'll leave while she's still here."

"I just got back from the only vacation I've taken since I got out of the hospital."

"Where did you go?"

"Colorado Springs to see my family. I was only there three days. My mother wished it had been longer, but I told her I had to get back to host the new family flying in."

"Do you have a large family?" Alex couldn't learn enough about him fast enough.

"Pretty big. Four brothers, all married with children,

and lots of extended family. I'll always like working with my hands the way they do, but you can't beat ranch living. I'm here to stay."

Alex knew she was taking a big chance to ask her next question, but something had come over her and she decided to risk it. "If you'd married your soul mate, would you be working with your father today?"

He slanted a look at her, one she couldn't decipher. "I'll never know the answer to that. The girl I loved married my brother, Sam."

No-o. *"Buck—"*

"Take that devastated look off your face. It happened twelve years ago while I was attending the University of Colorado at Boulder on scholarship. They didn't mean for it to happen. I'm glad they got together before we ever made it to the altar. It saved everyone a world of pain and trouble."

Even so, she was sick for the hurt he'd had to endure at the time.

"I can read your mind, Alex, but seeing Melanie and Sam together has nothing to do with my only staying in Colorado for a few days."

"I believe you."

"By the time I'd been deployed to Afghanistan, I'd gotten over it and gave them my full blessing. It's ancient history and there've been plenty of women since then."

Alex didn't doubt it.

"Melanie was my high school love, but we were never meant to be. Not very many high school affairs last."

"I know what you're saying. Kyle and I had no destiny. At the time it killed me, but it's amazing how time heals those wounds."

"Amen to that. The only reason I didn't take a week off to be with the family is because the guys and I are doing everything possible to make our venture work. I love my family and during the winter when we don't have so many guests, I'll spend more time with them."

"Thanks for telling me, Buck. When Jenny learns you don't have plans to leave the ranch anytime soon, she'll stop fretting. Since her mother and father died, she's turned into a worrywart."

"I've noticed. This morning when I bumped into her and Johnny in the back hall, they wanted to drive to the building site with me. I told them they couldn't because the workers were there and it was in the hard-hat stage. She promptly asked me if I wore one. When I said yes, she made me promise to keep it on the whole time. She's a sweetheart."

Her darling granddaughter was watching out for him. Jenny had never shown that kind of worry over Frank when he'd had a bad case of bronchitis, or when he'd slipped on the tennis court and had to be hospitalized for a torn leg muscle.

While she was cogitating on that fact, they both heard Johnny's blood-curdling cry for help, followed by Jenny's screams. Buck took off so fast Alex didn't have time to blink. With her heart in her throat, she raced after him. A dozen horrifying scenarios passed through her mind, giving her feet wings.

Buck was already there. Jenny was standing on top of a big beaver dam while Johnny stood on the grassy bank beside it. It appeared as if Jenny's leg had gone through part of the wooden structure. "I can't get out!"

she cried in a terrified voice. "It hurts! Come and get me, Buck! Come and get me!" Tears streamed down her cheeks.

He was already in the water. Alex could imagine him as a frogman, swimming against the fast current toward her granddaughter with torpedo-like strength. "I'm almost there. Easy does it, Jenny. Don't move."

Alex ran down to Johnny and put her arms around him, hugging him tight. "She's going to be all right."

Johnny had gone pale. "I was going to come and get you, but she begged me not to leave her."

"You did exactly the right thing."

"I told her she shouldn't walk on it, but she wouldn't listen to me. She lost her hat when her leg fell through. It's floating down the river."

"Don't worry about that. We can always get her a new one. What's important is that she's going to be okay." Knowing Buck was there made all the difference. Without him, Alex would be hysterical.

"Dad said it was dangerous. He wasn't kidding!"

"No, he wasn't, and now I'm afraid Jenny's had to learn a lesson the hard way."

"Are you mad at her?"

"Oh, no, honey. Accidents happen."

"You're nice." He hugged her hard.

"So are you," she whispered. Alex loved this boy who'd been through the same grief as Jenny.

For the next few minutes, Alex held her breath while Buck dug through the debris on his stomach to reach Jenny and extricate her leg. When he got her free, she howled in pain. He comforted her the best he could while he swam with her to the shore with her arms clutched around his neck.

"Alex?" he called to her. "Phone the ranch and tell someone to come in one of the vans stat! We need to get her to the hospital pronto. She's injured her ankle."

Alex did his bidding, and in a minute she got Tracy who said she'd be right there. By the time the van arrived, Buck had brought Jenny to shore and carried her up the incline to the road leading into the building site.

While Johnny climbed in front with his mom, Alex sat on the bench in back next to a dripping wet Buck and Jenny. Jenny lay across them with a pinched white face, still hugging Buck for dear life. Alex supported her legs. Her right cowboy boot was still on, but the left boot was missing and her ankle looked swollen.

"It hurts so much, Nana."

"I know it does, brave girl, but thanks to Buck nothing worse has happened. The doctor will fix you up in no time."

"Try to lie still," Buck encouraged her. "You know something?" He kissed her cheek. "The next time I see that beaver, I'm going to have to teach him how to build a better dam so there won't be any holes in it."

Jenny actually giggled before she started crying again. Before long they reached the hospital in Jackson.

An attendant brought over a gurney and Jenny was wheeled inside a cubicle. Soon she was getting fed through an IV and given something for her pain. The nurse changed her out of her wet clothes and put her in a hospital gown. After the initial examination by the doctor, she was taken to X-ray. Alex had to stay behind. The wait seemed to take forever until she was wheeled back in.

"Nana—"

"I'm right here, sweetheart." Alex sat on a chair next

to her and held the hand that was free of the IV. "I love you and I think you were very courageous while you waited for Buck to rescue you."

"It doesn't hurt as much now. Where is he?" She sounded sleepy.

Alex had no idea. "I'm sure he'll be back in a few minutes."

"Okay." Her eyes closed.

Tracy peeked around the curtain and came in. Alex got up and they hugged. "Thank you for bringing the van so fast."

"I'm just glad I was available to help. Are you all right, Alex?" she asked quietly.

"Yes, but we wouldn't be without Buck. I don't know what I would have done if we'd been alone. That darling son of yours yelled loud enough for us to hear him. You never saw anyone react to an emergency so fast or expertly as Buck."

"As we both know, that comes from his military training."

"Where is he?"

"He took Johnny with him to give the information to triage. He knew Jenny wouldn't want you to leave her side."

"Oh, Tracy, I'm so thankful for him," she whispered. "When I think what could have happened..."

"But it didn't."

She wiped her eyes. "He just dived into that water—wallet, cell phone, watch and all."

"Those things are replaceable."

"I know, b-but he needs a change of clothes." Alex felt jittery.

"I've already talked to Carson. He'll be here shortly with some things for him and Jenny."

"Oh, thank you. I only remembered now that we left the horses at the building site."

"Ross is taking care of that. You just concentrate on Jenny. I'm going to slip out and see if they've arrived yet. I'll be right back."

Alex sat back down and clung to Jenny's hand. In a minute the doctor came in. "Mrs. Wilson? Your granddaughter has an ankle fracture. The good news is, the fracture isn't badly displaced, so we'll splint her instead of applying a cast. That way it will allow more room for swelling, should it continue."

"Thank goodness it's not too serious."

"We'll keep her overnight. You can ask for a cot to be brought into the room for you."

"I appreciate that."

"In the morning we'll send her home with crutches. Keep her leg elevated as much as possible for the first twenty-four hours. Apply cold compresses at intervals if necessary. She can take ibuprofen and return to normal activity, except for sports, in another day."

"How long will she have to use crutches?"

"We'll want to see her in outpatient in ten days, and then we can tell you better. Most ankle injuries take four to eight weeks to heal. She's young, so she'll probably recover faster than an adult."

"I surely hope so."

"You're welcome to stay while we splint her."

"Thank you so much."

Twenty minutes later Jenny was ready to be wheeled out of the E.R. and into a private room. When Alex emerged from the cubicle, Buck was there waiting for them, dressed in dry jeans and a T-shirt. No one had ever looked so wonderful to her. His compassionate eyes sought hers before he leaned over Jenny and kissed her forehead.

"Hey, Red—"

Alex watched her granddaughter's eyelids flutter open. "Buck—"

"How are you doing?"

Tears filled her eyes. "The doctor says I can't go home until tomorrow. Will you stay with me and Nana?"

"What do *you* think?"

Jenny sniffed, struggling to hold back from crying. Alex was struggling herself.

The orderlies wheeled Jenny along until they arrived at her room and transported her to the bed. A different nurse came in to elevate her leg and make her comfortable.

After she left, Jenny asked, "Is Johnny here?"

"No," Buck answered. "His parents took him home, but we'll see him tomorrow."

"I wish he didn't have to go. The accident was my fault."

"You know what? I always did want to walk on top of the dam so I could watch that beaver. It's a good thing I didn't. Otherwise I'd have fallen right through it." A wan smile came and went. "Was it fun before you got trapped?"

"No. It was scary. Is my cowboy boot still stuck in the dam?"

"Afraid so. We'll get you another pair. I think you're the bravest girl I've ever known."

"Thanks, but I shouldn't have done it. Johnny told me not to. Thanks for saving me."

"It was my pleasure."

"You looked like a fish coming through the water." He grinned. "Yeah?"

"But I wasn't scared, because I knew it was you." Buck could do no wrong.

The nurse chose that moment to come in again with some apple juice for Jenny. She looked at Alex. "We're serving dinner now, if she's hungry. I can bring it out to you."

"I can't believe it's that late already. Thank you— that sounds great."

The nurse returned a few minutes later with two trays. Buck arranged the chairs on both sides of the bed and the three of them settled down to eat.

"Does this roll look good? You can have it. I'll get myself another one," Buck said.

Jenny nodded and bit into it. "It tastes nummy. Thanks."

Her granddaughter might not have wanted it if Alex had been the one to offer it. She could see the hero worship in Jenny's eyes as she gazed at Buck.

"Do you know something?" he said. "You don't look sick. In fact, you don't look like you should be in the hospital."

"You were in a hospital, too, huh?"

"Yes. That's where I met Ross and Carson."

"I know. Did you have to be in it a long time?"

"Five weeks."

Jenny made a face. "I get to go home tomorrow."

"That'll make Johnny happy."

"Buck, do you have a girlfriend? Johnny says you have lots of them."

Alex almost choked on her roast beef.

"Yes. In fact, I've got a special one now."

His answer trapped Alex's lungs in a vise.

"You do? What's her name?"

"Red."

Jenny giggled, but after she quieted down, she looked at him with a serious expression. "Are you ever going to get married? Johnny heard his parents say you're getting old."

"Johnny shouldn't repeat everything he hears," Alex muttered, but no one was listening because Buck had broken into laughter. It rebounded off the hospital room walls.

"You're never too old to get married, Jenny."

"My daddy got married at seventeen."

"Sometimes you meet the right woman fast. Sometimes it takes a long time to meet her."

"Johnny asked me how old Frank was. I told him fifty-five. He said that's as old as his Grandpa Baretta."

Alex couldn't take any more of this conversation. "Jenny? Are you hungry for anything more?"

"No."

"In that case, I'm going to lower the head of your bed so you can relax and go to sleep. You've had a big day and need your rest so that ankle will get better faster."

"The doctor said I have to see him in ten days. That means we'll have to stay at the ranch longer."

Sensing where this conversation was headed, Alex said, "We'll talk about all that tomorrow. Say goodnight to Buck."

"But I thought he was going to stay with us tonight."

"He can't, sweetheart." She spoke before Buck could. "He has work to do back at the ranch. Carson and Ross are relying on him."

Buck put his tray on the cart and leaned over her. "I'll be here in the morning to drive you home. How does that sound?"

"Good," she answered in a tremulous voice, and kissed his cheek. "Thank you for saving me. I love you."

No-o. The words had slipped out from Jenny's heart. She'd never said them to Frank. Alex groaned because she had the strongest conviction she never would.

"I love you, too. You're my best girl, remember?"

"Yes."

He stood. "Good night, Alex. Call if you need anything." She watched his tall form disappear out the door, leaving her in utter turmoil.

Chapter Six

"There she is in a wheelchair!"

His pulse raced. *And there's Alex.*

Buck had prevailed on Tracy to let Johnny come in the van with him. She said she was afraid to take advantage of him, but he insisted Johnny was a joy to be around, which was the truth. He could also cheer Jenny up better than anyone. And from a selfish standpoint, Johnny would provide the buffer Buck needed to keep his emotional distance from Alex.

He understood why she wanted to marry Frank. In addition to love and affection, he could offer her stability. He was a bank vice president and could provide her with a nice home, spending money and all the benefits that came with marriage.

When Jenny had brought up the question of a girl-friend last night, he realized he was hardly in a position to ask anyone to marry him. He was a vet with a disease, only a small nest egg and a job that might turn into a lifelong career as a rancher, but these were early days. He lived upstairs in the ranch house. Had no place of his own.

It was a good life, but hardly one he could share with a woman who wanted and needed all the things a man like Frank could supply.

That time he'd spent in the hospital with the guys had given him focus and a reason to get on with life. He'd been doing fine since coming to Wyoming. There'd been women. There'd be more of them as soon as Alex and Jenny went back to Sacramento.

Only four more days left to endure this fatal attraction. He could handle that. Stick to groups. Keep Johnny close. Not spend any alone time with her. Then she'd be out of sight. Hopefully, after a while, she'd be out of mind. It terrified him that he might not be able to forget her.

Buck pulled up to the entrance. "Johnny? If you'll open the back door, I'll lift Jenny inside."

"Okay." The boy jumped down from the passenger side, while Buck got out of the van and went around.

"Good morning, you two."

Both females flashed him a smile. "Thanks for coming to get me, Buck."

"I couldn't wait." It was the truth. He'd spent a restless night anticipating the morning to come.

Johnny looked at the splint. "Does it hurt?"

"A little bit."

"Come on. Let's get you inside so we can all go home."

The nurse steadied the wheelchair for Buck while

he picked Jenny up and placed her on the seat. Alex climbed in back next to Jenny, carrying a plastic bag that probably held her other clothes. He fastened Jenny's seat belt, taking care with her injured ankle. There was nothing he'd rather do than fasten her nana's, but that was out of the question.

Johnny climbed in and sat opposite them while Buck shut the door. Getting behind the wheel, he called out, "Who wants doughnuts?"

"I do!" the kids shouted at once.

He headed for the drive-through and picked up half a dozen doughnuts before they drove back to the ranch. The conversation between the kids was hilarious and prevented Buck from having to say anything. By the time he pulled up to the cabin, the doughnuts had been eaten and everyone was happy to go inside.

Jenny looped her arms around Buck's neck as he carried her into the living room and laid her down on the couch. Alex propped up her leg and head with pillows. Johnny brought in the crutches and tried using them. After a couple of failures, he got the knack.

"Hey—this is easy."

"Jenny can try it tomorrow. Today she needs to rest."

Johnny laid the crutches on one of the chairs and walked over to her. "Do you want to watch cartoons or movies?"

"Can you get that Hopalong DVD?"

"Yeah! I'll go get it right now."

"I'll drive you," Buck volunteered. It was time to get out of there before he started enjoying himself too much.

"Can't you stay?"

He'd expected that from Jenny. "I'll come back with

lunch for everybody. Right now, I've got to get some work done."

"Okay, but hurry."

"You know I will. Come on, Johnny."

He left without looking at Alex, but she followed him out to the van. "Wait—"

Buck rolled down the window. "What's wrong? If there's something you need, say the word and I'll get it."

"I know you will. That's what's wrong." Her incredible blue eyes searched his as if she were looking for something, but couldn't find it. "I'm afraid the Forrester family has turned into the ranch's biggest liability. My debt to you and your partners has gotten out of hand with her hospitalization, for which I refuse to let your insurance pay. I have insurance.

"Last night while Jenny was asleep, I looked into flights leaving for Salt Lake. Jenny and I are taking the 10:00 a.m. flight out tomorrow morning and we'll make a connecting flight to Sacramento. Frank is meeting us at the airport."

Buck froze. "Your vacation isn't over until Saturday morning. Yesterday you told me you planned to stay the whole week."

She moistened her lips—out of nerves, he presumed. "It ended when she got hurt. I thought if I gave you a heads-up, you'd be able to plan accordingly. We'll need to be at the airport by eight-thirty."

"Alex—"

"The accident disrupted everyone," she interrupted. "We're leaving so this cabin can go to the next lucky child on your list who'll be able to enjoy everything this dude ranch has to offer."

What she was saying didn't sound like the Alex he'd

come to know. The woman who'd been so grateful for the opportunity afforded them that she'd expressed her gratitude constantly.

Something else was behind her sudden decision to go back to California and she was using Jenny's accident as the excuse. Frank hadn't wanted her to come in the first place. If he was behind this, she'd never tell Buck.

"Alex—tomorrow she'll be able to get around on her crutches. We have several cars here for the benefit of the guests. You can keep one and use it to take her places. That way you won't be inconveniencing anyone."

"I can't ask that."

"Not even for your granddaughter?" Maybe if he played on her guilt. "Jenny hasn't begun to see everything yet. We've planned an overnight campout at Secret Lake, Johnny's favorite spot. The drive is beautiful, and she'll be able to sit on a lounge chair and fish to her heart's content."

Alex rubbed her temples, leading him to believe she had a headache. He would be amazed if she didn't have one after yesterday's trauma. "I appreciate what you're saying and it all sounds amazing, but I've already made plane reservations."

He bit down so hard, he almost severed his tongue. "I'm sorry to hear that."

"I—I need to ask something else of you." Her voice faltered. "It'll be the last favor, I promise."

Buck struggled to keep his emotions under some semblance of control. "What is it?"

Her chest rose and fell as if what she was about to say was causing her great distress. "I would rather you didn't bring us lunch. Jenny thinks you're her personal genie. We had a good breakfast at the hospital. When we're hungry again, I'll walk to the ranch house and get us some food. Johnny will stay with her long enough for that."

Before Buck could get another word out, she hurried up the steps into the cabin and shut the door.

He closed his eyes tightly for a minute before starting the engine. Halfway to the ranch house, he felt something stir at his side.

Damn if it wasn't Johnny, who'd been sitting next to him quietly the whole time, listening. Buck slammed on the brakes. When he looked over, he saw tears in the boy's soulful brown eyes. "I don't want Jenny to leave."

"You're not the only one, sport, but you heard her nana."

"Can't you make her stay?"

After a burst of coughing, he said, "Could you have stopped Jenny from climbing on the beaver dam?"

"I could have tackled her."

He probably could have, being a little taller and heavier than Jenny. Despite his pain, Buck laughed. "You think that's what I ought to do? Tackle Alex?" The thought brought on a whole fantasy he needed to delete from his mind forever.

"We've got to do something! Jenny loves it here! She told me she never wants to go home."

Johnny was as upset as Buck.

"There's a reason why I can't stop her. She and Jenny came on vacation, but Jenny can't do any sports for a while."

"That doesn't matter."

"It does to Alex. She would rather take care of her granddaughter at home where she has all her things to keep her entertained. She doesn't want to be a burden around here." *And there was always Frank waiting in the wings.* Buck's hands gripped the steering wheel so tightly, it was a miracle he didn't break it.

"What's a *burden?*"

"She doesn't want us waiting on them when we have other things to do."

"What other things?"

Another laugh escaped his lips. Oh, to be a child again where everything was so simple.

"If they go, she'll miss my birthday party. Mom's got all this stuff planned. We're going to the Funorama. Jenny would love it there."

"I'm as sorry as you are, Johnny. You have no idea."

On that note, he drove the rest of the way to the ranch house and pulled onto the parking area to let Johnny out. "Let your mom know you're back before you go looking for that DVD. I'm headed for the building site."

"Okay." He got out of the Jeep and started walking. There was a slump to his young shoulders. Johnny looked the way Buck felt.

When Alex had asked him not to bring them lunch, she'd really been telling him he'd done enough for them. Other than giving them a ride to the airport in the morning, she didn't expect to see him again. He understood she didn't want to make things more difficult for Jenny.

Buck got it, and he'd honor her wishes. But he didn't have to like it.

After turning on a cartoon for Jenny to watch, Alex went into the bathroom to shed the clothes she'd slept in at the hospital and take a shower. Her body trembled beneath the water as she washed her hair.

That speech she'd made to Buck before she could

take the words back had been one of the hardest things she'd ever had to do in her life. But last night, while she'd tossed and turned on that hospital cot, she'd had an epiphany and a clear grasp of her situation.

If she loved Frank the way she'd thought she loved him before arriving at the ranch, then meeting Buck wouldn't have made any kind of impact. But the truth was, she was conflicted about her feelings because of Buck. For him to affect her this fast and this strongly made Alex realize she wasn't in love with Frank the way she needed to be and couldn't possibly marry him.

For both their sakes, their relationship needed to end immediately so he could meet someone else. Frank had enjoyed a happy marriage and wanted to have that again. Naturally, he did.

Alex had been alone for so long, it had felt good to have a man she cared about and trusted in her life. She'd wanted to get married and would have done so when Jenny was more amenable.

But then she'd met Buck Summerhayes. He had had such a profound effect on her already that she was shaken to the core. Through no fault of his own, Buck had been the catalyst that reminded Alex of the girl she'd once been. The girl with stars in her eyes who'd once been passionately in love. Being with him these past few days had brought back all those intense feelings of breathlessness and excitement, the element of wonder and the anticipation of new possibilities that made you thankful to be alive.

All of that had been missing from her life since Kyle had abandoned her, only to be resurrected by one ex-marine who was carving out a new life for himself in the Tetons with his partners. It was clear from their conversation that he wasn't ready for marriage yet. He had girlfriends and was still enjoying his bachelor life.

If Buck could produce these feelings in her without even trying or being aware of it, then so could another man, but she needed to put herself in a position to find him. On this trip Alex had found out she *wanted* to experience those feelings again.

Last night she'd done a lot of heavy thinking. If she lived to be eighty or even ninety, then she needed to fill the next forty or fifty years with new adventures. She had no idea when or if this special man would come along, but she planned to find out.

First of all, she was going to give her two weeks' notice at the bank. She had enough savings for her and Jenny to live off while she looked for a new job. Something different that would challenge her and give her a new perspective.

That was what Buck had done after returning from war. Instead of going back to the family business, he'd joined forces with Carson and Ross. Anyone could see how happy and fulfilled he was.

Maybe it would require a move to a different city. Her parents had been retired for a few years and lived on the California side of Lake Tahoe. They came every three weeks or so for a visit. Maybe Alex would look for work there. Jenny would be so glad she wasn't marrying Frank, and she'd love being closer to her great-grandparents.

Once Alex had finished getting dressed and had blow-dried her hair, she walked into the living room. "Sweetheart? How's the pain?"

"It doesn't hurt now. I wish I could get up."

"I'm glad your leg's feeling better. If you rest today,

then tomorrow you can use your crutches to get around. Do you mind if I turn off the TV? I want to talk to you before Johnny comes back."

"What about?"

Alex shut the television off with the remote and sat in a chair next to her. "I've got a plan, but you need to listen until I'm through talking. Will you do that for me?"

A worried look crossed over her granddaughter's face before she nodded.

"First of all, you need to know we're flying back to Sacramento tomorrow." Instantly, tears sprang from the girl's eyes. "Here's the reason why."

Without discussing Buck, Alex laid it out that she wasn't going to marry Frank after all. "And I'm going to make you a promise. As soon as your splint comes off, we'll fly back here and finish the rest of our vacation. I bet it can come off in a month. We'll bring some presents for Johnny and throw him a surprise birthday party. But it will be our secret for now. Okay?"

That brought a glimmer to her eyes. After a long silence, she said, "You really promise?" Her question told her that Jenny was overjoyed Frank wouldn't be in their lives anymore. It also meant she'd accepted the change in plans to leave tomorrow instead of Saturday.

"I've never lied to you, have I?"

"No." Her answer coincided with a knock on the door.

"That'll be Johnny. I'll get it." Alex hurried to open it and discovered Tracy had come with her son. She was carrying a sack.

"Hi! I came to see how our famous patient is doing."

"She's fine. Please, come in."

"Johnny and I decided to bring Popsicles and potato

chips. We also brought a couple of his board games and some DVDs."

"Fantastic. I'll put the Popsicles in the freezer for now."

Tracy walked over to the couch. "How are you feeling, honey?"

"Good. My leg doesn't hurt."

"That's the best news we've heard."

"Do you want to watch Hopalong?" Johnny asked.

"Yes."

"Well, have fun, everyone. I'll come back in a while and see how you're all doing."

Alex walked her to the door. When they were out of earshot of the children, Tracy turned to her. "Is it true you're leaving tomorrow?"

"Yes. I need to get her home and check in with the doctor there. Her friend Mandy will be happy to see her."

"I understand there's a man in your life. No doubt he'll be anxious to have you back, too."

Alex nodded, not wanting to get into it. She had to end it with Frank before she told anyone else, except Jenny of course. "I talked to my parents early this morning. They're going to come and stay at the house with us for a week."

"I'm happy for you, but sorry for Johnny. He's taken such a liking to Jenny. We've got a whole month before he's back in school and able to make new friends."

"I know how that goes, and the feeling's mutual, believe me, but under the circumstances it's for the best we get back home. You have to know we've had the time of our lives here. What your husband and the others are doing for children like Jenny is so noble, I tear up thinking about it."

"I felt the same way when I got the letter. It was overwhelming."

Alex nodded. "And look what happened when you brought your Johnny to the ranch." She smiled at Tracy, who blushed.

"From anguish to pure joy. That was how it felt after I met Carson."

"They're remarkable men. Buck was positively heroic yesterday. This grandma will never forget what he did." Alex emphasized the word *grandma* to help keep her mental distance from the man who'd lit up her life over the past few days.

Tracy shook her head. "No one would believe you're a grandmother. My husband says you're way too young and beautiful."

"He doesn't see me when I first wake up in the morning." They both chuckled.

"Jenny and I will never be able to thank him or the rest of you enough."

"It's been our pleasure. Send Johnny home when he's worn out his welcome. He can talk your ear off," Tracy said with a laugh before she left.

Alex leaned against the closed door. Johnny usually had a lot to say, but not right now. Both children watched the cowboy video without saying a word. It was Alex's fault, and yet the strongest emotion she felt at the moment was relief that she'd set their plans in motion and Jenny wasn't fighting her.

After a sleepless night, Buck needed coffee. He leaped down the stairs three at a time and headed for the kitchen. Pouring himself a cup, he strode through the hall to the office. He didn't know if Alex had asked for a wheelchair, but in case she hadn't, he'd called the airport to reserve one for her ahead of time.

"Morning."

He reared his head when he discovered he wasn't alone. "Hey, guys." Carson and Ross were both drinking coffee, too.

Carson flashed him a curious glance. "You weren't at dinner last night and we didn't hear you come in."

"I searched along the river for Jenny's cowboy hat. I thought if I found it downstream, I'd give it to her for a souvenir, but I didn't have any luck."

"Some guest from the ranch will probably fish it out next spring," Ross murmured.

By then it would be too late. Far too late.

"How soon will you be taking our guests to the airport?"

He eyed Carson. "Their plane leaves at ten. I'll call her at seven-thirty to alert her." It was almost that time now. "We'll leave at eight."

"With Johnny's birthday coming up, it's a shame to see them go so soon. Tracy has already put plan B into action by arranging for Cory, his favorite cousin in Cleveland, to fly out and stay for a week. Hopefully the surprise will offset his disappointment."

Disappointment didn't begin to cover what Buck was feeling. "Does Johnny want to come to the airport with me?"

"That's up to you."

"The more the merrier."

"I'll tell him to get dressed and eat some breakfast quick. Be right back."

Buck felt Ross's eyes on him after Carson walked out. "What?"

"How come you're letting her leave?"

He swallowed the rest of his coffee. "What are you talking about? She's a grown woman who came at our invitation and now she's going home to marry her boyfriend. She wants to get Jenny back in familiar surroundings."

"And that's okay with you."

Ross could be relentless. This time he'd struck a nerve. "Frank's waiting for her."

"Frank wasn't on her mind when I took dinner to her and Jenny. Last night she opened her door expecting to see you. If you could have seen the look of pain in her eyes…"

"Shut up, Ross."

"It's the kind I see in yours right now," he persisted. "Why in the hell aren't you going to do something about it?"

"Like what?" he bit out angrily.

"Tell her how you feel!"

"I would if she'd given me *one* signal."

"She's been throwing them out right and left, but for some reason I can't understand, you've refused to read anything into them. What are you afraid of?"

"The truth is, I don't want to be the guy responsible for interfering with her relationship with Frank. I was on the receiving end of a similar situation once, remember?" The guys had shared everything when they'd been hospitalized together. There were few secrets left.

"This is different. And Alex doesn't have a ring on her finger yet."

"So that makes her fair game?"

"You know it does!"

Maybe, but that wasn't all of it. Buck hadn't had these kinds of feelings for a woman since Melanie. The idea of risking everything again only to be rejected, terrified him. "I don't want to talk about it."

"That's too bad. I feel for you. Let me know if there's anything I can do." He started out the door.

At the last second, Buck called after him. "Ross?" His friend hesitated. "Thank you."

"Don't mention it."

No sooner had he left than Johnny came running in. "Dad said I could go with you. Is that okay?"

He gave Johnny a hug. "I want you to come. It'll make it more fun for Jenny." *And save my life.* "We'll take the van so she can prop her foot on the seat. First I have to let Alex know we're coming."

"Okay."

Buck picked up the house phone receiver and rang through to the cabin. It wasn't long before she answered. "Hello?" He felt her voice snake through him.

"Alex? It's Buck. How's Jenny this morning?"

"She's doing better than expected."

"And you?"

"I'm fine." Code for any number of things she wasn't about to reveal to him.

"That's good. Have you eaten breakfast?"

"We filled up on fruit and granola bars. I even stuffed some of those homemade packets of pine nuts in our pockets."

"Those nuts are addictive." He couldn't handle this unsatisfying conversation any longer. "If you're ready, Johnny and I will come by for you."

"I'm glad he's coming. I think we're all packed."

"Then we'll be there shortly." He hung up. "Let's go!"

Within a few minutes, he'd started up the van and they headed for the cabin. Buck tried not to think that when they got back from the airport, another guest would take up residence and there'd be no evidence that the Forrester family had ever stayed there. At the thought, the hollow feeling inside threatened to envelop him.

Once he pulled up in front, Johnny scrambled out of the front seat and ran up to the door. Buck followed, but his legs felt like lead.

When Alex opened the door, she was dressed in the outfit she'd worn on the plane, looking elegant and completely gorgeous. He quickly averted his eyes and walked over to Jenny who was half lying on the couch.

"Hey, Red. Guess what? It's beautiful weather outside. No storm anywhere. When you fly out, you'll be able to see the mountains and the ranch. I'll be watching from the building site when your plane takes off. Look out the window at five after ten and I'll wave to you. When you see me, wave back."

She smiled. "I will."

"Promise?" he teased.

"Yes."

"Okay. Put your arms around my neck and I'll carry you out to the van. You should save using your crutches until you're back home in Sacramento."

Johnny helped Alex carry out their two bags and the crutches. Buck helped settle them in the back. When everyone was strapped in, he swung the van around and they drove out to the highway. He avoided looking through the rearview mirror in case he wouldn't be able to take his eyes off Alex.

The kids talked about the ponies and Moppy, while Buck and Alex put in a word here and there.

"I never got to see her."

"Maybe she's been playing with some squirrels in the other trees."

"But I didn't see any other squirrels."

As soon as Buck pulled up to the terminal, he told everyone to stay put while he went to get the wheelchair. It was such a novelty, the children were excited. After Buck had helped Jenny into it, Johnny volunteered to push her inside. Buck grabbed the bags and the four of them entered the terminal.

"Hey, Buck!"

Out of the corner of his eye, he saw Janie Olsen smiling at him. She worked for one of the airlines. They'd had a couple of dinner dates, but he hadn't followed up.

"How are you doing, Janie?" he said, but he kept walking past her to the counter where he checked in Alex's bags and the crutches. In return, he got their boarding passes. They had an hour's wait.

A TV was playing in the lounge. Since no one was watching, Buck flipped the channel to the cartoon network for the kids. Jenny shared her pine nuts with Johnny while they laughed at the antics on screen.

Buck looked down at Alex, who'd taken a seat next to her granddaughter. "If you'll tell me what airline you'll be connecting with in Salt Lake, I'll ask the employee at the counter to arrange ahead for a wheelchair at both ends."

Her eyes were a more intense blue than usual. "That's so thoughtful of you, Buck. It's Skyways."

"I'll be right back."

With that errand taken care of, he returned and

pulled one of the seats around so they could talk. He handed her the passes. "How are you going to manage work with Jenny incapacitated?"

"My parents are coming from Lake Tahoe tomorrow to help for a while."

He knew next to nothing about her parents. They were Jenny's great-grandparents. Amazing. There was still so much he didn't know about her life. *And never would.* He coughed. "I'm glad you're going to have help."

"I'll phone her friend Mandy's mom and see if she can't spend some with Jenny, but I know she's going to really miss Johnny. Tracy came over yesterday morning and we both agreed the children had a great time together. Too much of a great time, perhaps," she said on a nervous laugh. "My granddaughter decided to show off in front of Johnny, to her peril."

Buck cocked his head. "Things like that happen when you're really having fun."

"I suppose."

The children grew bored and Johnny started pushing Jenny around in the wheelchair. "Look at them."

She nodded. "They're a pair, aren't they?" After a silence, she added, "Thank heaven you were there, Buck." It came out as a sudden torrent of words. "She's the luckiest little girl in the world to have been rescued by you. My heart almost failed me when I saw her on top of that dam. If she'd fallen off into the current…"

"She couldn't have. Her boot was wedged in that hole too tightly."

"But you knew exactly what to do, while I stood there in absolute panic. You have my undying gratitude for everything you've done for us from the mo-

306

ment you picked us up here. We'll never forget you. As for Jenny, you have a special place in her heart." Her voice wobbled.

"That goes both ways."

"Except for her daddy and my father, she's never told another man she loved him. So you see, that letter from the ranch inviting us here truly did bring her great happiness despite her accident. The Daddy Dude Ranch achieved its objective. Please let Ross and Carson know that."

It was a good thing their flight was announced right then because Buck's endurance had worn out. He got up and went over to the children. "It's time for you to board."

"I wish you didn't have to go," Johnny said, taking hold of one of the wheelchair's handles. Buck took the other and they rolled her to the entrance where one of the attendants took over. Other passengers had queued up. "See ya, Jenny."

"See ya, Johnny." Her eyes filled with tears. "Bye, Buck."

"So long, Red." He kissed her on the forehead. "Take care of that ankle."

"I will."

Alex grabbed Johnny and gave him a big hug. When she lifted her head, her wet eyes met Buck's. "*You* take care of that cough."

Twenty minutes later Buck watched the jet take off from the building site and waved. The pain in his gut was unreal.

Chapter Seven

The orthopedic surgeon reentered the examination room, smiling at Alex and Jenny. "Are you two ready for the good news?" Jenny nodded. "I've seen the X-ray we just took and your ankle has healed beautifully. We can take off the splint."

Jenny beamed.

He put her up on the end of the exam table and proceeded to remove it. Then he helped her down and asked her to walk around. "Your leg's like brand-new. No more need for crutches."

"Can I ride my pony again?"

My pony—

Alex gasped quietly, realizing her granddaughter had been living for this day for a month. She now expected Alex to honor her promise to take them back to the Tetons. Jenny's recovery had happened even faster than Alex had anticipated. The rapid rise of her pulse made her dizzy with excitement when she imagined seeing Buck again.

"I didn't know you had one."

"Her name is Mitzi."

"Well, the answer to your question is yes. You can do everything you did before the accident."

Alex shook his hand. "Thank you for all your help, Doctor."

"Good luck to you."

Jenny thanked him, too, and they left the office, but as Alex walked down the corridor, it was *her* legs that felt unsteady. Her granddaughter kept up as if the accident had never happened. On their way to the car, Alex turned to her. "Do you think Johnny's back in school yet?"

It was August 23. "Probably not for a few more days."

"Can we fly to the ranch today?"

"Sweetheart—I don't know if we could get a flight that soon. I don't even know if there'd be a guest cabin free when we get there."

"Couldn't we stay at a motel? Johnny's grandma and grandpa stayed at one when they visited him."

Alex couldn't believe how much those two children had shared. But she had to admit the mention of a motel sounded like a good idea. That way they wouldn't be putting anyone out at the ranch.

When she thought about it, she realized it *was* a Friday. If they went for this weekend plus another day, Jenny would only miss school today and Monday. Her job hunt wasn't going well. There was nothing in Lake Tahoe that interested her. Four more days over a weekend before she renewed her search in the Sacramento area wouldn't make any difference.

After they got in the car, she said, "I'll call and see if we can get a flight." It was nine-thirty. There'd be a lot of flights to Salt Lake before evening. Most likely one of them would have seats available. The problem was trying to connect to a flight leaving for Jackson that wouldn't require a long layover.

Her hand actually shook as she called information for Skyways. She found out they could take a flight out at two o'clock and make a connecting flight that would put them in Jackson at 6:10 p.m. They'd need a rental car when they got there.

It meant they'd have to be at the airport in two and a half hours. If they threw a few things in one suitcase and locked up the house, they could manage it and park her car in short-term parking until they got back.

The biggest problem was finding a place to stay. After an exhaustive search of every hotel or motel in the area, she was able to reserve a room for three nights at a place called the Teton Shadows. Unfortunately it was still high season with summer rates, but she'd promised Jenny. After thinking it over, she decided this would be the best time to leave Sacramento.

If Frank broke down again and came over to see her this weekend, he wouldn't find her home. That was a good thing. He'd taken her rejection extremely hard and still called her, begging her to reconsider. She assured him she still loved him in her own way, but she would never change her mind about marrying him.

It astounded her that she hadn't missed him at all this past month. To her shame, her thoughts had been all about Buck. She'd had more sleepless nights than she cared to remember wondering how he spent his evenings.

Alex remembered the attractive woman at the airport counter in Jackson. She'd devoured Buck with her eyes when they'd wheeled Jenny into the terminal. Something in her look told Alex she'd been with Buck before. Wherever he went, women noticed him or went out of their way to get his attention. The poor girl at the Boot Corral....

That night at the pool, the female guests hadn't been able take their eyes off him. Alex was one of those guests. She'd been the worst.

Though they were returning to the ranch because she'd made a deal with Jenny, Alex could no longer lie to herself about Buck. She wanted to see him again and hopefully be alone with him, if only to find out if this longing was all on her part.

The trickle-down effect of Kyle's rejection had done its damage in her early years, but that period had long since passed. She didn't know if she could say the same thing when it came to Buck. If she learned he was already in a relationship with someone new, she might never recover and wondered if it were possible to die of jealousy.

What is wrong with you? She was a grandmother, not a starry-eyed teenager. But right now Alex didn't feel any older than seventeen with her hormones firing on all cylinders.

She hung up the phone. "Guess what, sweetheart? It looks like we're going to the Tetons. We'll have to rush home and get packed."

"I'm glad we already have Johnny's present."

"He'll love it." The first week after getting back

home, they'd bought a tan T-shirt featuring a snake. It had been Jenny's idea to have the words Fred's Dad printed on it. So silly and funny. Just the kind of thing to make Johnny laugh. Those two found the same things amusing and were in tune with each other on a level that surprised Alex.

But she had a secret she'd kept from her granddaughter. She'd had two T-shirts made up for Jenny and Buck, both in red. On the front, the white lettering said: Teton Valley Ranch Water Fight Champions.

"I can't wait to go back, Nana."

"Neither can I." *Neither can I.*

By a quarter to seven that evening, they'd checked in to their motel. Jenny wanted to call Johnny and surprise him. That was fine with Alex. She used the landline so the motel number would show up on the caller ID and pressed the digits for the ranch. Then she handed the receiver to Jenny.

Her eyes twinkled as she looked at Alex. "Hi—I want to speak to Johnny Lundgren." After a pause she said, "It's Jenny Forrester." Another pause. "Yes. My ankle's all better now." One more pause. "Me, too. But don't tell him it's me."

She held the receiver to her chest. "It was Willy at the desk. He said to wait just a minute."

Alex bet Willy couldn't believe who was calling. "Okay. Then you listen and wait."

Jenny nodded.

Alex was so nervous, she jumped up from the side of the bed and started pacing.

The guys had formed a line moving boxes of possessions into the Lundgrens' new house from the last truckload for the day. Tonight, Carson's family would be sleeping under their new roof for the first time. Not everything was done yet, but the house was ready enough for them to move in and be comfortable.

Johnny was in the kitchen with Tracy, putting the kitchen utensils away in drawers. Buck was happy for Carson's family and secretly envious of their joy. He knew Ross was, too. But no matter how many hours of hard work Buck had put in during the past month so he wouldn't let his mind wander, his emptiness had grown. Something had to be done about his mental state.

While he and Carson were carrying in the last heavy case of books, Carson's cell phone rang. They lowered the box to the floor so he could answer the call.

Buck saw a surprised look cross over his friend's face. "Hey, Johnny—the phone's for *you.*"

He came running. "Is it Cory or Grandpa Baretta?"

"Neither. Willy says it's a girl."

He frowned. "A girl?"

The guys grinned. At this point they were all curious.

"Here." He handed the phone to him.

"Hello?"

As he listened, there was an instant change in the boy's expression. His brown eyes rounded before he looked up at Carson in disbelief. "It's *Jenny!* Her leg's all better. She's in Jackson at a motel!"

Buck's next heartbeat practically knocked him to the floor. Alex had said she didn't want to inconvenience the staff any more than necessary. That had been a month ago. It appeared she still meant it. His thoughts spun out of control.

"Well, keep talking to her, sport," he said, eyeing

Tracy with a grin. Between them and Ross, they were trying hard not to laugh at Johnny's excitement.

After a minute, he said, "Hey, mom—can she have a sleepover with me tonight in the loft? We'll be good and go right to sleep."

Carson burst into laughter because Johnny was so predictable. It spread like contagion, pulling Buck out of his shock. He joined in with the others, but in letting go like that, the guys paid the price by ending up with coughs. For a minute it sounded like their former hospital ward.

With a tender smile, Tracy walked over to her son. "Ask Jenny to put Alex on the phone, honey."

"Okay, but please, please, please tell her she has to let Jenny come."

Buck watched Tracy wander into the kitchen out of earshot.

"Dad—" Johnny jumped up and down holding on to his arm. "The doctor said she can ride Mitzi again. Yippee!" He was so happy, he did a little dance in front of them.

Buck knew exactly how he felt. He'd given up on ever seeing that family again. In the past month, no one on the ranch had received word from Alex. It was as if she and Jenny had disappeared off the face of the earth. The past thirty days without them had been brutal.

"How many more signals do you need?" Ross had come up behind him.

"It's a moot point if she's officially engaged," Buck muttered, his body in turmoil. He was still reeling to think Alex was actually in Jackson.

Tracy came back in the room and walked over to Johnny. "Her grandma said yes. I told her we had a guest room for her to stay in, but she turned me down." Another clap of thunder resounded in Buck's chest. She handed the phone to Carson. "Alex has a rental car. She'll drive them here in a few minutes."

"Does she know I'm at my new house?"

"Yes. But I need you to keep something in mind."

"What?"

"They can only stay until Monday."

Johnny's face fell like a loose shingle off a roof. "How come?" Buck could relate. They were both suffering from too much good and bad news in the same breath.

"It has to be a quick trip for them, honey. You know Alex has to work, and Jenny's been in school since she went home. But before they left the ranch, Alex promised that once her ankle was better, she'd bring Jenny back to finish their vacation." Alex never told Buck that! "They missed your birthday party and wanted to make sure they celebrated with you another time."

"Hooray!"

"Evidently, the splint was just removed this morning and they decided this weekend would be the best time for them to come."

Was that because Alex was eager to get back here, too? Or had Jenny finally accepted Frank into their lives and this was the duty visit Alex had promised her granddaughter before they got married? How soon would it happen? Until Buck had answers, his emotions would be all over the place.

"But that's not long enough, Mom."

You can say that again.

"By then you'll be in school, too, honey."

Carson reached for Johnny and hoisted him on his

shoulders. "We'd better get your bed made up for her. We'll put down the air mattress and sleeping bag for you."

"I don't know where that stuff is."

"We'll find it in one of the boxes. Let's go."

"I'll help look," Buck offered, needing to channel his energy before he jumped out of his skin waiting for Alex to get there.

The air felt a little cooler than a month ago. Jenny and Alex decided to dress in matching navy turtleneck cotton sweaters and jeans to keep them warm. Alex left her hair loose and Jenny copied her. On their way out of town, she found the drive-through they'd been to before and picked up a dozen chocolate doughnuts with chocolate icing, the kind she knew Buck liked.

After learning Tracy and her family had been moving in to their new house all day, Alex had said she wouldn't dream of interfering with their first night. But Tracy insisted that everyone was thrilled to know they were there and that it would make Johnny's night to have Jenny sleep over. Alex caved and realized they'd all be hungry for a treat. It was the least she could do.

The sight of the Grand Teton ruling over the Snake River valley with the starlit sky overhead was so beautiful it hurt. What a difference from a month ago when they'd flown in with the storm. She still couldn't believe that Buck had just been sitting a few rows behind them on the plane, but they'd had to land before he'd introduced himself. While Alex drove, Jenny talked nonstop about how he'd saved her from falling in the current. She wondered where her cowboy hat had gone and chatted about Moppy and the ponies. When they entered the dude ranch property, the feeling of coming home was so overpowering, Alex only took in a portion of what her granddaughter was saying.

Would Buck treat her the same way as before?

Of course he would.

The morning Alex and Jenny had left the ranch, he didn't know she was going home to end her relationship with Frank. But he'd never given her a clue as to how he really felt about her. Alex's fears didn't stop there. He would never have feelings for her if his mind wouldn't allow him to see her as anything but Jenny's grandmother!

As her father would say, Buck played his cards close to the chest. So close it had given her terrible angst. Once he learned Frank was no longer part of her life, he might still treat her like the woman at the airport counter, or the girl at the Boot Corral. The thought was so crushing, Alex couldn't bear it.

She took the last curve on the dirt road that wound through the trees. Blood hammered in her ears as they came out on the other side where the newly constructed house was all lit up. It was a masterpiece of rustic and contemporary. There were several trucks and cars parked in front.

"Nana—their house is all done!"

She parked the car and turned off the ignition. "Can you believe it's finished already?" Before she could hear Jenny's answer, Johnny came running down the porch steps toward them. For once, he wasn't wearing his cowboy gear. Her granddaughter scrambled out of the front seat.

"Hi!"

"Hey—you can walk! Come on in the house and I'll show you where we're going to sleep."

Just like that, they were off in their own world. Alex got out of the car and reached in back for the box of doughnuts and the plastic bag with the things Jenny would need for the night.

"Would you like some help?"

Attractive as he was, the wrong man had appeared out of nowhere. *You've got your answer about Buck. Keep smiling.* She shut the door. "How are you, Ross?"

"Couldn't be better." He walked into the house with her. "You should have heard Johnny when he found out Jenny was in town."

"It was the same excitement on my end when she talked to him."

Tracy hurried over to give her a hug. "Welcome back. We're so thrilled you're here."

"So are we." She handed her the doughnuts. "These are for you."

"Thank you. You couldn't have brought us anything we'd love more right now."

"That's what I was hoping."

"Nana?" Alex looked up to see Jenny in the loft overhang. "You've got to come up and see Johnny's room. It's huge!"

"Okay. I'm coming."

Once she reached the top of the stairs, she could see Carson making up the queen-size bed. Not until she took a few more steps did she spy Buck on the other side. He was sitting against the far wall with his long, rock-hard legs extended, blowing up an air mattress. While the kids ran around, she felt his piercing gaze travel up her body until their eyes met.

"It's good to see you again, Alex." That deep voice of his was unforgettable.

Her heart throbbed in her throat, making it difficult to talk. "It's wonderful to see all of you." Her smile took in Carson.

"Your arrival has made this a red-letter night for our son."

"We had no idea your house would be finished this soon."

He flashed Buck a glance. "The taskmaster made certain the job got done in record time."

She didn't doubt it. "That's what best friends are for. Your home is breathtaking." Unfortunately she was out of breath and needed to go back downstairs away from Buck where she could get a grip. "I brought doughnuts in case you'd like some."

"In case?" Carson laughed. "Did you hear that, Buck?"

The gorgeous male in question was still filling the mattress with air and simply nodded. She didn't wait to watch anymore and hurried to join Tracy in the kitchen below. "Can I do anything to help?"

"Thank you, but no. We've all had it." She finished off her doughnut. "Come and sit down in the living room. As soon as Carson has Johnny's room sorted out, we'll get the kids to bed. Whether they can stop talking long enough to go to sleep is anyone's guess, however."

Alex chuckled. "They're a riot together. Oh, Tracy, you must be so happy to be in your new house at last!"

"It's a dream come true. But I was just watching Jenny dash up the stairs and can only imagine your relief that she's made a full recovery."

"You'll never know, but I'm nervous she'll forget and do something that injures it again."

"I have the same fear with Johnny. He keeps trying to imitate Carson's trick riding stunts. One of these days it'll be our turn to rush him to the hospital with a broken leg or arm."

"Let's hope not."

While they laughed, the men came down the stairs to the living room with the kids. Carson sat next to Tracy and pulled her to him, giving her a kiss. "The loft is ready for occupancy."

Alex looked at Jenny. "Did you hear that? No doubt everyone is exhausted and anxious to go to bed. Come here, sweetheart. Your jammies and toothbrush are inside the bag. Why don't you run in the bathroom and change before I leave for the motel."

"Okay."

Tracy eyed her son. "Now's a good time for you to do the same thing."

"I'll be right back."

Johnny bounded up the stairs and returned in record time, wearing camouflage pajamas. Pretty soon Jenny came back in. Alex got to her feet and gave her a hug. "Be sure to mind Tracy and Carson. They've had a long day moving and everyone's tired."

"I know."

"I'll miss you."

"Me, too."

"Tomorrow I'll drive to the ranch house for breakfast and we'll make plans for the day." They kissed each other. "Have fun. Good night, sweetheart."

"See you in the morning, Nana."

Alex gave Johnny a quick hug. "Good night."

Once the children disappeared upstairs, Alex turned to the others. "Thank you for making her feel so welcome. Since I know you weren't expecting visitors, I'm going to leave now. I'm in room fourteen at the Teton Shadows if you need to get ahold of me."

Carson gave Buck an odd glance before he and Tracy got up and walked her to the front door. Ross and Buck brought up the rear. Both of them were eating doughnuts. She heard Buck's voice. "I'll follow you back to town, Alex."

Her heart pounded with unmerciful force. "Thank you, but I'll be fine."

His eyes blazed an intense green in the porch light. "You're still my responsibility while you're here at our invitation. We don't want you driving the ranch roads alone this late at night."

Except that she wasn't staying at the ranch now. But to argue with him in front of the others would only create a fuss for nothing. He'd offered because it was his duty. No one else thought anything about it.

"If you're sure, then I'd appreciate it. See all of you tomorrow."

After everyone said good-night, she stepped off the porch and walked to her rental car. Once she'd started the engine, she noticed Buck climb in one of the trucks. Soon it was just the two of them making their way to Jackson in the moonlight.

Knowing it was his headlights reflected in the mirror, a rush of heat invaded her body. But her euphoria over being alone with him didn't last long. The thought occurred to her that he could have a late date in town with some beautiful girl and would have been driving there anyway. For the rest of the short trip, she tried without success not to think about his love life.

Jackson was lit up for the weekend with tourists. It was stop-and-go traffic until she reached the motel. When she'd been told she could have a room for all three nights, she should have known it would be on the ground floor at the end. Some guys were partying outside one of the rooms. They saw her pass in the car and let out with wolf whistles and catcalls.

To her chagrin, someone had taken her parking space in front of the door. She had no choice but to park farther away. Buck pulled up next to her and got out. The catcalls ended when he walked over to her wearing a black T-shirt and jeans. It was a sin for any man to look so good.

"I'll go inside with you to make sure you're safe." A familiar cough punctuated his declaration. The silent exchange between Carson and Buck was no longer a mystery. There was a reason why Alex had been able to get a motel for three nights during high season. It also explained why Buck had decided to follow her.

At times he had an authoritative way about him. This was the second time tonight she chose not to challenge one of those moments. "Thank you."

Alex rummaged in her purse for the key and they headed for her room. When they reached the door, he took it from her fingers and inserted it in the lock. The door opened to generic knotty pine walls and two double beds.

She laid her purse on the counter by the TV before turning to him with a smile. "As you can see, there's nothing sinister here."

"It's not what's on the inside that bothers me. Those

guys are out for a good time and they'll come around when they know I'm not here."

"I appreciate your concern, but I'll be fine."

His expression remained sober. He lounged against the closed door, scrutinizing her. "I had no idea you were coming back to finish your vacation with us. It's been a while. How's the situation with Jenny? Is she learning to accept Frank?"

Frank who?

Alex was so aware of him, she could hardly breathe. "No."

Buck's brow furrowed. "I'm sorry to hear that. It must be very hard on all of you."

Alex folded her arms against her waist. "When we went home, I ended our relationship."

The man staring at her didn't move a muscle, but his eyes suddenly charged with a new energy. "Why?"

She took another quick breath. "On the first night at the cabin, you told me there's something about being at the ranch that gives you a new perspective. After Jenny and I flew back to California, I realized what you'd said was true.

"When I saw Frank again, certain things were made clear to me that had nothing to do with Jenny's lack of acceptance. We'd both been friends who'd leaned on each other while we went through our grieving periods. He surprised me by asking me to marry him. I did love him, but I wasn't in love with him. Otherwise I wouldn't have let Jenny's objections stand in the way."

"It must've been devastating for him."

"It was bad," she admitted. "He still hasn't accepted it and keeps calling. Needless to say, Jenny couldn't be happier it's over."

He straightened. "Do you still work at the bank with him?"

She shook her head. "After we got back, I gave the manager my two weeks' notice. He knew how difficult it was for me to be in the same building with Frank and let me go after a week. Since then, I've been looking for another kind of job, even in Lake Tahoe where my parents live, but I haven't found one that appeals to me yet. Knowing the statistics about the process taking six months to two years, I'm not too hopeful about it happening anytime soon."

"Are you going to be all right financially?"

"Yes. I'll keep hunting for a job until I find something suitable. That's why I decided to take advantage of this weekend so Jenny could enjoy the rest of her vacation. She was having the time of her life here—it seems so cruel what happened."

"I would wager that the mood couldn't be happier at the Lundgren house tonight." She felt his gaze on her mouth. "I'm glad you came back, Alex." His voice sounded husky and made her feel light-headed.

"I am, too."

"Let's get out of here. I know a place where we can have a drink and listen to a live band."

As good as that sounded, she would have rather been alone with him. "You don't have other plans?"

"There's no woman in my life at the moment if that's what you mean."

It was exactly what she meant. "You're not too exhausted after the big move?"

He inhaled sharply, bringing on a cough. "No, but it sounds like you're tired after your flight and want to call it a night."

"You've misunderstood me. I just didn't want you to feel you had to entertain me."

"What if I want to?"

That was the first overt sign that he felt something for her that was separate from his job as her host. Her body trembled. "Then, with Jenny safe and sound at the Lundgrens', I'd love to go with you. Do I need to change?"

"No. You're perfect just as you are."

So are you.

He opened the door. "We'll go in the truck."

She grabbed her purse and walked out. He pulled the door closed and locked it. The party crowd had moved on. Alex was finally going on a date with the man she'd been fantasizing about for over a month. Their arms brushed while he was helping her into the truck's cab. It felt like liquid fire.

Once they left the motel, he maneuvered them through the maze of vehicles lining the streets, but they eventually got stuck in a traffic jam. "I'm taking you to the Million Dollar Cowboy Bar, if we can ever get there. You sit on a saddle to have a drink at the bar. There's a stuffed grizzly bear. It's a must-see for out-of-towners like yourself."

"Do you go there a lot?"

"I've been once."

"Then once was obviously enough and it's not your thing." He shot her a surprised glance. "I'd rather do something you'd like. What's *your* idea of a good time, Buck?"

"That depends on the female."

"Seriously, if you had your druthers."

"My druthers?" His brows lifted. "That would be telling secrets."

She smiled. "Don't hold back on me. Nothing you could say would surprise me. I'm a grandma and have lived longer than you."

Tension filled the cab. "Is that really how you see yourself?"

"It's what I am and you're evading my question."

"Right. My idea would be to camp out under the stars with the smell of pine filling the breeze. A beautiful woman would be in my arms and we'd have a whole night with nothing to do but enjoy each other."

"That sounds amazing." The tremor in her voice infuriated her.

"There were times overseas, breathing those toxic fumes, when I would have killed for one night like that."

"No wonder you got so excited about the idea of coming to work at the ranch." She shifted in her seat. "Buck? It's so busy here. When we get to the corner, let's go back to the motel, and I'll buy you a soda from the machine." At least they could have privacy, even if the surroundings left a lot to be desired.

"You really don't want to go to the bar? There's line dancing."

"Not tonight." She didn't want noise or other people around. She only wanted time alone with him.

Chapter Eight

Did he just blow it? It was time to try another tack.

"I've got an even better idea. Let's check you out of there. We'll grab your suitcase and head for the ranch." His jaw tightened. "That motel is no place for a good-looking woman on her own, let alone for Jenny. I'll follow you to the ranch in your rental car. You can park around the side with the other cars."

"But where will Jenny and I stay? You weren't expecting us."

"You saw Johnny's new furniture at the house. His old room still has the twin beds and matching dresser. Carson wants it to be used as an extra guest room when we have an overflow. I can't think of anyone better than you to christen it."

It would mean being in the ranch house with Buck

until Monday. She got a fluttery sensation in her chest. "If you're sure."

He made no further comment. By the time they reached the motel, it was out of her hands. Buck waited for her to gather up her things, and then he walked to the office with her while she checked out. For the second time that night, she found herself en route to the ranch, but this time Buck was driving right behind her and she felt as though she was floating.

She reached the parking area and locked up the car. Buck was there waiting for her and took her suitcase. "Tell me what kind of job you're looking for."

Alex didn't want to think about that tonight, but he'd asked. "I don't know. Something different. A new adventure. Breaking up with Frank has given me a sense of freedom I haven't known before. Now that Jenny is in school full-time, I don't want to do the same thing anymore. Would you think it odd if I told you I've left my old life behind and am ready to begin the next phase? It's kind of exciting to think about since I have no idea what's ahead."

Alex felt his eyes on her. "Would you believe I said those exact words to my parents after I got home from the hospital? The world I'd left behind no longer appealed in the same way. If anyone understands how you feel, *I* do."

She breathed in the scent of sage, something she would always associate with the ranch. "You've found a wonderful life here." The moon over the Grand Teton made the scene surreal.

"Would you be willing to uproot if you had to?"

"You mean, sell the house and put Jenny in a different school?"

He nodded.

"If I found the right job and situation, I'd do it in a heartbeat. My granddaughter is so happy with the way things have turned out, I'm sure she'd be amenable to a move if it meant Frank couldn't drop by unexpectedly anymore."

"Has he done that since you ended it?"

"Yes, but this weekend he won't find me home. Of course, my parents would like me to keep looking in the Tahoe area. But to be honest, after staying there for a few days while I searched for work, I realized it's their retirement dream, not mine."

"You've got years before you have to think about retirement."

"According to the great thinkers of our country, we should be worrying about it from the time we get our first paycheck."

Buck laughed softly as they made their way around the corner of the house. "It looks like we're alone tonight, because I don't see Ross's truck. If he's gone out, who knows when he'll be back."

"Is he involved with anyone special?"

"Nope."

"The bachelor life. I never thought it fair that the powers that be set it up so the guy had to be the one to make things happen."

His lips twitched in reaction. "It's not all joy. The female can choose not to cooperate."

"I don't imagine you or Ross have run into that experience often."

"What makes you say that?"

"Just an observation. I remember two women in par-

ticular when I was here last month who were just waiting for you to do more than simply acknowledge them."

"Is that right?"

"I notice you're not denying it."

His veiled eyes revealed little. "We'll go in through
the rear door. Except for Willy manning the front desk,
we have the place all to ourselves—a new experience
for me now that Carson's moved out. I'll fix you a cup
of coffee in the kitchen."

"That sounds better than any drink at a bar."

"My sentiments exactly."

He let her in through the back door. This was a portion of the ranch house she'd never seen before. After
locking it, he led her down a hallway in the dark. "I feel
like we're playing house," she said.

"That's the idea." He put the suitcase down in the
hall outside what she presumed was Johnny's old bedroom. Before she could take another breath, he grasped
her upper arms and backed her against the wall. "Since
Ross could come home at any time, let's take advantage
of our privacy. I'd like to properly welcome you back
to the Tetons, if that's okay with you."

"It's okay with me," she answered with a boldness
she'd blush over tomorrow. She wanted his kiss so badly
she could taste it before his beautiful mouth closed over
hers.

She moaned as he wrapped his arms around her and
pulled her against his rock-hard body.

There was no space between them. His male scent
mixed with the faint smell of the soap intoxicated her
to the core of her being. Her heart thundered against
his while they kissed with sensuous abandon, the way
they couldn't have done if they'd gone dancing in public.

Alex had dreamed of this moment for so long and now she found herself going with it, praying he'd never stop. His lips and hands brought pleasure to die for. This was ecstasy so beyond anything she'd felt at seventeen that she was in shock.

He finally lifted his head enough for them to breathe. "I've been wanting to do this since I first saw you in the airport."

A little cry escaped her. "Would you think I was terrible if I admitted to the same thing? I tried to fight what I was feeling. You can't imagine my guilt."

His hands tightened on her shoulders. "Frank has to be out of his mind with pain over losing you. It's no wonder he hasn't given up yet." He kissed her again with near-primitive passion.

If she didn't miss her guess, Buck was under a false impression about her relationship with Frank. This time she was the one to pull away first, but he didn't give her up willingly. "We never slept together," she admitted on a ragged breath.

A stillness surrounded them. His eyes traveled over her features. "But you were together for two y—" A cough cut his words off.

"We were friends for most of it," she explained. "I told him I wouldn't sleep with him until we were married."

He blinked. "Then all these years—"

"I've been the virgin grandma." She half laughed. "Even though I made the mistake with Kyle that resulted in my pregnancy, I still felt virginal. The truth is, we only made love one time before my parents found out and put an end to it. I'm afraid the experience was experimental at best."

A tremor passed through Buck's solid frame before he drew her back in his arms, burying his face in her hair. "You've had a rocky path for too many years."

"That's why I've decided I'm due for a change. Coming here again marks the beginning of my new adventure."

She heard him utter her name before pressing kisses over her hair and face. Once again, he found her mouth. Alex helped him, because her hunger matched his and had grown beyond caution. His short, rough beard was a reminder of his masculinity and whipped up her senses. In the middle of her delirium, a light went on in the hall. She heard footsteps.

"Hey, buddy—I saw your truck around the side." Ross's voice galvanized her into action and she tried to tear her lips from Buck's. "What are you doing back here? I figured you'd still be in—"

Too late, he saw them in an embrace. Buck let her go with reluctance and turned to Ross with a calm that astonished her. "After I saw what was going on in town, I decided to put Alex and Jenny up in Johnny's old room. The Teton Shadows leaves a lot to be desired on a Friday night, if you follow my meaning."

"Carson and I weren't thrilled to hear you were staying there, either." He drew closer. "Welcome to the ranch house, Alex. All day, Buck and I wondered how we were going to handle being orphans in this big old place." A smile lit up his eyes. "Now we don't have to worry."

She edged away from Buck. "You're all so nice, you would never admit that my surprise visit disrupted you."

Ross shot Buck another mysterious glance. "We like surprises. Ask Johnny."

For a little while she'd actually been able to forget about the kids. "Did they ever settle down?"

"No. They were still talking a mile a minute when I left."

"That's what I was afraid of."

Buck grinned. "Want to join us for a cup of coffee before we all turn in?"

"Not me. I've had enough for tonight. See you guys in the morning." He disappeared behind a door down at the other end of the hall.

As much as Alex didn't want to say good-night to Buck, Ross's unexpected appearance had brought her to her senses. He had to have seen how they were clinging to each other. Left alone with Buck again, she knew she'd lose control. This wasn't the time or the place. He'd had a long, tiring day and they couldn't be private in the ranch house. Carson could decide to come back for something.

She looked up at him. "Buck?"

"I know what you're going to say, and I'm way ahead of you," his voice rasped. "I wanted an excuse to be with you any way I could, but it's best you go to bed now while I'm still willing to let you." His words thrilled her. "Housekeeping gave Johnny's room and bathroom a thorough cleaning. The beds have been freshly made up. You'll be comfortable and safe."

"Thank you," she whispered.

"Don't look at me like that or I'll forget every good intention. If you should get hungry or thirsty during the night, help yourself to anything in the kitchen." She nodded and he added, "Have breakfast with me in the morning." She smiled. "I'll look for you in the dining room. Good night."

When she could no longer hear his footsteps, she went inside Johnny's room and got ready for bed. Her body was so wired, she knew it would be a long time before she fell asleep.

After she got into bed, she noticed how a shaft of moonlight fell across the wood floor. She loved everything about the ranch and the house itself. Built in true Western style, Carson had inherited a fabulous legacy, one he was sharing with Ross and Buck and, ultimately, the lucky guests like Alex and her granddaughter.

She lay back against the pillow, still tasting Buck on her lips. If it had been a mistake to kiss him tonight because she wouldn't be seeing him after Monday, she didn't regret it. He'd made her come alive so she didn't even recognize herself anymore.

Her thoughts stretched back to her early years. She'd been five years old when Buck was born. They'd gone through life with a five-year age difference. Even if they'd attended the same high school, she would have graduated before he'd started his sophomore year. It took growing up and becoming adults for the disparity in their ages to no longer matter.

Alex marveled over the painful twists and unexpected turns of both their lives that had brought them together at this particular moment in time. All because of Jenny. But for her father who'd been killed in war, Alex would never have met Buck or his partners.

She made a promise to herself to enjoy the few days she had left with Buck to the fullest.

Don't think beyond Monday, Alex. Just don't think.

Buck turned out the lights in the hall and walked up the stairs. Each step took him farther away from her, but he had little choice. Tomorrow night he'd get her alone where there was no possibility of anyone bothering them.

Ross heard him coming and walked out in the hall. They eyed each other before Buck said, "Can I talk to you for a minute?"

"If you didn't want to talk, I couldn't have handled it because I'm already exploding with curiosity. Come on in." They both went inside Ross's room. Buck hooked a leg around one of the chairs and sat backward while Ross sank down on the side of his bed to stretch his limbs. "Have you recovered from shock yet?"

He shook his head. "When I heard it was Jenny, calling from a motel in Jackson no less, you could have knocked me over."

"That made two of us. So cut to the chase. What's going on with her and Frank?"

Buck's head flew back. "He's permanently out of the picture."

"Yeah?" Ross grinned. "The news gets better and better."

"She gave up her job at the bank and is looking for a new one, not necessarily in banking. She's even willing to uproot herself and Jenny if she can find the right situation. I'm going to stick my neck out here and ask what you'd think if we hired her to take Susan's place at the front desk.

"Since she left for college, we've been lucky Willy has volunteered to help out until we find a replacement. But let me assure you, Alex has no idea that I've been thinking about asking her."

Ross's smile faded. "You're serious about this."

"I've never been so serious in my life. Whether she'd

be interested is an entirely different matter. The pay wouldn't be near what she's been making as a loan officer. Chances are, she won't even consider it. She has a granddaughter to raise and get through college."

Unable to sit still, Buck got up from the chair. "I wanted to talk to you about it before I run it by Carson. Naturally we'd all have to be in agreement before the position was offered to her."

"You're talking permanent, like as in full time, year round."

Year-round forever. "Yes. But that brings us to another problem. We won't know if we'll have broken even for at least a year. And we still haven't decided if we're going to keep the ranch open as a dude ranch through the winter. If not, we wouldn't need anyone at the desk."

"True. We're still in the experimental stage." Streams of unspoken messages passed between them before Ross whistled.

"I know," Buck muttered as he walked over to the doorway. "While your mind is considering all the logistics, my mind has been making its own list of imponderables. It's a mile long already."

Ross got up from the bed and looked him squarely in the eyes. "I like her a lot. Even if you have to work things out a different way and she gets a job in town, if it's what you want, I'm all for it. You know that. Good luck getting to sleep tonight."

"That's not going to happen, but thanks for your vote of confidence, Ross. It means everything. See you in the morning."

To Buck's surprise, he actually did get some sleep, but he was awake by six-thirty. Knowing Alex was under the same roof caused his adrenaline to kick in and gave him a reason to spring out of the sack.

After a shower and shave, he put on a polo shirt and a pair of jeans. The last thing he did was pull on his cowboy boots. He'd be taking Alex and Jenny on an overnight campout, but he didn't know if it would be today or tomorrow. They still had plans to make. In any case, they'd do some riding both days.

He heard a knock on the door. "Uncle Buck?"

Who else but Johnny. "Are you up already?"

"Yep. Jenny's with me. We've got to talk to you. Can we come in?"

Something was cooking. It always was with Johnny. "Sure."

His young gunslingers walked in looking so cute he couldn't believe it. There was no sign Jenny had ever hurt her ankle. "Hey—I like those new cowboy boots you've got on."

"Nana bought them for me. Hi, Buck!" She ran over and gave him a big hug that warmed his heart.

"Hi, Red." He kissed her forehead. "How was the sleepover?"

A smile broke out on her face. "Really fun."

"I wish we could do it every night."

Johnny was so predictable. Buck had to be careful not to laugh out loud. "I hear you, sport. So tell me what's on your mind."

"We want to camp out at Secret Lake tonight, but mom says everyone's too tired after yesterday's move. Are you too tired?"

"No, but your folks are, so I have a better idea. They need a day to rest, so let's plan to take the horses up there tomorrow and camp out. Today we'll do something else. How does that sound?"

"I guess that's okay. Can Jenny see the cows after breakfast?" She nodded with a look of anticipation.

A drive up to the pasture with Alex would give him time alone with her while the kids sat in the back of the truck. "Sounds like a plan. After we get back, there's plenty for you guys to do around here."

"We want to ride our ponies and catch bad guys."

"And then we'll go to Funorama!" Jenny looked up at Buck with imploring eyes. "Are you going to eat with us?" She had on another princess top with a ruffle over the waistband of her jeans. This one was pink.

"I'm right behind you. Lead the way."

"Goody!" they said in unison.

There was a full house in the dining room. Business was booming. After being open for only three months, it was the best of signs and proved they were attracting business. In time, their experiment might really grow into something. Nothing would make Buck happier. The thought of doing any other kind of work at this point was anathema to him.

He spotted Ross, who'd beaten him downstairs and was sitting at one of the tables with Alex. Buck's heart practically stopped beating. She'd caught her hair on top of her head with a clip and was dressed in a cream-colored Western shirt with fringe. Ross couldn't take his eyes off her and no wonder.

"That's a sensational outfit," Buck murmured after sitting down next to her. He saw the pulse at the base of her throat start to throb.

"I just finished telling her the same thing," Ross said.

"I bought the shirt at the Boot Corral on the way in

to town. We're staying at a dude ranch so I figured I'd better look the part."

"Nana bought me some new cowboy boots. See?" Jenny walked around the table so Ross would take notice.

"You and your nana light this place up like a Christmas tree."

Johnny giggled. "You're silly, Uncle Ross."

Since the surprise arrival of their guests last night, a whole new mood of excitement permeated the place. Halfway through their meal, Carson and Tracy walked in. The waitress took their orders.

"Excuse us for being late." They'd had the house to themselves on their first morning in their new home. Carson finally had his privacy and looked beyond happy. So did Tracy.

"Guess what?" Johnny exclaimed. "Uncle Buck's going to drive us to the pasture after breakfast."

Buck glanced at Alex. "Want to come?"

Her eyes met his. "I'd love to see more of the ranch." Then she looked around. "Since we're discussing plans, now might be the time to invite everyone to a party at the Funorama at five this afternoon. Jenny and I made the reservation to celebrate Johnny's birthday. We're sorry we had to miss his first one."

"Huh?" Johnny's eyes rounded. "Another party?"

Alex smiled at him. "Absolutely. Turning seven is a big deal and it's on us. Pizza and presents."

Buck wished he could have recorded Johnny's yelp of joy.

"I got you my present last month," Jenny informed him.

"You did? Will I like it?"

Buck was afraid to look at the others while he tried to control his amusement.

She giggled. "Yes. It's funny."

"Can I open it now?"

"Johnny Lundgren—" This from Tracy. "Where are your manners?"

"Sorry."

Carson grinned. "We'll all have to wait in suspense until the party. I've got to hurry and get my work done before then."

"How come you always have to work?" Johnny had posed a rhetorical question so full of disappointment it made everyone burst into laughter.

Alex had to wipe her eyes before she got up from the table. "Jenny? If we're going on a drive, we'd better freshen up first."

"I'll pick you up in front in ten minutes," Buck said.

She nodded and left the dining room with Jenny. His gaze followed her out of the room. Then it switched to Carson.

"Can I talk to you in private for a moment?"

"Sure."

"Come on, Johnny." Tracy was a quick study. "You need to visit the restroom before you leave."

"Thanks, Tracy."

He wanted to broach his idea to Carson while his partner was still available. After telling Ross to stay put, he related what he'd told Ross last night and asked him how he'd feel about offering Alex the front-desk job.

"I want your gut response, but I don't need an answer right now. If Johnny hadn't been around, I would have asked your wife to stay to give her input. Just think about it and talk it over with her and Ross. Alex knows nothing about this and she never will if you don't feel good about it."

The waitress refilled their coffee. Carson took a few sips. "This is déjà vu for me. I wanted to keep Tracy and Johnny around and offered them the use of one of the cabins while we got to know each other better. Instead we got married, but there's no reason why Alex and Jenny can't stay in one of the cabins for a temporary period whether she works for us or not."

"If things worked out that way, I've got a little money put away and would take less of a salary so it wouldn't hurt the business."

Carson studied him for a minute. "Just so you guys know, I've been looking over the books, and I say we keep the dude ranch open over the winter and see what happens. We've already had guests call us about doing some hunting in the winter months and have booked a couple of the cabins."

"That's the kind of news I've been hoping for." He knew Ross felt the same way.

"Heaven knows the staff needs the work in this economy. Any one of them would help run the desk. As for Alex, it's *your* life we're talking about here. I don't need to think about it. Do you, Ross?"

He shook his head. "I gave him my seal of approval last night."

"Johnny's is a given," Carson added with an infectious grin.

Buck's throat clogged up. "Thanks. It was my lucky day when I was sent to that hospital and got you two for roommates." He finished off his coffee and rose to his feet. "See you guys later." Now that he had the all-clear, he could choose the moment to feel her out. Maybe tomorrow night under the stars.

He made a detour to the kitchen and chatted with the cook while he put some bottles of water and apples in a bag. With that accomplished, he went out to the truck and swung by the barn where they stored the hay on pallets for the winter. Buck threw half a dozen of the smaller bales into the back of his truck. The kids could sit on a couple of them during the drive. As for the rest, the hands working the herd could spread it around.

After wishing Alex would come back every day for the past month, he found it difficult to believe it was really her and Jenny waiting in front of the ranch house with Johnny and Tracy. He jumped down from the cab and lowered the tailgate so he could lift the children inside.

"Do you need a ride back home, Tracy?" he asked as he closed the gate.

"No, thanks. I brought the car." She looked up at Johnny. "Be sure to mind Buck and Alex. I'll meet you back here at lunch."

Buck heard Johnny say okay, but the kids were already trying to choose which bale to sit on and weren't paying attention.

"Hey, guys. You need to sit where you can hold on to the side of the truck. All we need is for one of you to flip out and break another ankle."

"I'll be careful," Jenny promised him.

"I know you will, Red."

"So will *I*," Johnny assured him.

"I can always count on you, sport. If you get thirsty or hungry, there are snacks in that plastic bag."

"Thanks!"

He waved Tracy off and climbed back in the driver's seat. Alex smelled delicious, like a fresh wild strawberry warmed by the sun. The day was heating up, and the most beautiful woman he'd ever met was strapped in next to him. A sage-scented breeze wafted through the windows. Carson wanted to keep the ranch open year round, for this year at least. What more could a man ask for, he thought to himself, as they reached the forest and headed up the mountain.

Unfortunately, the answer that came back was *a lot more*.

The possibility that Alex wouldn't be interested in his proposition was enough for him to keep his boots planted on the ground. While he was experiencing alternating feelings of euphoria and fear, he heard her cell phone ring.

"That's probably my parents." She reached in her purse and checked the caller ID, and then put the phone back.

"Frank?"

She nodded. "He called earlier, but I didn't pick up. One of these days he'll have to give up, but I hate hurting him."

"It would have been worse to marry him and then discover it was a mistake."

"You're so right."

"I've learned the hard way that when something's truly over, it can't be resurrected, and you have to move on for your own sanity."

"Agreed."

They could hear the kids' talking in the back, mostly Johnny's. "By the time we reach the herd, Jenny's going to be a living encyclopedia of knowledge."

Alex had a warm laugh he loved. "I have to say, the boy's an original and a constant source of fascination."

They drove deeper into the forest. "While we're alone to talk, have you given any more thought to what you'd like to do for a living?"

"It's on my mind constantly," she said. "If we moved, I'd still need hours that coincided with Jenny's school day, and I'd want to live close by. If I could do it all over again, I would have gone into teaching."

"You still could." He said it without enthusiasm.

She sighed. "Yes, but that would mean several more years of college to get a teaching certificate. I'll worry about it after we get home. It's not your problem."

The hell it wasn't! "What about a job in a different bank?" he persisted. They had banks in Jackson.

"Buck…" She chuckled. "Didn't you hear what I said?"

"Yes, but you've got all that schooling in finance that shouldn't go to waste."

"True, but I'd want part-time work until Jenny's out of high school. To my knowledge, it's the rare bank manager who would hire anyone part-time regardless of their years of experience."

He didn't doubt that she was right, but it wouldn't hurt to inquire. The guys did all their business at the Moran Bank of Wyoming. Buck knew the bank manager well and could find out if they hired part-time employees. It was worth a shot.

"I'm going to make sure I know what's going on in Jenny's life so I can guide her. It's a promise I made to Christy before she died. I want to sign her up for piano lessons, dance, art lessons, all of it, so she gets exposed to lots of different things.

"By the time she's in high school, I'd like to see her involved in working on the school newspaper. Or I'd love to see Jenny on the debate team. She's smart and could work toward a scholarship. Maybe the third time's the charm for the females in our family and Jenny will wait till she's in her twenties before she wants to get married."

"I'm afraid she's already cursed with that Wilson-Forrester beauty, so I wouldn't hold my breath." Johnny had fallen under her spell. When he darted her a glance, he saw that color had crept into her cheeks. "Do you have a picture of your daughter?"

As she pulled a wallet out of her purse, he stopped for a minute. She handed him two photos. "That's Christy at seventeen. The other one shows her with Daniel, holding Jenny after she was born."

Buck heard the love in her voice. "She's lovely, just like you and your granddaughter."

"Hey—" Johnny cried out. "What's wrong?"

"We're just looking at a picture of Jenny when she was born," Buck called back.

"I have a baby monkey face in that picture," Jenny said.

"A monkey?" Johnny laughed. "I want to see it, Uncle Buck."

"Later, guys." He handed Alex the photos and started driving again.

It was clear to Buck that Jenny was Alex's raison d'être. That promise to her daughter was sacrosanct. Jackson was a small community. No doubt the schools offered some of the opportunities she'd mentioned, but not on the larger scale available in a city like Sacramento. The winters could be brutal here. Both she and Jenny would hate the isolation.

Neighbors might be next door, but they were separated by acres of ranch land. The front-desk job would never satisfy a woman with her curiosity and education.

No matter how much he wanted her in his life, he had nothing to offer her at the moment, only the good will of Carson and Ross. A year from now, he hoped to be in a different place financially, but no one could predict the future.

Last week his father had phoned, urging him to come home at the end of the summer and join the family business. There was more behind the call. Buck knew his father needed to slow down. The conversation had come at the precise moment when Buck had been missing Alex like crazy and was at a low point. He'd told his dad that if it appeared the dude ranch project was losing too much money, he would have to end the partnership and return to Colorado.

When they emerged from the trees and came to the pasture, Buck was asking himself what in the hell he'd been thinking, imagining that he and Alex could have a good life living together at the ranch.

In a different mood than when they'd started out, he lowered himself from the truck and helped the children down. Johnny led Jenny around to look at the new calves. Alex followed and acted interested, but Buck wasn't an idiot. One trip up here to see the herd was more than enough. By Monday, she would have seen all the sights the dude ranch had to offer and be glad she was flying home to civilization.

Chapter Nine

The difference in Buck from last night to right now was palpable. She'd been breathless when he'd walked in the dining room this morning and had sat next to her. The smoldering look in his eyes had sent a wave of heat through her she could still feel.

So what had happened on the drive over to make him withdraw from her?

Alex walked through a section of the herd with him and the children, but that feeling of emotional intimacy was gone. Vanished! She kept running their conversation through her mind, trying to pinpoint the moment everything changed.

It had to have been the photographs.

They were a graphic reminder that she'd been a mother and was now a grandmother. Buck was a red-blooded, virile bachelor who last night in the dark had succumbed to the novelty of indulging himself with an older woman until Ross had interrupted them. But in the light of day, reality had asserted itself and it was back to the business of being the congenial host until she and Jenny left the ranch.

That was how gorgeous bachelors like Buck and Ross survived to live another day. They were the opposite of Frank who should have known better than to go after a woman years younger, but at least he'd wanted to get married. She couldn't fault him for that. In Buck's case, a serious relationship wasn't a priority and hadn't been, not since the woman he'd loved had married his brother.

"Have you guys seen enough?" he asked.

"Yes," Johnny said. "But Jenny wishes we could take a calf home with us."

"The calf's mother wouldn't let us. She loves her too much."

"Oh," Jenny murmured.

"Can we go riding now, Uncle Buck?"

"We'll do whatever you guys want." They started back to the truck.

"Nana? Can I ride in front with Buck on the way home?"

He had to be relieved to hear that. "If it's all right with him."

"I was just going to tell you to hop in, Red."

There was her answer.

"Johnny and I will sit in back and see who can spot the most animals," Alex said. "How about the winner has to give the other one a treat."

"Yippee!" Johnny cried. The boy was always up for a competition. Buck lowered the tailgate and gave Alex an impersonal leg-up before lifting Johnny into the truck bed. In a few seconds they were off.

By the time they'd driven through the forest and reached the sagebrush, they'd counted a total of twenty-three animals, with Johnny spotting the most. He'd spotted a rabbit in the underbrush she hadn't seen.

She smiled at him. "What kind of a treat would you like?"

"Could I have another roll of caps for my gun? Or do they cost too much?"

"That's an easy request to grant."

"Thanks."

Unbeknownst to him she'd already bought a box of caps for him for the belated birthday party. He stared at her for a second. "Hey, Alex?"

Uh-oh. His tone had a serious inflection. "Yes?"

"Do you like it here?"

"I love it." *I love it more than you can imagine.*

"Jenny wants to live here."

"I know."

"Could you move here? My mom and I did."

Oh, boy. The children had been doing a lot of talking. But this was Buck's territory, with a no-trespassing sign he'd erected on the drive over.

"I'm afraid we can't. Remember, I'll be getting a job pretty soon. But maybe you and your parents could come down to Disneyland before Christmas and we could meet you there. Jenny would love that."

Before she could get an answer out of him, they'd pulled to a stop in the parking area outside the ranch house. Buck came around to lower the tailgate. "Time for lunch before we do anything else."

"Yum! I'm hungry." Johnny was such a character, it killed her. "Thanks for taking us, Uncle Buck."

Alex added her voice to his. "We had a wonderful time."

"So did I," Johnny said.

While Buck lifted him to the ground, Alex jumped down so he wouldn't be forced to help her. She started walking around the front of the ranch house with Jenny. "After playing with those calves, we need to wash our hands."

"They were so cute."

"Not as cute as you," Buck said loud enough for her to hear.

"Thanks." Her granddaughter loved his attention. Who wouldn't?

Alex led her to the rear of the ranch house.

"I've never been in here before."

"Carson and his family lived back here before they moved. This is Johnny's old room. Buck moved us out of the motel so we could sleep in here until we have to leave. Go ahead and use the bathroom first, then we'll eat."

In a few minutes they went back to the dining room to join Buck and Johnny. "We're staying in your bedroom," Jenny announced. "Which bed was yours?"

"I slept in both of them!"

Johnny's answer was so unexpected that the adults broke out laughing.

"No, you didn't." She giggled.

"Actually he did, but not at the same time, of course," Buck explained after a cough.

Jenny's eyes widened. "Why?"

"'Cause it's fun."

More laughter ensued while they ate lunch. After-ward, they walked to the barn and went riding. When everyone was good and hot, they decided to go swimming. Tracy brought Johnny's suit over and swam with them, while Buck disappeared.

Alex had been trying to ignore the change in him, but it was impossible. After last night, she was devastated to think he could shut off his feelings so quickly. He probably thought, now that she was free of Frank, she'd turned to Buck on a rebound. It was too embarrassing.

Having a baby at seventeen and the challenging years that followed had prevented her from enjoying a normal social life. She didn't know how to act around Buck. It sickened her to think she was giving off needy vibes that he'd picked up on without her realizing it. The way she'd clung to him last night must've made her seem desperate.

She'd prided herself on being mature and in charge of her life, but in that one area where she'd made her first mistake by getting involved with a guy way too early, she still hadn't learned anything. A smart woman would have recognized what was going on with Frank and wouldn't have allowed things to progress as far as they did. She could have saved all of them a lot of grief.

An even smarter woman would have said "No thank you" to Buck when he'd suggested they leave the motel and go get a drink. He was a typical single guy who went through women like water. It wouldn't have bothered him if she'd said she was too tired. *But you wanted to be with him any way you could.* In the end he'd gotten what he wanted and it was enough for him. To her humiliation, it wasn't enough for her, but today he'd made it clear it *had* to be.

She swam over to Jenny. "Come on, sweetheart. It's after three. We need to shower and wash our hair. After we're ready, we'll drive over to Funorama to set everything up for the party." Alex was glad she had the rental car and they could leave on their own without asking Buck for a ride.

On the night they'd flown in, they'd done a few errands that had included buying some extra balloons to be blown up. She'd also ordered a birthday cake from the Millhouse Bakery that needed to be picked up. She'd gone to the extra trouble because she and Jenny were crazy about Johnny. It was also her way of thanking Carson and his partners for inviting them to the ranch in the first place.

Jenny was excited and looked around for Johnny. "I have to go in now!" she shouted. "See ya at Funorama."

"Okay! See ya later!" Tracy waved in acknowledgment.

Funorama was a noisy place with rides and slides and games for kids. The party rooms were down the corridor. A teenager at the front counter showed Buck where to go. He'd come into town early to buy Johnny another gift and figured a water gun would be fun for him to have at the lake tomorrow. He'd bought one for Jenny, too, but was saving it until they got up there.

Once the party was over, he assumed Jenny would ride back to the ranch with Carson's family and spend another night in the loft. That would give Buck time to follow Alex to the car-rental place and return her vehicle. Then he'd get her alone and they'd have a serious talk. All day he'd gone back and forth about her and needed to speak his mind to her tonight. As Carson had said, Buck's whole life was at stake here. To put it off until tomorrow night would be pure torture.

When he entered, everyone else was already there. The room had been decorated to the hilt with balloons. He put his gift for Johnny on the table with the others, and then looked over at Alex, who'd changed into a yellow pullover and jeans. She'd washed her hair and tied it back at the nape. Another stunning look for her.

Their gazes met for a brief moment. He couldn't read what was in those beautiful eyes before she clapped her hands. "Now that we're all here, Jenny and Johnny want to eat now and then play. So, everyone, please be seated and we'll let the festivities begin. The decorations were all her idea." Everyone cheered. "We want the birthday boy to sit up here by the cake."

"Yay!" Johnny cried, and scrambled to the table covered in red paper with white number sevens that they'd cut out and pasted on it.

Jenny sat opposite him. "Come and sit by me, Buck." There was a light in her eyes that touched his heart. In a very short time he'd learned to love Alex's granddaughter. Nothing thrilled him more than to play substitute daddy to her. It occurred to him then that it would be easy to do so on a permanent basis.

Alex served the pizza and drinks. His sideward glance took in her profile and incredible figure. He had to hold back from grabbing her around the waist and pulling her into his lap so he could kiss the daylights out of her.

The discussion centered on the drive to the pasture and the calves. Carson wanted to know if Jenny had seen a blue-eyed one. That question prompted another discussion about the rarity of a calf being born with eyes that color. Pretty soon it came time for the dessert. Alex took the cake out of the box. A plastic figure had been set on it inside a minicorral. The frosted wording read Happy 7th Birthday, Johnny.

The boy's smile was so wide, there was no more room for expansion. "It's a cowboy with a pony like mine!"

Alex lit the red candles. "Okay—make a wish."

He closed his eyes. "I wish Jenny and Alex could stay on the ranch forever!"

Buck stopped breathing.

Johnny blew out the candles in one go. The silence was deafening.

"Hey, sport," Carson murmured, "in the future, remember you're supposed to keep your wish a secret."

"How come?"

"It might not come true if you say it out loud."

"But I didn't want it to be a secret."

Buck watched Alex cut pieces of cake for everyone. He noticed her hands tremble as she passed the plates around. Johnny could have no idea how deeply his words had penetrated.

"Okay, sweetheart," Alex said. "Start bringing his presents over."

Jenny slipped off the bench and found one in the pile wrapped in white paper with gold ribbon. "I want you to open mine first."

With cake icing clinging to the edge of his mouth, Johnny eagerly unwrapped the gift and pulled out a T-shirt with a snake on it. "Look, mom, it says Fred's Dad."

Everyone roared with laughter, including Buck.

"I don't believe it," Tracy blurted. "You couldn't have gotten him anything more perfect!"

"Yep." Carson nodded. "That tops anything I've seen."

"It was my granddaughter's brainchild, not mine."

Everyone was still laughing as Jenny brought Johnny his next gift. "This is from Nana."

"A box of caps!" he cried, after he'd torn off the paper. "I can shoot my gun two hundred times! Thanks, Alex!"

That set everyone off again. Soon he'd opened all the presents.

Just when Buck thought the fun was over, Alex made an announcement. "I have one more surprise. Jenny—there's another bag with some gifts. Will you get them?"

Her cute face beamed as she did her grandmother's bidding. To Buck's surprise, she handed one to him. Then she pulled out the other one. "Hey—this is for me!"

"That's right."

They were wrapped in that same white paper with gold ribbon. When Buck opened his, he discovered a red T-shirt with the words Teton Valley Ranch Water Fight Champions printed on it in white.

He pinned Alex with his gaze. She'd remembered that night and had gone to the trouble to get them a prize before she'd even returned to the ranch. His heart beat unnaturally fast while Jenny tore hers open and lifted out the same T-shirt with a cry of delight.

"I love it, Nana!"

"So do I, *Nana*," he half whispered.

She lowered her eyes. "You two deserved a prize."

"Did you hear that, sport?" Carson turned to Johnny.

"We're declaring a rematch before this weekend is over!"

"Yeah. And this time we'll win!"

"The guys have gone to play with the kids. Let me help you clean up."

"Thanks, Tracy, but you don't have to. It's my turn."

"I want to. Except for the time I told Johnny I loved Carson, I've never seen my son this happy. Your presence has brought a new element into Johnny's life. His cousin was here a few weeks ago and they had a wonderful time, but Johnny has changed. He loves this ranch and is going in a different direction from Cory. You don't know what this means to Carson. He so desperately wants Johnny to be happy here."

"Carson's an exceptional man. Johnny adores him."

"I keep telling him that, but deep inside he still has some demons to conquer. And then along came Jenny. I guess what I'm trying to say is that Johnny has found a new life here and really feels it's his home. He wants everyone else to love it, too."

Alex's eyes smarted. "Jenny couldn't wait to come back. She's been happier than I've seen her in several years. Her friendship with Johnny is very sweet. When your husband and his partners were inspired to do such a noble thing, they couldn't have known how deeply their goodness would affect the children. The fatherless kids of the world need more selfless men like the daddies on this dude ranch."

They stared at each other. "It's true."

She nodded. "I wish my daughter could have been the one to bring Jenny."

"Your pain must be terrible at times."

"In the beginning, yes, but time has brought healing. Jenny's my joy."

"So's my son, who has a terrible habit of running his mouth when he shouldn't. I'm trying to work on that with him. He mentioned you're…not getting married. I hope that decision has made life better for you."

"It definitely has. I didn't love Frank the way I should, and Jenny never took to him."

"Then I'm happy for you."

"Thank you." But now Alex had a new problem because Jenny liked Buck *too* much.

As for Alex's feelings for him… She looked around. "Why don't I help you take his presents and the rest of the cake to your car? Then we can go in and watch the kids until they're completely worn out and want to go home."

"That's so nice of you. Do you mind if Jenny sleeps over again tonight? Johnny begged me to ask you."

"She begged me, too. Do we have a choice?"

"Not with those two."

Once they'd taken everything out to Carson's SUV, they went back inside. Tracy gave Alex an impish look. "That giant slide looks fun. Shall we try it?"

"Why not?" She'd just seen Johnny go down it between Carson's legs, followed by Jenny between Buck's. Ross didn't seem to be around. Being a Saturday night, he probably had plans with a woman.

Alex hurried up the steps behind Tracy. The kids saw them and waved. Alex sat and pushed off. Buck was there to catch her as she reached the bottom and helped her to her feet. The contact caused a jolt of electricity to run through her.

When their eyes met, she saw the unmistakable glaze

of desire in his and realized he'd been affected, too. The change in him from earlier in the day confused her.

His hand closed over hers almost possessively. "Come on," he said in a husky voice. "Let's you and I go down together this time. You first."

The kids had already gone up again. Shaking like a leaf from his touch, Alex started up the steps once more, aware of him right behind her. When they reached the top, he sat first and pulled her down in front of him, encasing her legs with his. Hunger for him licked through her veins as his strong arms slid around her waist. The feel of his well-defined chest against her back sent shivers through her.

"Ready?" he whispered the word against her neck where his lips grazed the skin.

She nodded, unable to speak.

"Do you have any idea how wonderful you smell?"

A gasp escaped her throat before he pushed off. As they flew down the chute, she realized that without a doubt she was wildly in love for the second time in her life. No longer a witless teenager who hadn't yet experienced life, she was a fully grown woman who knew exactly what she wanted. How deep the feelings of this bachelor ran for her, she didn't know. But the chemistry was there and couldn't be denied. He wanted her. *And I want him.* She couldn't blame this on widow's hormones, because she'd never been a widow, never been married and was never going to be.

At the bottom of the slide, Jenny begged Buck to go down with her again. It was fine with Alex, who stood watching in a daze. Her mind harked back to high school. There'd been chemistry between her and Kyle and she'd let it take over.

Now here she was again twenty-four years later, in danger of making the same mistake again with a man who only had to touch her to turn her insides to liquid. Was this to be the pattern of her life? Make love with a man once every quarter of a century?

She needed to decide what she intended to do. Tonight Jenny would be sleeping over at Johnny's house again. Alex and Buck would have the whole night to themselves. Would she go home on Monday having known his possession? And then what? They'd both go their separate ways? She'd never see him again? The mere idea was enough to drive her mad.

She needed to get out of there. Get away from Buck so she could think. When he alighted once more at the bottom of the chute with Jenny, she turned to her granddaughter without looking at him. "It's getting late and we have a big day tomorrow if we're going to go camping. Tracy asked if you could sleep over again and I said yes, so I'll drive you to Johnny's house right now."

Jenny turned to Johnny. "Nana says I can stay at your house."

He'd been complaining that he didn't want to go yet, but knowing that Jenny would be sleeping over got him to agree to it.

"Come on, sweetheart." Alex took her hand and they walked out to the car.

"What about my T-shirt?"

"It's in my purse." Not looking back at the others, she drove out of the parking lot.

Twilight was turning into night. Crickets chirped in the pine-scented air. Lights twinkled between the trees and the last tinge of violet hadn't quite faded in the western sky. All of it just increased her longing to be in Buck's arms.

"Nana?"

Jenny's voice jerked her out of her thoughts. "Yes? Did you have a good time tonight?"

"It was the best! Buck's so nice. I love him." Alex had expected her to talk about Johnny, but it was Buck who was on her granddaughter's mind. "Johnny's afraid he's going to go back to Colorado. He doesn't want him to go. I don't, either."

Alex's hands tightened on the steering wheel. That was news to her. She'd gotten the impression that leaving the ranch would be the last thing he'd do. "Maybe Johnny misunderstood."

"No, he didn't. He heard him on the phone."

"Johnny shouldn't listen in on other people's conversations. I'm sure he's wrong."

"You sound cross."

She took a fortifying breath. "Do I? I'm sorry."

"Guess what? Buck has four brothers and Johnny has four uncles. That's funny."

"Because there aren't any girls?"

"Yes. Buck says I can be his little girl anytime."

Thank heaven the new house had come into view. At this point, Alex was afraid to say anything her granddaughter could misconstrue. Carson's SUV was right behind them.

She stopped the car. "Listen, sweetheart—I'm going to say good-night to you here. I need to get back to the ranch house and call Mom. She's been waiting all day to hear from me."

"Okay." Jenny undid her seat belt and leaned over to

kiss her. "Good night, Nana. Johnny said he loved his party and he really likes you."

Her eyes smarted. "Thank you for telling me." She took the T-shirt out of her purse and handed it to her. "See you in the morning."

With a nod, Jenny jumped out of the car and joined the others. Alex waved before turning the car around. She drove to the ranch house in turmoil. She didn't see the truck Buck had brought to the party. Fiercely disappointed to think he might have joined Ross and headed out instead of wanting to be with her, she hurried inside the front door.

Willy waved to her from the desk as she passed him on her way to her bedroom in the rear. She did owe her parents a callback, but after what Jenny had confided to her in the car, she was too shaken to make it.

How could Buck consider going back to Colorado? After putting the past behind him, what would be the reason to change his mind? She'd believed him when he'd told her he loved his life here. Alex couldn't figure him out. As much as she wanted to believe that Johnny was wrong about what he'd heard, that little guy was smart as a whip and had the inside track on what went on around the ranch.

The news shouldn't matter to her, but it did. Everything to do with him affected her because she was painfully in love with him.

Too wired to sleep yet, she slipped out into the hall and set out for the kitchen. Buck had told her she should feel free to use it. Caffeine wouldn't help her nerves, but it was coffee she wanted. After finding a jar of the instant stuff, she made herself a cup and microwaved it.

As she started back to her room to drink it, the overhead lights went on.

"Buck—"

He stood in the doorway with his hands on his hips, all male from his powerful thighs to the contours of his hard jawline. "Willy told me you'd come in. Since you weren't in the bedroom, I hoped I'd find you in here. Why in the hell did you run away so fast?" he asked. "One minute, you were there, the next you were gone."

"It was rude of me. Forgive me."

Buck's eyes wandered over her, missing nothing. "I didn't think you had a rude bone in your body, so tell me what's going on."

"A lot of things," she answered honestly. "Too many." She drank part of her coffee before putting the mug on the counter of the island.

"Am *I* one of those things? Is that why you fled into the night?"

"I didn't flee—"

"You could have fooled me. Am I so terrifying?"

She looked away. "You already know the answer to that question."

"On the contrary. It seems to me the minute I touch you, you do a disappearing act."

Her pulse was running away with her. "You mean, the way you disappeared on me during the drive over to the herd?"

His brows furrowed. "Explain that remark."

He wanted answers. She'd give them to him. "After I showed you the pictures in my wallet, you became a different person. Standoffish. Why? The night before, I thought we were enjoying ourselves. The chemistry felt obvious. But I can only think that in the light of day with certain proof before you, the idea of being with an older woman—a *grandma*—didn't hold the same appeal."

His eyes flickered with a strange light. "You couldn't be more wrong."

As long as she was feeling this brave, she would dare to say what else was on her mind. "Is it true what Johnny told Jenny?"

"About what?" He sounded impatient.

"That you might be going back to Colorado?"

He rubbed the back of his neck, as if he needed to plan his answer carefully. "You mean, for another trip?"

"No. Permanently. It's evident Johnny was worried enough about it to voice it to my granddaughter."

Buck rubbed his lower lip with his thumb. "He must have heard me on the phone with my father a couple of weeks ago. He's had to slow down and wants me back home."

Her heart lurched. "You must be so conflicted."

"That's putting it mildly, but not for the reasons you're thinking." He walked over to the island and looped his arms around her shoulders. "Look at me, Alex." His mouth was only inches from hers.

"I *am* looking." Her voice trembled.

"How do you feel about me?"

She groaned inside. "After what happened last night, it should be clear to you."

His features hardened. "That was chemistry. According to you, I can turn it off and on at will. Let's get past the discussion of our physical attraction to each other and dig deeper to find out what's going on inside of you. Why would it matter to you if I go back to Colorado or stay here?"

"Because I know how much the ranch means to you."

His breath was warm on her lips. "It means a hell of a lot, but some things are even more important."

She could hardly swallow. "Your family has to have missed you all these years."

"I've missed them, but I'm talking about the relationship between a man and a woman. If it's right, then it trumps everything else in importance. Don't you agree?"

Alex thought she was going to faint. "Yes, although I can't speak from personal experience because my only experience was with a boy and it never turned into a relationship."

"Then it's time you found out what a real one could be like." Suddenly the room tilted because he'd picked her up in his arms. His mouth took hers in a long, hungry kiss that still didn't satisfy either of them. At the doorway, he turned out the light and carried her down the hall to Johnny's bedroom.

His rock-hard body followed her down on top of the bed. He tangled her legs with his and smoothed the hair away from her temples. In the semidarkness, his eyes were alive with desire. "I want you more than I've ever wanted a woman in my life. Everything about you appeals to me. But it goes much deeper than the physical.

"I have this impossible dream of sharing my life with you, of having a baby with you. My mom had me at forty." She gasped. "I'm glad if that shocks you. Now you know how far my fantasy has taken me."

"Fantasy?" she whispered, out of breath.

"Yes." He covered her face in kisses. "I don't have anything to offer you and Jenny. A man needs something solid behind him." He had to be talking marriage, but hadn't said the words. The joy of it overwhelmed her. "I'm not Frank—I can't offer you the security you deserve. That takes time to build."

"If I'd wanted Frank, I would have married him."

"Be honest, Alex. You need much more than a ranch hand can deliver. While the guys and I were in the hospital, we felt it was pretty much the end of our lives. We had no expectations except to survive and try to do some good."

"You've done a lot more than that!" she cried from her soul, kissing him with abandon to convince him.

Buck was the one who eventually brought them down to earth. After relinquishing her mouth, he turned on his side, running his hand up and down her arm. "When you look at me like that, you have no idea how much I'd love to ravish you, but I'm not going to do it."

Giving her arm a squeeze, he rolled away from her and got off the bed. She hated that shuttered look hiding his eyes from her while he stood there rocking on his cowboy boots. "See you in the morning." He started for the door.

In panic, she sat up. "There you go again, Buck, distancing yourself from me. I'm not Melanie."

Her comment caught him on the raw. He turned to her. Lines marred his handsome features. "Where did that come from?"

"She didn't wait for you to finish college because she wasn't a risk-taker. Instead, she married your brother who already had job security working in the family construction business. She was blind not to realize that you instill security by simply being who you are.

"Your old girlfriend didn't know the Buck Summerhayes I know. Otherwise she would have realized what a rarity you are. It wouldn't matter what you did for a living or how long it took. You're a survivor and a hero who takes care of everyone else and went to my granddaughter's rescue without giving it a second's thought.

"There's greatness in you. Carson recognized it when he met you. No wonder your family wants and needs you back. It's because you're a remarkable man who's true to himself."

Even from the distance, she felt his body go rigid. "That was a speech any red-blooded man would be proud of, ma'am. Good night."

Oh, no, you don't!

She rushed out into the hall in time to hear a door bang shut in the distance.

With her heart racing, Alex dashed down the corridor and out the rear door after him. The headlights to his truck went on. He started to back out. "Buck? Wait—" She took a flying leap to reach the door handle on the passenger side.

He slammed on the brakes. She took advantage of the moment to open the door and climb inside the cab. His expression looked like thunder. "What in the hell do you think you're doing?" He was out of breath. "Don't you know you could have gotten dragged, even killed?" The pulse at the corner of his mouth was throbbing.

"You're worth the risk."

"We've already said good-night."

"No," she fired back. "You walked out on me while I still had more to say. I think the term *slippery slope* was invented when someone tried to get up close to you and failed. This pattern you have of bolting like an unbroken stallion at the first sign you might be in danger is

disconcerting to say the least. Last year I watched Hugh
break one in and can see the similarity in behavior."

His expression grew as dark as a thundercloud. She'd
made him angry again. The next thing she knew, he'd
pulled the truck closer to the house and shut off the
engine.

"Since you love this ranch so much, why don't you
drive us to a favorite spot I haven't seen before? In case
you're worried, I'm not tired in the least."

"That wouldn't be a good idea." His voice sounded
like gravel. "We have a big day planned for tomorrow.
I've got a lot of gear to get together."

"Of course." His work was never done.

Silence stretched between them. "What did you want
to say?"

She took a shaky breath. "It can wait until tomorrow
evening when we're at the lake and you're able to relax."

"In that case, I have things to do now." He reached
across to open the door for her. His arm brushed against
her in the process, turning her body to a mass of jelly.
"I'll wait till I know you're safely in the house. Lock
the door behind you."

"I will."

Chapter Ten

Buck waited until Alex had gone inside.

In the bedroom, she'd sung his praises. It had reminded him of a glowing eulogy to a dead marine.

But not one word of love had come from her lips.
Not one declaration that she shared his dream for a life
together.

Holding her in his arms, exulting in the rapture of
her kisses, he'd forgotten to be cautious and had been
all kinds of a fool to have opened up to her. How could
he forget it had taken Frank two years to make a dent....

Buck didn't have years. He'd been given only eight
days, if you combined the two times she'd come to
the ranch. After her experience with Kyle, she'd been
guarding her heart all this time. To suppose or even
hope she would blurt out that she was in love with Buck

in such a short amount of time was ludicrous. He really was out of his mind.

He took off for the shed where they kept the camping supplies. There were tents, water toys, fishing poles, lanterns, sleeping bags and feed for the horses to load in the back of the truck. A couple of guys from the staff would drive up to the lake early with the food.

It was close to midnight when he drove back to the ranch house and went inside. Ross caught up to him at the top of the stairs. His brows knitted together. "You look gutted. What's wrong?"

"I blew it tonight and told her how I felt."

"And?"

He sucked in his breath. "She gave me some spiel about what a great man I am."

"You are."

"Thanks, buddy," he said with a mirthless smile, "but you know damn well that kind of talk is a death sentence."

"I don't get it. I thought—"

"So did I," Buck cut him off, and then had a coughing spell. "But being on fire for each other doesn't mean she's ready for anything else. She couldn't bring herself to marry Frank, who hung in there for two years. I'm not made like him.

"I can't believe I'm saying this, but I'm glad she's flying out of here on Monday. Do me a favor tomorrow and ask Tracy to stick with her while we entertain the kids?"

Ross nodded. "What time do you figure we should get away?"

"After breakfast. I've asked Bert to get the horses saddled and ready."

"Carson checked the weather forecast. There could be light rain later in the day."

Buck frowned. "Jenny's afraid of storms. Last month our plane flew right into one over the Tetons."

"I remember. If it doesn't look good, we'll come back early."

"That's all we can do. Under other circumstances I'd cancel the outing, but I know Jenny's got her heart set on it. She and Johnny have made all sorts of plans."

"Don't I know it."

"I'll ask a couple of the hands to bring up an extra truck for us in case we need to drive the kids back."

"Sounds like you've got everything covered."

"Except that we can't count on the weather report ever being accurate," Buck muttered.

"We'll play it by ear. Get some sleep."

"You, too."

They parted company and went to bed. For the first time in over a month, Buck wasn't fighting the urge to seek out Alex, whether she slept in the guest cabin or in the ranch house. Nothing could have cooled his blood faster than to realize his dream had no possibility of coming to fruition.

When he awakened the next morning, he looked out the window. An overcast sky greeted him and appeared as grim as his mood. He turned on the TV to the weather channel. Just as he'd feared, the earlier forecast hadn't been specific enough. A storm front would move in by evening and bring wind and heavy rainfall.

After he'd showered and shaved, he got dressed in jeans and a flannel shirt. When he was ready, he went down to the dining room. Ross was there talking to some of the guests.

While Buck ate, he phoned Carson. His friend had been outside already and was in agreement that they would have to cancel the campout portion of their outing. If they got up to the lake early to swim, they would have time to ride back home before the storm started.

The kids wouldn't like the news, but for once, their disappointment wasn't foremost in his mind. All he could think of was that now he wouldn't have to spend a night in the rain aching for Alex who would be asleep in one of the tents only a stone's throw away from his.

Once he'd finished eating, he pulled Ross aside. "I just talked to Carson. We've decided to call off the camping-out part of the trip."

"I looked at the sky a few minutes ago. It's a good idea."

"Since the others haven't come to breakfast yet, I'm going to use this time to drive back to the shed and unload everything from the truck. It needs to be done and I'd rather do it now. I'll coordinate with the staff about just bringing lunch for us."

"Do you want help?"

They eyed each other. He could always count on Ross to know exactly what was going on with him. "Bring everyone to the barn. I'll be there to meet you and we'll head out."

There was no sign of Alex yet, which was good. He hurriedly left the dining room and headed out to the truck. Twenty minutes later, he'd finished the job and climbed back in the cab. There was a message waiting for him on his cell. His mother had phoned. On the drive over to the barn, he called her back.

As their party came out of the trees Jenny cried, "Secret Lake looks like a silver dollar!"

"Told you," Johnny said after they'd dismounted.

The small mountain lake with its stretch of beach was perfectly formed. With a pine forest surrounding them, the place looked enchanting and would have been an ideal spot to spend the night, if not for the impending storm.

Alex glanced at the sky for the dozenth time. It was noon. She'd been hoping for a break in the clouds, but no such luck. Thankfully, with the three men doing their best to keep the kids entertained, the children seemed to have gotten over their disappointment at not being able to camp out.

It was Alex who was still suffering over the way things had ended before she'd gotten out of Buck's truck last night. He'd been charming and friendly to her this morning. From his surface behavior you would never have known what had transpired the night before.

But Alex knew he'd retreated deep within himself. She feared it might be impossible to reach him once she nabbed some time alone with him today. So far, there'd been no opportunity for that. The men stuck together as they chaperoned the children.

Tracy stayed at Alex's side and they rode the entire way together. She found out that Tracy had been a technology specialist for the school district where Johnny had gone to school in Sandusky, Ohio.

They talked about jobs and the necessity of finding the kind of work that coincided with the kids' school day. Little by little, Alex learned about the pain Tracy and Johnny had gone through when her first husband was killed.

"Johnny changed. He retreated into his shell and had no confidence. He didn't want to play with his friends. By the time that letter from Carson arrived, I was pretty

frantic. I didn't think Johnny would agree to go. If we
hadn't…"

Alex understood and could hardly believe the boy
her friend was describing was the same little cowboy
with the shining brown eyes who was showing Jenny all
the ins and outs of the ranch as if he owned the place.

In turn, Alex admitted to Tracy how her granddaughter had suffered after losing both parents. She feared
that her sadness would rob her of the happy childhood
she deserved.

"Buck was the first one to make her laugh since her
mother's death. The night we drove to the ranch from
the airport, she was scared because of the storm. He
kept chatting with her and told her about Moppy the
squirrel. It was like magic the way she responded—he
helped her forget her fear. Then she met Johnny and
they laugh all the time."

"I know. To be honest, I'm dreading you leaving tomorrow. Johnny told me again this morning he wishes
you'd get a job in Jackson."

Alex almost moaned out loud. "I'm afraid Jenny had
something to do with that."

"Do you know the only thing saving me is that we
have a back-to-school information night on Thursday?
I'm praying Johnny makes some new friends soon, but
Jenny will be a hard act to follow. She's wise for her
age and I think that intrigues him."

"Jenny thinks he's the funnest, funniest person on
Earth."

"He has his father's personality. The first time I met
Tony, my girlfriends and I were having a picnic at Lake-
front State Park in Cleveland when a crew of firefight-
ers pulled up to eat their lunch and play some football.

The cutest guy in the group started flirting with me. I secretly called him Mr. Personality. He told me after our first date he was going to marry me."

Alex smiled. "I can hear him through Johnny. That first morning he came to our cabin door, he spoke right up and said, 'Hi! I'm Johnny Lundgren. Are you Jenny?' My granddaughter was so stunned, she could only nod. Then he said, 'Do you want to have breakfast with me?'"

Both women's laughter drew the guys' attention. Alex felt Buck's gaze on her. They were setting up a table and chairs that one of the staff members had driven up with the food for their lunch. The children had run over to the water's edge and stripped down to their bathing suits to go wading.

"What's so funny?" Carson called to his wife.

"Just the kids. I'll tell you later." In an aside to Alex, she said, "Carson is so different. He was much more guarded when we first met. I had to read between the lines."

"I know what you mean. That's a trait all three of the guys seem to share," Alex murmured. "Buck was hurt long before he went to war."

"You're talking about Melanie."

"Yes."

"He got over her years ago, but unfortunately he doesn't have a lot of faith in a woman's staying power. The fear of committing again without a guarantee still looms large for him."

Alex's heart rate increased. Last night was proof of what Tracy had just confided to her. Buck was so convinced he didn't have enough to offer a woman that the thought was entrenched in him. Alex had thought about it all night and her illuminating conversation with Tracy just now had her mind spinning with an idea.

Deep in thought, she barely heard Tracy add, "Then there's Carson who suffered *after* he came home from war because he felt he'd deserted his grandfather. He's still trying to get over the guilt."

"Those poor guys. And on top of everything else, they have to cope with their disease. It isn't fair."

"No kidding."

"Food's ready. Come and get it!" Ross announced, jarring Alex back to the present. The guys were trying to hurry things up. Alex sensed they didn't trust the timing of the storm and wanted to make sure they started on their way back in plenty of time.

She and Tracy rounded up the kids. They took them behind some bushes where they could take off their wet bathing suits and get dressed. Once that was done, they all sat down to eat sloppy joes and potato chips. After finishing three of the hot beef sandwiches, Carson stood.

"As much as I wish we could stay here until tomorrow, I'm afraid we can't. As soon as everyone's through eating, we'll head back to the ranch and finish our party in the swimming pool. It's time for a water-fight rematch!"

"Yippee!" the children cried in unison.

Once Johnny and Jenny had wolfed down their cookies, Carson and Ross helped them get back on their ponies.

"The kids are really getting a workout."

"So are we," Tracy quipped. "I'm going to be sore after this."

"Tell me about it." But Alex's physical discomfort

would be nothing compared to the mental agony she was suffering from.

Out of the corner of her eye, Alex watched Buck assist with the cleanup and put the camp furniture back in the truck. She mounted her mare and caught up to Tracy for the ride home. Carson led them out. Ross and Buck were bringing up the rear, or so she thought. But when she looked back, there was no sign of Buck. Ross was trailing Buck's horse behind him. She stared at him. "Where's Buck?"

"He left with Randy to get back to the ranch sooner. A call came in early this morning. His father's in the hospital. He had some minor chest pain. Nothing serious so far." A small cry escaped Alex's throat. "We told him to fly home and be with his family."

"Of course." Her concern for him sent her heart racing. He'd hidden his emotions so well, no one had suspected anything was wrong. He was a master at it. "Why did he come on the trip, Ross?"

"He didn't want to disappoint Jenny."

Alex loved him too much. Tears filled her eyes. She looked away, but not before both Ross and Tracy had seen them.

"Carson and I decided we won't tell the kids the real reason he left until we get back." He coughed. "Let them think Randy needed his help."

"That was a good idea," she said through wooden lips.

Jenny would be inconsolable when she learned she wouldn't be able to say goodbye to him before they left for California in the morning. Ditto for her.

Oh, Buck.

It didn't take her granddaughter long to notice Buck

wasn't with them. Ross's explanation didn't take away her disappointment. After that, the subdued atmosphere among their group matched the elements. Naturally, Jenny expected to find Buck at the barn when they returned, but he wasn't there.

"Sweetheart?" Alex took her aside. "I just found out Buck's father is ill, so that's why he left the lake in the truck with Randy. He's taken a flight to Colorado to be with his family."

"In the storm?" The alarm in her voice spoke volumes.

"It's not a bad storm like the one last month. He'll be fine."

"When will he be back?"

"I don't know."

Her face crumpled before the tears came. "Then we won't see him again."

Alex knew exactly how she felt. There were no comforting words. All she could do was hug her for a long time.

"Do you want to go swimming until it rains?" Johnny could be so sweet.

"No," her granddaughter sniffed.

Tracy suggested they walk to the ranch house for some hot chocolate. Halfway there, the wind picked up and there was a noticeable drop in temperature.

A shiver ran down Alex's back. She prayed Buck's father would be all right. He *had* to be. If anything happened to him, Buck would carry around the same kind of guilt that plagued Carson.

After their hot chocolate, Tracy and Alex went into the games room with the kids to watch them play Ping-Pong. When that activity no longer appealed, they ate a meal in the dining room without much enthusiasm, and then went back to the games room to watch a movie. No one could concentrate. It had started raining but there was no lightning or thunder, for which Alex was grateful. And still no news from Buck.

By nine o'clock, Carson suggested Alex get her suitcase and come back to the house with them so the kids could get ready for bed. Tracy put an arm around her. "Plan to stay with us tonight. We have two guest bedrooms. That way when Buck phones, we'll all hear any news he has to share. In the morning, we'll drive you to the airport."

"Thank you, Tracy."

A half hour after the children went to bed in the loft, Buck phoned Carson. After he hung up, Carson turned to them. "His father's undergoing a series of tests with an important one scheduled for tomorrow. He isn't sure how long he'll have to be away from the ranch." Carson eyed her. "If he can, he'll phone you and Jenny in the morning to say goodbye. I need to let Ross know." He kissed his wife. "I'll be in the den."

Everyone was worried about Buck, but no one more so than Alex. He was in pain, not only because of what was going on with his father, but because of the way things had been left last night before he'd driven off. She felt him slipping away from her emotionally with every tick of the grandfather clock in the hallway.

Alex couldn't stand it any longer and jumped up from the loveseat. "Tracy—"

"What is it?"

"I—I need a favor," she stammered. At this point it didn't matter if she revealed what was going on inside her to Johnny's mother.

"Anything."

"I should get Jenny back in school, but I can't leave Wyoming without seeing Buck again. A phone call won't do. Last night he left the ranch upset before we could finish talking and I've been in agony ever since.

"I'd like to fly out to Colorado early in the morning and be back by evening. I still have my rental car. If you could watch Jenny for that long, you'd have my eternal gratitude and I'd make it up to you. Jenny thinks the world of you and your family and is totally comfortable with you."

"We'd love to take care of her. Johnny will be so excited when he finds out she can stay another day."

Alex smiled. "Thank you so much. I know it's a huge imposition, but if anything happens to Buck's father, I want to be there. He shouldn't be alone. But I don't want him to know I'm coming. That would put added pressure on him. I'd rather just show up."

Tracy got to her feet and walked over to her. "I'm glad someone's going to be there for him. He's usually the one helping everyone else. You've been through so much yourself. I think you're exactly what he needs."

"I hope that's true, because what you said about him earlier today definitely is. He doesn't believe that a woman will stick by him when the going gets tough. That old wound of his runs deep. I'd like to prove him wrong if he'll let me."

There was a new sweetness in Tracy's smile. "You love him."

Moisture wet her cheeks. "I do."

Now Tracy teared up. "You have no idea how much that thrills me. Buck deserves to be loved by a wonderful woman like you. Please don't worry if you can't get back to the ranch tomorrow. We're not going anywhere."

"You're an angel."

"Let's go in the den so you can make your plane reservations. Carson will give you the name of the hospital and Buck's cell-phone number."

"First, I'd better go up to the loft and run this by Jenny. If she doesn't think she can stay here on her own, then I'll take her with me."

"Go ahead. I'll tell Carson your plans."

It was 10:30 a.m. when Alex arrived at Memorial Hospital in Colorado Springs. She hurried inside to get the room number for David Summerhayes. The central bank of elevators was close by. She took a lift to the third floor. There was a no admittance sign on the door to his room. Fearful of what it could mean, she went down the hall to the nursing station.

"What can you tell me about Mr. Summerhayes's condition?"

The nurse looked up from the chart. "Are you a member of the family?"

"No. A...friend."

"I'm sorry. The best I can do is direct you to the visitor lounge at the other end of the hall. Perhaps you'll see a family member there."

"Thank you."

Alex should have phoned Buck, but she'd wanted to know his father's status first so she'd be better prepared to talk to him. With her heart in her throat, she walked down the corridor where she could see a room with half a dozen people sitting at random while they waited. A

TV was on, but no one seemed to be watching it. A few people looked as though they'd been up all night.

She sat for a few minutes, but soon realized that wasn't going to get her anywhere so she went back down the hall. Since she couldn't use her cell phone in the hospital, she decided to go outside and try to reach him. If that failed, she could call his parents' home and leave a message. Carson had given her the number, but she worried Buck might not like her doing that.

After pushing the button, she waited impatiently for the elevator going down. To her chagrin, it stopped at every floor. Finally, the doors opened to a full car, but some people made room for her. After she got on, she turned around to face the doors.

Across the hall, a tall, muscular guy in a crewneck sweater and jeans had just stepped onto another elevator opposite hers. The cough sounded familiar. Then he faced forward.

"Buck—"

His eyes swerved in her direction as her doors closed. The elevator started to descend.

Please stop at the next floor.

But this time it didn't. The minute the doors opened onto the main floor, she looked for the stairway sign and opened the door to go back up. Although she was still sore from yesterday's ride, she paid no heed as she dashed up the first flight.

As she rounded it to start up the second, she heard someone coming down. She lifted her head and her eyes collided with his. He slowed to a stop a few steps above her. *"Alex—"* She thought he'd paled a little. "I thought I was hallucinating just now. What are you doing here?"

"I—I came to be with you." Her voice faltered.

He rubbed his chest absently. "You're supposed to be on your way to California."

She shook her head. "Something more important came up."

There was a silence before he said, "When I couldn't get you on the phone this morning to say goodbye, I called the ranch. Tracy told me you'd left for the airport early. No wonder I couldn't reach you." He acted dazed. "Where's Red?"

Alex loved his nickname for her granddaughter. "Back at the ranch with Johnny."

"You came without her?" He sounded shaken.

"She understood I needed to see you alone. Buck—" Her voice throbbed. "Tell me about your father. The no-admittance sign on his door worried me and the nurse at the nursing station couldn't tell me anything because I'm not family."

"The sign was put there because dad has too many friends. His doctor insisted everyone stay out of the room until all the tests were done. It seems he had a severe panic attack that mimicked all the signs of a heart attack. He needs medication to get his anxiety under control. The recession hit him harder than any of us realized because he knows my brothers' families depend on the construction company being successful. But the doctor says he's going to be fine."

"Oh, Buck—that's wonderful news!" She couldn't stop the tears. "You must be so relieved."

"Relieved doesn't begin to express what I'm feeling right now," he said. "He's going to be released later today."

"Thank heaven!"

A smile curved one corner of his mouth. "We're all pretty happy. Especially my mom."

"I can only imagine. Is everyone here?"

"Not yet. They were all here yesterday. I stayed with Dad during the night. Before he fell asleep a minute ago, he told me to go back to the ranch where I belong."

Alex had trouble swallowing. "He said that?"

Buck nodded. "We did a lot of talking and came to a new understanding. For one thing, I've promised him I'll come home more often. I would introduce you to him right now, but the medication they gave him will keep him asleep for several hours."

"Are you going to your folks' house now?"

"No. I'm on my way to the airport. If I take the next flight to Denver, I can make a connecting flight to Jackson. I've left the guys in the lurch long enough."

"Buck—they understand. As long as you're here, don't you want to take another day to visit with your family?"

He shook his head. "I had my private time with Dad. Now I've got something more important to do."

"What's that?"

"You'll find out after we grab a taxi." He reached her in one step and swept her down the stairs to the main floor. They practically ran to the front exit.

"Didn't you bring any luggage?"

"No. I was in too big a hurry last night. Where's yours?"

She bit the underside of her lip. "I only planned to stay long enough to offer my support."

"So you have a return ticket for today?"

"Yes. I couldn't ask Tracy to watch Jenny any longer than that."

"Perfect. Things couldn't have worked out better."

He detained a taxi that had just dropped off an older man with a cane. "We need a ride to the airport," he called to the driver, before helping Alex into the back-seat.

Once he'd shut the door, he turned to her and crushed her in his arms. He was so strong, he didn't know he was nearly suffocating her, but she didn't mind. This was where she wanted to be for the rest of her life.

"We've got a lot to talk about, but right now this is what I'm dying for." His voice shook before he kissed her with almost savage hunger. She was so consumed with happiness that the driver had to tell them they'd arrived at the terminal. Even then, several seconds elapsed before they could stand to pull apart from each other long enough to get out of the taxi.

"You blush beautifully," he whispered after he'd paid the driver. "Come on. We've got a plane to catch."

Chapter Eleven

The seat-belt sign had just flashed on, warning them they were about to land at Jackson airport. When he wasn't kissing her, Buck hadn't been able to take his eyes off the gorgeous woman who was wearing his favorite outfit, the one he'd first seen her in.

He needed to get her alone, pronto. He was relieved when she told him she'd brought her rental car to the airport. They wouldn't have to call anyone and could take their time before they drove home.

Alex gave him the car keys before he could ask for them. He reached for her hand and clung to it all the way to the ranch entrance. But instead of taking the road to the ranch house, he turned onto a side road that wound around to the far side of the property.

"Where are we going?"

"There's something I want to show you." He squeezed her fingers. "It's my favorite spot."

When they came upon a whole hillside of quaking aspen surrounded by dark pines, he heard her gasp of wonder. "Oh, Buck—it's beautiful!" The late-afternoon sun had set the yellow leaves on fire. "If I were an artist..."

"I know what you mean." He turned off the engine and pulled her across to him so she was half lying in his arms. "When I was telling you about my fantasy, this was part of it, with a home set right in the middle of all that color." Her neck was so delectable, he couldn't resist kissing it.

"Carson has told me repeatedly that if I want to go into business with him permanently, this parcel of land is mine."

She turned in his arms and looked up at him with her vivid, dark blue eyes. "Is that what you want to do?"

"It's what I always wanted to do, now more than ever. That's because of you and your belief in me."

"I love you, Buck. I'm so in love with you, it hurts."

"Finally she tells me." He lowered his mouth to hers. For a little while, time and place had no meaning as he absorbed those precious words into his heart. When he was halfway coherent again, he said, "I have a small nest egg, as my dad calls it. I've held on to it, waiting to use it for something worthy. If I built that house, would—"

"Yes—" She cut him off. "I'll marry you under any circumstances. Does that answer your question?"

"Darling—" Once again they were devouring each other. "I told my parents I'd met the woman I wanted to marry. You've brought this bachelor to his knees."

She kissed his features. "It wasn't easy."

Buck let out a harsh laugh. "What are you talking about? I was nailed the second I saw your long, shapely legs walking in front of me."

Alex raised her head. "What do you mean?"

He told her everything. "When I left the hospital, I had plans to fly directly to Sacramento and bring you and Jenny back home."

She cupped his face in her hands. "There aren't enough words to tell you how much I love you. Whether you build us a house, or we rent one in Jackson, I'm planning to get a job there to help support us for as long as it takes. Tracy put me on to an idea without her realizing it. She used to work for the school district in technology. I'm going to apply for an accounting job with the school district here in Jackson. If they don't have an opening, I'll find something else."

"Alex—" he said, his voice full of emotion. Her love was blowing him away.

"If I put my house on the market right away, we can use the money from the sale. It won't be a lot, but it will all help, because you and I are in this together for the long haul."

Her declaration humbled him, but there was still something else bothering him. "Alex?"

"What is it? You sound worried. How can you be worried about anything right now?"

"It's Jenny. She—"

"She loves you."

"I want to believe that, but she didn't want you marrying Frank."

"You're not Frank. You're Jenny's superhero. She wanted to fly to Colorado with me because she's absolutely crazy about you. When you didn't come back from the lake with us, she became a ghost of herself. If you don't believe me, ask Tracy. And there's more. When you told her you'd like her to be your little girl, she took that to heart."

Buck buried his face in her hair. "I pray to God you're right about that. I couldn't lose you now. I just couldn't."

"You'll never have to. But to help you feel better, why don't we go pick her up so you can find out for yourself and be happy."

"I *am* happy. Too happy. I'm afraid I'm going to wake up."

"Well, I can tell you this. You *are* awake and have been kissing me until my lips are swollen, my hair is a complete mess and your beard has given me a rash. While we drive home, I need the time to make myself somewhat presentable. You know Johnny. He'll take one look at us and know exactly what we've been doing. That child is positively dangerous."

Laughter pealed out of Buck. Life didn't get better than this. He wrapped his arm tightly around her shoulders. With the taste of heaven on his lips, he started the engine. It took a while for them to reach the turnoff for Carson's new house. He couldn't get enough of Alex. Before they came out of the trees, he stopped the car while they kissed as if they were making up for years of deprivation. Her passion had set him on fire.

Suddenly, there was a knock on the window. Buck was so far gone, Alex was the one who had to separate them. He raised his head and looked around. Two cute faces stared at them through the window on the front passenger side of the car. Buck lowered it.

Johnny's eyes had rounded. "Whoa, Uncle Buck!"

"Hey, sport. How's everybody?"

"Good."

"Hi, Buck."

"Hi, Red."

"Is your daddy okay?"

"He's going to be fine."

"That's good." A smile broke out on her face. "I'm glad you're back."

"We are, too." Alex opened the door so Jenny could climb in and hug her.

Johnny looked as if he was going to explode. "I've got to tell Mom and Dad! I'll be right back." He took off running, six guns and all.

Buck was glad the three of them were alone for a moment. "What have you and Johnny been doing all day?"

"We watched Moppy for a long time."

"So she finally came out of hiding?"

"Yes. Carson told us where to sit and wait."

Buck grinned. "What else did you do?"

"We looked for bad guys."

"Is that what you were doing just now?"

"Yes."

He leaned over to kiss the tip of her nose. "I hope you didn't think your nana and I were bad guys."

A giggle escaped her. "No."

"So you like me a little bit?"

"A lot."

"Well, guess what?"

"What?"

"I love you."

"I love you, too," she said back to him without missing a beat.

His heart was melting. "Do you love me enough to

let me marry your nana and we'll all live at the ranch together?"

Her face lit up with joy. "I *want* you to get married."

"Then if it's all right with you, that settles everything."

"Goody!" She sounded like someone else he knew. "Now I'll have my own daddy. I've got to go tell Johnny!" She kissed his cheek, and then her nana's, before she backed out the door and raced away.

Alex leaned over to kiss his lips. "I guess you got your answer, *Daddy.*"

"I guess I did."

"I think maybe we'd better drive to the house before we get caught again by the big guys because we're doing something we shouldn't be."

"Wouldn't Carson just love that—I'd never be able to live it down." After a cough, Buck started the car. When they arrived in the clearing, the whole family was outside waiting for them. He kissed one corner of her luscious mouth. "There's no rest for the wicked."

She laughed gently. The minute she got out, Alex ran over to hug Tracy and thank her for watching Jenny. Carson just stood there with a huge grin on his face. "What did I hear about a wedding?"

"It's not going to happen for a while."

Johnny frowned. "How come?"

"Because we have a lot to figure out."

"No, you don't. Dad says you can live in the downstairs of the ranch house now that we've moved out."

That kid killed him. Buck exchanged an amused glance with Carson. "We're thrilled to hear the good news about your father."

"Me, too. Thanks for everything, for keeping Jenny

happy. Now it's our turn. Do you two gunslingers want to come with us? I'm going to follow Alex into town in the Jeep so we can return her rental car. While we're there, we'll grab a hamburger. How does that sound?"

"Hooray!" The kids were ecstatic.

"I'll keep Jenny with me tonight," Alex said. "There's a lot we have to discuss and we need to tell my parents." She looked down at the girl. "Your great-grandparents are going to be overjoyed."

"*Great*-grandparents?" Johnny piped up.

"That's right, sport," Carson spoke up. "You have to remember Alex is a grandmother. So her parents are Jenny's great-grandparents."

"Then they're really, really old."

Alex gave Johnny a hug. "I think they're about the same age as your Grandma and Grandpa Baretta. When they come to the wedding, you'll see for yourself."

Buck laughed. "Don't try to figure it out, Johnny. I still haven't."

And I don't care because I'm so happy I'm going to burst.

"Darling?"

She heard Buck's whisper from the hallway. There'd been so much excitement all evening, Jenny had barely just fallen asleep.

Alex tiptoed out of Johnny's old bedroom but didn't shut the door. Buck drew her across the hall to the master bedroom. "We need to leave this door open, too, in case she wakes up and calls out."

"Let's hope she doesn't." He gathered her in his arms and gave her a long, languorous kiss. The absence of desperation was heavenly. She'd gone after

Buck today and had found him with split-second timing. The thought of him chasing her clear to California was too much to comprehend. For the first time in her life she felt complete.

"I love, love, love you, Buck Summerhayes. I only have one concern."

"What?" He drew her down on the king-size bed and stretched out beside her.

"Did you mean it when you said we wouldn't be getting married for a while? You know I'm planning to get a job right away. We'll be able to afford it, or is there something you're not telling me?"

"That's not it." He kissed her throat, and then her mouth. "I don't want you to feel rushed."

She rolled over so she was half lying on top of him. "I'm almost forty-one, and time is flying by. You wouldn't be getting cold feet all of a sudden, would you?"

"Cold feet? Woman, what you talking about?"

"You still haven't answered my question."

"I'd marry you tomorrow if it were possible."

She took a shaky breath. "Then let's do it, if not tomorrow then the next day."

He rolled her back over and stared down at her. "You're serious…"

"Yes. I want your baby. It's been my fantasy since I met you. I've given it a lot of thought and have decided Jenny needs a sibling."

"I had no idea this was going on in your mind."

"All it took was meeting the man of my dreams. As soon as I got pregnant with Christy, Kyle left the state. I never knew what it was like to have a husband who loved me and would help me raise our child. When

Frank asked me to marry him, I put away any thoughts of having a baby, because he was too old to start over again on a second family."

"You'd really be willing to go through another pregnancy?"

"For you, I'd do anything. I don't know how come I'm so lucky that you came into my life. That's why I don't want to wait a couple of months for a ceremony. If we got married this week, we could be expecting a baby in that amount of time. Your mom had you at forty. Why can't I? I'm in excellent health and had no problems carrying Christy. Am I moving way too fast for you? It's just that you're going to be the most spectacular father."

He clutched her to him. "You've made me the happiest man alive. We'll see about getting a wedding license tomorrow. Carson will know of a justice of the peace."

"I'm so glad you're okay with that." She kissed him over and over again.

Buck started to laugh.

"What?" She smiled.

"If we're blessed enough to have a baby soon, be it a boy or girl, then he or she will be Jenny's aunt or uncle. But Jenny will be almost eight years older. Can you imagine Johnny having to wrap his mind around that when he's still struggling over the great-grandparent thing?"

Alex buried her face in his shoulder, trying not to laugh out loud. But that didn't stop the bed from shaking.

Alex was manning the front desk at the ranch house when the landline phone rang. She picked up. "Teton Valley Dude Ranch."

A woman with a voice Alex didn't recognize asked to speak to Mr. Lundgren.

"I'm afraid he's out of town at the moment." Carson had gone back to Cleveland with Tracy and Johnny to visit the Baretta side of the family for a few days. "This is Alex Summerhayes." She and Buck had been married by a justice of the peace a little over three weeks ago. "May I help you?"

"My name is Kit Wentworth. My son and I are scheduled to fly in this Friday from Maine, but there's been a problem and I'm afraid we won't be able to come until Saturday. If that's impossible for you to change now, I'll certainly understand."

Alex remembered this was the third war widow who'd received a letter from the ranch. She immediately felt a connection to the woman. "I can't answer for him. If you'll give me your number, I'll have Mr. Livingston, his partner, call you back as soon as possible." He'd be taking care of this family.

"Thank you very much."

"You're welcome."

After hanging up, she tried reaching Ross on his cell phone. She got his voice mail and left a detailed message. Buck had taken some guests down the Snake to shoot the rapids and wouldn't be back for another hour.

It was almost time to check on the kids, who'd been swimming in the pool. To her relief, Willy breezed into the foyer. "Hi, Alex."

"Hi, yourself. I'm glad you're here. I'll see you later." She had something important she had to do before she got Jenny.

Alex rushed to the back of the ranch house and pulled a home pregnancy test out of the dresser drawer. For the past few days, she'd been sleepier than usual and remembered she'd felt that way before she found out she was pregnant with Christy.

This was her third day of testing. If an obstetrician knew what she was doing, he'd tell her she'd put way too much pressure on herself and was bound to be disappointed. She promised herself that if she got another negative reading, she'd let a week go by before trying it again.

Fearful of the same result, she waited a few minutes, and then looked at it, bracing herself.

Pregnant.

No. She didn't believe it. But there it was. The instructions said the result was 99% accurate.

A new kind of happiness permeated her body.

Where was her husband? She had to tell him! He'd go crazy when he found out he was going to be a father. While her mind spun with all the changes that would be taking place in their lives, it dawned on her she needed to check on the children.

She ran out of the bedroom and down the hall to the back door, almost colliding with Buck. "Oh—you're back!"

"Whoa, darling—" He caught her in his arms. "What's the big hurry?"

"The kids are still in the pool."

"They'll be fine." He kissed her soundly. "Let me wash my hands and then I'll go with you."

Uh-oh. "You can't go in our bathroom. Use Jenny's."

"Why?" He coughed.

"Just because."

"Just because you told me not to, I'm going in."

"No, Buck. Wait—" She wanted to plan something

special for tonight to give him the news, but he was gone in a flash.

She started down the hall after him.

There was no sound. Maybe he hadn't seen the test, but she'd been in such a hurry, she'd left it in plain sight.

When she walked into the bedroom, her husband was just coming out of the bathroom. He reached her in two long strides and drew her into his arms. For a full minute he just rocked her. His quiet sobs of joy told her that he knew what it was like to feel complete. This was only the beginning.

* * * * *

YOU HAVE
JUST READ A
HARLEQUIN®
SPECIAL
EDITION
BOOK.

Discover more heartfelt tales of **family, friendship** and **love** from the Harlequin Special Edition series. Be sure to look for all six Harlequin® Special Edition books every month.

SPECIAL EXCERPT FROM

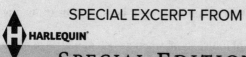

SPECIAL EDITION

*Cole Dalton thought letting Vivienne Shuster
plan his wedding—to no one—would work out just
fine for both of them. But now not only are they getting
caught up in a lot of lies, they might just be getting
caught up in each other!*

Read on for a sneak preview of
the next **MONTANA MAVERICKS** story,
THE MAVERICK'S BRIDAL BARGAIN
by *Christy Jeffries*.

"You're engaged?"

"Of course I'm not engaged." Cole visibly shuddered.
"I'm not even boyfriend material, let alone husband
material."

Confusion quickly replaced her anger and Vivienne
could only stutter, "Wh-why?"

"I guess because I have more important things going
on in my life right now than to cozy up to some female
I'm not interested in and pretend like I give a damn about
all this commitment crap."

"No, I mean why would you need to plan a wedding if
you're not getting married?"

"You said you need to book another client." He rocked
onto the heels of his boots. "Well, I'm your next client."

Vivienne shook her head as if she could jiggle all the
scattered pieces of this puzzle into place. "A client who
has no intention of getting married?"

"Yes. But it's not like your boss would know the difference."

"She might figure it out when no actual marriage takes place. If you're not boyfriend material, then does that mean you don't have a girlfriend? I mean, who would we say you're marrying?"

Okay, so that first question Vivienne threw in for her own clarification. Even though they hadn't exactly kissed, she needed reassurance that she wasn't lusting over some guy who was off-limits.

"Nope, no need for a girlfriend," he said, and she felt some of her apprehension drain. But then he took a couple of steps closer. "We can make something up, but why would it even need to get that far? Look, you just need to buy yourself some time to bring in more business. So you sign me up or whatever you need to do to get your boss off your back, and then after you bring in some more customers—legitimate ones—my fake fiancée will have cold feet and we'll call it off."

If her eyes squinted any more, they'd be squeezed shut. And then she'd miss his normal teasing smirk telling her that he was only kidding. But his jaw was locked into place and the set of his straight mouth looked dead serious.

Don't miss
THE MAVERICK'S BRIDAL BARGAIN
by Christy Jeffries,
available June 2018 wherever
Harlequin® Special Edition books and ebooks are sold.

www.Harlequin.com

Looking for more satisfying love stories
with community and family at their core?

Check out **Harlequin® Special Edition**
and **Harlequin® Western Romance** books!

New books available every month!

CONNECT WITH US AT:

Harlequin.com/Community

 Facebook.com/HarlequinBooks

 Twitter.com/HarlequinBooks

 Instagram.com/HarlequinBooks

 Pinterest.com/HarlequinBooks

ReaderService.com

**ROMANCE WHEN
YOU NEED IT**

HFGENRE2017R

Reward the book lover in you!

Earn points from all your Harlequin book purchases from wherever you shop.

Turn your points into *FREE BOOKS* of your choice OR
EXCLUSIVE GIFTS from your favorite authors or series.

Join for FREE today at
www.HarlequinMyRewards.com.

Harlequin My Rewards is a free program (no fees) without any commitments or obligations.

MYR17